St Clare's

Enid Blyton

Enid Blyton

St CLARE'S
The Middle Years

3 books in 1

EGMONT

ST CLARE'S

Enid Blyton

EGMONT
We bring stories to life

Second Form at St Clare's first published in Great Britain 1944
The Third Form at St Clare's first published in Great Britain 2000
Kitty at St Clare's first published in Great Britain 2008
First published as *St Clare's: The Middle Years* 2013
by Egmont UK Limited
The Yellow Building, 1 Nicholas Road, London W11 4AN

ISBN 978 1 4952 6856 1

www.egmont.co.uk

A CIP catalogue record for this title is available from the British Library

Printed and bound in Great Britain by the CPI Group

55945/5

Contents

Contents

1.

Off to school again

The last week of the summer holidays flew by, and the twins, Pat and Isabel O'Sullivan, seemed to be in a rush of buying clothes, fitting them on, looking out lacrosse sticks, finding lacrosse boots, and hunting for all kinds of things that seemed to have completely disappeared.

'Where *is* my knitting-bag?' said Pat, turning a whole drawerful of things upside down. 'I know I brought it home at the end of last term.'

'I can only find *one* of my lacrosse boots,' wailed Isabel. 'Mummy, have you seen the other?'

'Yes, it came back from the bootmaker's yesterday,' said Mrs O'Sullivan. 'Where did you put it?'

'Packing to go to school is always much more muddling than packing to come back home,' said Pat. 'I say, Isabel – won't it be fun to be in the second form this term?'

'Who is your form teacher there?' asked their mother, unpacking half Pat's things and packing them all over again.

'Miss Jenks,' said Pat. 'I'll be sorry to leave Miss Roberts and the first form, in some ways. We did have fun there.'

'I bet we'll have some fun in Miss Jenks's class too,' said Isabel. 'I don't think she's quite so strict as Miss Roberts.'

'Don't you believe it!' said Isabel, trying to cram a tin

of toffees into a corner. 'She may not have Miss Roberts's sarcastic tongue – but she's all there! Don't you remember how she used to deal with Tessie when Tessie used to try on her pretend-sneezes?'

'Yes – sent her to Matron for a large dose of awful medicine, supposed to stop a cold!' giggled Pat. 'All the same, I bet we'll get away with quite a lot of things in Miss Jenks's form.'

'I hope you mean to work,' said Mrs O'Sullivan, putting in the top tray of Isabel's trunk. 'I was quite pleased with last term's report. Don't let me have a bad one as soon as you go up into another form, will you?'

'We'll work all right, Mummy,' said Pat. 'I can tell you, the teachers at St Clare's aren't easy-going where work is concerned. They keep our noses to the grindstone! Mam'zelle's the worst. She really seems to think we ought to learn to talk French better than we speak English!'

'No wonder your French accent is so much improved, then,' said Mrs O'Sullivan, with a laugh. 'Now Pat – let me see if I can possibly shut your trunk. You'd better sit on it whilst I try to shut the clasps.'

The trunk wouldn't shut. Mrs O'Sullivan opened it again and looked inside. 'You can't take all those books,' she said, firmly.

'Mummy, I *must*,' said Pat. 'And I simply must take those games too – we love jigsaws in the winter term.'

'Well, Pat, all I can say is, you'd better take books, games, toffees, biscuits and knitting things, and leave behind your clothes,' said the twins' mother. 'Now – be sensible – take out three books and we can shut the trunk.'

Pat took out three books, and, when Mrs O'Sullivan was not looking, put them hurriedly into Isabel's trunk. Her own trunk now shut down fairly easily, and was locked. Then Mrs O'Sullivan went to Isabel's.

'This won't shut, either,' she said. 'Gracious, the things you girls take back with you to boarding school nowadays! When *I* . . .'

'When *you* were a girl you only took a small case, and that held everything!' chanted the twins, who had heard these remarks before. 'Mummy, we'll *both* sit on Isabel's trunk, shall we?'

Mrs O'Sullivan opened the trunk and firmly removed three books from the top layer. She looked at them in surprise. 'I seem to have seen these before!' she said. The twins giggled. They sat on the trunk and it shut with a groan.

'And now to pack your hand-bag with night-things in,' said Mrs O'Sullivan, looking at the school-list to make sure nothing had been forgotten. 'That won't take long.'

Nightgowns, tooth-brushes, face-flannels and sponges went into small bags. Then the twins were ready. They were both dressed neatly in their school winter uniforms of grey, with blue blouses and scarlet ties. They put on grey coats and grey felt hats with the school ribbon round, and looked at each other.

'Two good little St Clare girls,' said Pat, looking demure.

'Not so very good,' said her mother, with a smile. 'Now – there is the car at the door, ready to take us to the station. Have we really got everything? You must write and tell me if you want anything else.'

'Oh, we're sure to want lots of things!' said Pat. 'You're a darling, the way you send us things. It's fun to be going back to St Clare's. I'm awfully glad you sent us there, Mummy.'

'And how you hated going at first!' said Mrs O'Sullivan, remembering the fuss the twins had made, because they had wanted to go to another, much more expensive school.

'Yes – we made up our minds to be so awful that the school wouldn't keep us,' said Pat. 'And we *were* awful too – but we couldn't keep it up. St Clare's was too much for us – we just *had* to be decent in the end!'

'Do come on,' said Isabel. 'We shall miss the train! I'm longing to meet all the girls in London, and see them again, aren't you, Pat? I do like the journey down to St Clare's.'

They were off at last. They had to travel to London, and go to the station where the St Clare train started. The whole train was reserved for the St Clare girls, for it was a big school.

There was a terrific noise on the platform, where scores of girls were waiting for the train. Their mothers were there to bid them goodbye, and teachers moved about, trying to collect the girls together. Porters shoved luggage into the van, and everyone was excited.

'Bobby! Oh, there's Bobby!' yelled Pat, as soon as they arrived on the crowded platform. 'And Janet too. Hi, Bobby, hi, Janet!'

4

'Hallo, twins!' cried Bobby. Her merry eyes crinkled up as she smiled.

'It's good to see your turn-up nose again,' said Pat, slipping her arm through Bobby's. 'Hallo, Janet! Got anymore tricks from that brother of yours?'

'Wait and see,' grinned Janet. A mistress came up at that moment and overheard the remarks.

'Ah – did I hear the word *tricks*, Janet?' she said. 'Well, just remember you're in *my* form this term, and there are really Terrible Punishments for tricks like yours!'

'Yes, Miss Jenks,' grinned Janet. 'I'll remember. Are all the others here yet?'

'All but Doris,' said Miss Jenks. 'Ah, there she is. Now we must get into the train. The guard is looking rather worried, I see.'

'Carlotta! Get into our carriage!' yelled Bobby, seeing the dark-eyed, dark-haired girl running down the platform. 'What sort of hols did you have? Did you go back to the circus?'

Carlotta was a source of great attraction and admiration to the girls, for she had once been a circus girl, and her understanding and handling of horses was marvellous. Now she had to settle down at St Clare's, and learn many things she had never heard of. She had found her first term very difficult, but at the end of it she was firm friends with most of her form, and the mistresses were pleased with her. She ran up to the twins and Bobby, her vivid little face glowing with pleasure.

'Hallo!' she said. 'I'll get into your carriage. Oh, look –

there's your cousin Alison. She looks rather miserable.'

'I *feel* miserable,' said Alison O'Sullivan, coming up, looking very woe-begone. 'I shall miss my friend Sadie dreadfully this term.'

Sadie had been an American girl with no ideas in her head at all beyond clothes and the cinema. She had had a very bad influence on Alison, but, as she was not coming back that term, it was to be hoped that the feather-headed Alison would pull herself together a little, and try to do better. She was a pretty little thing who easily burst into tears. Her cousins welcomed her warmly.

'Hallo, Alison! Don't fret about Sadie. You'll soon find other friends.'

They all got into the carriage. Doris arrived, panting. Hilary Wentworth, who had been head of the first form, flung herself down in a corner seat. She was very much wondering if she would be head of the second form. She was a trustworthy and responsible girl who liked being head.

'Hallo, everybody,' she said. 'Nice to see you all again. Well, Carlotta – been riding in the ring, I suppose! Lucky kid!'

'You know I don't belong to a circus any more,' said Carlotta. 'I went to spend my holidays with my father and my grandmother. My father seems to like me quite a lot – but my grandmother found a lot of fault with my manners. She says I must pay more attention to them this term even than to my lessons! You must all help me!'

'Oh, no!' said Pat, with a laugh. 'We don't want you

6

any different from what you are, my dear, hot-tempered, entirely natural, perfectly honest little Carlotta! We get more fun out of you than out of anyone. We don't want you changed one little bit! Any more than we want Bobby changed. We shall expect some marvellous tricks from you this term, Bobby.'

'Right,' said Bobby. 'But I tell you here and now, I'm going to work too!'

'Miss Jenks will see to that,' said Hilary. 'Remember we shall no longer be in the bottom form. We've got to work for exams and pass them!'

'We're off!' said Pat, leaning out of the window. 'Goodbye, Mummy! We'll write on Sunday!'

The train steamed slowly out of the station. The girls drew in their heads. All the carriages were full of chatterers, talking about the wonderful hols they had had, the places they had been to, and what sort of term it would be.

'Any new girls?' said Isabel. 'I haven't seen one.'

'I think there's only one,' said Bobby. 'We saw a miserable-looking creature standing a little way up the platform – I don't know whether she'll be second form or first form. Not second, I hope – she looked such a misery!'

'Alison's doing her hair again already,' said Pat. 'Alison! Put your comb away. Girls, I think we'll have to make it a rule that Alison doesn't do her hair more than fifty times a day!'

Everyone laughed. It was good to be back, good to be all together once more. The winter term was going to be fun!

2.

In the second form

It was very strange at first to be in the second form, instead of the first. The twins felt very important, and looked down on the first formers, feeling that they were very young and unimportant. But the third formers also looked down on the second form, so things soon shook themselves out, and everyone settled down.

'It's funny to go to the second-form classroom instead of to Miss Roberts's room,' said Pat. 'I keep on going to the first-form room, as I always used to do.'

'So do I,' said Janet. 'Miss Roberts is beginning to think we're doing it on purpose. We'd better be careful.'

'There's a whole lot of new girls in the first form, after all,' said Pat. 'Miss Roberts must have collected them altogether on the train. That's why we didn't see them. There's about twelve!'

'I shall never know all their names,' said Isabel. 'Anyway – they're only little kids – some of them not yet fourteen!'

'All the first formers have been moved up,' said Bobby. 'Except young Pam – and she's only just fourteen. I bet she'll be head of the first form!'

Pam Boardman had been new the term before, and

was a very hard-working child. As Bobby said, she was made head of the first form, and was extremely proud of the honour. She had many new girls under her, and was eager to help them all.

Only two girls had been left down in the second form – Elsie Fanshawe and Anna Johnson. The girls who had just come up were sorry to see them there, for they were not much liked. Elsie Fanshawe was spiteful, and Anna Johnson was lazy.

'I suppose one of them will be head girl,' said Hilary, with a grimace. 'Well – I don't fancy either of them, do you, Bobby?'

'They both think themselves very superior to us,' said Bobby. 'Just because they've been second formers for a year.'

'*I* should be ashamed,' said Carlotta. 'I would not like to spend more than a year in any form. But Anna is so lazy she will never get up into the third form, I'm sure!'

'I believe Miss Jenks didn't send them up because she hoped they'd buck up a bit if they were heads,' said Pat. 'I rather think she's going to make them joint head girls. We shall have to look out if Elsie's head – she's really catty.'

'We've got that Misery-girl in our form after all,' said Bobby, looking at the new girl, who was standing mournfully not far off, looking at nothing. 'She never says a word, but looks as if she'll burst into tears at any moment!'

The Misery-girl, as the others called her, was named Gladys Hillman. The girls tried to make her talk and Bobbie did her best to make her laugh, but Gladys took no

9

notice of anyone. She walked by herself, seemed to dream all the time, and hardly spoke a word.

'Better leave her alone,' said Hilary. 'Perhaps she's homesick.'

Not many of the St Clare girls felt homesick when they returned to school, because it was all so jolly and friendly, and there was so much to do that there seemed no time to miss home and parents. The beginning of term was always fun – new books given out, new girls to size up, new desks to sit in, and sometimes new forms to go to.

'There's a new mistress,' said Bobby, in excitement. 'She's to take elocution and drama! Look – there she is – isn't she dark?'

Miss Quentin certainly was dark, and extremely good looking. She had black piercing eyes, and a beautiful voice. Alison thought she was wonderful.

'You *would*!' said Bobby. 'You'll be doing your hair like Miss Quentin next, swept over your brow and round your ears. There'll always be someone for you to copy, my dear Alison! Do you remember last term how you copied everything your dear friend Sadie did?'

Alison flushed. She was always being teased and she never seemed to get used to it. She turned away with a toss of her pretty head. The others laughed at her. There was nothing bad in Alison – but on the other hand there was nothing very good either. She was, as Pat so often said, 'just a pretty little feather-head!'

The second form soon settled down with Miss Jenks. At first it seemed strange to them not to have Miss Roberts teaching them for most of the morning. They missed her dry remarks and crisp words of praise. Miss Jenks was not so shrewd as Miss Roberts, nor was she so cool when angry. She could not bear the slightest hint of rudeness, and she had no sympathy at all for 'frills and fancies' as she put it. No girl dared to fuss her hair out too much, or to wear anything but a plain gold bar for a brooch in Miss Jenks's class.

'Alison is in for a bad time!' grinned Bobby one morning, when Alison had been sent to remove a bow from her hair and a brooch from her collar.

'So is Carlotta!' said Pat. 'Miss Jenks doesn't like frills and fancies – but she doesn't like untidiness either! Just *look* at your hair, Carlotta. It's wild enough in the ordinary way – but it looks like a bird's nest at the moment.'

'Does it really?' said Carlotta, who never cared in the least what she looked like. 'Well, those sums we had to do were so hard I just had to clutch my hair all the time!'

'Old Mam'zelle's still the same,' said Isabel. 'Funny, old, hot-tempered, flat-footed thing – but I like her all the same. She always gives us *some* excitement – and I bet she will this term, too. Do you remember how she and Carlotta nearly came to blows last term?'

Yes – the summer term had been a very exciting one. The girls looked at Mam'zelle and remembered all the jokes they had played on her. Dear old Mam'zelle, she always fell for everything. She was very terrifying when she lost her temper, but she had a great sense of humour, and when her short-sighted eyes twinkled behind their

11

glasses, the girls felt a real fondness for her.

'Ah,' said Mam'zelle, looking round the second form. 'Ah! You are now the second form – very important, very responsible, and very hard working, *n'est-ce pas*? The first formers, they are babies, they know nothing – but as soon as you arrive in the second form, you are big girls, you know a great deal. Your French will be quite per-r-r-rfect! And Doris – ah, even Doris will be able to roll her 'r's in the proper French way!'

Everyone laughed. Poor Doris, always bottom at oral French, could never roll her 'r's. Doris grinned. She was a dunce, but nobody minded. She was a wonderful mimic and could keep the whole form in roars of laughter when she liked.

'R-r-r-r-r-r!' said Carlotta, unexpectedly. She sounded like an aeroplane taking off, and Mam'zelle frowned.

'You are now in the second form, Carlotta,' she said, coldly. 'We do not do those things here.'

'No, Mam'zelle,' said Carlotta, meekly. 'Of course not.'

'Tricks and jokes are not performed in any form higher than the first,' warned Mam'zelle. 'Whilst you are first-form babies, one does not expect much from you – but as soon as you leave the bottom form behind, it is different. We expect you to behave with dignity. One day the head girl may be one of you here, and it is not too soon to prepare for such an honour.'

Winifred James, the much-admired head girl, had left, and Belinda Towers, the sports captain, had taken her place. This was a very popular choice, for Belinda was well known by the whole school, and very much liked. As sports captain she knew practically all the girls, and this would be a great help to her as head girl. She was not so gentle and quiet as Winifred, and many girls were afraid of her out-spokenness, but there was no doubt she would make an excellent head girl.

Belinda visited every common-room in turn and made the same short speech to the girls there.

'You all know I'm head girl now – and I'm still sports captain too. You can come to me if you're in a spot of trouble at any time and I'll help if I can. You'll all have to toe the mark where games are concerned, because I want to put St Clare's right on the map this winter, with lacrosse. We must win every match we play! We've got some fine players for a school team, but I want every form to supply players for the second and third match-teams too. So buck up, all of you, and practise hard.'

Alison groaned as Belinda went out of the second-form common-room. 'Why *do* we have to play games?' she said. 'They just make us hot and untidy and tired.'

'You forget they do other things as well,' said Janet. 'We have to learn to work together as a team – each one for his side, helping the others, not each one for himself. That sort of thing is especially good for *you*, my dear Alison – you'd sit in a corner and look at yourself in the mirror all day long if you could – and a fat lot of good that would do you or anybody else.'

'Oh, be quiet,' said Alison. 'You're always getting at me!'

It *was* fun to be back again, and to hear all the familiar

school chatter, to groan over prep, to eat enormous teas, to talk about lacrosse, to laugh at somebody's joke, and to look forward to the class you liked the best – painting, maybe, or music, or elocution – or even maths!

There was a surprise for the second form at the end of the first week. Another new girl appeared! She arrived at tea-time, with red eyes and a sulky mouth. She looked defiantly at everyone as she took her place at the second-form table.

'This is Mirabel Unwin,' said Miss Jenks. 'She has arrived rather late for beginning of term – but still, better late than never, Mirabel.'

'I didn't want to come at all,' said Mirabel, in a loud voice. 'They tried to make me come on the right day but I wouldn't. I only came now because my father promised I could leave at half-term if I'd come now. I suppose he thought once he got me here I'd stay. But I shan't.'

'That will do, Mirabel,' said Miss Jenks, soothingly. 'You are tired and over-wrought. Don't say any more. You will soon settle down and be happy.'

'No, I shan't,' said the surprising Mirabel. 'I shan't settle down and I shan't be happy. I shan't try at anything, because what's the use if I'm leaving at half-term?'

'Well, we'll see,' said Miss Jenks. 'Be sensible now and eat some tea. You must be hungry.'

The girls stared at Mirabel. They were not used to people who shouted their private affairs out in public. They thought Mirabel was rather shocking – but rather exciting too.

'I thought she was another Misery-girl at first, but I believe she's just spoilt and peevish,' said Pat. 'I say – the second form is going to be quite an exciting place this term!'

3.

Two head girls and
two new girls

Miss Jenks made both the old second formers into joint head girls of the form. She and Miss Theobald, the head mistress, had had a talk about them, and had decided that perhaps it would be the making of them.

'Elsie is a spiteful type,' said Miss Jenks. 'She has never been popular, though she would have liked to be – so she gets back at the others by being spiteful and saying nasty things. And Anna is bone-lazy – won't do a thing if she can help it!'

'Well, a little responsibility may be good for them,' said Miss Theobald, thoughtfully. 'It will give Elsie a sense of importance, and bring out any good in her – and Anna will have to bestir herself if she wants to keep her position. Let them both try.'

'I don't know how they will work together,' said Miss Jenks, doubtfully. 'They don't like each other very much.'

'Let them try,' said Miss Theobald. 'Elsie is quick, and she may stir Anna up a bit – and Anna is too lazy to be spiteful, so perhaps she will be good for Elsie in that way. But I too have my doubts!'

Elsie Fanshawe was delighted to be a joint head girl – though, of course, she would very much rather have been the only one. Still, after being thoroughly disliked and kept down by the whole of the second form, it was quite a change to be top-dog!

Now I can jolly well keep the others down and make them look up to *me*, thought Elsie, pleased. I can get some of my own back. These silly little first formers, who have just come up, have got to learn to knuckle under a bit. I can make Anna agree with all I do – lazy thing! I'll have every single one of the rules kept, and I'll make a few of my own, if I want to – and I'll report anyone who gets out of hand. It's worthwhile not going up into the third form, to be top of the second!

The others guessed a little what Elsie was thinking. Although they had not known the girl very well when they were first formers, they had heard the others talking about her. They knew Elsie would try to 'get her own back'.

'Just what a head girl shouldn't do,' said Janet. 'She should try and set some sort of example to the others, or what's the use of being a leader? Look at old Hilary, when she was head of the first form! She was a good sport and joined in everything – but she always knew where to draw the line without getting our backs up.'

'I can't bear Elsie,' said Carlotta. 'I would like to slap her hard.'

'Oh, Carlotta! Have you still got that habit?' said Bobby, pretending to be shocked. 'Really, a second former, too! What *would* Elsie say?'

Elsie overheard the last remark. 'What would I say to what?' she asked, coming up.

'Oh, nothing – Carlotta was simply saying she'd like to slap someone,' said Bobby, with a grin.

'Please understand, Carlotta, that you are in the second form now,' said Elsie, in a cold voice. 'We don't even *talk* of slapping people!'

'Yes, we do,' said Carlotta. 'Wouldn't you like to know whom I want to slap, dear Elsie?'

Elsie heard the danger-note in Carlotta's high voice, and put her nose in the air.

'I'm not interested in your slapping habits,' she said, and walked off.

'Shut up now, Carlotta,' said Bobby. 'Don't go and get all wild and Spanish again. You were bad enough with Prudence last term!'

'Well, thank goodness old Sour-Milk Prudence was expelled!' said Carlotta. 'I wouldn't have stayed if she had come back!'

It was the hour when all the second form were in their common-room, playing, working or chattering. They loved being together like that. The radio blared at one end of the room, and Doris and Bobby danced a ridiculous dance to the music. Gladys Hillman sat in a corner, looking as miserable as usual. Nobody could make anything of her. Isabel looked at her and felt sorry. She went over to her.

'Come and dance,' she said. Gladys shook her head.

'What's the matter?' asked Isabel. 'Are you homesick? You'll soon get over it.'

'Don't bother me,' said Gladys. 'I don't bother you.'

'Yes, you do,' said Isabel. 'You bother me a lot. I can't bear to see you sitting here all alone, looking so miserable. Haven't you been to boarding school before?'

'No,' said Gladys. Her eyes filled with tears. Isabel felt a little impatient with her. Hadn't she any courage at all?

'You don't seem to enjoy a single thing,' said Isabel. 'Don't you like any lesson specially – or games – or something?'

'I like acting,' said Gladys, unexpectedly. 'And I like lacrosse. That's all. But I don't like them here. I don't like anything here.'

She wouldn't say any more, and Isabel gave her up. She went across to Pat. 'Hopeless!' she said. 'Just a mass of self-pity and tears! She'll fade away and we'll never notice she's gone if she doesn't buck up! I'd almost rather have that rude Mirabel than Gladys.'

Mirabel had been the source of much annoyance and amusement to the second form. She was rude to the point of being unbearable, and reminded everyone every day that she wasn't going to stay a day beyond half-term.

'Don't tell me that any more,' begged Bobby. 'You can't imagine how glad I am you're going at half-term. It's the only bright spot I can see. But I warn you – don't be too rude to Mam'zelle, or sparks will fly – and don't get on the high horse too much with our dear head girl, Elsie Fanshawe, or you'll get the worst of it. Elsie is pretty clever you know, and you're rather stupid.'

'No, I'm not!' flashed Mirabel, angrily. 'I only seem

19

stupid because I don't want to try – but you should hear me play the piano and the violin! *Then* you'd see!'

'Why, you don't even *learn* music!' said Bobby. 'And I've never seen you open your mouth in the singing class. We all came to the conclusion that you couldn't sing a note.'

'That's all *you* know!' said Mirabel, rudely. 'Golly, what a school this is! I always knew boarding school would be awful – but it's worse than I expected. I hate living with a lot of rude girls who think they're the cat's whiskers just because they've been here a year or two!'

'Oh, you make me tired,' said Bobby, and walked off. 'Really, what with you and the Misery-girl, and spiteful old Elsie, we're badly off this term!'

Miss Jenks kept a very firm hand on Mirabel. 'You may not intend to work,' she said, 'but you are not going to stop the others from working! You will do one of three things, my dear Mirabel – you will stay in the classroom and work – or you will stay in the classroom and do nothing at all, not even say a word – or you will go and stand *out*side the classroom till the lesson is finished!'

At first Mirabel thought it was marvellous to defy Miss Jenks and be sent outside. But she soon found it wearisome to stand there so long, waiting for the others to come out. Also, she was always a little afraid that the head mistress, Miss Theobald, would come along. Loudly as Mirabel declared that she cared for nobody, nobody at all at silly St Clare's, she *was* in awe of the quiet head mistress.

'Did you tell Miss Theobald that you didn't mean to

stay here longer than half-term?' asked Pat. Every girl had to go to see the head mistress when she arrived on the first day.

'Of course I did!' said Mirabel, tossing her head. 'I told her *I* didn't care for anyone, not even the head!'

This was untrue. Mirabel had meant to say quite a lot – but Miss Theobald had somehow said it first. She had looked gravely at the red-eyed girl when she had come in, and had told her to sit down. Mirabel opened her mouth to speak, but Miss Theobald silenced her.

'I must finish this letter,' she said. 'Then we will talk.'

She kept Mirabel waiting for ten minutes. The girl studied the head's calm face, and felt a little awed. It would be difficult to be rude to someone like this. The longer she waited, the more difficult it would be to say what she had meant to say.

Miss Theobald raised her head at last. 'Well, Mirabel,' she said, 'I know you feel upset, angry and defiant. Your father insisted you should come away to school because you are spoilt and make his home unbearable. You also domineer over your smaller brother and sister. He chose St Clare's because he thought we might be able to do something for you. No – don't interrupt me. Believe me, I know all you want to say – but you don't know what I have to say.'

There was a pause. Even defiant Mirabel did not dare to say a word.

'We have had many difficult girls here,' said Miss Theobald. 'We rather pride ourselves on getting the best

21

out of them. You see, Mirabel, difficult children often have fine things hidden in their characters – things that perhaps more ordinary children don't possess . . .'

'What things?' asked Mirabel, interested in spite of herself.

'Well – sometimes difficult children have a great talent for something – a gift for art or drama, a talent for music – or maybe they have some great quality – outstanding courage, perhaps. Well, I don't know if this is the case with you, or whether you are just a spoilt and unruly girl – we shall see. All I want to say now is – give yourself a chance and let me see if there *is* anything worthwhile in you this half-term. If there is not, we don't want you to stay. We shall be glad for you to go.'

This was so unexpected that Mirabel again had nothing to say. She had meant to say that nothing on earth would make her stay at St Clare's beyond the half-term – but here was Miss Theobald saying that she didn't want to keep her longer than that – unless – unless she was worthwhile! Worthwhile!

I don't care if I'm worthwhile or not! thought Mirabel to herself, indignantly. And how dare Daddy write and tell Miss Theobald those things about me? Why couldn't he keep our affairs to himself?

Mirabel voiced this thought aloud. 'I think it was horrid of my father to tell you things about me,' she said, in a trembling voice.

'They were said in confidence to someone who understood,' said Miss Theobald. 'Have you kept your own tongue quiet about *your* private affairs this afternoon, Mirabel? No – I rather think you gave yourself away to the whole school at tea-time when you arrived!'

Mirabel flushed. Yes – she had said far too much. She always did. She could not keep control over her tongue.

'You may go,' said Miss Theobald, picking up her pen again. 'And remember – it is not *St Clare's* which is on trial – it is *you*! I hope I shall not say goodbye to you and rejoice to see the last of you at half-term. But – I shall not be surprised if I do!'

Mirabel went out of the room, her ears tingling, her face still red. She had been used to getting all her own way, to letting her rough tongue say what it pleased, and to ruling her parents and brother and sister as she pleased. When her father had at last declared in anger that she must go away, there had been a royal battle between them. The spoilt girl had imagined she could rule the roost at St Clare's too. But she certainly could not rule Miss Theobald!

Never mind – I'll lead everyone else a dance! she thought. I'll show Daddy and the others that I mean what I say! I won't be sent away from home if I don't want to go.

And so Mirabel set herself to be as annoying as possible, to spoil things for the others, and to try and domineer in the classroom, as she had always done at home. But she had not bargained for the treatment she got at last from an exasperated class.

4.

Mirabel is a nuisance

The second form did not so much mind when Mirabel was annoying in classes they disliked, such as the maths class, which they found difficult that term – or even in Mam'zelle's class when she took irregular French verbs, hated by every girl. But they did dislike it when she spoilt, or tried to spoil, the English class, or the art class.

'It spoils our reading of *The Tempest* when you make idiotic remarks, or flop about in your seat and make Miss Jenks keep on saying, "Sit up!" ' said Hilary, angrily. 'Either behave badly enough to get sent out of the room at once, idiot, or else keep quiet.'

'And if you dare to upset your paint-water all over somebody again, and make us lose ten minutes of the art class whilst we all get ticked off by Miss Walker, I'll throttle you,' said Carlotta, all in one breath. 'We wouldn't mind so much if you did something really funny, like Bobby or Janet did last term – what you do *isn't* funny – just idiotic, spoiling things for the whole class.'

'I shall do what I like,' said Mirabel.

'You will not,' said Elsie, spitefully. 'I'm head girl of this form – with Anna – and we say you are to behave yourself, or we'll know the reason why.'

'You do know the reason why,' said Mirabel, pertly.

'Anyone would think you were six years old, the way you behave,' said Bobby, in disgust. 'Well – I warn you – you'll be sorry if you keep on like this. We're all getting tired of you.'

The explosion came during the drama class. This was taken by the new teacher, Miss Quentin, and was really rather an exciting class. The girls were to write and act their own play. Dark-eyed Miss Quentin was full of good suggestions, and the play was almost written.

The new teacher was not much good at discipline. She relied on her good looks and rather charming manner, and on the interest of her lessons, to help her to discipline her classes. Alison adored her, and, as the girls had already foreseen, was copying her in everything, from her little tricks of speech, to the way she did her hair.

Most of the girls liked Miss Quentin, though they did not very much respect the way she coaxed them to behave when they became a little unruly. They really preferred the downright methods of Miss Roberts or Miss Jenks. Mirabel, of course, soon found that Miss Quentin was quite unable to keep her in order.

'Your turn now, Mirabel dear,' Miss Quentin would say, smiling brightly at her. Mirabel would pretend not to hear, and Miss Quentin would raise her voice slightly.

'Mirabel! Your turn now, dear!'

The class disliked Miss Quentin's 'dears' and 'lambs' and other names – except Alison. She loved them. They all looked at Mirabel impatiently. She was always losing time like this, when they wanted to get on.

Mirabel would pretend to come back to earth with a start, fumble for the place, be gently helped by Miss Quentin, and at last say something, usually incorrect. When there was any acting to be done she came in at the wrong moment, said the wrong lines, and altogether behaved in a most annoying manner. Miss Quentin was at a loss to know how to deal with her.

'Mirabel! I have never yet sent a girl out of my class,' she would say, in such a sorrowful voice that it quite wrung Alison's heart. 'Now come – pull yourself together and try again.'

One morning Alison was waiting to act a part she loved. She had rehearsed it over and over again to herself, acting it, as she thought, to perfection. She was longing for her turn to come, so that she might gloat over the sugared words of praise she felt sure would drop from Miss Quentin's lips.

There were ten more minutes to go – just about time for Alison's turn to come. And then Mirabel chose to be stupid again, saying her lines incorrectly, doing the wrong things so that Miss Quentin had to make her speak and act two or three times. The teacher, following her usual rule of being patient and encouraging, wasted nearly all the precious ten minutes on Mirabel.

Alison cast her eye on the clock, and bit her lip. All her rehearsing would be wasted now. How she hated that stupid Mirabel, holding up every class in order to be annoying.

'Now, Mirabel *dear*,' said Miss Quentin, in her

charming, patient voice, 'say it like this . . .'

It was too much for Alison. She stamped her foot. 'Mirabel! Stop fooling! It's hateful the way you take Miss Quentin in – and she's so patient too. You've wasted half the time – and now I shan't have my turn.'

'Poor little Alison!' said Mirabel, mockingly. 'She so badly wanted to show off to her precious Miss Quentin, and hear her say, "Well done, *darling*!" '

There was a dead silence. Then Alison burst into a flood of tears, and Carlotta trod on Mirabel's toe very neatly and smartly. Miss Quentin stared in horror.

'Girls! Girls! What are you thinking of? Carlotta! You amaze me. I cannot have this behaviour, I really cannot. Carlotta, apologize at once to Mirabel.'

'Certainly not,' said Carlotta. 'I don't mean to be rude to *you*, Miss Quentin – but you must see for yourself that Mirabel deserved it. I knew no one else but me would dare to do it – and it's been coming to Mirabel for quite a long time.'

The bell rang for the next class. Miss Quentin was most relieved. She had no idea how to tackle things of this sort. She gathered up her books quickly.

'There is no time to say any more, girls,' she said. 'I must go to my next class. Carlotta, I still insist that you put things right with Mirabel by apologizing.'

She went out of the room in a flurry. Carlotta grinned round at the others. 'Well,' she said, 'don't stand staring at me like that as if I'd done something awful. You know quite well you've all wanted to chastise Mirabel yourselves. We're as tired of her as we can be. It's a pity half-term isn't here and we can see the back of her.'

'Carlotta, you shouldn't do things like that,' said Janet. 'Alison, for pity's sake, stop howling. Mirabel, you deserved it, and now perhaps you'll shut up and behave properly.'

Mirabel had gone rather white. She had not attempted to hit back at Carlotta. 'If you think that will stop me doing what I like to spoil things for anybody you're mistaken,' she said, at last, in a tight kind of voice. 'It'll make me worse.'

'I suppose it will,' said Hilary. 'Well – I'll give you a warning. If you don't stop being an idiot, we shall make things uncomfortable for *you*. I don't mean we shall thump you. We shan't. But there are other ways.'

Mirabel said no more – but as she made no attempt that day or the following to behave sensibly, the girls made up their minds that they must carry out their threat.

They met in one of the music-rooms. Elsie Fanshawe was pleased. This excited her – it gladdened her spiteful nature, and added to her sense of importance, for, as she was one of the head girls, she could direct everyone in what they had to do.

'We've met together to decide how to get back at Mirabel,' she began.

Hilary interrupted her. 'Well – not exactly "get back", Elsie,' she said. 'It's more to prevent her from going on disgracing herself and our class.'

'Call it what you like,' said Elsie, impatiently. 'Now – what I propose is this: we'll take her books from her desk and hide them. We'll make her an apple-pie bed each night. We'll stitch up the pockets and sleeves of her outdoor coat. We'll put stones into her Wellingtons. We'll . . .'

'It all sounds rather spiteful,' said Hilary, doubtfully. 'Need we do quite so many things? I know Mirabel is perfectly sickening and needs a good lesson – but don't let's make ourselves as bad as she is!'

'Well – do as you like,' said Elsie, rather sneeringly. 'If you're too goody-goody to follow the lead of your head girls, well, there will be plenty of us who'll do what I say.'

'I bet Anna didn't think of any of those things,' said Bobby, looking at the plump, placid Anna, sitting beside Elsie.

The meeting discussed the matter a little more, and then, at the sound of a school bell, broke up. Only Gladys had said nothing. She had sat, as usual, in a kind of dream, paying hardly any attention to what was said. The girls were becoming so used to the Misery-girl, as they called her, that they really hardly noticed whether she was there or not.

'Well,' said Hilary, as the girls ran off to change for games, 'I suppose we must do something to teach Mirabel that two can play at being annoying – but somehow a lot of spitefulness seems to have got mixed up in it.'

'It's bound to, with Elsie Fanshawe to lead us!' said Bobby. 'I wish she wasn't our head girl. She's not the right sort. As for Anna, she's no use at all – just a lazy lump!'

'Mirabel's going to have a few shocks from now on,' said Alison, who was more pleased than anyone to think of the tricks that were to be played on Mirabel. 'I for one will do everything with the greatest pleasure!'

'I hope your darling Miss Quentin will be pleased with you!' said Bobby, with a grin, and scampered off to the field before Alison could think of any reply.

5.

Mirabel and the Misery-girl

It was not pleasant to be thought a tiresome nuisance by girls and teachers alike. Mirabel was getting tired of her defiant pose. Nobody had ever thought it was funny, as she had hoped. Nobody had ever laughed. They had just got impatient. The girl began to feel sorry she had ever started her irritating behaviour.

A great feeling of misery overtook her the evening of the day Carlotta had turned against her. She felt that no one liked her, and certainly no one loved her. Hadn't her own father sent her away? And her mother had agreed to it! How could she put up with that? There was no way to answer things like that except by being defiant.

Mirabel felt that she did not want to be with the others that evening in the noisy common-room. She stole away by herself to one of the music-rooms. She had spoken truly when she had told Bobby that she could play the piano and the violin. She loved music, and was a really good performer on the piano, and a beautiful player of the violin. But because of her defiant obstinacy, she had refused to learn either of the instruments at St Clare's, when her father had spoken to her about them.

'You can learn well there,' he had told her. 'There are excellent teachers of both.'

'What's the use?' Mirabel had flashed back at him. 'I'm only going to be there for half a term – and you don't want to have to pay full fees for two lots of music lessons, do you, as well as full fees for the ordinary lessons?'

'Very well. Have it your own way,' said her father. So nothing had been said about learning music, and the girl had missed her weekly lessons very much. Music had always helped her strong, domineering nature – and now, without it, she felt lost. She was depressed and unhappy tonight – her mind longed for something to fasten on, something to love. She thought of her violin at home, and wished with all her heart that she had brought it with her.

It was dark in the music-room. Mirabel did not turn on the light, for she was afraid somebody passing might see her, and she did not want any company just then. She leant her arms on a little table and thought.

Her hands touched something – a violin case. Something in the feel of it stirred her, and suddenly, with hands that trembled a little, she undid the strap and took out the violin inside. She put it lovingly under her chin, and groped for the bow.

And then the little dark music-room was full of music, as Mirabel played to herself. She played to comfort herself, to forget herself, and the notes filled the little room, and made it beautiful.

'That's better,' said Mirabel at last. 'That's much better! I didn't know how much I'd missed my music. I wonder whereabouts the piano is. I'll play that too. Why didn't I think of this before?'

She groped her way to the piano, and began to finger the notes gently in the darkness. She played from memory, and chose melodies that were sad and yearning, to match her own mood.

She thought she was alone, and she put her whole heart into her playing. Then suddenly she heard a sound in the room beside her, and she stopped at once, her heart thumping. She heard a stifled sob.

'Who's there?' said Mirabel, in a low voice. There was no answer. Someone began softly to grope her way to the door. Mirabel felt a stir of anger. Who was it spying on her? Who had come into the room like that? She jumped up and grabbed wildly at the someone near the door. She caught a blouse sleeve and held on.

'Who is it?' she said.

'Me – Gladys,' said a voice. 'I was in here alone – when you came in. I didn't know you were going to play. But you played such beautiful music I had to stay – and then it got sad, and I cried.'

'You're always crying,' said Mirabel, impatiently. 'What's the matter?'

'I shan't tell you,' said Gladys. 'You'll only tell the others, and they'd laugh. They call me Misery-girl, I know. It's hateful. They'd be Misery-girls too if they were like me.'

'Like *you* – why, what's the matter with you?' asked Mirabel, her curiosity aroused. 'Look here – tell me. I shan't jeer at you or anything.'

'Well, don't turn on the light then,' said Gladys. 'You'll think I'm very feeble, so I'd rather tell you in the dark.'

'You *are* an odd fish,' said Mirabel. 'Come on – what's the matter?'

'It's my mother,' said Gladys. 'She's awfully ill – in hospital – and I don't know if she'll get better. I simply can't tell you how much I love her, and how much I miss her. I haven't a father, or brothers or sisters – only my mother. I've never been away from her even for a night till now. I know it sounds silly to you – you'll call me babyish and mother's girl – and so I am, I suppose. But you see, Mother and I haven't had anyone but each other – and I'm so terribly, terribly homesick, and want to be with Mother so much . . .'

Gladys burst into sobs again, and cried so miserably that Mirabel forgot her own troubles for the moment and put her arm awkwardly round the girl. She saw how little courage Gladys had got – she saw how little she tried to face what had come to her – and she felt a little scornful. But no one could help feeling sorry for the miserable girl. Mirabel had no idea what to do for the best.

'Well,' she said, saying the first thing that came into her head, 'well, how would you like to be *me*? Sent away from home by your mother and father because they didn't want you, and said you upset your brother and sister and made everyone unhappy! That's what *I've* got to put up with! I'm not so lucky as you, I think!'

Gladys raised her head, and for the first time forgot her unhappiness in her scorn of Mirabel.

'*You* unlucky! Don't be silly – you don't know how lucky you are! To have a father *and* a mother, a brother *and* a sister, all to love and to love you. And I only have my mother and even she is taken away from me! Mirabel, you deserve to be sent away from home if you can't understand that families should love one another! I can tell you, if I had all those people to love *I* wouldn't behave so badly to them that they'd send me away. You ought to be ashamed of yourself.'

Coming from the silent Gladys, this was most astonishing. Mirabel stared into the darkness, not knowing what to say. Gladys got up and went to the door.

'I'm sorry,' she said, in a muffled voice. 'You're unhappy – and I'm unhappy – and I should be sorry for you, and comfort you. But you made your own unhappiness – and I didn't make mine. That's the difference between us.'

The door banged and Mirabel was alone. She sat still in surprise. Who would have thought that Gladys could say all that? Mirabel thought back to her own home. She saw the golden head of her little sister, the dark one of her brother, bent over homework. She saw the gentle, patient face of her mother, who always gave in to everyone. She remembered the good-humoured face of her father, changed to a sad and angry countenance because of her own continual insistence on her own way.

It was Mother's fault for giving in to me, she thought. And Harry and Joan should have stood up to me. But it's difficult for younger ones to stand up for themselves – and after all, I *am* difficult. I wish I was home now. I'm lonely here, and I've behaved like an idiot. I know Mother would always love me – and yet I've been beastly to her – and turned Daddy against me too. Harry and Joan will be glad I've gone. Nobody in the world wants me or loves me.

Self-pity brings tears more quickly to the eyes than anything else. Mirabel put her head on the table and wept. She forgot Gladys and her trouble. She only felt sorry for herself. She dried her eyes after a while, and sat up.

I shall stop behaving badly, she thought. I shall leave at half-term and go back home and try to do better. I'm tired of being silly. I'll turn over a new leaf tomorrow, and perhaps the girls will feel more friendly.

She got up and switched on the light. Her watch showed five minutes to nine – almost bed-time. She sat down at the piano and played to herself for a while, and then, when the nine-o'clock bell sounded, made her way upstairs to bed, full of good resolutions. She began to make pictures of how nice the girls would be to her when they found she was turning over a new leaf. Perhaps the twins would find she was somebody worth knowing after all.

Poor Mirabel! When she got into bed that night, she found that she could only get her legs half-way down it! The girls had made a beautiful apple-pie bed, and, not content with that, Elsie had put a spray of holly across the bend of the sheet. Mirabel gave a shout of dismay as the holly pricked her toes.

'Oh! Who's put this beastly thing into my bed? It's scratched my foot horribly!'

Mirabel had never had an apple-pie bed made for her before. She could not imagine what had happened. She tried to force her legs down to the bottom of the bed, but only succeeded in tearing the sheet.

The girls were in fits of laughter. They soon saw that Mirabel had not experienced an apple-pie bed before, and had no idea that the top sheet had been tucked under the bolster, and then folded in half, half-way down the bed, and brought back to fold over the blanket. Doris rolled on her bed in glee, and even placid Anna squealed with joy.

'Golly! You'll have to report that tear to Matron in the morning,' said Elsie, when she heard the sheet torn in half. 'You idiot! You might have guessed that would happen. You'll spend the next sewing-class mending a long rent.'

Mirabel threw the holly at Elsie. She had now discovered what had happened, and was angry and hurt. She got into bed and drew the covers round her. The others chuckled a little and then one by one fell asleep.

In the morning Mirabel awoke early. She lay and thought over what she had decided the night before. It wasn't going to be easy to make a complete changeover, but she didn't see anything else to do. She simply could *not* go on being idiotic. Once you were ashamed of yourself, you had to stop. If you didn't, then you really were an idiot.

So, full of good resolutions still, Mirabel went to her classes. She would work well. She would give Mam'zelle a great surprise. She would please Miss Jenks. She would make up for her rudeness to Miss Quentin. She would even be decent to that wild little Carlotta, and forgive her for treading on her toe. The girls would see she wasn't so bad as they thought she was, and they would turn over a new leaf too, and be friendly to her. Everything would be lovely again – and at the half-term she would leave, and people would be sorry to see her go!

It was with these pleasant thoughts that poor Mirabel entered on a day of horrid shocks and unpleasant surprises!

A day of shocks and surprises

Alison and Elsie were the two who enjoyed punishing Mirabel more than any of the others – Elsie because she was naturally spiteful, and Alison because she had been so annoyed at losing her turn in Miss Quentin's class.

'I'll sew up the sleeves of Mirabel's coat,' said Alison to Elsie. 'I'll do them awfully tightly. She'll be furious!'

'I'll take out some of her books and hide them,' said Elsie. 'Anna, go and find Mirabel's Wellington boots and put small pebbles inside – right in the toes.'

'Oh, can't someone else do that?' said Anna. 'I shall have to go down to the games-room to get the boots. Bobbie, you go.'

Elsie went to the classroom before morning school and removed various books and exercise papers. There was no one else in the room. The girl spitefully dropped ink on to a maths paper that Mirabel had done. 'This will teach her to behave better!' said Elsie to herself. 'Now – where shall I put the books?'

She decided to put them at the back of the handwork cupboard, and cover them with the loose raffia there. So into the cupboard went the books, and then Elsie, having a few minutes to spare, looked round for something else to do.

She saw the list of classroom duties hung up on the wall and went to read them. It was Mirabel's turn that week to keep the vases well-filled with water. Elsie pursed up her lips spitefully.

I'll empty out the water – and then, when the flowers begin to droop, Miss Jenks will notice and Mirabel will get ticked off for forgetting the water, thought Elsie. So out of the window went the water from the four big vases. The flowers were hurriedly replaced just as the first bell went for lessons.

The second form trooped in to take their places. Alison went to hold the door for Miss Jenks. Mirabel took a look round at the girls, hoping to get a smile from someone. She was longing to say that she meant to turn over a new leaf. But nobody looked at her except Elsie, who nudged Anna and then turned away.

'She's coming!' hissed Alison. The class stopped lounging over their desks and talking. They stood up and waited in silence. Miss Jenks was very strict about politeness and good manners in her class.

'Good morning, girls,' said the mistress, putting her books on her desk. 'Sit, please. We will . . . good gracious, Alison, what is that you are wearing on your left wrist?'

'A bracelet,' said Alison, sulkily. The girls looked at it and giggled. It was very like one that Miss Quentin wore. Alison loved to wear anything that even remotely resembled her beloved Miss Quentin's belongings.

'Alison, I am getting tired of asking you to remove bows and brooches and bracelets and goodness knows what,' said Miss Jenks. 'What with putting up with Mirabel's stupidities, and your vanities, I'm going really grey!'

Miss Jenks had flaming red hair, with not a scrap of grey in it. The girls smiled, but were not certain enough of Miss Jenks's temper that day to laugh out loud.

'Bring me that bracelet, Alison,' said Miss Jenks, in a tired voice. 'You can have it back in a week's time providing that during that time I haven't had to remove any other frills and fancies from you.'

Alison sulkily gave up the bracelet. She knew it was the rule that no jewellery should be worn with school uniform, but the little feather-head was always trimming herself up with something or other.

'And now please get out your maths books and the exercise you did for prep and we will go on to the next page of sums,' said Miss Jenks. 'It's much the same as the one we did yesterday. Work them out, please, and if there is any difficulty, let me know. Come up one by one as I call you, with your maths exercise paper, and I will correct it at my desk with you.'

The class got busy. Desks were opened and books got out. Pencils were taken from boxes. Exercise books were opened, and there was a general air of getting down to hard work.

Mirabel hunted all through her desk for her maths book. How curious! It didn't seem to be there. 'Have you borrowed my maths book?' she asked Janet in a whisper.

'No whispering,' said Miss Jenks, who had ears like a

lynx. 'What is it, Mirabel? One of your usual interruptions, I suppose.'

'No, Miss Jenks,' said Mirabel, meekly. 'I can't find my maths book, that's all.'

'Mirabel, you're always pretending you can't find this and that,' said Miss Jenks. 'Get your book at once and begin.'

'But, Miss Jenks, it really isn't here,' said Mirabel, hunting frantically through her desk again. The girls nudged one another and grinned. They all knew where it was – at the back of the handwork cupboard. Mirabel might look through her desk all day but she wouldn't find her book.

'Share Janet's book, then,' said Miss Jenks, shortly, only half-believing Mirabel. Mirabel heaved a sigh of relief, and opened her arithmetic book to copy down the sums from Janet's textbook. She put ready her maths paper, which she had done in prep the night before, to show to Miss Jenks. But as she turned it over the right way, she stared at it in horror. It was covered with ink-spots!

Just as I've made up my mind to turn over a new leaf, all these things happen! thought Mirabel in dismay. I can't imagine how I got that ink on my paper. Miss Jenks will never believe I didn't know it was there.

Mirabel was right – Miss Jenks didn't believe it! She looked in disgust at the untidy paper. She would not even correct it.

'Another of your nice little ways, I suppose,' she said. 'Do it again, please.'

'Miss Jenks, I really didn't make all those ink-spots,'

said Mirabel. But she had given in too many badly done papers before, on purpose, for Miss Jenks suddenly to believe her now.

'I don't want to discuss the matter,' said Miss Jenks. 'Do it all again, and let me have it this evening, without any mess on it at all.'

Mirabel went back to her desk. She caught Elsie's spiteful smile, but she did not guess yet that there was a campaign against her. She sat down, angry and puzzled.

The French class came next, and Mirabel discovered, to her dismay, that not only her French books, but also the French paper she had written out the day before as homework, had disappeared. She hunted through her desk again and again, and Mam'zelle grew sarcastic.

'Mirabel, is it possible for you to come out of your desk before the lesson is ended? Soon I shall forget what your face is like.'

'Mam'zelle, I'm sorry, but I can't seem to find the French paper I did yesterday,' said Mirabel, emerging from her desk flushed and worried.

If there was one thing that Mam'zelle could not stand, it was the non-appearance of any work she had set the class to do. She frowned, and her glasses slid down her big nose. The girls watched gleefully. The knew the signs of gathering wrath. Mam'zelle replaced her glasses on the bridge of her nose.

'Ah, Mirabel! You cannot seem to find the work you did, you say? How many times have I heard that excuse since I have been here at St Clare's? A thousand times, ten thousand times! You have not done the work. Do not deny it, I know. You are a tiresome girl – you have been tiresome ever since the first day you came. You will always be tiresome. You will give me that work before the end of the morning or you will not play lacrosse this afternoon.'

'But, Mam'zelle, I really *did* do it!' protested Mirabel, almost in tears. 'I can't find my ordinary French books, either. They're gone.'

'Always this Mirabel holds up my class!' cried Mam'zelle, raising her hands to the ceiling and wagging them in a way that made Doris long to imitate her at once. 'She loses things – she looks for them – she makes excuses – I cannot bear this girl.'

'Nor can anybody,' said Alison, delighted at the success of the trick. Mirabel flashed an angry glance at her. She was beginning to wonder if the girls had had anything to do with the mysterious disappearance of her things.

It's too bad all this happening now, she thought. Mam'zelle might believe me. I really am speaking the truth.

But Mirabel had so often been silly and untruthful that she had only herself to blame now if no one believed her when she did actually tell the truth. She tried once more with Mam'zelle.

'Please do believe me, Mam'zelle,' she begged. 'Elsie saw me doing the paper last night. Didn't you, Elsie?'

'Indeed I didn't,' said Elsie, maliciously.

'Ah, this untruthful Mirabel!' cried Mam'zelle. 'You will do me the paper once because you have not done it –

and again you will do it for me because you have told an untruth.'

Mirabel saw her time at break going. She would have to do the two papers then. She looked round the class for sympathy. Usually, comforting glances were sent from one girl to another when somebody got into trouble. But there were no comforting glances for Mirabel. Everyone was glad that the Nuisance was in trouble.

Poor Mirabel! Her troubles were never-ending that morning. Miss Jenks noticed all the drooping flowers in the waterless vases during the next lesson, and spoke sharply about it.

'Who is Room Monitor this week?'

'I am,' said Mirabel.

'Well, look at the flowers,' said Miss Jenks. 'It doesn't seem as if they can have a drop of water in the vases, by the look of them.'

'Why, I filled them all up yesterday,' said Mirabel, indignantly. 'I did really.'

Miss Jenks went to the nearest vase and tipped it up. 'Not a drop of water,' she said. 'I suppose you will suggest next that somebody has emptied all the vases, Mirabel?'

It flashed across the girl's mind that someone might actually have done that, to pay her back for all the annoying things she had done. But it seemed such a mean trick – to make flowers die in order to get somebody into trouble! She flushed and said nothing.

'I suppose you thought I would let you miss part of the lesson whilst you filled up the flowers,' said Miss Jenks, in

45

disgust. 'Hilary, have you finished answering the questions on the blackboard? Good – then just go and get some water for the vases, will you?'

Mirabel spent the whole of break doing the French paper twice over. She guessed now, by the grins and nudges among the girls, that most of her troubles were due to them, and she was angry and hurt. Just as I had made up my mind to be decent! she thought, as she wrote out the French papers quickly. It's beastly of everyone.

She was late for games because she could not put on her coat in time to go to the field with the others. Alison had sewn up the sleeves well and truly – so tightly that it was impossible to break the stitches. Mirabel had to go and hunt for a pair of scissors to cut the sewn-up sleeves. She was almost in tears.

And then, when she put on her Wellingtons to go across the muddy field-path, she squealed in pain. Nasty little pebbles made her hobble along – and at last she had to stop, take off the boots, and empty the pebbles into the hedge.

Miss Wilton, the sports mistress, had already started the lacrosse game going. 'You're late, Mirabel,' she called. 'Stand aside until half-time. If you can't bother to be in time, you can miss part of the game.'

It was cold standing and watching. Mirabel felt miserable. Everybody and everything was against her. What was the use of trying to be different?

Miss Wilton took her to task at half-time. 'Why were you so late? You know the time perfectly well. You were almost fifteen minutes after the others!'

She waited to hear Mirabel's excuse. The other girls listened. They had not bargained for Miss Wilton enquiring into the matter. Alison felt uncomfortable. She didn't want to get into trouble for sewing up Mirabel's coat-sleeves. She did not want another bad report. Last term's had been very poor, and her father had had a good many things to say that were not pleasant to hear.

Mirabel opened her mouth to pour out her woes – how her coat-sleeves had been sewn up – stones put into her Wellingtons – and goodness knows what else done to her! Then she shut her mouth again. How often had she scolded her young brother and sister for telling tales of her when she had made things unpleasant for them? She had always said that a tale-bearer was someone quite impossible.

The girls deserve to have tales told about them, thought Mirabel, but I shan't make myself into something I hate just to get back at them.

So she said nothing at all.

'Well,' said Miss Wilton, impatiently, 'as you have no excuse, it seems, take off your coat and join in the second half of the game. But next time, if you are late, you will not play in the game at all – you can just go back to school and ask Miss Jenks to give you something to do.'

The game went on. One or two of the girls began to feel uncomfortable. It was decent of Mirabel not to give them away. You couldn't attack people if they behaved well. It's time we stopped going for Mirabel, thought Hilary. I'll tell Elsie so tonight!

7.

A meeting in the common-room

Another meeting, this time called by Hilary, was held that night. It was held in the common-room. Everyone was there but Mirabel, who was doing her maths paper all over again in the classroom.

'What's the meeting for?' asked Elsie, half-indignant that anyone but herself should call a meeting.

'It's about Mirabel,' said Hilary. 'You know, she didn't split on us when she had the chance to – so I vote we stop playing tricks on her now. Anyway, we pretty well put her through it today!'

'We're certainly not going to stop,' said Elsie, at once. 'What, stop when she's only just begun to learn her lesson! She'll be as bad as ever if we don't go on showing her we can make things just as tiresome for her as she has made them for us!'

'No, we've done enough,' said Hilary. 'It makes me feel rather mean. I rather wish we hadn't done *quite* so many things – and anyway, I don't know who spilt ink over her maths paper, and took the water out of the flowers. We didn't arrange that. Who did it?'

There was a silence. Elsie went red. She did not dare to say she had done anything more than had already

48

been arranged – the others might think her spiteful, or mean.

'I believe it was Elsie!' said Carlotta, suddenly. 'Look how red she's gone!'

Everyone looked. Elsie scowled. 'Of course I didn't do anything,' she said. 'I don't think we did nearly enough. I think a girl who openly says she's jolly well going to make herself too beastly to stay more than half a term ought to be well shown up!'

'Well, she *has* been shown up – by her own self!' said Janet. 'No one would have known anything about her or her private affairs if she hadn't gone round yelling them out! I think Hilary is right – we won't do anything more.'

'You talk as if Hilary is head girl,' said Elsie, spitefully.

'Well – so she was in the first form,' said Bobby, losing her temper. 'And let me tell you she was a much better one than you, Elsie.'

'Don't forget that Anna is head girl too,' said Pat. Anna smiled sleepily. Bobby turned on her at once.

'As if anyone can remember that Anna is head girl, or anything! What's the good of a head girl who is always too lazy to do a single thing? We've got two head girls in this form – and one is spiteful and catty and overbearing – and the other is fat and lazy!'

'Shut up, Bobby,' said Hilary, uncomfortably. 'It's no good losing your temper like that. Let's get back to the point – and that is, we're not going to persecute Mirabel any more. Let's give her a chance and see if today's lessons have taught her anything. She knows well enough we have all been working against her – and that must be a very horrid experience.'

'Hilary Wentworth – if you don't stop talking as if you were head of this form, you'll be sorry,' said Elsie, angered by Bobby's candid speech. 'Anna – for Heaven's sake sit up and back me up.'

'But I don't think you're right,' said Anna, in her gentle voice. 'I don't want to persecute Mirabel, either. I don't feel spiteful towards her now.'

'You're too lazy to feel anything,' said Elsie, surprised and furious at Anna's unexpected refusal to back her up. 'You know perfectly well that as head girls we must work together – and it's an unwritten rule that the form go by what we say.'

'Well, I can't work with you in this,' said Anna. 'I may be fat and lazy and all the other things you probably think about me, and don't say – but I am not catty. So I say, as head girl of the form – we will not continue with our tricks against Mirabel.'

'Well,' said Pat, 'this is going to be difficult – two head girls, each saying different! I suppose we'd better put it to the vote, which girl we follow. Now – hands up for Anna and doing what she says!'

Every single hand went up at once. Anna grinned and for once sat up really straight. Elsie went white.

'Now – hands up those who wish to follow Elsie,' said Pat. Not a single hand went up, of course. Elsie stood up angrily.

'This is what comes of having to stay down with a lot

of half-baked first formers!' she said, her voice trembling. 'Well – I'll tell you who emptied the water out of the vases – and dropped ink on Mirabel's maths paper – it was your precious Anna! If you want to follow a girl who does things like that, and then is ashamed to own up to them, well, you can!'

She flung herself out of the room and slammed the door loudly. Anna raised her well-marked eyebrows.

'Well, girls,' she said, in her rather drawling voice, 'I assure you I am not guilty.'

Everyone believed her. Anna might be lazy and not bother herself or undertake any kind of responsibility – but at least she was truthful and honest.

'I'm not going to count Elsie as head girl any more,' said Isabel. 'We'll have only Anna. Come on, Anna – stir yourself, and settle things one way or another.'

'Poor Anna – she will have to open her eyes and wake up at last,' said Carlotta's high voice, rather maliciously. Anna stood up suddenly.

'Well – I'm just as tired of Elsie's spite and cattiness as you are,' she said. 'So if you'll do with just me as head girl, I'll wake up a bit. It's not been easy trying to work with Elsie. I'm not going to give her away – but I just can't bear some of the things she says and does. Now – it's not enough just to stop persecuting Mirabel – can't we do something positive – I mean, something to put her right, instead of just stopping her being wrong?'

Everyone gaped at Anna. This was the first time the big, sleepy-eyed girl had ever made such a long speech, or suggested anything of her own accord. Hilary thought her suggestion was excellent.

'Yes – that's the way to do things really,' she agreed. 'It's not enough to stop things going wrong – you've got to set them going the other way – on the right road. But I don't for the life of me see how. Mirabel is terribly difficult. I can't see that she's any good at anything at all. There isn't anything to work on.'

'She's bad at lessons – no good at games – hopeless at art – poor at gym,' said Isabel. 'If there was *some*thing she was good at, we could make it our starting-point – you know, praise her up a bit, and give her some self-respect. That's what people need when things have gone wrong.'

Then the second form had a great surprise. The Misery-girl spoke, in her rather timid little voice!

'Mirabel *is* good at something! *Awfully* good!'

Everyone stared at Gladys in double-amazement, astonished that she should have spoken at all, and amazed to hear what she said. Gladys seemed to shrink under the gaze of so many pairs of eyes. She wished she had not spoken – but she had been interested, in spite of herself, in the scene that had been going on – and she had suddenly felt that she would like to help stupid Mirabel. After all – she had put her arm round her the night before, and had been kind in her own awkward way.

'What do you mean?' said Anna.

'Well – she's frightfully good at music,' stammered Gladys, horrified now to think she had to speak to so many girls at once.

'How do you know?' asked Janet. 'She's never played any instrument here – and she doesn't even open her mouth in the singing-class.'

'I know because I've heard her,' said Gladys. 'She was in the music-room last night – you know, the one next to the boot-cupboard – and first she played a violin – oh, most beautifully – and then she played the piano. And it was all in the dark too.'

'In the *dark*!' said Carlotta, in surprise. 'Whatever were you two doing there in the dark? How odd! Do you usually go and sit in the music-rooms in the dark?'

Gladys didn't know what to say. She couldn't confess that she often went to the lonely little music-rooms by herself when she felt extra-homesick – the girls would laugh at her, and she couldn't bear that. She stared at Carlotta and said nothing.

'Well, can't you answer?' said Carlotta, impatiently. 'Do you often go and listen to Mirabel playing in the dark?'

'No – of course not,' said Gladys. 'I – I just happened to be there – when Mirabel came in – and she didn't see me. So I heard her playing, you see.'

The girls looked at one another. So Gladys disappeared into the dark little music-rooms at night – all alone. What a strange girl she was! They looked at her thin white little face, and two or three of them felt a pang of sympathy for the Misery-girl and her lonely thoughts, whatever they might be. Nobody laughed or teased her about being in the dark in the music-room. Even downright Carlotta made no remark about it.

'You know,' said Janet, looking round at the little company of girls, 'Mirabel reminds me in some ways of the O'Sullivan twins!'

'What do you mean?' said Pat, indignantly.

'Well – don't you remember how awfully difficult you were a year ago, when you first came to St Clare's?' said Janet. 'You just made up your minds to be awkward, and you were! You ought to understand Mirabel's point of view, and be able to tell us how to tackle her. What made you two change your ideas and want to stay here?'

'Oh – as soon as we realized we were acting stupidly – and you were friendly to us – we just sort of settled down and loved everything,' said Pat, trying to remember that first exciting term.

'Right,' said Anna, taking charge of the meeting again. 'That's just what *we*'ll do! We think Mirabel was decent for not splitting on us today – so we'll be friendly towards her now instead of beastly – and perhaps if we get her to play to us, and praise her up a bit – she'll settle down too. What about it?'

'Yes, Anna!' said everyone, Gladys too. Hilary gazed in surprise at Anna. She would never have thought that sleepy Anna could have come to the fore like this – why, she really seemed to be taking a keen interest in everything! And taking the lead too. Perhaps it would be a good thing that the class had broken away from Elsie's leadership. Anna seemed as if she was going to take the chance offered to her by the unexpected quarrel.

'Sh! Here comes Mirabel!' said Pat, as the door opened.

At once the girls began to chatter and gabble about anything that came into their heads. Mirabel looked at them suspiciously. She felt sure they had been discussing her! Horrid things. Well – if they had been planning fresh tricks to play on her, she would go back to her old ways and upset every single class she could!

8.

Mirabel gives the
form a surprise

The twins talked together that night when they were in bed. Their beds were next to one another and they could whisper without anyone else hearing what they said.

'We ought to have a few excitements now!' whispered Pat. 'I bet Elsie won't sit down under this! She'll find some way of getting back at Anna – and all of us as well!'

'I hope Mirabel will be sensible now,' said Isabel. 'She looked most suspiciously at all of us, I thought – and she hardly answered Janet at all when she spoke to her.'

'Well, I'm not surprised, really,' said Pat, with a yawn. 'After all – we did do an awful lot of things to her today. It was funny at first – but I didn't like it much afterwards – even though I must say I think Mirabel deserved a little rough-handling. I say – didn't you think it was funny, Gladys speaking up like that – and admitting she was in the music-room all alone? Funny kid, isn't she?'

'Pat, what Janet said was quite true,' said Isabel, speaking rather loudly.

'Sh! Don't speak so loud,' whispered Pat. 'What do you mean?'

'Well, you know – we did behave a little bit like Mirabel – and we did hate it when everyone disliked us – it was a miserable feeling,' said Isabel. 'So let's make a bee-line for Mirabel tomorrow, and buck her up a bit. St Clare's has done a lot for us – let's do a bit for Mirabel.'

'Pat! Isabel! If you don't stop talking at once, I'll report you to Miss Jenks tomorrow!' suddenly came Elsie's sharp voice through the darkness.

'You can't. You're not head girl,' came Carlotta's cheeky voice, before the twins could answer.

'I'll report you too, for untidy drawers and cupboard,' said Elsie, furiously.

'Well – it will only be the fiftieth time, I should think,' said Carlotta, lazily. 'Go ahead, Miss Catty Elsie!'

There was a delighted squeal of laughter from the dormitory at this. Elsie sat up in bed, furious.

'Carlotta! If you dare to talk like a low-down circus girl to me . . .' she began. But at that everyone sat up in bed, indignant.

'Listen,' began Bobby, 'anyone who calls Carlotta low-down deserves a good scolding! We're all proud of Carlotta – remember how she saved Sadie from being kidnapped last term! It's *you* who are low-down, Elsie! Now – just you remember what I said about that scolding!'

Elsie was furious. She began to tell Bobby exactly what she thought of her. She forgot to keep her voice low, and when Miss Jenks came along to see that all was quiet in the dormitory, she was amazed to hear a voice going on and on in the darkness – an angry voice, a spiteful voice!

57

She switched on the light and stood in silence by the door. Every girl was sitting up in bed. Elsie's voice died away in horror. She stared wide-eyed at Miss Jenks.

'Who was that talking just now?' enquired Miss Jenks, in her cool voice.

Nobody answered. Elsie simply could not bear to own up. She swallowed hard, hoping that Miss Jenks would deliver a general lecture and go. Miss Jenks didn't. She just stood and waited.

'Who is in charge of this dormitory?' she asked. 'Oh you, I suppose, Elsie – as you are one of the head girls for this form. Well – as the culprit does not seem to have enough courage to own up, perhaps you, as head girl, will see to it that the girl is punished by going to bed one hour earlier tomorrow. Will you?'

'Yes, Miss Jenks,' answered Elsie, in a very subdued tone. There was a smothered giggle from Carlotta's bed, hurriedly turned into a loud cough.

'You seem to have a cold, Carlotta,' said Miss Jenks, pretending to be quite concerned. 'Perhaps you had better go to Matron tomorrow morning and get a dose of medicine for it.'

'Oh, I shall be quite all right tomorrow morning, Miss Jenks, thank you,' Carlotta hurriedly assured her.

'Good night, girls,' said Miss Jenks, and switched off the light. As soon as her footsteps had died away, the girls began to giggle and whisper.

'Elsie! See you put yourself to bed an hour earlier tomorrow!' whispered Carlotta.

Elsie lay in bed, her cheeks burning. Why hadn't she owned up? Then she wouldn't have been so humiliated! She jolly well wouldn't go to bed early the next night, anyway. She shut her ears with her fingers, so as not to hear what the girls were whispering. She did not dare to tell them to stop – and as for threatening to report them – well, that would make them laugh all the more!

Everyone felt scornful of Elsie – but they also thought the whole thing was funny. The girls were quite determined that Elsie *should* go to bed early the next night. They were not going to let her off the punishment she had meekly promised to wreak on the culprit!

The next day the twins gave Mirabel a cheerful grin at the breakfast-table. She smiled back, surprised and warmed. She had been expecting a few more tricks, and the unexpected smile surprised her very much.

After breakfast Pat and Isabel spoke to Mirabel. 'Did you hear about the row in our dormitory last night?' asked Pat.

'I knew there was something up,' said Mirabel. 'I heard the others talking about it. What was it?'

The twins told Mirabel about Elsie and Miss Jenks, and the girl smiled. 'Thanks for telling me,' she said, 'it was funny. I say – is the form going to do beastly things to me today? You know, I'd just decided to turn over a new leaf – when you did all those things.'

'Had you really decided to change?' said Pat, in surprise. 'Well – don't worry – we're not going to get back at you anymore. But for goodness' sake do your bit too.

It's pretty sickening having class after class upset, you know. You may feel in a temper about your home-affairs – but that really isn't any reason for venting your temper on the class!'

'No – I see that now,' said Mirabel. 'I'm an idiot – always have been. Well – I bet you'll be glad to see the back of me at half-term.'

'Wait and see,' said Isabel. 'I say – our form is giving a concert next week, in aid of the Red Cross. Everyone is to do something. Could you play the violin for us, do you think? And perhaps the piano too?'

'How do you know I play?' asked Mirabel, in surprise. But at that moment Miss Jenks bustled the whole class off for a nature-walk, and Mirabel found herself walking with the timid Gladys, who, remembering the night in the dark music-room, felt afraid to say a word. Mirabel felt awkward too, so the two hardly exchanged a single word.

The twins, when the chance came, hurriedly told the rest of the form that they had asked Mirabel to play at the concert planned for the following week. Every form had been asked to get up something in aid of the Red Cross, and this was to be the second form's contribution.

'Did she say she would?' asked Bobby.

'No – but we'll put her name down on the programme,' said Pat. 'I bet she will! She was quite nice this morning.'

Mirabel found her books back in her desk that day. Anna had taken them from their hiding-place and put them back. Elsie had scowled, but had said nothing. She didn't know whom she hated most – Anna – or that saucy Carlotta!

When the programme for the Red Cross concert was drawn up that evening, Isabel called across to Mirabel.

'Hi, Mirabel! I've put you down for a violin solo, and a piano solo. What will you play? Can you tell us the names of the pieces?'

'I haven't my violin here,' said Mirabel hesitatingly.

'Pooh – you can easily send a message home for it,' said Pat. 'And Anna will lend you hers to practise on this week – won't you, Anna?'

'Of course,' said Anna. 'I'll go and get it now and you can see if you like the feel of it. It's a good one.'

Anna went to fetch her violin. She took it out of its case and put it into Mirabel's hands. As she had said, it was a good one. Mirabel drew the bow across it lovingly.

'Play something,' said Isabel. And then, as in the dark music-room, Mirabel played some of the melodies she loved. She forgot the girls in the common-room, she forgot St Clare's, she forgot herself. She was a real little musician, and she put all her heart into the music she loved.

The girls listened spell-bound. Two or three girls in the school played the violin very well – but Mirabel made it speak. The notes rang out pure and true, and Anna was amazed that her violin could produce such music.

When Mirabel stopped, everyone clapped frantically. 'I say! You *are* marvellous!' said Pat, her eyes shining. 'Golly – you'll make everyone sit up at the concert next week, I can tell you. Now go and play something on the piano. Go on. You simply must!'

Mirabel looked round at the admiring audience, with flushed cheeks and bright eyes. Only Elsie Fanshawe did not applaud. She sat at a table, reading a book, taking no notice at all.

'Go on, Mirabel – play us something on the piano!' insisted Pat.

Mirabel went across to the old piano in the common-room. It was there for the girls to strum on, if they wanted to. Usually dance music or popular songs were hammered out on it – but tonight something quite different was played!

Mirabel's long, sensitive fingers ran over the notes, and one of Chopin's nocturnes filled the quiet common-room. Most of the girls loved good music, and they listened in delight. Gladys shut her eyes. Music always stirred her very much, though she learnt no instrument, and knew little about it.

The notes died away. The girls sat up, pleased. 'Look here – play that at the concert next week,' said Hilary. 'It's heavenly. I heard it on the radio in the hols – but you play it much better!'

'I don't,' said Mirabel, red with embarrassment and pleasure. 'All right – I'll play it. And if you really want me to play something on the violin too, I'll send a message tomorrow asking for my own violin to be sent. Anna's *is* a lovely one – but I'm more at home with my own.'

'Good,' said Isabel. 'I say – aren't you a dark horse –

never saying a word about your music – keeping it up your sleeve like that! You've got a real gift. I wish *I* had a gift. You're lucky!'

Mirabel went to help Isabel to draw up the programme. Her words echoed in her mind. 'You've got a real gift!' She remembered Miss Theobald's words too. 'Difficult children often have some hidden quality – some gift – something to make them worthwhile!'

Nobody at home thought her worthwhile – or surely they wouldn't have sent her away! But she *was* worthwhile! See how the girls loved hearing her play. It was a pity she hadn't accepted her father's offer to learn music at St Clare's. She had no other gift but music, and she had refused to develop that, out of obstinacy.

'I bet you could pass any music exam you went in for,' said Isabel, handing Mirabel a few programmes to print. 'Nobody in our form is specially good at music. It's a pity you don't learn. You would be a credit to us – you'd make some of the top formers sit up, I bet! And I guess you'd win the music-prize.'

'Well – I'll certainly send that message tomorrow,' said Mirabel, printing the programmes neatly. She felt happy for the first time that term. It was nice to be working in friendliness with someone like Isabel. It was lovely to be praised for something. Nobody thought a great deal of her music at home, because none of them were musical – except her brother – and dear me, how she snubbed him! Mirabel felt annoyed with herself when she remembered that. She ought to have encouraged him.

I really must have been tiresome, she thought. Well – going away from home does make you see things clearly. When I go back at half-term I'll show them I'm not as bad as they think!

That night, at eight o'clock, all the second form winked at one another. If Elsie was going to bed an hour earlier, it was time she went. But she showed no sign. She had come back from supper and had settled down to read again, saying nothing to anybody.

'Bedtime for little girls!' said Carlotta. Elsie took no notice.

'Naughty girls must go to bed early,' said Bobby, loudly. Elsie did not move.

The girls looked at one another. It was quite clear that Elsie was not going to get up and go. She had not only been afraid to own up to Miss Jenks the night before – but she was now going to evade the punishment!

To everyone's surprise Anna spoke. 'Elsie!' she said. 'You know perfectly well what you have to do. Don't make us all ashamed of you.'

'You can't talk to *me* like that!' said Elsie, turning over a page.

'I can,' said Anna, calmly. 'I am head girl of the form. I have the right to tell you what to do.'

'You haven't,' said Elsie, furiously. 'I'm head girl too.'

'You're not, you're not!' cried a dozen voices. 'We only recognize Anna as head girl now. We don't want *you*!'

'Only Miss Jenks can decide a thing like that,' said Elsie, looking round at the girls.

'Perhaps you are right,' said Anna, in her slow voice. 'Come with me and we will let Miss Jenks decide.'

Hilary looked at Anna in admiration. She knew that this was the one thing that would defeat Elsie. On no account would Elsie go to Miss Jenks at the moment! It would be far too humiliating.

Elsie hesitated. The girls waited. They knew Elsie would not consent to go with Anna. Anna stood up as if she was going.

'I'm not going to Miss Jenks,' said Elsie, in a low voice.

'I thought not,' said Anna, and sat down again. 'Well – either Miss Jenks decides this matter or the girls do. I don't mind.'

'*We*'ll decide – we've already decided!' said Janet. 'Anna is our head girl, and we don't want Elsie. And that being so, Elsie – you'll just do as Anna says, and go off to bed. It's your own silly fault.'

That was too much for Elsie. Her obstinacy rose up and she pursed her thin lips. 'I'm not going,' she said. 'I'm not obeying Anna. She may be your head girl – but I won't admit she's mine!'

'Right,' said Carlotta, cheerfully, getting up. 'Come on, Bobby – Janet – twins. Get hold of Elsie, and we'll bump her all the way upstairs to bed! We can't have her disobeying Miss Jenks's orders like this! My word – won't the third form stare when we go by with poor Elsie!'

'No – don't!' cried Elsie, in dismay, jumping to her feet. She knew the wild little Carlotta would stop at nothing. 'I'll go. I'll go. But I hate you all!'

She burst into tears, and with loud sobs went to the door. Carlotta sat down. When Elsie had gone, she looked round.

'I didn't really mean us to bump her up the stairs to bed,' she said, 'but I guessed she'd go of her own accord if I suggested it.'

'She'll be awful tomorrow,' said Bobby. Anna shook her big head.

'No,' she said. 'I know Elsie. She will begin to feel a martyr, and terribly sorry for herself. She will try to get our sympathy by being subdued and meek.'

'Yes – I think you're right,' said Janet. 'Well – the best thing is not to take any notice of her at all. We don't want to get spiteful – just let's leave her alone and take no notice at all.'

'That's the best thing,' said Anna. She took up her knitting again. 'Oh, dear – being the only head girl is very wearing. There seem so many things to decide!'

9.

Anna sees the head mistress

The next morning Mirabel wanted to send for her violin. Anna told her what to do.

'You'll have to go and get permission from Miss Theobald.'

Mirabel went to ask permission. She knocked at Miss Theobald's door and was told to come in. The head mistress looked up. She did not smile.

'What is it, Mirabel?' she asked.

'Please, Miss Theobald, may I send a message home?' asked Mirabel.

Still Miss Theobald did not smile or unbend in any way. She looked really stern. Mirabel began to feel very uncomfortable.

'What is the message about?' she asked. 'You know that you cannot leave before half-term.'

'It's nothing to do with my leaving,' said Mirabel. 'It's – it's – well, Miss Theobald, I just want to ask my mother if she'll send my violin, that's all.'

The head looked surprised. 'Your violin?' she said. 'Why? You don't learn music, do you?'

'No,' said Mirabel. 'I wish I did now. But I wouldn't when Daddy gave me the chance. You see – the second form are giving a concert for the Red Cross next week – and I said I would play for them. I'd like my own violin to play on. It's a beauty.'

Miss Theobald looked at Mirabel. 'So you *have* a gift, Mirabel!' she said. 'You remember what I said to you? I wonder if there is anything worthwhile in you after all!'

Mirabel went red. She stood on first one foot and then on the other. She felt certain that Miss Theobald had had bad reports of her from every mistress.

'I'm not sure that I shall let you ask for your violin,' said Miss Theobald at last. 'I hear that you misbehave at practically every class. You try to spoil everything, it seems. How do I know that you will behave at the concert?'

'I will,' said Mirabel, earnestly. 'You won't believe me, perhaps – but I've turned over a new leaf now. I've got tired of being silly.'

'I see,' said Miss Theobald. 'You've stopped misbehaving just because you're tired of it – not because you're ashamed of it, or want to do better, or want us to think well of you. Only just because you're tired of it. You disgust me, Mirabel. Go, please. I'm disappointed in you. I had hoped that possibly you might turn over a new leaf for some better motive. I thought I saw some courage in you, some real intelligence that might help you to realize your foolishness and selfishness in behaving as you did. Now I see that you have none – you only stop because you yourself are tired of misbehaviour and, possibly, are tired also of having the others unfriendly towards you. Please go.'

Mirabel was struck with horror at the cold, stern words. She had felt so pleased with herself to think she was turning over a new leaf. She *had* been ashamed of herself. She hadn't only got tired of being silly. She opened her mouth to defend herself, but the sight of Miss Theobald's stern face frightened her. She went out of the room without a word.

Miss Theobald sat and thought for a few minutes. Then she sent a message to ask Miss Jenks to come to her for a few minutes.

Miss Jenks soon appeared. 'Sit down for a moment,' said Miss Theobald. 'I want to talk to you about Mirabel Unwin. I have had continual bad reports from you about her. Is there any improvement at all?'

'Yes,' said Miss Jenks at once. 'She seems suddenly to be settling down. I don't quite know why. Has anything happened? I saw her just now, and she looked as if she had been crying.'

'Probably she had,' said Miss Theobald, and told Miss Jenks what had just passed between her and Mirabel.

'I should like to know if the girl has suddenly changed for the right reasons, or the wrong ones,' she said. 'Perhaps the head girls could tell me. Send them, will you?'

'There seems to be some sort of upset between the two head girls of my form,' said Miss Jenks. 'I don't think Elsie Fanshawe has gone down very well with the first formers who came up into my form. But Anna seems unexpectedly to be showing some signs of responsibility and leadership. I'll go and send the two girls to you.

Perhaps they can tell you more about Mirabel. Personally I think we might give her a chance now, and let her have her violin.'

She left the room and went to find Anna and Elsie. They were in the common-room with the others. As the door opened and Miss Jenks appeared all the girls rose to their feet and stopped chattering. Janet turned off the radio.

'Miss Theobald wants the two head girls to go to her for a few minutes,' said Miss Jenks in her cool voice. 'Will you go at once, please?'

She left the room. There was a silence. Anna stood up to go. So did Elsie. But quick as thought Carlotta pulled her down again to her chair.

'You're not head girl, Elsie. You know you're not. We won't have you – and if we won't have you, then Anna is the only head girl. You are not going to Miss Theobald!'

'Don't be an idiot!' snapped Elsie, scrambling up again. 'You know I've got to go. I can't tell Miss Theobald I'm no longer head girl.'

'Well, Anna can,' said Hilary. 'It's unfortunate, Elsie – but we all happen to think the same about this. You were a bad head girl – and we won't accept you. You wouldn't let Miss Jenks decide it – you accepted *our* decision – and you've got to abide by it. Anna must go alone.'

'She's not to, she's not to,' said Elsie, half-crying. 'It's shameful. What will Miss Theobald think?'

'You should have thought of these things before,' said Hilary. 'Anna, go. Say as little as you can about Elsie, of course – but please let it be understood that you are the only head girl of the second form now.'

Anna went. Elsie saw that the whole of the second form would stop her by force if she tried to follow. So she lay back in her chair, looking as forlorn and miserable as she could, letting the tears trickle down her cheeks. She hoped that the girls would feel uncomfortable, and very sorry. But nobody did. In fact, they took no notice of her at all, and went on cheerfully chattering among themselves. It was Saturday morning, and except for an hour's lessons, they were free to do as they chose.

Mirabel was not there. She had had a shock, and it had upset her very much. She did not want anyone to see that she had been crying, so she had gone to the cloakroom to bathe her eyes. She came out of the room just as Anna passed it on her way to the head. Anna spoke to her.

'Hallo! Did you get permission from the head to send for your violin?'

'I didn't get permission,' said Mirabel, miserably. 'Anna, Miss Theobald was awful to me. She thinks I've only turned over a new leaf because I was tired of being an idiot. But I haven't. I'm awfully ashamed of myself now. It was dreadful having you all doing beastly things to me the very day I'd made up my mind to do better – and now even Miss Theobald is against me. What's the use of trying? It's just no good at all. I shan't play at the concert. I shan't do anything.'

Anna stared at Mirabel, surprised. 'Look here, I can't wait now,' she said. 'I've been sent for by the head. But I'll

71

have a talk with you afterwards, see? I'm awfully sorry, Mirabel. Really I am. Cheer up.'

She ran down the passage to Miss Theobald's sitting-room and knocked.

'Come in!' said the head's pleasant voice. Anna entered, half-scared. Miss Theobald was kind and just – but her wisdom and dignity awed every girl, and it was quite an ordeal to go for any kind of interview.

'Good morning, Anna,' said Miss Theobald. 'Where is Elsie Fanshawe?'

'Elsie isn't head girl now, Miss Theobald,' said Anna, feeling awkward. Miss Theobald looked most surprised.

'I hadn't heard this,' she said. 'Why isn't she?'

'We all decided that she wasn't quite fit to be at present,' said Anna, finding it difficult to explain without giving Elsie away too much.

'Miss Jenks knows nothing of this,' said the head. 'Why didn't you ask her advice?'

'Elsie didn't want us to,' said Anna. 'She said she would rather accept our decision, without us taking matters any further. It's – it's rather difficult to explain, Miss Theobald, without telling tales.'

'Did Hilary Wentworth and the O'Sullivan twins agree to this?' asked the head. She had great faith in the fairness and common sense of these three girls.

'Oh, yes,' said Anna. 'I wouldn't have done it myself – I'm too lazy, I'm afraid. But once the girls wanted me to accept responsibility and carry on without Elsie, I had to take it.'

'Of course,' said Miss Theobald, sensing in Anna something better and stronger than she had known before in the lazy slow-moving girl. 'Well – I won't ask any more questions, Anna. I think probably the second form are right – all I hope is that some good will come out of this for Elsie. I can see an improvement in *you* already!'

Anna blushed. Responsibility was a nuisance – but it did bring definite rewards, not the least of which was an added self-respect.

'Anna, I sent for you because I want to ask you about Mirabel Unwin,' said Miss Theobald. 'I always take the head girls of any form into my confidence, as you know. Will you tell me what your opinion is of Mirabel – whether it is bad or good – anything that can help me in dealing with her. You know all the details as to why she was sent here because she has told the whole school!'

Anna seldom wasted words. She said shortly what Miss Theobald wanted to know. 'Mirabel has been awfully tiresome, and the second form punished her for it. She's ashamed of herself now – and she wants to show us she's some good. Could you let her send for her violin?'

'Very well,' said Miss Theobald, smiling at Anna's directness. 'I refused her permission a little while ago. Will you, as head girl, tell her I have changed my mind, and she can send for her violin. Tell her, too, that I shall like to hear her play at the second-form concert.'

'Yes, Miss Theobald,' said Anna. 'Thank you.' The girl left the room, pleased. For the first time in her lazy life she felt that she had some importance. The head had sent for her and actually listened to her. It was worth making an effort if people like Miss Theobald appreciated it.

She went to look for Mirabel. She found her in the common-room, reading rather soberly, her eyes still red.

'Mirabel! Miss Theobald says you may send for your violin. And she says she looks forward to hearing you play at the concert next week.'

Mirabel looked up, astonished and delighted. This was a lovely surprise after having her hopes dashed and her good resolutions misunderstood. She stood up, glowing.

'Anna! It's because of you Miss Theobald said I could send for it. Thanks awfully. You're a brick.'

'It wasn't altogether me,' said Anna. 'Hurry up and get that message sent off.'

The message caused much surprise in Mirabel's home!

'She wants her violin!' said her mother, in astonishment. 'Why, she must be settling down a bit. I *am* glad!'

So the violin was packed up, registered and sent off at once. It arrived on the Monday of the week following, and Mirabel unpacked it joyfully. Her own violin! Now she would be able to play beautifully. She would show the second form what real music was!

And I'll astonish Miss Theobald a bit too, thought Mirabel. She'll see I have a real gift – even if I haven't anything else! I'd like her to think I was worthwhile – I really would.

10.

Gladys is surprising

The second form were very busy preparing for their concert. They were going to charge fifty pence for the tickets, and all the first form, most of the third form, and even a few of the higher-form girls had promised to come. All the mistresses had promised too. It was to be quite a big affair.

The girls were to manage everything themselves. They prepared the programmes and the tickets. Isabel drew a fine big poster and coloured it. She put it up in the big assembly room where everyone could see it.

The concert was to be held in the gym, where there was a fine platform. The second form grew quite excited about it. Too excited for Mam'zelle's liking. She could not bear to feel that the class were thinking about something else in her lessons.

'Isabel! Pat! Did you not sleep last night, that you dream so this morning? What was the question I have just asked the class?'

The twins stared at Mam'zelle in alarm. Neither of them had heard the question. Carlotta whispered softly.

'She said, "Has anyone here seen my glasses?"' whispered Carlotta, grinning. This was quite untrue, as everyone knew! But the twins fell into the trap at once. They stared innocently at Mam'zelle, seeing her glasses perched as usual on her big nose.

'Well?' said Mam'zelle, sharply. 'What did I ask the class?'

'You asked if we had seen your glasses anywhere,' said Pat, 'but they are on your nose, Mam'zelle.'

There was a squeal of laughter from the class. Mam'zelle banged on her desk angrily. '*Ah, que vous êtes abominable*!' she cried. '*Insupportable*!'

The twins glared at Carlotta, who was holding her sides. She shook her head at them, tears of laughter in her eyes. 'Wait till break, you wretch!' said Pat.

'*Taisez-vous*!' said Mam'zelle. 'Pat! Isabel! Of what were you thinking just now when I addressed the class? Be truthful!'

'Well, Mam'zelle – I was thinking of the concert our form is holding on Saturday,' said Pat. 'I'm sorry. My thoughts just wandered away.'

'So did mine,' said Isabel.

'If they wander away again I shall not come to the concert,' threatened Mam'zelle. There was a loud and universal groan.

'We shan't hold the concert unless you come!'

'You *must* come, Mam'zelle! You laugh louder than anyone!'

'I will come if you write me a nice composition,' said Mam'zelle, suddenly beaming again. 'You shall write me a beautiful essay and tell me all that is to happen at this wonderful concert. With no mistakes at all. That will please me greatly. That shall be your prep for tomorrow.'

The girls groaned again. French essays were awful to do – and this one would be difficult. Anyway, the idea had put Mam'zelle into a better temper, so that was something!

Two girls were doing nothing in the concert at all. Elsie had refused to do anything, and had announced her intention of not even coming. And nobody had asked the little Misery-girl to do anything. Everyone felt certain that Gladys would not and could not do a thing. They thought it would be kinder to leave her out altogether.

Gladys was hurt because she was not asked, yet glad that she was not pressed to do anything. She shut more and more up into herself, only spoke when she was spoken to, and was so quiet in every lesson that the teachers hardly knew she was there. Only in Miss Quentin's class did she show any real animation. Not that Miss Quentin ever asked her to act a part, because, like everyone else, Miss Quentin always passed over Gladys, thinking that such a little mouse could never do anything!

But Gladys watched the others acting, and for once in a way forgot to brood over her troubles when she saw Bobby strutting across the room as a king or duke, and Carlotta playing the part of a jester.

Alison adored Miss Quentin's classes. She really did work hard in those – harder than she worked in anyone else's. For one thing she was pretty and graceful, and parts such as princesses or fairies were given naturally to her, and for another thing, she lived for Miss Quentin's words of praise. She thought Miss Quentin was 'just wonderful'!

The preparations for the concert went on well. Doris was to give some of her clever imitations. She meant to mimic Mam'zelle, who had all kinds of mannerisms which were a joy to the class. She meant to imitate Clara, the cook, a jolly, rough-and-ready person much liked by the girls. And she meant to dress up as Matron, and imitate her doling out advice and medicine to various girls.

'Doris, you really are a scream,' said Bobby, enjoying the girl's clever performance in rehearsal. 'You ought to be on the stage.'

'I'm going to be a doctor,' said Doris.

'Oh – well, you'll be a jolly good one because you'll make all your patients scream with laughter!' said Bobby.

Everyone was doing something – either reciting, playing the piano or violin, singing or dancing – everyone, that is, except Elsie and Gladys. Carlotta was going to give a display of acrobatics. She was marvellous at such circus tricks as turning cartwheels, walking on her hands and so on.

'You and Doris, Carlotta, will be the hits of the evening,' said Pat. She and Isabel were going to give a dialogue, supposed to be funny, but they both felt it was not nearly so good as anyone else's contribution. Bobby was to do conjuring tricks! She was very good at these, and had a lot of idiotic patter that fell from her lips in a never-ending torrent.

'I bet Mirabel will be a hit too,' said Janet, after the girl had played her concert piece to them, during rehearsal. 'Good thing we found out she could play!'

'By the way – how *did* you find out?' asked Mirabel, putting her violin into its case. 'I kept meaning to ask you. I didn't think anybody knew.'

'Yes – somebody did,' said Janet, looking round to see if Gladys was in the room; but she was not. 'It was Gladys who told us.'

'*Gladys*!' said Mirabel, suddenly remembering the night in the dark music-room. 'Yes – of course – she heard me that night.'

'She said you were in the dark,' said Pat. 'So that means she was too. Funny kid, isn't she, sitting about in dark rooms all by herself. She really is a little misery. I can't think what's the matter with her. She never tells anyone. If she did, we might help her a bit – get a smile out of her occasionally, or something.'

'Oh – she told me what's the matter,' said Mirabel, remembering everything Gladys had said.

'*Did* she?' said Bobby, in surprise. 'Well, what *is* the matter with her?'

'It's her mother,' said Mirabel. 'She's in hospital – awfully ill – perhaps she's going to die. Gladys said she's only got her mother – no father or brothers or sisters – and they were sort of all-in-all to one another. She'd never been away from her mother even for a night till she was sent here when her mother went to hospital. She said she was awfully homesick, and missed her mother terribly. I suppose she thinks every day she may hear bad news or something.'

The girls heard all this in silence. They felt sorry and uncomfortable. The little Misery-girl really did have something to worry about. Everyone there but Carlotta had mothers they loved – and fathers – and most of them had brothers and sisters. Even slow-minded Anna, who had little imagination, knew for one short moment the sort of heartache that Gladys carried with her day and night.

'Why didn't you tell us this?' asked Bobby.

'I didn't remember it till now,' said Mirabel.

'Well, I think you should have told us at once,' said Hilary. 'We might have been decenter to Gladys. She's a poor little thing, without any courage or spunk – but we haven't exactly made things any easier for her. You really are to blame for not having told us, Mirabel.'

Mirabel was really conscience-stricken. She couldn't think how she could have forgotten Gladys's troubles. She had been so wrapped up in her own, and then, when the girls had become friendly and helped her, she had been so happy that she had not given a thought to the little Misery-girl. She stared unhappily at Hilary.

'I'm sorry,' she said. 'I *should* have told you. All the same, I don't think Gladys would like it if she knew that everyone knew about her troubles. So don't tell her you know. Just be nice to her and notice her a bit.'

The second form received this advice in silence. Mirabel sensed that they did not think very much of her for forgetting another person's troubles. She said no more, but went off to put her violin away.

I wonder where Gladys is, she thought. I've a good mind to hunt for her and ask her if she's heard any news of her mother lately. After all, it might help a bit if someone shares the news with her.

Mirabel went to look for Gladys. She could not seem to find the girl anywhere. It was puzzling.

'Well, she simply *must* be somewhere!' said Mirabel to herself. 'I wonder if she's up in the box-rooms. I saw her coming down from there the other day and wondered whatever had taken her there.'

She went up the stairs to the top of the school. Trunks and bags were kept in the attics, but little else. There was a light showing under the door of one of the attics – and from the room came a voice.

It didn't sound like Gladys's voice. It was deep and strong. Mirabel listened in surprise. The voice was declaiming one of the speeches in *The Tempest*, which the second form were taking that term with Miss Jenks.

That's not Gladys, thought Mirabel. I wonder who it is. Ah – now there's a different voice. There must be two or three people there. But who can they be? Only the second form are doing *The Tempest* this term – and all but Gladys were at rehearsal this evening.

A third voice spoke, gentle and feminine. Mirabel could bear it no longer. She really must see who the speakers were. They were declaiming Shakespeare's words beautifully.

She opened the door. The voice stopped at once. Mirabel stared into the room, expecting to see three or four people there, rehearsing the play. But there was only one person there – Gladys!

'Golly! It's only you!' said Mirabel, in astonishment. 'I thought there must be lots here. I heard all kinds of different voices. Was it *you*?'

'Yes,' said Gladys. 'Go away. Can't I even do this in peace?'

'What are you doing?' asked Mirabel, going into the room and shutting the door. 'Do tell me. It sounded fine. Do you know it all by heart?'

'Yes, I do,' said Gladys. 'I love acting. I always have. But Miss Quentin never gives me a chance in the drama class. I could act the parts well. I know I could. You see me act Bobby's part in that play we're doing with Miss Quentin!'

And before Mirabel's astonished eyes, the girl began to act the part that had been given to Bobby. But she acted it superbly. She was the part! The little Misery-girl faded, and another character came into the attic, someone with a resonant voice, a strong character, and a fierce face. It was extraordinary.

Mirabel stood and gaped. Her astonishment and admiration were so plain that Gladys was impelled to show her another part in the play – Carlotta's part. Here again she was twice as good as the fiery Carlotta, and her voice, wild and strong, quite different from Gladys's usual meek, milk-and-water voice, rang through the attic.

'Gladys! You're simply marvellous!' said Mirabel.

'You're to come and show the girls. Come on. Come on downstairs at once. I never saw anything like it in my life. *You* to act like that! Who would have thought it? You're such a mouse, and your voice is so quiet – and yet, when you act, you're Somebody, and you quite frighten me. You simply *must* come down and show the girls what you can do.'

'No,' said Gladys, becoming herself again and looking half the size she had seemed two minutes before.

'Oh, Gladys,' said Mirabel, suddenly remembering why she had been looking for the girl. 'Gladys – how's your mother? I do hope you've got good news.'

'Thank you – it's just about the same,' said Gladys. 'Mother can't even write to me, she's so ill. If I could just get a letter from her, it would be something!'

'Does she get *your* letters?' asked Mirabel.

'Of course,' said Gladys. 'I keep telling her how much I miss her, and how lonely and unhappy I am without her.'

'But, Gladys – how silly!' said Mirabel.

'What do you mean?' asked Gladys, half-indignantly. 'Mother wants to know that.'

'I should have thought she would have been much gladder to think you were trying to settle down and be happy,' said Mirabel. 'It must make her very miserable indeed to feel you are so lonely and sad. I should think it would make her worse.'

'It won't,' said Gladys, her eyes filling with tears. 'If she thought I was happy here, and getting other interests, she would think I was forgetting her.'

'I do think you're silly, Gladys,' said Mirabel, wishing she was Hilary or Anna, so that she might know the best way of tackling someone like Gladys. 'Don't you want your mother to be proud of you? She'll think you are an awful coward – no spunk at all – just giving in like this, and weeping and wailing.'

'Oh, you *are* hateful!' cried Gladys. 'As if my mother would ever think things like that of me, ever! Go away. I won't come down with you. And don't you dare to tell anyone what you saw me doing. It's my secret. You'd no right to come spying like that. Go away.'

Mirabel looked at Gladys's angry little face, and wondered what to do or say. She hadn't done any good, that was certain. I suppose I haven't got the character to help people properly, like Hilary or Anna, thought Mirabel, going soberly downstairs. I've got a lot to learn. When I go home at half-term next week, I'll really try and do better.

She went down to the library to get a book. But, as she hunted through the shelves, she kept thinking of Gladys. She couldn't just do nothing. If she, Mirabel, couldn't help Gladys, maybe somebody else could. Hilary could. She was always so sensible. So was Bobby – and the twins, too. She would go and tell them what had happened, and leave it to them to do what they could. Mirabel was beginning to have a very low opinion of herself and her powers.

She left the library and went to find Hilary. She was lucky enough to see her in a music-room with

Bobby, Janet and the twins, practising something for the concert. Good! This was just the chance to tell them what had happened!

A disappointment for
the second form

'I say!' said Mirabel, opening the door. 'Can I interrupt a moment?'

'I suppose so,' said Bobby. 'What's up?'

'It's about Gladys,' said Mirabel, and she told them how she had found the girl acting all by herself in the box-room. Then she went on to tell them what she had said to Gladys, and how she had failed to help her – only made her angry.

'Well,' said Hilary, listening intently. 'I think, Mirabel, you gave Gladys some very sound advice. Really I do. Of course Gladys ought to stop moaning to her mother. She must find a little pluck somewhere, or she'll go to pieces. You did right to say that it would help her mother if she knew Gladys was settling down, and trying to do well.'

'Oh – I'm glad you think that,' said Mirabel. 'I'm not so good as you are at knowing what to do for the best for people. By the way – Gladys said she didn't want me to tell everybody.'

'Well, you haven't,' said Hilary. 'You've only told us five – and we understand perfectly. But, Mirabel, as it seems that Gladys has taken *you* into her confidence and nobody else, I think you'd better go on tackling the matter!'

'Yes!' said all the others.

'Oh, *no*,' said Mirabel, horrified. 'I came to ask *you* to help. I'm no good at this sort of thing.'

'Well, it's time you were,' said Hilary, firmly. 'Now come on, Mirabel – we all tried to help you when you needed it – you've got to do the same to Gladys. Be friends with her, and buck her up – and if you can persuade her to show us how she can act, we'll all listen and applaud – and she must be in the concert!'

'She can't be. It's the day after tomorrow, and all the programmes are written out,' objected Isabel. 'We really can't write them all out again.'

'She wouldn't want to be in the concert, anyhow,' said Mirabel. 'All right, Hilary – I'll do what I can. But I really am very bad at this sort of thing.'

It was distasteful to Mirabel to mention the matter to Gladys again. She always felt awkward at anything involving tact or understanding another's troubles. She would very much rather have left it to the others. Still, once she said she would do a thing, she did it.

Gladys was surprised, and not too pleased to find Mirabel always at her elbow the next day. 'Gladys, I didn't mean to make you angry,' Mirabel said, when they were alone for a few minutes. 'I'm clumsy in what I say. I know I am. But I really and truly am sympathetic. I don't expect I can help at all – but I'd like to.'

'Well,' said Gladys, looking at Mirabel's earnest face,

'I *was* angry yesterday. Nobody likes being told they're cowardly. But I thought it all over and in some ways I think you're right. I shouldn't keep writing to my mother and telling her how miserable and lonely I am. I know it would worry her – and that might keep her from getting well.'

'Yes, it might,' said Mirabel, pleased that what she had said had, after all, had some effect on Gladys. 'I say – look here – wouldn't she be *thrilled* if she knew you were in the concert – acting like that – being clapped by everybody! I do wish you'd let the girls see you act.'

Gladys hesitated. She did know, quite certainly, that her mother would be pleased to hear of any success she made – but she was such a mouse, so afraid of everything – it would be a real ordeal to show off in front of the girls. And, of course, she couldn't possibly be in the concert! She would be scared out of her life!

Mirabel saw her hesitate, and she went on pressing her. 'Gladys! Come on – be a sport. Look – if you'll show what you can do, and get the girls to put you into the concert, *I'll* write to your mother myself and tell her how well you did. See? Because I know you'll do well. And then think how pleased she'll be!'

The thought of Mirabel actually writing to her mother for her touched Gladys more than anything else could have done. She stared at Mirabel's earnest face, and tried to blink back the tears that came far too easily.

'You are a good sort,' she said, rather chokily. 'You really are. I thought at first you were such a selfish, cold-hearted sort of girl – but you're not. Be friends with me, Mirabel. You haven't any friend here and neither have I. I'll do anything you ask me, if you'll be friends.'

'Well,' said Mirabel, remembering that it was the half-term the following week, 'I'm leaving soon, you know – at half-term. I never meant to stay longer than that. So it's not much use your being friends with me really – because I'll soon be gone.'

'Oh,' said Gladys, turning away. 'That's just my luck. People I like always go away.'

'Now don't start that sort of thing again,' said Mirabel, half-impatiently. 'All right. I'll be your friend till I go – but mind, you've got to be sensible and do what I say. And the first thing I say is – you've got to show the girls how you can act!'

It was quite pleasant to have someone taking such an interest in her! Gladys felt warmed, and looked gratefully at Mirabel. She was a weak, timid character – Mirabel was strong and decided, even though she was often wrong.

'Yes – I will show the girls if you want me to,' Gladys said.

'Well, after tea, in the common-room this evening, you show them,' said Mirabel. 'I'll clap like anything at the end, so you needn't be afraid. Perhaps the girls will put you in the concert after all, when they see how good you are. Isabel said something about not being able to alter the programmes – but I'm sure it could be done. I could help.'

Mirabel felt rather proud of having got her own way with Gladys. She told Hilary and the others, and they looked forward with interest to seeing what Gladys could do that evening.

It certainly was a surprise to everyone! Gladys looked terribly nervous at first, and her voice shook. But in a minute or two, as she forgot herself, and threw herself heart and soul into the part she was acting, it seemed as if the little Misery-girl was no longer there – but someone quite different, that nobody had seen before!

Gladys acted many parts from different Shakespeare plays – Lady Macbeth – Miranda – Malvolio – Hamlet. She knew them all by heart. Her mother had been very fond of Shakespeare's works, and the two of them had studied them together evening after evening. Gladys's dead father had been a fine actor, and Gladys had inherited the gift.

Gladys stopped at last, changing from Bottom the Weaver to her own timid self. The girls roared with delight at her, and clapped loudly.

'You monkey! Fancy not telling us you could do all that!' said Pat. 'You'll bring the house down at the concert! I say – we simply MUST put her in! Can't we possibly?'

'Please, please don't,' begged Gladys in alarm. 'I couldn't possibly do it in front of most of the school. Well, I might, if I'd more time to rehearse with you. But the concert's tomorrow. I should die if you made me be in it! Please don't!'

'Well – if you feel so strongly about it, I suppose we'll have to leave you out,' said Janet. 'Is there, by any chance, anything else you've kept us in the dark about?

Can you paint marvellous pictures – or work wonderful sums in your head?'

Gladys laughed – the first laugh since she had been at St Clare's. 'There's only one other thing I'm good at,' she said. 'That's lacrosse.'

'Well, you don't seem to have shone there to any great extent,' said Bobby, in surprise.

'I know. I didn't bother,' said Gladys. 'I just didn't care whether I ran fast or not, or scored a goal, or anything. That's why Miss Wilton kept making me goalkeeper, I expect. She thought I was only good for stopping goals, not for anything else. But I *can* play well, if I try. I was in the top team at my day school.'

'Good,' said Mirabel. 'We'll make you shoot dozens of goals and then you can write that to your mother, too.'

'Sorry about your mother, Gladys,' said Hilary. 'Tell us any news you get. We're all interested.'

Gladys went to bed really happy that night. She had a friend. She had been clapped and applauded. She had thrown off her reserve, and let the other girls speak to her of her mother. Things didn't seem so bad now. For the first time she fell asleep without laying and worrying.

In the middle of the night, five of the girls lay and tossed restlessly. Pat and Isabel, Doris, Bobby and Carlotta could not sleep. Their throats hurt them. They coughed and sneezed. It was most annoying – because the concert was to be the next evening!

I shan't be able to speak a word, thought Doris, as she tried to ease her throat. This really is bad luck. I can't possibly be in the concert. Blow! I was so looking forward to it.

In the morning all five went along to Matron, feeling very miserable and sorry for themselves. She took their temperatures.

'You've got the horrid cold that has been running round the school,' she said, briskly. 'You've all got temperatures except Carlotta – and it would take a lot to give *her* one! But she can go to bed just the same. To the sickbay, all of you.'

'But, Matron – it's the concert tonight!' said Bobby, hoarsely. 'We can't possibly go to bed.'

'Put your coats on and your hats and scarves,' said Matron, taking no notice of Bobby at all. 'And go across to the sickbay, immediately. You've all got the same feverish cold, that's plain – caught the chill watching lacrosse in that cold wind the other day, I suppose – so the germ found you easy prey. Bobby, are you deaf? Go and get your coat and hat at once and don't stand arguing.'

It never was any good trying to argue with Matron. She had dealt with girls for many, many years, and bed and warmth and the right medicine in her opinion cured most things very quickly. So, concert or no concert, the five girls were bundled into bed in the sickbay, and there they lay, moaning about the concert and wondering what was going to happen.

It didn't take the rest of the form long to decide what was to happen.

'We can't *possibly* hold the concert without those five!' said Hilary.

'Doris was one of the stars,' said Janet.

'*And* Bobby,' said Hilary. 'And Carlotta too. It would be a very weak affair without those three. We'll have to postpone it. We'll have it just before half-term.'

'We can't,' said Anna. 'The third form are having theirs.'

'Well, the week after then,' said Hilary. 'That will give the invalids time to get over their colds. I hope nobody else feels like sneezing or coughing! If they do, for goodness' sake go to the sickbay, and get it over, so that we can have the concert all right in a fortnight's time!'

'Gladys can be in it this time!' said Kathleen. 'That makes another good performer.'

'Oh, good!' said Anna, looking at Gladys. 'That will be fine. You'll have loads of time to practise and rehearse now, Gladys.'

Gladys couldn't help feeling thrilled. She did love acting – and it would be fun to rehearse with the others. It hadn't been nice to be left out. Now she would be able to join in, and would be clapped just as the others were. There would be a lot to tell her mother when she wrote. She felt a wave of gratitude welling up for Mirabel. It was Mirabel who had made all this possible for her.

She went up to Mirabel and slipped her arm through hers. 'It's a pity about the others, isn't it?' she said. 'But they'll be better in a fortnight – and I *shall* like being in the concert now. I shall clap like anything when your turn comes, Mirabel. I think you'll be the best of us all.'

Mirabel did not smile. She looked rather cold and blank. Gladys wondered what the matter was.

'How many pieces are you going to play?' she asked. 'Do you want me to turn over the pages for you at the piano?'

'I shan't *be* in the concert,' said Mirabel, in a funny, even voice. 'You know I'm going home at half-term – and by the time the concert comes, I'll be gone. I feel disappointed, of course – so don't keep on rubbing it in!'

She took her arm from Gladys's and walked off. How sickening everything was!

12.

Gladys tackles Mirabel

The second form seemed to have dwindled considerably now that five of them were away. Hilary and Alison went down with the cold the next day, so there were many empty desks. The concert was put off for two weeks, and the second-form girls felt very flat and gloomy.

Elsie was the only one who was at all pleased. She had consistently refused to take any interest at all in the concert, and she felt glad that this disappointment had come upon the others. As Anna had predicted, Elsie had adopted a martyr-like attitude, looking left-out and miserable all day long. But no one took the slightest notice of her.

The girl's pride was hurt. She had not liked to ask Anna what she had said to Miss Theobald on the day when both of them had been sent for. But it was clear to her now that not only did the girls no longer regard her as one of their heads, but Miss Jenks also appeared to think that only Anna was head girl. It was most exasperating. Elsie sometimes wished she was like Carlotta and could scold people when she felt like it! She would scold everyone in the form!

The seven girls in the sickbay had a bad time for

95

the first day or two, and then, when their temperatures went down, they sat up and recovered their spirits. It was fun for so many to be together. They could play games and talk.

'It's half-term next week,' said Isabel. 'Our mother's coming over to take us out.'

'So's mine,' said Doris. 'Carlotta, is your father coming to take you out?'

'Yes – and my grandmother too,' said Carlotta, gloomily. 'I get on with my father all right now – but I just seem to go all common and bad-mannered with my grandmother. I remember all my circus ways, and she just hates them. Oh, dear – I meant to try and get terribly good-mannered this term, and not scold anyone or lose my temper or anything.'

'Mirabel is supposed to be going at half-term, isn't she?' said Bobby, suddenly. 'She won't be in the concert then – and she won't know if she's been chosen to play in any of the lacrosse matches, either – and she'll miss the birthday feast that Carlotta's going to give.'

'She's an idiot,' said Doris. 'She can't think straight. That's what's the matter with her.'

'She wouldn't be a bad sort if she made up her mind to shake down and be sensible,' said Pat. 'I quite like her now. And I must say she's good to that timid little Gladys. When Kathleen came in to see us yesterday, she said that Mirabel really does look after her and walk with her – and Gladys is like a little dog with her – trots after her and does everything she's told.'

'Well, who would have thought that those two would pair up?' said Isabel. 'And there's another astonishing thing too – who would have thought that lazy old Anna would pull herself together as she has done?'

Before long the seven invalids were very much better. They could not possibly have attended the concert, if theirs had been postponed only a week, so it was just as well that it had been put off for two weeks. They would be well enough to go to the third form's concert, which was on the Thursday before half-term.

Mirabel was looking very glum. Half-term seemed to be coming quickly. The postponing of the concert had been a bitter disappointment. It was dull without half the class at lessons.

The only bright spot was her new friendship with Gladys. The girl was showing unsuspected sides of her character to Mirabel. She could make excellent jokes, and had a fine sense of humour. She was fun to walk with because she could keep up a merry chatter. She seemed to have quite thrown off her preoccupation with her own troubles. She really was very fond of Mirabel, and the girl, although embarrassed by any show of affection in the ordinary way, liked to feel Gladys slipping her arm through hers.

'Mirabel! You won't really go home at half-term, will you?' Gladys said that week. 'There are only a few days more. It's lovely being friends with you. Don't go, will you?'

'Of course I'm going,' said Mirabel, impatiently. 'I told

you I'd made up my mind to go at half-term, even before I arrived here! And I'm not going back on that. I never go back on what I've said.'

'No. I know you don't,' said Gladys, with a sigh. 'It's only people like me who change their minds and alter what they meant to do. But I do wish you weren't going, Mirabel.'

Gladys said the same thing to Hilary that day, when she went to see her in the sickbay. 'I do so wish Mirabel wasn't going,' she said. 'I feel a different person since she was nice to me, and all of you clapped me that time I acted for you.'

'What's she got to go for?' said Hilary. 'She has settled down all right. She's happy. She's one of us now, and she enjoys life here. Whatever does she want to go home at half-term for, now she's all right?'

'Well, you see,' said Gladys, earnestly, 'she can't go back on what she said. She *said* she was going home at half-term – she made up her mind about that – so she can't *possibly* change her mind, can she? She's such a strong character, you see.'

'Well, it's strong characters who ought to be able to change their minds at times,' said Hilary. '*I* call it weak to stick to something when you know it's silly. And it is silly for Mirabel to go back home now. We want her for the concert. She knows that. She's just being weak, not strong!'

Gladys was astonished to hear this. It seemed to make things quite different. Weak little Gladys had thought that strong characters must be able to make right decisions and carry them out – but now she saw that a strong character could do something wrong or stupid because it was too proud to unmake a decision! It was something quite new to her. She stared at Hilary.

'I wish you'd say that to Mirabel,' she said.

'Say it yourself,' said Hilary. 'You're her friend, aren't you? Well, *you* tell her!'

'She wouldn't listen to *me*,' said Gladys.

'What you mean is – you're afraid to tackle her!' said Hilary, with a laugh. 'Go on, Mouse – take the bull by the horns – and if you really do care for Mirabel and want her for your friend, don't be afraid of telling her what you think. Get a little spunk!'

Poor Gladys! Everyone always seemed to be telling her to get a little 'spunk'. It was something she was sure she would never possess. She had been such a mother's girl that now it was difficult for her to stand on her own feet.

All the same – it's no good having a friend unless you'll do something for them, thought Gladys, trying to screw up her courage. I shall lose Mirabel if I don't tackle her – and if I lose her because she's angry with me for tackling her, well, I shan't be any worse off. So I'll do it.

It wasn't easy. It never is easy for a timid person to tackle a strong one, especially if it is to point out that the strong one is wrong. Gladys went to Mirabel and slipped her arm through hers.

'Mirabel,' she said, 'I've been thinking over what you said about going home – and not changing your mind and all that – and I really do think you're wrong.'

'That's my own business,' said Mirabel, rather roughly.

'No, it isn't. It's mine too,' said Gladys, hoping her voice would not begin to tremble. 'You're my friend, and I don't want you to go.'

'I've told you I can't change my mind. I never do,' said Mirabel. 'Don't bother me.'

'If you were really as strong a character as you make out, you *would* change your mind,' said Gladys, boldly. 'You know you could stay here happily now – but you're too proud to own you've been silly – and you call it being strong enough not to change your mind!'

'Gladys! How *dare* you talk to me like this?' cried Mirabel, astonished and angry. 'Anybody would think you are Miss Theobald – picking me to pieces – telling me I'm no good – not worthwhile!'

'I'm not telling you that,' said Gladys, getting distressed. 'I'm only saying – don't let your pride stand in the way of your happiness. That's all.'

Mirabel wrenched her arm out of Gladys's and walked off, red in the face. How dare Gladys say things like that to her? She put on her hat and coat and went out into the school grounds, fuming.

Gladys stared after her, miserable. I knew it wouldn't be any good, she thought. Of course Mirabel wouldn't let me say things like that. Now she won't even be friends with me for the last two or three days before she goes!

Mirabel walked round the grounds, hot and angry. But, as her anger died, her mind began to work more calmly. There was a great deal in what Gladys had said. 'Though how that timid little thing ever thought that all out beats me!' said Mirabel to herself. 'There must be more in her than I thought. And the way she stood up to me too! She *has* come on. She must like me a lot to make up her mind to go for me like that, in order to try and make me change my mind, so that she can still have me for a friend.'

The wind cooled her hot cheeks. She sat on the wall and looked down over the valley. It was very pleasant there. It would be marvellous in the summer. St Clare's was fun – there was no doubt about that.

'Now, let's think things out calmly,' said Mirabel to herself. 'I was angry because my family sent me away because I didn't fit in at home – and I vowed to get back as soon as I could just to show them they couldn't send me away! Now I like being here – and I see that I *am* better away from home, and shall go back really thrilled to see everyone. I dare say I'll learn lots of things here I ought to have learnt before – thinking of other people, not always having my own way and things like that. Well, then – what is stopping me from staying here?'

She gazed down on the valley, and did not like to think out the answer. But she had to.

'All that is stopping me is, as Gladys pointed out, my pride. I'm too proud to tell Daddy that I'll stay. I was so angry at being sent away that I wanted to pay them out by coming back as soon as possible and being beastly. And I think I'm a strong character! Golly, all this makes me sound as hateful as catty Elsie!'

She stayed for a few minutes longer and then she

sprang down from the wall. She went into the school building and took off her outdoor things. She went straight to Miss Theobald's room and knocked at the door.

'Come in!' said Miss Theobald. She was talking to Miss Jenks and Mam'zelle. Mirabel was a little taken aback when she saw all three teachers there – but what she had come to say had to be said, no matter how many people were in the room.

'Miss Theobald,' she said, rather loudly. 'May I stay on, please, and not go home at the half-term? Would you let me? I like being here, and I'm sorry I was so silly at first.'

Miss Theobald looked at the girl, and smiled her nicest smile, warm and friendly.

'Yes – we shall be very glad to have you,' she said. 'Isn't that so, Miss Jenks – Mam'zelle?'

'It is,' said Miss Jenks and nodded kindly at Mirabel.

'Ha!' said Mam'zelle. '*C'est bien, ça*! I too am pleased.'

'I will telephone your parents,' said Miss Theobald. 'I am glad, Mirabel, that you have something "worthwhile" in you – no, I don't mean your music! Something better than that. Well done!'

Praise like this was very sweet. Mirabel walked out of the room, warm and happy. She knew she had a great deal to learn – things would go wrong, and she would make mistakes – but nothing could take that moment from her.

She went to find Gladys. She found her curled up in a corner of the common-room, looking rather small and woe-begone. She went over to her and gave her an unexpected hug.

'Well, old thing! I'm staying on! I've just been to tell Miss Theobald. And all because you ticked me off like that, and set me thinking!'

Half in tears Gladys returned the hug. It was marvellous. She, a weak person, had summoned up enough strength to tackle a strong one – and had actually got what she wanted. It was too good to be true.

'You'll be in the concert!' she said. 'And you'll come to Carlotta's feast. What fun we'll have! Oh, Mirabel I'm so proud of you!'

'I'm rather proud of you too,' said Mirabel, awkwardly. 'You gave me a surprise, telling me home-truths like that. You're a good sort of friend to have.'

'What a lot I shall have to write and tell my mother!' said Gladys. 'And I say – won't everyone be pleased you've changed your mind and are staying on!'

The girls *were* pleased. They had begun to like Mirabel now, and they admired her for being able to alter her mind and own that she had been wrong. Soon they would forget Mirabel's extraordinary behaviour the first few weeks of the term.

Only one girl was displeased. That was Elsie. Why should such a fuss be made of that ridiculous Mirabel, who had behaved so badly, and who had been partly the cause of Elsie's disgrace? Elsie brooded over this and cast many spiteful glances at Mirabel, wondering what she could do to pay her out for being popular, when she,

Elsie, was never taken any notice of at all!

But Mirabel was thick-skinned. She neither saw nor felt Elsie's hostility, but looked forward happily to the remainder of the term at St Clare's.

13.

Half-term holiday

Half-term came and went. It was a pleasant break for everyone. Most parents came to take out the girls for some kind of treat, and those that lived near enough went home for a day or two. Alison's parents were away so she went out with the twins and their mother.

'Well, how are you all getting on this term?' asked Mrs O'Sullivan. 'Working hard, I hope?'

But nobody said anything about work. The twins poured out their news about the concert, and about lacrosse, and how Carlotta was going to have a feast on her birthday. Alison talked of nothing but her beloved Miss Quentin.

'She's awfully clever,' said Alison. 'It's lovely learning drama under her. She says I have the making of a good little actress.'

'Oh, do shut up talking about Miss Quentin,' groaned Pat. 'Mummy, last term Alison was all over Sadie Greene, that American girl – who, by the way, has never even *written* to you, Alison! And this term it's Miss Quentin! Isn't there any medicine or pill we can give Alison to stop her raving about people?'

Alison had been very hurt that her 'best' friend, Sadie,

had not taken the trouble to write to her at all. She thought it was mean of Pat to remind her of it.

'Well, Miss Quentin wouldn't be like that,' she said. 'I've made her promise to write to me every week in the holidays. She's loyal, I know. I think she's marvellous.'

'She's beautiful, she's wonderful, she's marvellous, she's magnificent,' said Isabel, with a grin. 'But the thing is – what does she think of *you*, Alison? Not much, I bet! You're always going about thinking somebody is wonderful – you never seem to imagine they might be bored with you.'

The idea of her beloved Miss Quentin being bored with her made Alison hot and angry. She glared at the twins. Mrs O'Sullivan saw the look.

'Now, now,' she said, 'don't let's waste our precious time in quarrelling, please. I've no doubt Miss Quentin is a very admirable person and I'm sure Alison works hard in *her* class, at least, if she doesn't in anyone else's.'

Mirabel's father and mother came over to see her at half-term, and took her out to lunch, a theatre, and tea afterwards. Mirabel was intensely excited at the thought of seeing them. She forgot all about the temper in which she had been when she had parted from them. She forgot the horrid things she had said, and the threats she had made. She stood at the front door, eagerly waiting for them.

When they arrived, they were startled by someone who hurled herself at them, flung her arms round them, and exclaimed in a choky voice, 'Mummy! Daddy! It's lovely to see you again!'

Her mother and father looked at the excited girl, whose eyes shone with welcome. This was a different Mirabel altogether! They hugged the girl, and looked with interest at the school. Neither of them had seen it. It had been a very sudden decision on Mirabel's father's part to send Mirabel away, and he had chosen a school recommended to him very highly by a friend. It had all been done in such a hurry that the parents had not had time to see the school itself.

'What a lovely place!' said Mrs Unwin. 'Is there time to look round?'

'Mummy, you simply *must* see everything,' cried Mirabel, and she dragged her parents all over the school, from top to bottom, even showing them the bathroom where she had her nightly bath. There was great pride in the girl's voice. Her parents exchanged happy glances with each other. It was quite plain to them that Mirabel was extremely proud of St Clare's already, and felt it to be her own splendid school.

'Daddy, I'm so pleased you chose St Clare's,' said Mirabel, when they came back to the front door at last. 'It's marvellous. It really is.' She looked at her parents and hesitated a little. She had something to say that was difficult. Mirabel hated saying she was sorry about anything.

'You know – I really am sorry I was so awful at home,' said the girl, rushing her words out. 'I can see you all better now, because I'm far away from you – and I think I was awful to everyone.'

'We've forgotten it all,' said her father. 'We shall never

remember it again. All that matters to us is that you are happy – and will be happy when you come home again. We felt so proud when Miss Theobald let us know that you wanted to stay on. She said one or two nice things about you.'

'Did she really?' asked Mirabel, pleased. 'I hated her at first – she said some awful things to me – but now I think she's fine. Oh, Mummy – I do wish you'd brought Joan and Harry with you! I did want to see them.'

'They wanted to see you too,' said her mother. 'But it was too far to bring them. Now – what about going? We shall never get any lunch if we don't start soon.'

'Mummy – would you do something for me?' asked Mirabel, suddenly. 'I've got a friend here – and her mother's ill in hospital, so there's no one to take her out for a half-term treat. Could she possibly come with us, do you think?'

'Of course,' said Mrs Unwin, surprised and pleased to think that her difficult daughter had actually made a friend. She wondered what the friend would be like. She had never liked Mirabel's chosen friends before – they had always been noisy, impolite and out-of-hand – a little like Mirabel herself.

'I'll go and get her,' said Mirabel. She ran off to find Gladys. She was getting ready for the school lunch, feeling a little lonely, for nearly all the other girls had left for the half-term holiday.

Mirabel rushed at her. 'Gladys! You're to come with me! Go and ask Miss Jenks if you can come, quickly!

Mummy and Daddy say you can come.'

A shock of joy ran through Gladys. She felt nervous of meeting Mirabel's parents – but to think that Mirabel wanted her to come was marvellous. Her depression fell away from her at once, and she stared in joy at her friend. She had had few treats in her life, and it did seem to her that going out to lunch and a theatre was too good to be true.

'Gladys, don't stand staring there!' cried Mirabel, impatiently. 'Hurry up. Go and find Miss Jenks. I'll get your outdoor things.'

In three minutes Gladys was at the front door with Mirabel, red with shyness, hardly able to say a word. Mr and Mrs Unwin took a look at the nervous girl, and were astonished. So this was Mirabel's friend – well, what a change from the tiresome girls she had chosen before! They took a liking to Gladys immediately, and Mrs Unwin smiled a motherly smile at her.

In some ways Mrs Unwin resembled Gladys's own mother. Both were the gentle, kindly type, and Gladys warmed to Mrs Unwin at once. In no time at all she was telling Mrs Unwin all about her own mother, revelling in the understanding and kindness of Mirabel's mother.

'I say! I do think you've got a nice mother!' she whispered to Mirabel, when they went to wash their hands at the hotel, before lunch. 'Next to mine, she's the nicest I've ever met. And isn't your father jolly? I feel a bit afraid of him but I do like him. Aren't you lucky?'

Mirabel was pleased. She was seeing her mother and

father with different eyes, now that she had been away from them for some weeks. It was pleasant to hear someone liking them so much. She squeezed her friend's arm.

'It's fun having you,' she said. 'I'm glad my people like you.'

A real surprise was in store for Gladys. When Mrs Unwin asked her what hospital her mother was in, she heard Gladys's answer with astonishment.

'Why – that's quite near where my sister lives. I often go over to see my sister – and perhaps I could go to the hospital and find out how your mother is. I might even see her, if she is allowed visitors.'

Gladys stared at Mrs Unwin, red with delight. It would bring her mother much closer somehow, if she knew someone was going to the very hospital where her mother was. And just suppose she was allowed to see her! Mrs Unwin could write and tell her about it.

'Oh, thank you,' said the girl. 'If you only could! It would be marvellous!'

The half-term went all too quickly. All the girls enjoyed it. It was a very pleasant break indeed, and they went back to school full of chatter about what they had done.

'Hallo!' said the twins, meeting Carlotta when they arrived back. 'How did *you* get on? Was your grandmother very stand-offish?'

'No – she seemed quite pleased with me,' said Carlotta, grinning. 'I didn't walk on my hands or do anything she disapproves of – and I made my hair so tidy you wouldn't know me. I was most frightfully polite to her, and my father was awfully pleased with me. He gave me a five-pound note for my birthday!'

'Gracious!' said Pat. 'What luck!'

'And my grandmother told me I could order anything I liked for my birthday party, at the shop in the town,' said Carlotta, her eyes lighting up with delighted expectancy. 'I say – won't we order lots of things! She gave me some things out of her store cupboard too. I've got a big box in the cupboard in our dormitory. I don't know what's in it yet, but I bet my grandmother has given me plenty.'

'How gorgeous!' said the twins. 'You sound as if you've got enough to feed the whole school.'

'No – just our form,' said Carlotta. 'And I'm not sure yet if we'll have it properly, in the afternoon at tea-time – or whether we'll make it really exciting, and go in for a midnight feast again. I think we ought to have a midnight feast every term, you know! School doesn't seem really complete without that!'

It looked as if the latter half of the term was going to be exciting. There was the concert to look forward to that week – several lacrosse matches – and now Carlotta's feast! All the girls glowed. What fun they had!

Bobby had a secret, and so had Janet. They had gone out together with Bobby's parents, and with Janet's brother, whose half-term holiday was the same weekend. He was as much of a monkey as Janet, always up to tricks. He had given Janet and Bobby an old trick to play on Mam'zelle. It was a curious-looking thing, consisting of a long stretch of narrow rubber tubing, with a little bladder on one end, and an india-rubber bulb on the other, which, when pressed, sent air down the tube into the little bladder, which at once expanded and became big.

'But what's it for?' asked the twins, in curiosity.

'You put the bladder under someone's plate at mealtime,' giggled Bobby, 'and run the tubing under the table-cloth. Then, when you press the bulb, the bladder fills and up tips the plate. Imagine Mam'zelle's astonishment when her plate starts dancing about! We shall all be in fits of laughter!'

This was really something to look forward to as well. Mam'zelle was a marvellous person to play tricks on. She was always taken in, and had caused more enjoyment than all the mistresses in the school put together.

'Oh, Bobby! Let's do it soon,' begged Doris. 'Do let's. We haven't played any tricks this term, at all.'

'Well, after all, we *are* the second form,' said Janet, teasingly.

'Bobby will be playing tricks when she's head girl!' said Isabel. 'I'm surprised she has gone as far as half-term without thinking of any.'

'Oh, I've *thought* of plenty,' said Bobby. 'But Miss Jenks isn't an easy person to play about with. She doesn't keep her temper like Miss Roberts did. She flares up suddenly, and I don't particularly want to be sent to Miss Theobald now I'm in the second form. It may have escaped your notice that I'm working hard this term! Don't forget I'm not Don't-Care Bobby as I was last term. I'm using my brains for other things besides tricks and jokes.'

112

'Let's have a rehearsal for the concert,' said Pat. 'We've only got a few days now. Bring your violin, Mirabel – and Gladys, make up your mind what you're going to act, out of all the hundreds of parts you seem able to play. Come on, everybody – let's enjoy ourselves!'

14.

A marvellous show

The days flew by, and the night of the concert came. Miss Jenks had to be lenient with the second form, because she could see that they really did mean their show to be a great success. Mam'zelle was the only teacher who would not make allowances, so the class groaned and worked for her as best they could.

'It is bad to have concerts in the middle of the term,' Mam'zelle grumbled to Miss Jenks. 'These girls, they think of anything but their work. Now, when I was a schoolgirl . . .'

'You worked all day, and you worked all night, you had no games, you prepared no concerts . . .' chanted Miss Jenks, with her wide smile. The teachers had heard a thousand times of Mam'zelle's hard-worked youth.

'There are other things as important as lessons,' said Miss Roberts. 'We are not out to cram facts and knowledge into the girls' heads all day long, but to help them to form strong and kindly characters too. This concert now, that you grumble at – it is making the second form work together in a wonderful way, it is bringing out all kinds of unexpected talent – look at Mirabel and Gladys, for instance – and it will help a great cause. It makes the girls resourceful and ingenious too – you should see the costume Doris has made for herself as Matron and as Cook.'

Mam'zelle did not know that Doris was going to imitate her as well. The other mistresses guessed it and they were looking forward to it. They all liked Mam'zelle, and admired her sense of humour. She could take a joke against herself very well.

'The third-form concert was quite good,' said Miss Lewis, the history teacher. 'But I think the second form will be more entertaining. The third form were rather high-brow, and didn't provide a single laugh for anyone. I fancy we shall find plenty to laugh at this Saturday!'

The second form were getting very excited. Only Elsie was apart from all the thrills and enjoyment. The girl still obstinately refused to take part in anything, and would not even be prompter.

'But Elsie, everyone will think it very funny that you are the only second former out of things,' said Pat, impatiently. 'We keep on offering you things to do, and you keep turning them down. I think it's very decent of us to be so patient with you.'

'I'll take part on one condition,' said Elsie, sullenly.

'What?' asked Bobby, coming up.

'That you let me be head girl again with Anna,' said Elsie. 'You've punished me for weeks now, by taking away my authority as head girl. Isn't it about time you let me have it back again?'

'Well – we'll ask the rest of the form,' said Pat. So that

night in the common-room, before a rehearsal was held, Anna put the question to the meeting.

'Elsie says she will take part in the concert if we let her be joint head girl again. What does everyone think about it?'

'Why should she bargain with us?' cried Carlotta. 'It is we who should bargain with her! We should say, "You can be head girl again if you show that you are worthy of it!"'

'Quite right,' called Doris.

'Look how she has behaved all these weeks,' said Janet. 'Has she tried to give us a better opinion of her? Has she shown us she could be trusted to lead us again? No – all she has done is to look spiteful, be catty when she has a chance, pose as a martyr and hope she'll get our sympathy. Well, she hasn't. We've just taken no notice at all, and she hasn't liked it.'

'I don't see why we should bother with her,' said Isabel. 'I really don't.'

'Will you show in the usual way whether you would like her again or not?' asked Anna. 'Hands up those who will give Elsie another chance as head girl.'

Not a single hand went up. Anna grinned. 'Well,' she said, 'that's that. Elsie will have to put up with it. She hasn't come at all well out of this, I must say. I would have been willing to work with her again, if you'd said so – but I'm glad I haven't got to.'

Elsie was not there, and nobody bothered to fetch her to tell her what had happened. They began their rehearsal and were soon busy criticizing and applauding as one after another performed. Gladys was by now used to an audience and she acted as naturally as everyone else. She and Doris were both natural actresses, though in a different way. Doris could imitate anyone she had seen, but not act a part – and Gladys, quite unable to imitate anyone around her, was excellent at interpreting any part in a play. The two admired each other and Gladys was fast making another friend.

'Well – I really think we've got everything all right now,' said Bobby at last. 'It *will* be fun! Doris, you'll bring the house down with your imitation of Mam'zelle. I only hope Mam'zelle won't mind. But I don't think she will.'

The door opened and Elsie came in. 'You held the rehearsal without me,' she said. 'What do you want me to do at the concert?'

'Well, Elsie – you said you would only be in it if we recognized you as head girl again,' said Anna, rather awkwardly. 'We put the question to the second form, and I'm afraid they decided not to give you the chance. So we didn't think you'd want to help with the concert, in that case.'

'Couldn't you have told me you wouldn't have me as head girl, and still let me be in the concert?' said Elsie.

The others stared at her. 'Don't be silly,' said Bobby, at last. 'That's not the point. The point is, you always refused, and then wanted to make a bargain with us – and we wouldn't make it. I suppose you're beginning to feel very awkward about being left out of the concert in front of the whole school, so you're climbing down a bit, and want to help even if we won't accept you as head girl again. Well – help if you like – but don't expect us to fall on your neck and give you a warm welcome, because we shan't.'

This was a long speech and Elsie listened to it in growing anger. All that Bobby said was true. Elsie was now beginning to feel horrified at being left out. Everyone in the school would notice it. They would whisper about her. They would nudge one another as she passed. Elsie couldn't bear it. But neither had she the strength to over-rule her rage and accept Bobby's luke-warm offer to let her help. She made a curious explosive noise of rage and walked out of the room.

Doris immediately imitated the explosive noise, and the whole form burst into laughter. Elsie heard the squeals, and stopped. She felt inclined to go back and hit out at everyone. Then a wave of self-pity overcame her and she burst into tears.

The concert was an enormous success. Half the school was there and all the mistresses. The curtain was drawn at exactly eight o'clock, and everything went like clock-work. The third form had been late in starting, and there had been long intervals between the various turns, which had bored the audience. But the second form were most efficient.

Turn after turn was put on and loudly applauded. Mirabel's playing was encored twice. The girl was so thrilled at her success that she could hardly speak for joy. Her piano-playing was really excellent, and as for her violin solo, it amazed everyone, even the four music teachers, who were by now used to gifted children springing up in their classes at times.

Carlotta's acrobatics were hailed with delight by the whole school. Everyone knew that Carlotta had once been a circus girl, and they clapped till their hands smarted when she did some of her graceful circus-tricks. The first formers gaped in admiration and secretly determined to try out all the acrobatics themselves.

Gladys got an encore too. When the nervous, white-faced girl stepped on to the stage, the audience waited, rather critical, expecting to be bored. But before their eyes the girl changed into the characters she acted, and held the whole school spell-bound. She was really gifted, there was no doubt about it.

The most surprised person in the whole of the audience was Miss Quentin. She took the drama class herself, and prided herself on knowing the capacities of everyone in the second form. Privately she had thought that Doris and Carlotta were the only ones worth teaching – and now here was the quiet little mouse, Gladys, bringing down the house with her polished and beautiful interpretations of many of the most difficult parts in Shakespeare's plays!

Miss Theobald leant across to Miss Quentin. 'I must congratulate you on one of your pupil's performances!' she said, in her quiet voice. 'I can see that you must have helped the child a great deal. She could never have done all this by herself. It is amazing.'

Miss Quentin was not honest enough to say that she was as astonished as Miss Theobald. She loved praise as much as Alison did, and she nodded her head, pretending that she had taught Gladys all that she knew. Secretly she made up her mind to cultivate Gladys Hillman and give her the most important part in the play the second form were doing with her. She knew Alison had hoped for it – but she couldn't help that. Gladys must certainly have it. Then Miss Quentin could take all the credit herself for the excellent performance she was sure Gladys would give!

The concert went on. The twins were applauded and so was Janet. The first formers loved Bobby's conjuring tricks, and her ceaseless, ridiculous patter, and gave her an encore! But it was Doris who was the real star of the evening!

When she stepped on to the stage, dressed up as the jolly, fat old cook, there was a roar of delighted laughter. Doris pretended to make a pudding, keeping up a monologue in the cook's Irish accent, bringing in all the phrases that the girls knew so well. They squealed with laughter.

Then she altered her cook's uniform deftly – and lo and behold, there was Matron! Bobby ran on with some big bottles of medicine and a thermometer, and Doris proceeded to imitate Matron interviewing various girls sent to her for treatment or inspection.

Matron was in the audience, shaking with laughter. The girls roared with delight, missing many of Doris's jokes because they could not stop laughing. She was extremely clever and extremely funny.

'She should be on the stage,' said Matron, wiping her streaming eyes. 'Oh, am I really as funny as that? It's time I retired if I'm such a joke. This girl will be the death of me! Wait till she comes for medicine! I'll get my own back then!'

Doris went off the stage, grinning. The audience looked at the next item she was to do – another impersonation. Who?

They knew as soon as she appeared again. She had made herself plump with padding. She had scraped back her hair into a bun, put on enormous flat-heeled shoes, secretly borrowed from Mam'zelle's room, and wore glasses crookedly on her nose.

'Mam'zelle!' shrieked the girls, in delight. 'Marvellous!'

Doris approached the edge of the stage and addressed the girls in Mam'zelle's identical voice, taking off her English accent to perfection. The audience roared with laughter as Doris scolded them for misbehaviour.

'C'est abominable!' she finished. Then she turned away, re-arranged some things on a desk behind, and proceeded to take a lesson in the way that Mam'zelle took it, with hands wagging towards the ceiling, and her glasses slipping down over her nose.

Everyone looked at Mam'zelle herself to see how she was taking it. Mam'zelle was lying back in her chair, helpless with laughter, tears pouring down her cheeks. The girls felt a warm wave of liking for her – how nice she was to laugh at someone taking off her little foibles and mannerisms! The girls had to laugh at Mam'zelle's squeals as much as at Doris's acting.

It was a marvellous show and a great success. Everyone had loved it, and crowded round at the end to clap the performers on the back, and congratulate them. It was pleasant for both Mirabel and Gladys to feel these pats and hear the generous words of praise.

'Mother will hardly believe it all,' said Gladys to herself, her face shining with delight. 'I must tell her every single thing. And wasn't Mirabel's playing good? I clapped till my hands were sore.'

'We've made ten-pounds-fifty by selling tickets, programmes and getting in extra subscriptions,' announced Anna. 'Isn't that good? I bet no form will do as well as that.'

The second form enjoyed coffee and biscuits for a treat after the show, generously provided by Matron and Mam'zelle. 'Though why we should do this for a form whose chief success is putting up Mam'zelle and myself to be laughed at, I really don't know!' said Matron, beaming round. 'By the way – where's Elsie? She wasn't in the concert, and I don't see her now.'

The second form were so elated by their success that they wanted Elsie to join in the coffee and biscuits. But she was nowhere to be found.

She was in bed, alone – but not asleep; the only girl who had not shared in or applauded her form's success! Poor Elsie – her thoughts were very bitter that night, as she heard the echoes of laughter from the concert-room!

15.

Elsie is foolish

The next big event was Carlotta's birthday. She was fifteen, and planned a really good feast. She had opened the box of goodies given to her by her grandmother, and it had proved to be even better than the second form had hoped.

'Sardines!' said Bobby, taking out three or four of the oblong tins. 'And what's this – an *enormous* tin of pineapple chunks. It's ages since I've tasted pineapple. And what a fine big tin!'

'Bars of chocolate-cream!' said Janet. 'Enough to feed the whole school, I should think!'

'Tins of prawns!' cried Hilary. 'I say – I do like prawns. Golly – prawns and pineapple – what a heavenly mixture that would be!'

'Here's a gingerbread cake,' said Alison. 'Isn't it big? Carlotta, I must say you own a first-class grandmother! Mine's good for a cake and a bottle of boiled sweets, but that's about all. Yours is super!'

'Well, she's only just begun to be super,' said Carlotta, with a grin. 'When she didn't approve of me, she handed me out ten pence and a new comb. See what happens when she *does* approve of me!'

'Let's teach Carlotta some really marvellous manners,' said Janet, 'so that she will make a wonderful impression on her grandmother in the Christmas hols. She'll come back with half a grocer's shop then, I should think!'

'Oh, I say – what's this?' said Bobby, pulling out what looked like a large medicine bottle full of a yellow liquid. She read the label on it, then laughed.

'Do listen. "One table-spoonful of this to be taken by each girl after the birthday feast!" Oh, Carlotta, your grandmother is a scream.'

'Did you say you could go down to the shop in the town and order anything else you liked for your birthday?' asked Hilary, looking at the fine selection of things spread out on the floor. 'I shouldn't think you want anything else, do you?'

'I'd like a good big birthday cake with fifteen candles on,' said Carlotta. 'I know candles are childish when you're fifteen, but I can't help it. I think a cake looks so pretty when they are all lit. And, if we have the party at night, we can let the cake-candles light us!'

'Are we *really* going to have the feast at night?' asked Mirabel, thrilled. 'I've often read of midnight feasts in school-stories, but I didn't really think they happened.'

'Of course they happen!' said Bobby. 'You wait and see what we'll do.'

'I must order heaps and heaps of ginger beer,' said Carlotta. 'I always feel I can drink a lot at night. And I'll get lemonade too. And buns we can butter and put jam on. I like those. It's a pity we can't cook kippers too. I do like kippers.'

Everyone laughed. Carlotta loved kippers and pine-apple, two things she had had a good deal of in her circus days. She had often described to the girls how lovely frying kippers smelt, being cooked on a stove in the open-air, in the dark of the night after a show.

'No, Carlotta – we must draw the line at kippers,' said Anna. 'The smell would wake the whole school. You know how we smell kippers frying even when Cook has the kitchen and the scullery door shut.'

Elsie heard all the talk about Carlotta's birthday. She knew there was to be a feast or a party of some sort. She saw the amount of goodies taken out of Carlotta's box, and she wondered if she was going to be asked or not.

The others debated the point when Elsie was not in the room.

'Are we going to ask Catty Elsie, or not?' said Pat.

'Not,' said almost everyone.

'Oh, yes, let's,' said easy-going Anna. 'She likes good things as much as anyone.'

'I dare say – but we don't want her spiteful face glowering at us all the time,' said Isabel.

At this moment Elsie came to the door of the common-room. She stood outside, listening. She was always wondering if the others were discussing her. This time they were!

'Well, as it's my birthday I can choose my own guests,' said Carlotta. 'It's for me to say whether I'll ask Catty Elsie or not.'

'Yes – all right – *you* say, Carlotta!' cried half a dozen voices at once.

'Well – I say this – I'll ask her, but at the same time I'll tell her she's got to drop this awful pose of being a miserable martyr and act sensibly,' said Carlotta. 'She goes about looking like a wet dishcloth. I'm sure everyone in the school must laugh at her. She's a disgrace to our form. Anyway, I'll ask her to the feast, and see if she's properly grateful, and will behave herself.'

'Yes, do that,' said Anna, who was as tired as anyone else of seeing Elsie walking about looking as if she was going to weep at any moment. 'Maybe she learnt her lesson when she was left out of the concert. Perhaps she will jump at the chance of being friends again.'

'Poor Catty Elsie,' said Doris, and she began to imitate Elsie's rather high, silly voice, tearful and excited. Everyone roared with laughter.

They had no idea at all that Elsie was outside the door, listening. They would have been very scornful of her if they had known that, for eavesdropping was not looked on favourably by any member of the second form. They had very strict ideas of honour and liked to keep to them.

Elsie forgot that those who listen behind doors seldom hear any good of themselves. She stood there, trembling with anger and self-pity, hating all the girls who tossed her name about so scornfully, and laughed at her so unkindly.

A movement towards the door made her hurry away quickly. She turned a corner and went into a cloak-room, pretending to fetch a pair of shoes. The second formers, pouring out of their common-room to go to a Nature meeting, did not guess that she had overheard nearly all they had said.

There was no time then to ask Elsie to the party, for the girls were already late for the meeting. Elsie joined them, and sat sulkily silent whilst the second and third formers decided various matters concerning the Nature Club. She didn't hear a word that was said. She remembered instead what she had just overheard, and looked with rage at Carlotta and the others. How she wished she could punish them in some way!

That night Carlotta went up to where Elsie was sewing in the common-room. 'Elsie! I expect you know I'm having a birthday soon, don't you?'

'I should think the whole school knows,' said Elsie, spitefully.

'Well – I'm having a party or a feast of some kind,' said Carlotta. 'And everyone is coming. The thing is – I'd like you to come too – but only if you'll pull yourself together and act sensibly. We're all tired of the way you're behaving. Come on, Elsie, now – can't you have a bit of common sense and be one of us? We don't like you a bit as you are now, but we are quite willing to change our ideas of you, if you'll be sensible.'

'Very kind of you, *very* kind of you indeed,' said Elsie, in a trembling, sarcastic voice. 'The great Carlotta is *most* bountiful and condescending! And I know I should be very grateful and bow before her, thanking her for her great kindness!'

'Don't be an idiot,' said Carlotta, uncomfortably.

'I'm not,' said Elsie, changing her tone of voice and almost snarling at the surprised Carlotta. 'I'm just saying – "No, thanks! *I'm* not coming to your beastly feast." Ho – be a good little girl and you can come to the party! That's what you've said to me – me, who ought to be your head girl! I would *hate* to come! And what is more, if you're going to hold it at night, Anna had better look out. You're second formers now, not first formers, and if you're caught, Anna will soon find *she* isn't head girl any more, either.'

'You're impossible, Elsie,' said Carlotta, in disgust at Elsie's tone of voice. 'Well, if you don't want to come, don't. I for one am pleased.'

'So are we all!' cried Pat, Isabel and a few others, who had listened in indignation to Elsie's stinging speech. 'Keep away, Elsie. The party will be better without you!'

Elsie went on with her sewing, pursing up her thin lips scornfully. She badly wanted to go to the party, for she loved good things as much as anyone else. But her spitefulness and obstinacy made it impossible for her to climb down and accept. She sat sewing, thinking that if she could possibly prevent the party from being held, she would.

If I could find out when and where Carlotta is going to hold it, I could drop a hint to Miss Jenks, she thought. Miss Jenks doesn't look kindly on things like that. I've only got to say a word – or write an anonymous note – and the feast would be stopped before it had begun. That would be fine!

But the others did not mean to let Elsie know when the feast was to be held! They felt certain she would try to spoil it in some way. They had decided to hold it on the night of Carlotta's birthday, in the common-room itself. If they drew the blinds, and shut the door, they were reasonably safe. The common-room was a good way away from any mistresses' room, and yet fairly near their own dormitories.

They talked about it with excitement whenever Elsie was not in the room. As soon as she appeared they dropped the subject at once. Not one girl, not even silly little Alison, mentioned the subject when Elsie was there, much as they sometimes wanted to.

Carlotta had been down to the shop in the town and ordered what she wanted. The cake was to be a magnificent affair, with fifteen coloured candles. It was to have pink icing, with roses round the edge, and silver balls and sugared violets for decoration. The candles were to be fixed in roses made of sugar. Everyone was very excited about it.

'The ginger beer has come,' announced Carlotta, gleefully. 'I got the boy who brought it to put it at the back of the bicycle shed. I was afraid Miss Jenks would have a fit if she saw all those bottles of ginger beer and lemonade arriving for me. We'll each have to bring in a bottle or two when it's safe.'

'It will be fun,' said Mirabel. She looked at Gladys, who was beaming too. 'I'm glad I stayed on. Fancy missing Carlotta's feast! I would have been an idiot.'

'You would,' said Gladys. The mouse-like girl was no longer the Misery-girl. She laughed and smiled with the rest, and followed Mirabel about like a shadow. The bigger girl was very fond of her, and the two were quite inseparable. St Clare's had already done a good deal for both of them!

'We'd better not cook anything at all,' said Pat. 'I remember when we fried sausages once in the middle of the night, they made a terrific smell. We'd better just be content with cold things. We'll borrow some plates from the dining-room cupboard. There are heaps of old ones on the top shelves that won't be missed for a day or two.'

It was fun to plan everything – fun to smuggle glasses and mugs, plates and dishes and spoons and forks into the common-room. Carlotta's birthday was coming nearer and nearer. The birthday cake was made and the girls went down to the shop to inspect it. It was marvellous.

'I wish your birthday night would come, Carlotta!' said Pat. 'What sport we'll have! And *what* a feast!'

16.

Carlotta's birthday party

The girls were gathered in their common-room, the day before Carlotta's birthday. Alison took a quick look round the room. Elsie was not there.

'What time's the feast tomorrow night?' she asked. 'Exactly at midnight? Let's make it *exactly*! It's much more thrilling. Miss Quentin calls it the "witching midnight hour", and somehow . . .'

'I suppose you'd like to ask your beloved Miss Quentin?' said Isabel, pulling Alison's curly hair. 'Can you see her sitting here in our common-room, her hair done up in curlers, her face shining with grease, eating pineapple chunks and sardines? I can't.'

'She *doesn't* do her hair in curlers,' said Alison, indignantly. 'She's got beautiful, naturally wavy hair. Why are you always so unkind about her? I wish she *could* come to the feast. I'm sure she'd love it.'

'Well, *we* shouldn't,' said Pat, who had no great liking for the rather affected teacher of drama. 'You make me sick the way you go mooning round after Miss Quentin. She's not so marvellous as you think she is. I think it was pretty mean of her to take the credit herself for Gladys's acting at our concert the other night.'

'Whatever do you mean?' cried Alison, indignantly.

'Well, Alison, you know when Gladys put up that grand performance of Shakespeare's characters the other night,' said Pat, who thought it was about time that Alison was cured of her senseless admiration for Miss Quentin.

'Yes,' said Alison.

'Well, at the end of it, Miss Theobald leant across to Miss Quentin and congratulated her on Gladys's performance and said she was sure she herself had coached her for it,' said Pat, mercilessly. 'And your wonderful Miss Quentin just nodded and smiled and looked pleased – and didn't say that she knew nothing about Gladys Hillman's acting powers at all! We all think that was pretty mean.'

'I don't believe it!' cried Alison, quick to defend the mistress she so much admired.

'Well, Pam Boardman was sitting near, and she heard it all,' said Pat. 'She told us. So now just stop thinking Miss Quentin is the world's greatest wonder.'

Alison changed the subject quickly. It really hurt her to hear such things of Miss Quentin. She was always one to shut her ears to possibly unpleasant things.

'To come back to what I was saying,' she said, 'what time's the feast tomorrow night?'

'Well, as you so badly want it at exactly midnight, we'll have it then,' said Carlotta. 'I've got a dear little alarm clock I'll set for the time – and one of you in the other dormitory can stick it under your pillow so that it'll wake you without rousing everyone in the building. I daren't put it under *my* pillow because Miss Catty Elsie sleeps near

132

me and would wake too. We want to be sure she doesn't know the time.'

'All right then – midnight exactly, tomorrow night,' said Doris, in her clear voice.

At that moment the door opened, and Hilary came in. She had been to the school library to choose a book. She looked round at the others.

'I hope you haven't been talking about anything that matters,' she said, 'because dear sweet-natured, honest-souled Elsie was outside the door, listening for all she was worth!'

The others stared at her in dismay.

'Blow!' said Carlotta. 'We *have* been talking – about the feast – and we said a good many times it was to be midnight tomorrow. Blow, blow, blow!'

'Well, Elsie will certainly do her best to spoil it for us tomorrow night,' said Pat. 'She's sure to split on us somehow – absolutely sure to.'

'I'm not *going* to have our feast spoilt,' said Carlotta, in a determined voice. 'Pat, go to the door and see if Elsie's anywhere about now. Stay by the door and warn us if she comes.'

Pat looked outside the door. There was no one there. Elsie had got the information she wanted, and was content!

'Now listen,' said Carlotta, 'the feast is off for tomorrow night – but it's *on* for tonight instead!'

'Goody, goody!' said everyone, pleased.

'We must make sure Elsie doesn't hear us creeping out of the room,' said Bobby.

'She sleeps very soundly,' said Carlotta. 'I think we can manage it all right. Now, not a word, anyone! We'll hold the feast tonight – and Elsie will get a frightful shock tomorrow when she finds it's all over, and she hasn't been able to spoil it!'

Elsie had no idea that the time of the feast was altered. She hugged her secret all day long, pondering how she could spoil the feast without anyone guessing it was she who had done so.

Should she tell Miss Jenks? That would certainly stop the feast, but Miss Jenks did not like tale-bearers. Should she write a note to Miss Jenks, informing her of the feast, but not sign her name? This seemed quite a good idea – but then Miss Jenks might throw the note into the fire and take no notice of it. Elsie had once heard her say that no one should ever take notice of anonymous letters – they were too despicable even to read.

It's no good writing a note that Miss Jenks won't read or take notice of, thought the girl. I wish I knew the best way to spoil the feast.

She thought about it earnestly – so earnestly that Mam'zelle nearly 'went up in smoke', as Bobby put it, because Elsie paid so little attention in the French class.

'Elsie! This is the third time I have asked you to come out and write on the blackboard,' said Mam'zelle, exasperated. 'Ah, I have the patience of a donkey or I would not put up with you.'

'You mean, the "patience of an *ox*", Mam'zelle,' chuckled Bobby.

'A donkey is patient too,' said Mam'zelle. 'I need the patience of cows, donkeys, sheep and oxen too, when I deal with such a person as this Elsie. You will either depart from this room, Elsie, or pay attention to what I say. I will not have inattention in my class.'

Elsie had to give her thoughts to the French lesson after that – but during prep time that evening she suddenly made up her mind what she would do.

I'll wait till they're all out of the room tomorrow night – then I'll slip along to Miss Jenks's room and say I'm very worried because all the others have vanished, thought Elsie. She'll come back to see – and will then go and hunt around, and find everyone feasting in the common-room. I can say I am afraid they've been kidnapped or something. After all, that American girl, Sadie, was nearly kidnapped last term – so I can pretend to be afraid it's happened again!

This seemed to Elsie a good idea. If she really pretended to be frightened that the others had been kidnapped, Miss Jenks would not think she was telling tales – and the others would not know she had given them away, because it would be Miss Jenks who suddenly came along and found them!

Elsie had no idea that the feast was for that night not the next. The second formers kept their secret well. In fact, Carlotta and Bobby went a bit further, and whispered loudly together, in Elsie's hearing, about all that was to happen the night following! Elsie took it all in, and grinned to herself. Just wait, you second formers, and see what happens to your wonderful feast tomorrow night!

That night Carlotta wound up and set her tiny alarm clock. She gave it to Kathleen, who slept in the next room with the others. 'Put it under your pillow,' she said. 'When it goes off, wake the others quietly. Then come and wake me in the next dormitory. I'll wake our lot and we'll all go to the common-room as quiet as mice.'

Kathleen put the clock under her pillow. She felt sure she would not need it, because she was too excited to sleep. But sleep overtook one tired girl after another, and soon both dormitories were peacefully dreaming.

Elsie was fast asleep too. She was a heavy sleeper, and sometimes snored. Tonight she was huddled up beneath her blankets, because it was cold. She meant to sleep well that night so that she would be well-rested, and able to keep awake the following night.

Everyone was asleep at midnight. The alarm clock under Kathleen's pillow suddenly went off with a tiny ringing noise. Kathleen woke with a jump. She put her hand under the pillow and stopped the alarm from ringing. No one else had woken up. Kathleen sat up in bed, hugging herself in joy. The midnight feast was about to begin!

She sprang out of bed and put on her slippers and dressing-gown. Then she went softly from one bed to another, shaking the sleepers, and whispering the magic words into their ears: 'Midnight feast! Midnight feast!'

Everyone sat up at once. Dressing-gowns and slippers were groped for in the dark. Excited whispering rose.

'I can't find my slippers!'

'Blow this dressing-gown! The belt's all tied in a knot!'

'Sh!' warned Kathleen. 'We've got to be careful not to wake dear Elsie, you know.'

She slipped into the next dormitory and made her way quietly to Carlotta's bed. Carlotta was under sheets and blankets, curled up like a little animal. Kathleen shook her gently. Carlotta shot upright in bed and Kathleen pressed her shoulder warningly.

'Midnight,' she whispered in Carlotta's ear. Carlotta's heart jumped for joy. Her birthday feast, of course! She padded round the dormitory as quietly as a cat, waking everyone but Elsie.

There was no whispering in that room, and not a single giggle! Each girl took slippers and dressing-gown and crept quietly to the door. Elsie snored a little, much to everyone's relief. Carlotta shut the door quietly – and locked it! She took out the key, and put it into her dressing-gown pocket. Now, if Elsie *did* wake up, she couldn't get out and spoil the feast!

Everyone went to the common-room. Not until the door was fast-shut and cushions put along the bottom to hide the crack of light, was the light switched on. Then what a whispering and giggling there was!

'Elsie snored as we went out!' giggled Carlotta. 'Such a nice, gentle little snore! Now – come on – set out the plates and things!'

Everything was taken from the hiding-places – from the bottom of cupboards, and the back of shelves, from tuck-boxes and tins, and from behind books in book-cases. Soon the common-room tables were set with the empty plates and dishes. The largest plate of all was put in the middle. That was for the lovely birthday cake.

'Now for a real, proper feast!' said Carlotta, happily. She and the others set out the goodies they had – the cakes and the buns, the biscuits and the sweets. They opened the tins and emptied the contents on to dishes – sardines, fruit salad, pineapple, prawns – the most wonderful selection of things imaginable!

Carlotta opened a dozen ginger beer bottles. At each pop there was a giggle.

'Here's to our dear, sleeping-beauty, Elsie!' said Bobby, with a laugh, and drank the fizzy ginger beer. 'Come on, everyone – let's really enjoy ourselves!'

17.

The second form play a trick

The second formers certainly *did* enjoy themselves. After a bit they forgot to whisper, and began to speak in their normal voices. It didn't matter, really. They were too far from any sleeping mistress to be heard. They giggled at everything, and laughed till the tears came at Doris and her idiotic antics with empty ginger beer bottles.

They ate everything. Carlotta even ate sardines and pineapple together. Alison tried prawns dipped in ginger beer, which Pat and Isabel said were 'simply super', but they made her feel sick taken that way. However, the others didn't mind, and mixed all the food together with surprising results.

'Nobody would dream that sardines pressed into gingerbread cake would taste so nice,' said Janet. 'My brother told me that and I didn't believe him. But it's true.'

The birthday cake was marvellous. It melted in the mouth! The candles were lit very soon and the light turned off. All the girls sat munching happily, watching the fifteen candles flicker and glow. It was lovely.

'A happy year to you, Carlotta!' said Pat, holding up her mug of ginger beer. 'It's your birthday now, because it's past midnight. Many happy returns of the day!'

'Thanks,' said Carlotta, her vivid little face radiant. Her dark eyes sparkled as she looked round at her friends. It was lovely to give people pleasure. She would tell her grandmother all about it.

'Happy returns!' said one voice after another. 'Happy birthday! Good old Carlotta!'

Carlotta cut second slices of her big birthday cake for everyone. There was a fairly big piece left, enough for two extra slices.

'Two more bits,' said Carlotta, slicing the piece in half. 'Who shall we give them to?'

'One to Miss Jenks!' said Pat. 'You needn't say we had the cake at midnight!'

'And one to Miss Quentin,' said Alison eagerly.

'Don't be silly,' said Carlotta. 'Do you think I'm going to waste my birthday cake on Miss Quentin! I'd rather give a slice to Elsie!'

'Well, let's,' said Anna, unexpectedly. 'It's supposed to be good for people to heap coals of fire on their head – you know, return good for evil – and anyway, what a shock for Elsie when we give her a bit – and she realizes we've had the party!'

'We'll give it to her after the next night then,' said Carlotta, grinning. 'Let her try and spoil the feast this coming night – and then the next day we'll present her with a bit of cake. That really would be funny.'

Everyone agreed to that – not that they wanted to make Elsie a present at all – they just wanted to see her face when she saw the piece of cake, and realized that the feast had been held in peace without her, and hadn't been spoilt.

'Well, one bit for Miss Jenks, and the other for darling Elsie,' said Carlotta, and put them away in a tin. 'Now, girls, is there anything else left to eat?'

There wasn't – and very little to drink either. 'It's a good thing,' said Anna. 'I simply couldn't eat another crumb!'

'Fancy *you* saying that, Anna!' said Pat, with a laugh, looking at the plump, round-faced girl. 'I should have thought you could have gone on eating till breakfast-time!'

'Don't be rude to your head girl,' said Anna, lazily. Nothing ever ruffled her good temper. 'Carlotta, we'd better clear up and get back. We've been here ages!'

'What a pity!' said Alison, with a sigh. She never liked clearing up. The girls set to work and stacked the dishes and plates neatly at the back of a cupboard, hoping they would be able to wash them and put them back into their proper places in the morning.

They swept up the crumbs and threw them out of the window. They put the ginger beer and lemonade bottles into a cupboard outside in the passage. Then they looked round the common-room. There was not a single sign of the lovely feast they had had.

'Good girls,' said Anna. 'Now come along – as quietly as you can, so as not to wake Elsie.'

The second formers crept quietly back to their rooms. Carlotta unlocked her dormitory door. The first sound that greeted her was the light snoring of the sleeping Elsie! She had not even stirred.

Good, thought Carlotta, cuddling into bed. Everything went off marvellously. Oh, I wish we could have it all over again tomorrow night!

The second formers were very sleepy the next morning. They found it difficult to get up. Alison said she felt sick, and so did Kathleen.

'Well, never mind, it was worth it, wasn't it?' said Pat. 'Do you want to go to Matron?'

'No,' said Alison and Kathleen together. Matron would only give them a large dose of nasty-tasting medicine. She had an unfailing way of knowing when a midnight feast had been held, and kept special medicine for girls who complained of feeling sick the next day!

Elsie did not for one moment suspect that the feast had been held. Nobody said a word about it in front of her. The common-room had been so well cleared up that there was not a crumb left to give the secret away.

Elsie looked at the second formers as they worked in Miss Jenks's geography class. You may think you are going to have a lovely time tonight, she thought, but you won't! Miss Jenks will come and spoil it all – and that will serve you right for being so mean to me!

Neither Alison nor Kathleen were sick after all, but because they would eat no breakfast and no dinner, Miss Jenks sent them to Matron. Matron took their temperatures, and found they had none.

'H'mmmm!' she said, thoughtfully. 'Anyone had a birthday in the second form?'

'It's Carlotta's today,' said Kathleen.

'I thought so,' said Matron. 'You are both suffering from Too-Much-To-Eat. A dose of medicine will soon put you right!'

That night the second form went to bed with giggles and nudges. They felt quite certain Elsie was going to give them away – or was hoping to. They had made a lovely plan.

'We'll all wake up at midnight and creep out of the room,' planned Bobby. 'Then, as soon as we're gone, I bet Elsie will go off to tell Miss Jenks, or even Miss Theobald! You never know! When we see her go, we'll all creep back into bed and be there, pretending to be sound asleep, when Miss Jenks comes. What a sell for dear Elsie!'

Everyone approved of this plan. Elsie saw them whispering and giggling, and felt certain it was about the feast that night! She made up her mind to keep awake, whatever happened.

Carlotta set her alarm clock for midnight once more – this time under her own pillow, as she wanted to make sure of waking Elsie up that night! It went off at twelve o'clock, and Carlotta sat up. She grinned to herself in the darkness.

She went from bed to bed, waking everyone up, making rather a noise. Elsie woke up too, for she had fallen asleep after all. She pretended to lie fast asleep, and did not stir until all the girls had crept out of the dormitory. Then she sat up and pulled on her own dressing-gown.

The beasts! Enjoying themselves without me! she

thought maliciously, forgetting that she could have joined in the party if she had said she would behave sensibly. Well, now I'll go and wake Miss Jenks – and pretend I'm frightened because the others have all disappeared!

She slipped out of the dormitory. Carlotta, who was hiding round a corner, saw her going down the passage in the opposite direction, on her way to Miss Jenks's room.

'Come along,' she whispered to the second formers, who were giggling nearby. 'She's gone! I bet Miss Jenks will be along in half a minute! What will she say to Elsie when she sees us all safe and sound in our warm beds!'

The girls took off dressing-gowns and slippers, and hurried back into their beds, which were still nice and warm. They cuddled down and waited, giggling every now and again when someone made a silly remark.

Meanwhile Elsie was knocking on Miss Jenks's door. There was no answer. She knocked more loudly. There was a creak from the bed and then Miss Jenks's voice. 'Who's there? What's the matter?'

Elsie opened the door. Miss Jenks switched on the light beside her bed. She saw Elsie, who had put on a very frightened expression indeed.

'Is somebody ill?' asked Miss Jenks, springing out of bed and dragging her dressing-gown on. 'Quick, tell me!'

'Oh, Miss Jenks – I'm so frightened,' stammered Elsie, filling Miss Jenks with foreboding, she looked so scared. 'All the girls out of my dormitory have disappeared – every one of them. Oh, Miss Jenks – do you think they can have been kidnapped? I feel so scared.'

Miss Jenks snorted. She had a wonderful snort which was often faithfully copied by Doris.

'My dear Elsie, don't be a ninny! As if seven or eight girls could be kidnapped in your room and you hear nothing! Use your common sense, for pity's sake!'

'Miss Jenks, they really aren't there,' said Elsie, looking more wide-eyed than ever. 'Not one of them. Where can they be?'

'It's Carlotta's birthday, isn't it?' said Miss Jenks, crossly. 'I suppose it's a feast. Just like you to try and spoil it!'

'Oh, Miss Jenks, I never thought of that!' cried Elsie, pretending to be astonished and hurt. 'Oh, so long as they aren't kidnapped!'

'You really make me cross, Elsie,' said Miss Jenks who, having had Elsie for more than a year in her form, knew her very well indeed. 'Well, come along – I suppose I'll have to look into this – but you'll just come along with me too, my girl – and the second form can see who's spoilt things for them!'

This was not what Elsie had planned at all! But it was no use, she could not draw back now. She had to go with Miss Jenks.

They went along to the dormitory where Elsie slept. The girls heard them coming and cuddled closer into bed, shutting their eyes tightly, hoping they would not giggle and give everything away. Doris gave one or two beautiful little snores, so real that Carlotta wondered if she could possibly have gone to sleep! Miss Jenks heard the snores. She switched on the dormitory light.

She stared in silence at the beds, all except Elsie's occupied by apparently sleeping girls. Doris gave another marvellous little snore, and then, with a realistic grunt, turned over in bed and settled down again. Miss Jenks watched her. She felt certain Doris was awake.

Elsie stared in the utmost astonishment and horror at the occupied beds. She simply could not understand it. She had not been more than three minutes away, surely – and yet here were all the girls asleep in bed. Could she have dreamt it all? Had the girls not stirred from their beds at all? What had happened?

'Well, Elsie,' said Miss Jenks, not troubling to lower her voice, for she felt certain every girl was awake, 'you appear to have brought me out on a wild-goose chase. We shall have to have a talk about this tomorrow, I think. I don't feel at all pleased to be woken up with a story of wholesale kidnappings, and then to find that the only girl out of bed is yourself. Not a very creditable performance on your part, I feel.'

Elsie got into bed without a word. Miss Jenks snapped off the light and went back to bed, shutting her ears to the giggling and whispering that immediately broke out. No one said a word to the cowering Elsie. Let her try to puzzle out what had happened! After ten minutes giggling the room went to sleep again – all but Elsie, who lay awake worrying about what was to happen to her the next day!

The first thing that happened had its funny side. Carlotta solemnly approached her and offered her a piece of the birthday cake. 'You weren't there, so we saved it for you,' she said, a very goody-goody expression on her glowing little face.

Elsie was startled out of her silence. She stared at the cake and said, 'So you *did* have the feast after all? When did you?'

'We had it when we were kidnapped,' said Carlotta, solemnly. 'Oooh, Elsie – it was thrilling! Somebody came in the middle of the night – and kidnapped us all – and took us away – but we offered them a bit of the birthday cake and they were so pleased with it that they set us free!'

'Don't tell such untruths!' said Elsie, angrily. There were squeals of laughter at this.

'Untruths! Why, who was it went and told Miss Jenks we had been kidnapped? *You* can't talk about untruths!'

Elsie turned away. She would not take the cake. She was sick at heart, and longed for a friendly look or a friendly word. Now she had to go and face Miss Jenks. That would be awful too. She had to go just before morning school, at ten minutes to nine in the classroom.

She went. Miss Jenks was there, busy as usual correcting piles of exercise books. On the desk in front of her was a most surprising sight – a large piece of birthday cake! It had been offered to her by Carlotta with a merry twinkle – and had been accepted with a merry twinkle also! Elsie stared at it and bit her lip. To think that Miss Jenks had accepted the cake! Why, she must have guessed about the feast – and here she was accepting a bit of the cake! It was too bad.

'Elsie, there is something seriously wrong with you this term,' began Miss Jenks. 'You had a great chance as head girl, and both Miss Theobald and I hoped you would take it. Apparently you haven't. None of the girls will accept you. Instead of standing up to things and realizing you had to do better and change your attitude, you chose to do stupid things like coming to me last night with a cock-and-bull tale, in order to spite the others. They were too smart for you, I am pleased to see. Now what is to be done? Are you going to go on like this for the rest of the term? Your report will not make pleasant reading if so. Or are you going to show that you really have a little courage and common sense in you, and try to make up for your silly behaviour before it is too late?'

Plain speaking was Miss Jenks's strong point. Elsie listened in silence. She looked at the calm eyes of her form mistress. There was absolutely nothing else to be done now but admit herself to be in the wrong, and say she had courage to do better. That was hard – but the alternative was harder – getting a thoroughly bad report, and having to bear the sneers of the girls for the rest of the term.

'I'll try to make up for being silly,' said Elsie, in a half-sulky tone.

'You've been more than silly,' said Miss Jenks. 'Pull yourself together. You know that St Clare's only keeps the girls it can do something with. The second formers are decent. If they see you showing a little courage and common sense, they will help you.'

'All right,' said Elsie, ungraciously. 'But, Miss Jenks –

don't make me tell them I'm sorry or anything. I can't do that. I really can't.'

'My dear Elsie, I haven't had you in my form for over a year without knowing that I can't expect you to have either the good feeling or the courage to say you're sorry,' said Miss Jenks, impatiently. 'Now here come the others. Go and get my books for me out of the mistresses' common-room, and put on a little brighter face. I simply cannot bear to see you looking like a hen left out in the rain any longer!'

Elsie went to fetch Miss Jenks's books as the second formers crowded into the room. They sat down at once, surprised to see their form mistress there before them.

'I want to say a word to you this morning,' said Miss Jenks. 'About Elsie. She has agreed to try and have a little courage and do better from now on – rather unwillingly, I must admit. She tells me she cannot possibly say she is sorry to you for her stupid conduct – and in any case, I don't think she *is* sorry – but try to act towards her in a way to help her efforts, not hinder them, will you? After all – you played a wonderful trick on her last night, didn't you?'

This unexpected ending made all the girls smile delightedly. So Miss Jenks guessed everything – and there was the birthday cake, sitting waiting to be eaten! Good old Miss Jenks! The girls were ready to do anything she asked them.

'All right, Miss Jenks – we'll put up with Elsie as graciously as we can,' said Hilary, smiling. 'We got our own back last night – so we can afford to be generous!'

Elsie came back into the room. She had tried to make her face pleasanter. She placed the books on the desk. 'Thank you, Elsie,' said Miss Jenks, in a pleasant tone, and gave her a smile. The girls saw it and approved. What Miss Jenks could do, they could do also. Things would be easier for Elsie than she deserved!

18.

An exciting match

The term went on its way, happy and busy with lessons, games and fun. Lacrosse matches were played, and the whole school turned out to watch and cheer at the home matches.

The second form were very proud of Gladys. Anna had told Miss Wilton, the games mistress, that she thought Gladys would be worth trying in some other position than goal-keeper, and Miss Wilton rather doubtfully agreed to try her.

'She has never shown any aptitude for running, catching or tackling,' she said. 'However – we will see.'

So Gladys, to her delight, was put in a position where running and catching would count, and after once or twice the girl proved herself to be very good. She was small, but very wiry and agile, and she was amazingly good at dodging the enemy and passing the ball quickly to someone else.

'Good, Gladys, good!' Miss Wilton said, time after time, one Monday afternoon. 'You *are* coming on!'

Gladys flushed with pleasure. She looked very happy these days. Miss Quentin was taking a good deal of notice of her in the drama class, and now Miss Wilton was praising her at lacrosse – the two things she liked most. She was writing very happy letters to her mother now, and although she still had no reply, she had had a letter from Mirabel's mother that had delighted her.

Dear Gladys [the letter had said],

I thought you might like to know that I was able to go today to the hospital your mother is in. The nurse actually allowed me to see her for two minutes, as it was one of her good days. I told her about you, and how you and my Mirabel were friends. She could not say much, but she did say how delighted she was to hear what a success you were at the concert. Perhaps you will be able to see her in the holidays. It is early days to say yet whether she is really making progress, but I think you may be hopeful. I will go to see her again if I can.

Give my love to Mirabel, and say I hope she is treating you properly! You are such a little mouse and Mirabel is just the opposite!

Love from

Elise Unwin

This letter Gladys treasured greatly. She thought with intense gratitude of Mrs Unwin. She began to hope that her mother really might get better. She knew that when she was well enough she had to have a serious operation, and this thought worried her greatly – but now that she was happier things did not seem so bad.

Meantime there was lacrosse, and the excitement of the next match, which was to be a home one, against St

Christopher's. Belinda Towers had let it be known that she would like to choose one girl from the second form for the team. No one in the first form was good enough as yet – but the second form were on the whole not at all bad at the game.

'*You* might be chosen, Gladys!' said Mirabel, half-teasingly. She did not seriously think that the shy girl would be picked out, for although she certainly was very good at the game now, she was not half the size of some of the other girls in the form.

'I wish I could!' said Gladys. 'But I know who will be – Hilary! She's terribly good, I think.'

Hilary certainly was very good – very sure and very swift. Her catching was graceful to watch, and it seemed certain she would be chosen for the match.

But two days before the match Hilary went down with a cold again. Matron popped her into bed, in spite of her wails about lacrosse.

'Belinda said I could play in the match!' she said. 'Can't I get up tomorrow for certain?'

'Nothing is certain with bad colds,' said Matron. 'So don't count on anything.'

Thus it came about that Hilary, although chosen by Belinda, could not play – and Belinda, running her pencil down the list of names in the second form, suddenly came to a stop by Gladys Hillman's name. She sat and thought.

That kid's good, thought the head girl. I watched her yesterday. She's fast – and jolly good at tackling although she is small. I've a good mind to try her.

So, when the list of names was put up on the big noticeboard, showing the girls chosen for the next match, Gladys Hillman's appeared at the bottom – the only one chosen from the second form! Mirabel saw it and went hurriedly in search of Gladys.

'Gladys! What do you think? You're down for the match!'

'Really?' said Gladys, her face flushing brightly. 'Oh – how marvellous! Golly, I *shall* be nervous, though!'

'No, you won't. You'll just remember that your mother is longing to hear that you've shot twelve goals for St Clare's, and that you've won the match for the school!' said Mirabel, laughing. 'Oh, I say – I *am* pleased. Good for you!'

Gladys was happy to see Mirabel's real pleasure. That was the best of friends – they shared your troubles with you, and they doubled your joys. It was good to have a friend.

The school turned out as usual to watch the match. The St Christopher girls came in a big coach, their lacrosse sticks beside them. The St Clare's girls gave them a cheer.

The game began. Belinda was referee, and blew her whistle sharply. There was the click of lacrosse sticks as the two girls in the centre of the field began the game. Then the ball was flicked quickly away, and Margery Fenworthy, of the third form, picked it up in her lacrosse net and flew down the field with it. She passed to Lucy Oriell, her friend, and then when Lucy was tackled, cleverly caught the ball once more and passed to Gladys, who was hopping about in excitement, ready for any chance.

Click! Gladys caught the ball, dodged a tackling enemy, and threw to Lucy. From one to another went the ball, and Lucy tried to throw a goal, which was deftly stopped by the St Christopher's goal-keeper.

The game was very even. The St Clare girls were better runners and catchers, but the St Christopher goal-keeper was marvellous. She had a quick eye, a firm wrist, and a real talent for stopping the ball every time the St Clare girls threw at the goal.

St Christopher's threw a goal first, and the St Clare girls clapped, though their faces were rather anxious. This was going to be a stiffer match than they thought. Thank goodness both Margery Fenworthy and Lucy Oriell were playing today – they were always first-class. Some of the St Clare girls looked doubtfully at Gladys Hillman. She seemed very small in comparison with the others. Margery Fenworthy, for instance, was a big strapping girl who over-topped Gladys by a head and a half!

'Play up, Gladys!' yelled Mirabel, every time her friend came near her. 'Go on – play up!'

And the whole second form would yell in chorus, 'Play *up*, Gladys! What about a goal from you?'

Half-time – and no goals for the St Clare girls! One-love! The St Clare girls who were watching crowded round their team, trying to buck them up and spur them on.

'You are doing well, Margery and Lucy,' said Belinda Towers, approvingly. Her eye caught the flushed face of Gladys Hillman, and she gave her one of her sudden wide smiles. 'You're not doing too badly either, kid! But keep a bit closer to Margery, will you? You might be able to score a goal off one of her passes to you.'

'Yes, Belinda,' said Gladys, happily. 'I'll try.' She kept her word. She hovered closer to Margery, and caught the ball slickly each time. Twice she was tackled and had to pass before she could shoot at the goal – but the third time she threw the ball with all her might at the net in the distance.

'Goal, goal!' yelled the St Clare girls. But no, the St Christopher goal-keeper deftly flicked the ball away. No goal – but a jolly good try!

'Go it, Gladys, go it!' yelled the second form, dancing about in excitement. 'Try again!'

Gladys did her best. She was everywhere, in and out, running, tackling, passing. Time slipped on, and still no goals were scored by St Clare's. On the other hand no more were scored by St Christopher's, either. It was the closest match the schools had ever played.

'Oh, golly, it's almost time!' groaned Mirabel, glancing at her watch. 'Gladys! Play up. There's only four minutes more!'

Gladys heard, and ran to tackle an enormous St Christopher girl. The girl dodged, and Gladys tripped. She wrenched her ankle, and gave a groan. It was going to be painful to run now. But she couldn't possibly give up!

The ball rolled near her. She nipped it up into her lacrosse net, and ran, limping, down the field. She passed to Margery, who at once passed back again when she was tackled. Gladys didn't catch the ball. It was neatly caught by a much taller girl, who leapt into the air. The ball fell into her net, and she turned to run down the field. But quick as thought Gladys hit her lacrosse stick upwards, and the ball flew into the air. Gladys caught it, and ran again. She shot for the goal.

It was not such a good shot as before – but the ball bounced over a tuft as it rolled towards the goal, and avoided the waiting lacrosse net of the goal-keeper. In the greatest dismay she saw it roll into the goal!

The St Clare girls nearly went mad with joy. The second form thumped each other on the back and yelled 'Good old Gladys' at the tops of their voices. It was all very thrilling.

The match was a draw – one all. The St Christopher girls went back to tea with St Clare's, and discussed the match at the tops of their voices. The second form treated Gladys to a special cake for making the score even.

'Good for you, kid!' said Belinda, as she passed. That was Gladys's biggest reward! Words of praise from the great head girl were words of praise indeed!

19.

Alison and Miss Quentin

The term hurried on its way. The girls began to talk about Christmas holidays and what they were going to do – pantomimes, parties and theatres were discussed. Gladys looked a little bleak when the girls began to talk excitedly about the coming holidays.

'Will your mother be well enough to leave the hospital and have you home with her?' asked Mirabel.

'No. I'm staying at school for the hols,' said Gladys. 'Matron will still be here, you know, and two girls from the third and fourth form, whose parents are in India. But I shall be very lonely without you, Mirabel.'

'Poor Gladys!' said Mirabel in dismay. 'I should hate to stay at school for the hols I must say. After all, most of the fun of being at boarding school is being with crowds of others, day and night – it won't be any fun for you being with one or two! Won't your mother really be better?'

'She's going to have a serious operation soon,' said Gladys. 'So I know quite well she won't be able to leave the hospital, Mirabel. But the operation may make her well again, so I'm just hoping for the best – and I'm quite willing to stay on at school for the hols if only I hear that Mother is getting better after the operation.'

Mrs Unwin had written to Mirabel about Gladys's mother. She had told Mirabel not to show the letter to Gladys.

'I feel rather worried about Gladys's mother,' she wrote. 'She is to have the operation soon – and I can't help wondering if she really will get over it, because she is very weak. If there is bad news, you must comfort Gladys all you can. She will be very glad to have a friend if sadness comes to her. I will let her know at once if the news is good.'

Mirabel said nothing to her friend about the letter – but she was extra warm and friendly towards Gladys. It was unusual for the rather selfish, thick-skinned Mirabel to think of someone else unselfishly and tenderly. It softened her domineering nature and made her a much nicer girl.

Gladys was pleased to be able to tell her mother about the match. She wished she had shot a winning goal – but it was something to shoot the goal that made a draw!

'*I* shall write and tell your mother too,' said Mirabel, who could not do enough for her friend just then.

'Oh, Mirabel – you are good!' said Gladys, delighted. 'You wrote to Mother after the concert, and I guess she was pleased to hear all you said. My word – what a silly I was at the beginning of the term, all mopey and miserable, couldn't take an interest in anything. I should think you hated me.'

'Well, I didn't like you very much,' said Mirabel, honestly. 'But I guess you didn't like *me* much, either!'

Gladys was shining not only at lacrosse but in the

drama class as well! Miss Quentin, who had been really amazed at Gladys's performance on the night of the concert, was making a great fuss of her and her talent. Alison didn't like it at all. She was jealous, and there were some days when she could hardly speak to Gladys.

The play was to be performed at the end of the term. Miss Quentin had tried out Alison, Doris, Carlotta and now Gladys in the principal feminine part. There was no doubt that Alison looked the prettiest and the most graceful, and that she was quite word-perfect and had rehearsed continually. But Gladys was by far the best actress.

Miss Quentin had given Alison to understand that she would have the chief part. She had not actually said so in so many words, but the class as a whole took it for granted that Alison would take the part. They found it quite natural too, for they knew how hard the girl had worked at learning the words, a task always difficult for her.

Alison was really silly about Miss Quentin. She waited round corners for her, hoping for a smile. She hung on every word the teacher said. She was worse than she had been with Sadie Greene the term before – for one thing Sadie had had a little common sense and often laughed at Alison, but Miss Quentin had no common sense at all! So Alison became worse instead of better, and the second formers became quite exasperated with her.

Then Alison heard some news that gave her a great blow – Miss Quentin was not coming back the next term!

'Are you sure?' asked Alison, looking with wide eyes at Hilary, who had come in with the news.

'Well, I heard Mam'zelle say to Miss Quentin, "Well, well – so you will be on the stage next term, whilst we are all struggling with our tiresome girls!" Apparently Miss Quentin had only just heard the news herself – she had a letter in her hand. I think she must only have been engaged for a term – it's the first time we've had a proper drama class. Perhaps Miss Theobald was trying out the idea.' Hilary looked at Alison, who had tears in her eyes. 'Cheer up, Alison – the world won't come to an end because your beloved Miss Quentin isn't here next term! You'll find someone else to moon round, don't fret!'

It was a great shock to Alison. She had dreamt of term after term in Miss Quentin's drama classes, with herself taking all the chief parts in every play, hearing honeyed words of praise dropping daily from the teacher's lips. She went away by herself and cried very bitterly. The silly girl gave her heart far too easily to anyone who attracted her, or made a fuss of her.

'What's come over Alison?' asked Pat, in surprise, when her cousin appeared with swollen eyes. 'Been in a row, Alison?'

'She's only sorrowing because her beloved Miss Quentin won't be here next term to pat her on the back and tell her she is very very good!' said Janet.

'Alison, don't be an idiot!' said Isabel. 'You know perfectly well Miss Quentin won't be much loss. We all think she's too soft for words! And think how mean she was in taking the credit for Gladys's performance at the concert.'

'I have never believed that,' said Alison, tears coming

into her eyes again. 'You don't know Miss Quentin as I do – she's the truest, honestest, most loyal person! I've never met anyone like her.'

'Nor have I!' said Pat. 'And thank goodness I haven't. Alison, why must you go and choose the wrong people to moon round? Sadie Greene was amusing but she hadn't anything in her at all – and neither has Miss Quentin. Now, take Miss Jenks for instance . . .'

'Miss Jenks!' said Alison, with an angry sniff. 'Who would want to moon round Miss Jenks, with her snappy tongue and cold eyes?'

'Well, I think she's pretty decent,' said Pat. 'Not that I should want to moon round her or anyone, for that matter. I'm only just saying you will keep on choosing the wrong people to lavish your affections on! Sadie has never even written to you – and I bet Miss Quentin won't, either!'

'She will! She's very fond of me,' said Alison.

The others gave it up. Alison would never learn sense! 'It's a pity she can't find out how silly her Miss Quentin really is – how undependable,' said Hilary. 'Your feather-headed cousin, Pat, wants to learn common sense – it's a pity she can't find out that all her ideas about Miss Quentin are only dreams – the real Miss Quentin isn't a bit as Alison pictures her!'

'Well, we can't teach her,' said Pat. 'She'll make herself miserable for the rest of the term now, and for all the hols too, I expect!'

Alison was really unhappy to hear that her favourite teacher was leaving. She thought she would hang about near the common-room of the junior mistresses, and watch for Miss Quentin to come out. Then she would tell her how upset she was.

So she went to a little lobby near the common-room, and pretended to be hunting for something there. She could hear Miss Quentin's voice talking to Mam'zelle, behind the closed door of the common-room, but she could not hear anything that was said.

Then someone opened the door and came out. It was Miss Lewis, the history teacher. 'Leave the door open,' cried Mam'zelle, 'it is stuffy in here!'

So Miss Lewis left the door open, and went off towards the school library. Alison stood in the little lobby, her heart beating fast, waiting for Miss Quentin to come out. Surely she would come soon!

The mistresses went on talking. Some of them had clear, distinct voices, and some spoke too low for Alison to hear anything. She did not mean to listen, she was only waiting for Miss Quentin – but suddenly she heard her own name, spoken by Miss Quentin herself. Alison stiffened, and her heart thumped. Was Miss Quentin going to praise her to the others? It would be just like her to say something nice!

'Alison O'Sullivan is going to get a shock,' said Miss Quentin, in the low, clear voice that Alison thought so beautiful. 'The silly girl thinks she's good enough to play the lead in the second-form play! She's been wearing herself out rehearsing – it will do her good to find she's not going to have the part!'

'Who's going to have it, then?' asked Miss Jenks.

'Gladys Hillman,' answered Miss Quentin, promptly. 'I've had my eye on that child ever since the beginning of the term. She's three times as good as anyone else. She will be marvellous as the Countess Jeannette.'

'I wish Alison worked as hard in my classes as she does in yours,' remarked Mam'zelle, in her rather harsh, loud voice. 'Ah, her French exercises! But I think, Miss Quentin, she really does work at drama.'

'Oh, well, she simply adores me,' said Miss Quentin, easily. 'I can always make her type work. She'll do anything for a smile or a kind word from me – like a dear little pet dog. But give me somebody like that wild Carlotta – somebody with something in them! Alison bores me to tears with her breathless, "Yes, Miss Quentin! No, Miss Quentin! Oh, *can* I, Miss Quentin?" It will be good for her to have a shock and find she has to take back place to Gladys Hillman.'

'I'm not so sure,' said Miss Jenks, in her cool voice. 'Shocks are not always good for rather weak characters, Miss Quentin. I hope you will break your news kindly to poor Alison – otherwise she will weep all day, and as exams are coming on tomorrow, I don't want bad work from her because of you!'

'Oh, don't worry! I'll just pat her curly head and say a few kind words,' said Miss Quentin. 'She'll eat out of my hand. She always does.'

Miss Lewis came back and shut the door. Not a word more could be heard. Alison sat on a bench in the lobby, sick at heart, shocked and hurt beyond measure. Her mind was in a whirl. She had not been able to help hearing – and once she had grasped that her idol, Miss Quentin, was poking fun at her, she had not even been able to get up and go. She had had to sit there, hearing every cruel word.

She was not to have the leading part in the play. Miss Quentin wasn't fond of her – only amused with her, thinking her a little pet dog, someone to pat and laugh at! Miss Quentin had told a lie – she had not noticed Gladys Hillman at all until the night of the concert! Miss Quentin was bored with her!

Alison was too shocked even to cry. She sat in the lobby quietly, looking straight in front of her. What was it that Miss Jenks had said? 'Shocks are not always good for weak characters!' Was she, Alison, such a weak character then? The girl rubbed her hand across her forehead, which was wet and clammy.

I have to think all this out, said Alison to herself. I can't tell anyone. I'm too ashamed. But I must think things out. Oh, Miss Quentin, how could you say all that?

Poor Alison! This was the greatest shock she had ever had in her easy-going life! All her admiration and love for Miss Quentin vanished at once – passed like a dream in the night. There was nothing of it left, except an ache. She saw the drama teacher as the others saw her – someone pleasant and amiable, but undependable, disloyal, shallow.

Alison was a silly girl, as changeable as a weather-vane, swinging now this way and now that, easily upset and easily pleased. As the others often said, 'she hadn't much in her'! But in this hour of horror – for it *was* horror to her – she found something in herself that she hardly knew she possessed. And that something was a sense of dignity!

She wasn't going to go under because of someone like Miss Quentin! She wasn't going to be a pet dog, eating out of her hand! She had too much dignity for that. She would show Miss Quentin that she was wrong. Hurt and shocked though she was, Alison had a glimmering of common sense all at once, and she held up her head, blinked away the tears, and made up her mind what she was going to do.

So it came about that when Miss Quentin broke the news to the drama class that Gladys was to have the leading part, and not Alison, the girl gave no sign at all of being disappointed. Her face was pale, for she had slept badly that night, but it had a calmness and dignity that astonished the watching girls.

'So Gladys is to have the part, you see,' finished Miss Quentin. She lightly touched Alison's curly head. 'I'm afraid my Alison will be disappointed!'

'Of course not, Miss Quentin,' said Alison, moving away from the teacher's hand. 'I think Gladys *should* have the part! She is the best of us all – and I am very glad.'

The girls stared at Alison in the greatest amazement. They had expected tears – even sulks – but not this cool acceptance of an unpleasant fact.

'Who would have thought Alison would take it like that?' said Janet. 'Well – good for her! All the same, I think it's a shame. Miss Quentin made us all think Alison would have the part.'

Alison would not meet Miss Quentin's eye. She played the part she was given very well, but seemed quite unmoved when Miss Quentin praised her. Miss Quentin was puzzled and a little hurt.

'Girls, I have something to tell you,' she said at the end of the lesson. 'I shall not be here next term. I shall miss you all very much – especially one or two of you who have worked extremely hard!'

She looked hard at Alison, expecting to see tears, and to hear cries of 'Oh, Miss Quentin! We *shall* miss you!'

But Alison did not look at the teacher. She gazed out of the window as if she had not heard. Hilary cleared her throat and spoke politely. 'I am sure we are all sorry to hear that, Miss Quentin. We hope you will be happy wherever you go.'

Miss Quentin was hurt and disappointed. She spoke directly to Alison.

'Alison, I know you worked specially hard for me,' she said.

'I worked hard because I like drama,' said Alison, in a cool voice, looking Miss Quentin in the eyes for the first time. This was a direct snub and the girls gasped in surprise. Whatever made Alison behave like that? They gazed at her in admiration. So Alison had seen through her beloved Miss Quentin at last – and instead of moaning and wailing, had put on a cloak of dignity and coolness. One up to Alison!

167

Miss Quentin retired gracefully to her next class, very much puzzled. The girls crowded round Alison.

'Alison! What's happened? Has your beloved Miss Quentin offended you?'

'Shut up,' said Alison, pushing her way between the girls. 'I can't tell you anything. I don't want to discuss it. Let me alone.'

They let her go, puzzled, but respecting her request. 'Something's happened,' said Hilary, watching the white-faced girl going out of the room. 'But whatever it is, it's for the best. Alison seems suddenly more grown-up.'

'Time she was,' said Pat. 'Anyway – if she stops mooning round somebody different each term – or at any rate chooses somebody worthwhile – it will be a blessing!'

Nobody ever knew what had made Alison 'grow up' so suddenly. Only Alison herself knew, and out of her hurt came something worthwhile, which was to help her in many years to come.

20.

An exciting end of term

Exams were being held, and girls were groaning daily over them. Mam'zelle was in a state of trepidation in case any of the girls fell short of pass-marks. The girls were in a far greater state, feeling quite certain that nobody at all would pass in French! Mam'zelle always threatened to give them such difficult papers – but when the time came, they were not so bad after all!

Gladys found the exams difficult because her mother was to have her operation that week. She was very anxious indeed. Mirabel did all she could to help her to prepare each evening. It was good to see the patience and kindliness of the bigger girl. The others warmed greatly to Mirabel because of it.

Even Elsie felt sorry for the anxious girl. 'I hope you'll hear good news soon,' she said. Gladys looked at her in surprised gratitude. Fancy Elsie saying anything kind! The others heard the low words, and looked at one another with raised eyebrows. They had kept their promise to Miss Jenks, and had not hindered Elsie in any way in her efforts to behave more reasonably.

But, on the other hand, no girl had been able to show any liking for Elsie. It was impossible. The girl had been too spiteful, too exasperating altogether to be liked now. She would be tolerated, but nothing else. Miss Jenks watched everyone's behaviour, and came to the conclusion that it was hopeless to expect any happiness or real help for Elsie from the second formers. On the other hand, the lazy Anna had been a great success as head girl of the form. She had thrown aside her laziness, and had come to the fore, taking responsibility and making decisions capably and quickly. Miss Jenks was pleased with her. She was now ready to go up into the third form, and take her part with the older girls there. Hilary Wentworth could be head girl next term.

Miss Jenks spoke to Miss Theobald about it and the head agreed. 'But what are we to do with Elsie?' she said. 'I will have a talk with her.'

So Elsie was sent for, and sat rather sullenly in Miss Theobald's sitting-room, expecting to be scolded, or something even worse – she might be told that St Clare's didn't want her any more!

'Elsie,' said Miss Theobald, 'I know you have found things difficult this term – mostly your own fault, as I think you will admit.'

Elsie looked at Miss Theobald's solemn face. 'Yes,' she said at last. 'I suppose things were mostly my own fault. The second form don't like me at all. They will never have me as head girl. They just tolerate me, that's all. It makes things hard for me. I feel I can never do anything to alter their opinion, and so I can't very well take any pleasure in being there.'

'You see, Elsie, one of the hardest things in the world to forget and forgive is spitefulness,' said Miss Theobald. 'Malice and spite rouse such bitter feelings in others. Other faults, such as greed, irresponsibility, silliness – these arouse disgust, but are forgotten and forgiven. Spite always rankles, and is never forgotten. I can see you will never do any good either to yourself or to others in the second form.'

Elsie waited, her heart sinking. This meant that she was to be asked to leave. She didn't want to do that. She did like St Clare's. She stared at Miss Theobald miserably. The head guessed what the girl was thinking.

'I'm not going to say you must leave St Clare's,' she said quickly. 'I think the school can do a lot for you, Elsie, and you may be able to do something for St Clare's too. No – you shan't leave! I think you must go up into the third form instead – leave behind the second formers who have seen such a bad side of your character – and go into the third form, which, next term, will have five or six new girls. You will have a chance then to show a different side of your character! You are not really ready to go up, either in your work, or in your behaviour – but I will send you up if you will tell me that you will take this chance, and work hard and, more important still, try to get the "cattiness" out of your nature that every schoolgirl detests!'

Elsie's heart lifted in relief. Go up into the third form – and leave behind the girls who would always dislike her! Wouldn't she work hard! Wouldn't she be kind and friendly and helpful to the new girls who didn't know anything about her! She smiled gladly.

'What about Anna?' she asked. 'Is she going up too?'

'Yes – but you can trust Anna not to give you away at all,' said Miss Theobald. 'She's a good girl – she really has turned out well as head girl. Now, Elsie – take this chance and make good!'

'I will,' said Elsie. 'Thank you, Miss Theobald. I never thought of going up into the third form! It makes all the difference in the world!'

The girl went out, pleased and hopeful. She saw Gladys Hillman in the passage and went up to her with a warm gesture of friendliness.

'Any news of your mother, old thing?' she asked.

'Not yet,' said Gladys, wondering whatever could have made Elsie look so friendly and glad. Elsie went on her way and met Bobby.

'I say,' she said, 'I saw poor old Gladys just now. Can't we do something to take her out of herself a bit? She's moping again.'

'Good idea!' said Bobby at once. 'I'll play that trick on Mam'zelle – you know, the trick that makes plates jump about! Mam'zelle is taking lunch today at our table, because Miss Jenks is going out. It will be sport!'

So the second formers were told that a trick was about to be played, and they all cheered up, forgot about exams, and looked at Bobby with bright eyes. The first trick that term! It was time one was played!

Mam'zelle was in a good temper. The first form had

done unexpectedly well in their French exam. She beamed at everybody. The second formers beamed back, and Doris gave a deep chuckle, exactly like Mam'zelle's.

'Ah, this bad Doris!' said Mam'zelle, clapping Doris on the shoulder. 'She can imitate me per-r-r-rfectly – but she cannot roll her 'r's yet in the true French way! Now – let us go to the dining-room. The bell for luncheon has gone. Today I take you for the meal, because the good Miss Jenks is out!'

The second form seated themselves at their table. Mam'zelle was at the head. Bobby was three places away from her. The others looked at her, grinning. They hoped she had been able to slip into the dining-room and lay her plans!

Bobby had prepared everything carefully. There was a pile of plates at Mam'zelle's place, ready for her to serve the stew for each girl. Bobby had removed the plates, and had deftly placed the long rubber tubing under the table-cloth, so that it ran from where the plates were to Bobby's own seat, and hung down under the cloth. The bladder-end was where the plates were, and the bulb to press was by Bobby's place. Bobby replaced the pile of plates over the bladder-end. The plates were too heavy to move when the bulb was pressed – but when all the girls were served and only Mam'zelle's plate was there, it would tip up beautifully as soon as Bobby pressed the bulb which filled the bladder-end with air!

Mam'zelle served out the stew rapidly. The girls began their meal hungrily, one eye on Mam'zelle's plate. It was the only one left now. Mam'zelle filled it with stew and gravy. She was very fond of gravy.

'At first,' said Mam'zelle conversationally, taking up her knife and fork, 'at first when I came to England I did not like this stew of yours! But now – ah, it is wonderful!'

Bobby pressed the rubber bulb she was holding under the cloth. The bladder-end under Mam'zelle's plate filled with air and became fat and big. Mam'zelle's plate tilted up on one side, gave a little wobble and subsided again as Bobby let go the bulb she was pressing.

Mam'zelle was overcome with astonishment. She felt her nose to see if her glasses were there. Yes, they were. But could she have seen right? Her plate had moved!

She took a quick look round at the girls. They seemed to have noticed nothing – though actually all the girls had seen the plate lift and wobble, and were fighting hard to keep from giggling.

Mam'zelle dismissed the matter from her mind. She had imagined it! She began to make conversation again.

'Tomorrow you second formers will have your French tests,' she said, smiling round. Then she tried to cut a piece of meat with her knife – whilst Bobby at the same moment pressed the rubber bulb. Air ran through to the bladder, and Mam'zelle's plate lifted itself up very suddenly, and spilt some gravy over one side.

Mam'zelle looked at her plate in alarm. It had done it again. It was alive! It had spilt its gravy on the cloth.

'*Tiens*!' said Mam'zelle, very much startled. 'What is this?'

'What is what, Mam'zelle?' asked Janet, with a solemn face.

'Nothing, nothing!' said Mam'zelle, hastily, not liking to say that she feared her plate was alive. But something certainly was the matter with it. She looked down at it, hardly daring to eat her meal.

Bobby gave the plate a rest. Mam'zelle looked at it warily for a little while, and then plucked up her courage to eat her meal once more. The plate seemed to be behaving itself. Then it suddenly went mad again!

It tipped up and down slowly and solemnly three times, then jerked from side to side spilling some more gravy. Mam'zelle grew really alarmed. She glanced at the girls. How strange that they did not seem to see what was happening! She must be going mad!

'Don't you like your stew, Mam'zelle?' asked Pat, solemnly. 'I thought you said it was wonderful.'

Mam'zelle looked suspiciously at her plate which was now quiet. Doris made a silly joke in order to let the girls laugh loudly, for two or three of them were almost hysterical by now, and would certainly have given the game away if they had not been able to laugh loudly.

The rest of the school looked in amazement at the bellowing girls. Miss Theobald, who sat at the head of the sixth-form table, was displeased.

'Quiet, please,' she called to the second formers. They choked and became quiet. Doris was purple in the face with trying not to laugh again. Mam'zelle looked round with a frown.

'Such a noise!' she said, reprovingly. But her attention was soon drawn to her plate again when it solemnly rose up and down twice, and then became quite still.

Mam'zelle frowned. This could not really be happening! Plates could not behave like that. It was nonsense. She would eat her dinner and not think about it.

'Don't do it again till the pudding comes,' whispered Carlotta to Bobby. 'We can't help squealing with laughter now. We shall get into a row. Give us a rest!'

So for the rest of the first course the plate behaved itself, and Mam'zelle was much relieved. But when the pudding arrived, and she had served it out, leaving only her own plate in its place, the fun began again. The pudding-plate leapt quite wildly, and Mam'zelle pushed her chair back with a scream. The girls choked and the tears ran down their cheeks.

'Ah! This plate!' cried Mam'zelle. 'It is as bad as the other one. See how it jumps!'

Bobby kept the plate quite still. Doris exploded into laughter and two or three joined her helplessly. Miss Theobald began to look really vexed. The rest of the school craned their necks to see whatever could be happening at the second-form table.

The plate moved again, and Mam'zelle backed away still farther. Miss Theobald, amazed and puzzled, left her place and walked over to the second-form table. Every girl was rocking in helpless laughter. Not even the presence of the head mistress could stop them. This was the funniest thing they had ever seen.

'Mam'zelle! What *is* the matter?' asked Miss Theobald, really annoyed. Mam'zelle turned to her wildly.

'My plate!' she said. 'My plate!'

'Well, what is wrong with it?' asked Miss Theobald, impatiently, thinking that Mam'zelle must really have gone mad. 'It seems all right to me.'

'Miss Theobald, it jumps, it dances, it leaps around the table,' said Mam'zelle, earnestly, exaggerating in the hope that Miss Theobald would be impressed. 'It is a mad plate. I cannot bear it.'

The head mistress looked at the plate of pudding. It lay quite still on the table, perfectly ordinary. She glanced round at the giggling girls. She supposed they were laughing at Mam'zelle's behaviour. Well, it certainly was extraordinary.

'You had better go and lie down, Mam'zelle,' she said at last. 'I think you can't be well.'

'*I* am well,' said poor Mam'zelle. 'It is the plate that is mad. You should see it jump, Miss Theobald.'

Miss Theobald looked doubtfully at the plate – and Bobby had a tremendous urge to make it jump again. She pressed the bulb hard, and the plate jumped up at once, wobbled and fell back again. Miss Theobald looked astonished and Mam'zelle gave another squeal. The girls screamed with laughter.

Miss Theobald lifted up the plate, and pushed back the table-cloth. There, underneath, was the little rubber bladder attached to the tubing that led to Bobby's place. Mam'zelle's eyes nearly fell out of her head when she saw it.

'I think, Mam'zelle, one of the girls is playing a trick on you,' said Miss Theobald. 'I will leave you to deal with it. I dare say Roberta can explain how it was done.'

The girls stopped laughing. They stared at Miss Theobald walking back to her seat. They looked at Mam'zelle, who glared at poor Bobby.

'What is this horrible trick?' she inquired in a loud voice.

Bobby explained, and Mam'zelle listened carefully. She removed the whole thing and looked at it. Then she put back the table-cloth and her plate and began to eat her pudding, looking straight in front of her with her sloe-black eyes.

The girls felt uncomfortable. Was Mam'zelle really offended, really angry? The trick was quite a harmless one. They finished their pudding and sat still.

Suddenly there came a snort from Mam'zelle and all the second formers looked up in surprise. Mam'zelle threw back her head. She roared, she bellowed! She laughed so much that the relieved second formers couldn't help laughing again too.

'It was a good trick,' said Mam'zelle at last, wiping her eyes. 'Yes, a good trick. I shall make my sister laugh till she cries when I tell her. When I think of that plate jumping at me like that – ah, *magnifique*!'

'I'll lend you the whole trick, if you like,' said Janet. 'It belongs to my brother. You can play the trick on your sister.'

Mam'zelle stared at her in delight. 'What a good idea!' she exclaimed, beaming. 'This will cheer my good sister immensely. You shall show me how it works.'

Miss Theobald smiled as she left the room. It really had been funny. What a good thing Mam'zelle had seen the funny side – but she could generally be trusted to. Poor Mam'zelle – the hundreds of tricks that had been played on her during her years at St Clare's! She would never learn to be suspicious of the girls!

'Marvellous!' said Janet, when the second formers were in their common-room again, discussing the affair. 'Simply super. Bobby, you did it awfully well. I thought I should have died, trying to keep in my laughter. Oh, dear – when I think of that plate jumping about – and Mam'zelle's horrified face – I want to scream all over again!'

Everyone was amused, and Gladys, who had seen few tricks played in her life, laughed as much as anyone. She forgot her worry for a while, and Mirabel was glad to see her smiling face as she listened to the talk.

The next day Mam'zelle gave out the French papers. They were much easier than the class expected and everyone gave a sigh of relief. Even Doris hoped she might get enough marks for a pass!

In the middle of the exam when everything was perfectly quiet, the door opened and a junior girl looked in. Mirabel glanced up. She looked across at Gladys. Gladys had gone white. She wondered if there was any news for her. 'Please could Gladys Hillman go to Miss Theobald,' she said. Gladys stood up, her knees shaking. She was sure that her mother was dead. She went out of the room as if she was walking in a dream. Mirabel stared after her, miserable. She feared the worst too.

But in two minutes Gladys was back! The door was flung open, and she burst into the room, her face beaming, and her eyes shining. She rushed to Mirabel.

'Mirabel! Mother's had the operation, and she's come through it wonderfully! She's going to get better! I'm to see her soon, just for an hour! Perhaps next week, Mirabel! Isn't it marvellous!'

Mirabel was as glad as if it had been her own mother. She forgot about the class, and put her arm round the happy girl.

'Oh, Gladys!' she said. 'It's marvellous! I *am* glad!'

'Hurrah!' yelled Bobby, as delighted as anyone. 'Good old Gladys!'

'I too am glad,' beamed Mam'zelle, forgetting all about the French exam, for a wonder. 'Such a surprise for you! Now you will be able to smile again!'

Gladys glanced round the room, suddenly remembering where she was. She had forgotten everything for the moment except that she must tell Mirabel, her friend, the great news. She went back to her seat, so happy that she felt she might cry with gladness at any moment.

'And now, we must look at our exam papers again,' said Mam'zelle, in a kindly voice. 'Gladys, you should do a wonderful paper, with such good news to help you!'

Everyone was glad. The term had only two more days to go, and the girls were pleased to think that Gladys had something to look forward to. They were as nice to her as they could be, even Elsie!

The last day came, and packing was begun. Gladys couldn't help feeling a little sad as she saw everyone preparing to go away for the holidays. She would have to stay at school – but, never mind, she would be able to see her mother soon. What a pity she was so far away – it would be difficult to see her more than once.

Just as the second form were in a complete muddle over their packing, Miss Theobald came into the room with a letter in her hand. She had just received it. The girls stood up and listened.

'Oh, Mirabel,' said Miss Theobald in her clear voice, 'I have just received a letter from your mother. She says you can take Gladys home with you for the holidays if I will give my permission, as then she can go to see her mother twice a week quite easily from your home, which is not very far from the hospital.'

Mirabel gave a shriek of delight. Gladys turned as red as a beetroot.

'Miss Theobald! How marvellous! Isn't mother a brick? Can Gladys come with me?'

'Of course,' said the head mistress, smiling at the bewildered, radiant Gladys. 'But she will have to pack very quickly. Hurry up, Gladys, and see if you can be ready by the time the school-coaches arrive!'

Ready! Of course she could be ready! Helped by willing hands Gladys flew here and there, cramming everything in, her heart singing with joy. To go home with Mirabel – see her friend's brother and sister – visit her own mother twice a week! What wonderful luck!

And if I hadn't tackled Mirabel that time, and got her to change her mind and stay on, nothing like this would have happened! thought the girl, packing her jerseys. It just shows you've got to have courage and go straight for things. Oh, it's too good to be true!

But it was true, and Gladys went off in the school-coach with Mirabel beside her, singing heartily with the others as they rolled down to the station. Alison clapped her on the back. 'Happy holidays, Gladys!' she said.

'Same to you,' said Gladys. Alison was changed. Not so silly, thought Gladys. I like her better now. I like lots of people better – but most of all Mirabel!

'Goodbye, everybody!' yelled the twins. 'Merry Christmas and Happy New Year when they come!'

'Goodbye! Don't eat too much Christmas-pudding, Anna!'

'Goodbye, Elsie! Happy hols!'

'Goodbye, Bobby! Think out a few more tricks. I say, *do* you remember Mam'zelle's face when the plate jumped?'

'Goodbye, Hilary. See you next term. Nice to think you'll be our head girl again!'

'Goodbye, everybody! Goodbye!'

Contents

1.

Back to school

'Not long now and we'll be back at St Clare's,' said Isabel O'Sullivan, glancing out of the car window.

'Yes. It feels as though we've been away for *months*, not just a few weeks,' said her twin, Pat.

'Anyone would think the two of you positively disliked coming home for the holidays!' said their mother from the driving seat.

'Oh, Mum, of course we love being at home!' cried Pat. 'It's just . . .' Then, in the mirror, she caught the twinkle in her mother's eye and laughed.

'I wonder who will be head of the form this term?' mused Isabel.

'One of you two, perhaps?' suggested their friend, Carlotta Brown. She lived several miles away from the twins and had been delighted when Mrs O'Sullivan had telephoned to offer her a ride back to school. Her father was away, and the girl hadn't been looking forward to making the journey in the company of her rather strict, disapproving grandmother. 'It certainly won't be me,' she went on now with a laugh. 'Miss Theobald thinks that I'm still too wild and irresponsible.'

'Perhaps she will choose you for that very reason,'

suggested Mrs O'Sullivan. 'A little responsibility might do you good and calm you down a bit.'

Carlotta looked doubtful. She wasn't at all sure that she *wanted* to be calmed down!

'I hope it's not you or me, Pat,' said Isabel. 'I'd be just green with envy if you were head girl. Yet I'd feel dreadful about you being left out if I was chosen!'

Pat laughed. 'Yes, that's exactly how I feel.'

'I shouldn't be surprised if it's Hilary again,' said Carlotta. 'She's certainly had plenty of experience and she's always done a marvellous job.'

'In that case, perhaps it's time someone else had a chance,' put in the twins' mother. 'Hilary's already proved that she can lead and accept responsibility.'

'Mm. Janet, perhaps?' said Isabel. 'Certainly not Bobby! When it comes to being wild and irresponsible, there's not much to choose between her and you, Carlotta!'

Carlotta grinned broadly at this then, suddenly, she gave a gasp, her dark eyes widening. 'Look – over there! Mrs O'Sullivan, would you mind stopping for a moment?'

The twins' mother pulled in to the grass verge, while Pat and Isabel turned their heads to see what Carlotta was so excited about.

'Why, someone has bought the Oaks!' exclaimed Pat. 'And they've turned it into riding stables. Wonderful!'

The Oaks was a large and very beautiful house a short distance from St Clare's, set in several acres of green fields. It had been standing empty and neglected for some time, but now the front door was freshly painted and the windows gleaming. More importantly as far as the girls were concerned, a series of jumps was set up in the adjoining field, and they could see a girl on a beautiful white horse cantering round.

'May we stop and take a look, Mum?' asked Isabel eagerly.

'Yes, we've plenty of time,' replied Mrs O'Sullivan. 'I'll wait in the car and read the newspaper.'

The three girls scrambled out of the car, going straight to the fence that bordered the field. The girl on horseback spotted them and immediately rode across, long brown hair streaming out from beneath her riding hat.

'Hallo there!' she called out with a friendly smile. 'Come to have a look at Snowdrop here?'

'If you don't mind,' answered Carlotta, liking the look of the horse at once. 'Hey, aren't you a beauty?' This last remark was addressed to Snowdrop, whose snow-white neck she at once began to stroke.

'You wouldn't be St Clare's girls, by any chance?' asked their new acquaintance, dismounting.

'We most certainly would,' said Carlotta. 'And, I can promise you, you'll be seeing several of us here regularly – me for one!'

The girl laughed. 'We might be seeing more of one another than you think! My cousin and I are starting in the third form – as day girls! Miss Theobald has agreed to take us at reduced fees. In return, my parents have agreed on special terms for any pupil who wishes to ride here. Oh, I'm Libby Francis, by the way.'

Delighted at this turn of events, the twins and Carlotta introduced themselves, Pat remarking, 'We're in the third too!'

'What a bit of luck!' exclaimed Libby. 'I'm afraid we won't be with you for very long, though. Fern – that's my cousin – is staying with us for a few months whilst her parents are abroad. And I'm due to go to America on an exchange scheme in the autumn.'

Just then a movement at the other end of the field caught everyone's eyes and they saw a girl and boy approach the gate there.

'Fern!' called out Libby. 'Over here!'

The girl opened the gate and began to walk across the field, while the boy turned away abruptly and made for the stables.

'My brother, Will,' explained Libby. 'He goes to day school in Lowchester, a few miles away.' She lowered her voice and went on, 'Fern absolutely idolizes him and makes a prize nuisance of herself hanging round him all the time. Will can't bear girls – apart from me – and he thinks that she's just too silly for words!'

'I'll bet he wasn't too pleased when he found out that she was coming to stay,' laughed Isabel.

'That's putting it mildly!' said Libby. 'You see, it all started when we were kids and I pulled the head off Fern's favourite doll. Will fixed it and, ever since, she's treated him like some kind of hero.'

Fern looked a little like a doll herself, thought Isabel as the girl approached. A very pretty china doll, with her pink and white complexion, golden hair and wide, blue eyes. Unlike her cousin, who was casually dressed for riding, Fern wore a pretty summer dress and high-heeled sandals, on which she teetered and stumbled over the uneven ground. Really, thought Pat, she looks as if she's going to a garden party!

'Fern, come and meet Carlotta, Pat and Isabel, from St Clare's,' said her cousin. 'We're all going to be in the third together.'

Fern said hallo in a high, pretty voice, and Pat noticed that she kept a cautious distance from Libby's horse, shying away nervously every time the animal tossed its head.

'Do you ride, Fern?' she asked.

'Oh, no!' The girl shuddered and shook her golden curls. 'Horses frighten me to death! I have other interests.'

Libby grinned fondly at her cousin and said impishly, 'Yes, Fern's interested in her hair, her nails, her clothes . . .'

Fern turned red and gave Libby a little push, while the twins exchanged grins. Winking at Carlotta, Isabel said smoothly, 'Our cousin Alison will be in the third too – and her interests are exactly the same as yours! I just bet the two of you will get on like a house on fire!'

'Oh, that would be great!' breathed Fern, her big blue eyes growing even rounder. 'To have a friend who likes the same things as I do.'

'Well, you and Alison are welcome to your fashions and fancy hair-dos,' said Libby bluntly. 'Give me my horses any day! How about you, twins? Are you interested in riding?'

'We've had a few lessons,' answered Pat. 'But we're not in Carlotta's league. She used to ride in a circus, you know.'

Libby looked at the dark girl with interest, exclaiming and pressing her to tell all about her life in the circus. Even Fern dropped her sophisticated pose and came out of her cloud of self-absorption to ask Carlotta several interested questions.

Just then the girls heard Mrs O'Sullivan calling and Carlotta, reluctant to leave, pulled a face. 'Back to school for us!'

'We don't start until tomorrow morning,' said Libby. 'It must be such fun, all of you being together all the time.'

'Yes, we have some good times,' laughed Pat. 'And we try to fit in a midnight feast each term!'

'Midnight feasts! How marvellous that sounds,' sighed Libby wistfully. 'But Fern and I will be here at home each night, and shan't be able to join in anything like that.'

Carlotta grinned wickedly. 'I wouldn't be too sure. At St Clare's, *anything* is possible!'

2.

Another new girl . . .

On the short drive from the stables to St Clare's, the girls chattered non-stop about the two day girls, thrilled that they had been the first to meet them.

'What a piece of news to tell the others!' said Pat.

'Yes, and what a term it's going to be,' Carlotta sighed happily. 'I don't know that I'll have time to fit any school work in. I shall be too busy riding!'

The twins laughed and Isabel said, 'Libby seems a good sort. I don't know that I'm too keen on Fern, though.'

'Me neither,' agreed Carlotta with a grimace. 'Still, with any luck we should be able to push her off on to Alison.'

'Oh, yes, Alison will think she's just too wonderful for words,' chuckled Pat. 'No doubt she'll spend the whole term in Fern's pocket.'

But the girls were in for a surprise once they reached St Clare's and had said goodbye to Mrs O'Sullivan. For there in the big hall was the twins' cousin, already arm in arm with another new girl. This one seemed the complete opposite of Fern, being dark and rather serious looking.

'Twins! Carlotta!' called out Alison, pulling her new friend forward. 'Enjoyed the holidays? Come and meet our new girl, Rachel Denman.'

The three girls introduced themselves and Rachel inclined her head graciously. The reason for her rather haughty manner was made clear when Alison said in hushed tones, 'Rachel is the daughter of Sir Robert and Lady Helen Denman, the well-known actors. What do you think of that?'

'Wow!' exclaimed Pat, very much impressed despite the fact that she hadn't taken to Rachel at all. 'Isabel and I saw one of their films at the pictures during the holidays and they were both just marvellous. It must be wonderful to have that kind of talent. Do you mean to follow in their footsteps?'

'Naturally I intend to become an actress,' answered the girl sharply, as though surprised that Pat should ask such a foolish question. 'Until recently I went to drama school in London.'

She had a beautiful speaking voice, low pitched, yet clear as crystal. Due to her drama coaching, no doubt, thought Isabel.

'What made you decide to leave and come to St Clare's?' she asked.

'My parents feel strongly that one must experience *real* life to be able to inject true emotion into one's acting,' she explained loftily. 'So for the next year I'm just to be an ordinary schoolgirl, like the rest of you.'

The twins and Carlotta stared at her hard. Her condescending manner really put their backs up. As though sensing that the others didn't think much of Rachel, and fearing that they might say something cutting, Alison said hastily, 'I'd better take you to Matron, then we'll see which dormitory we're in. I do hope we're together.'

'I suppose we "ordinary" mortals ought to pop along to Matron too,' remarked Carlotta as Alison and Rachel walked away. But before they had a chance, the girls heard their names called and turned to see Janet Robins and Bobby Ellis walking towards them.

'Hallo! I see you've met the actress. What do you think of her?' asked Janet with a wry grin.

'So good of her to come down and live among us little people,' said Bobby, a scornful look on her freckled face. 'My word, if she puts on her high and mighty airs with me she'll learn all about true emotion, all right!'

The others laughed. Rachel was the kind of girl who brought out the worst in the forthright Bobby. She just couldn't bear airs and graces, as she called them.

'Trust your cousin to latch on to her,' remarked Janet drily.

Pat gave a chuckle. 'Don't be surprised if Alison changes her affections tomorrow, Janet. We've two more new girls starting then – and one of them is just Alison's cup of tea!'

'Hallo, what's this?' The dark, good-looking Hilary Wentworth came up, accompanied by Doris Elward. 'Who's Alison's cup of tea? Tell us!'

'Hilary!' cried the girls. 'And Doris!'

'Just arrived back?'

'Good to see you both again!'

Once the girls had greeted each other, Janet nudged

Pat and said impatiently, 'Go on! Let's hear all about these new girls.'

So Pat, with much eager assistance from Isabel and Carlotta, told the listening girls all about Libby and Fern, extremely gratified at the reaction their news produced.

'Day girls! How thrilling!'

'And riding stables right on our doorstep. Brilliant!'

'Looks as if it's shaping up to be a fab term!' remarked Hilary. 'And we've got the glorious summer weather too, which means plenty of tennis and swimming. Come on, let's hurry along to Matron and give her our things. If we're quick there might just be time to take a look at the swimming-pool before tea. I know we won't be able to go in, but just looking at that clear blue water lapping at the sides makes me feel all nice and summery!'

Everyone agreed with this and, picking up their night-cases, they sped along to Matron's room. But they never did get to visit the swimming-pool, caught up in the first-day bustle of unpacking, finding their dormitories, greeting girls, mistresses – and Miss Theobald, the wise, kindly head mistress, of course. Then the bell sounded for tea, and before the girls knew what had happened, the day was over and it was bedtime.

Alison, to her great disappointment, wasn't in the same dormitory as Rachel, but had been allocated a bed next to Mirabel Unwin. This didn't thrill her at all as Mirabel was rumoured to snore loudly! She sought out Mirabel's best friend, the quiet little Gladys, who was in Rachel's dormitory, and whispered, 'Gladys! How about you and I swapping places? Then you can be next to Mirabel.'

'Why, that's very kind of you, Alison!' exclaimed Gladys, quite unaware that Alison had her own reasons for wanting to change places. 'But aren't we supposed to ask Matron if we want to move dormitories?'

'Yes, you are,' said Hilary, coming up with Janet and overhearing this. 'What's up, Gladys? Do you want to go in with Mirabel?'

'Well, it was Alison's idea,' replied Gladys, anxious to give credit where it was due.

'Really,' said Hilary drily. 'I wonder why?'

Alison blushed and said hastily, 'I was only thinking of Gladys, and how nice it would be for her to be next to Mirabel.'

'And I suppose this has nothing to do with the fact that your precious Rachel is in the other dormitory?' put in Janet with a grin.

'Alison, if you want to change with Gladys, kindly make your request through Matron tomorrow,' Hilary said with calm authority. 'Now it's bedtime, so I suggest you go and get ready – quickly!'

'Spoken like a true head girl,' said Janet with a chuckle as Alison, rather sullenly, went into her dormitory.

Hilary laughed. 'Perhaps, but I'm not head girl.'

'You will be tomorrow,' said Janet confidently. 'Once Miss Adams has made the announcement.'

'I don't think so,' responded Hilary thoughtfully. 'I overheard Miss Jenks saying last term that she thought it was time someone else had a chance.'

'Really? Won't you mind standing down?' asked Janet curiously.

'Not at all,' answered Hilary. 'I thoroughly enjoyed being head girl and appreciated what an honour it was. But it's a big responsibility and I'll be quite happy to sit back and let someone else take it this term.' She paused and looked thoughtfully at Janet. 'You, perhaps?'

'Never!' Janet dismissed this with a laugh. 'I'm too fond of jokes and tricks to make a good head girl.'

'Yes, but you're also a born leader and a strong character,' pointed out Hilary. 'Anyway, we'll find out tomorrow.'

'Yes,' said Janet slowly, Hilary's words making her think.

The girls, worn out by their long journeys and the excitement of the day, fell asleep quickly. All except two of them. One was Rachel Denman, who lay staring miserably into the dark, aware that she had made a bad start with the girls.

It's all so very different from my drama school, she thought unhappily. Only Alison seems to like me. Still, I suppose that's my fault for getting on my high horse. But somehow I just find myself going all defensive and can't seem to help it. Sighing heavily, the girl turned over in her bed. If only they knew it was my stupid pride making me act like that, she thought. But I can't bring myself to tell them the truth.

The other girl was Janet, who lay awake for a very different reason – excitement! Until that conversation with Hilary, it had never occurred to her that she might be in the running for head of the form. But now that she came to think about it, why shouldn't she be? After all, she, Hilary and Doris had been at St Clare's longer than any of the others. Well, Hilary had had her turn, and as for Doris – Janet grinned to herself – Doris, the duffer, would run a mile if the honour was offered to her. There wasn't an ounce of conceit in Janet's nature, but the more she thought about it, the more she saw herself as the obvious choice for head girl. At last she drifted off to sleep, her thoughts pleasant. Tomorrow . . . she thought drowsily. Tomorrow she would know.

3.

. . . And a head girl

When the laughing, chattering stream of third formers made their way into the classroom after breakfast next morning, Fern and Libby were already there, looking out of the big window at the gardens. They turned as the girls entered and Pat called out, 'Hi! You two are keen!'

'We wanted to make a good impression on our first day,' said Libby with her ready grin. 'Fern's been up since the crack of dawn doing her hair and nails!'

Fern blushed and Alison, looking at the pretty, dainty girl with approval, stepped forward.

'Fern!' she said with her charming smile. 'What a pretty name!'

Fern smiled back, recognizing at once in Alison many of the traits that were in her own character.

'You must be Alison,' she said. 'The twins have told me all about you.'

Alison looked rather doubtful at this, casting a suspicious glance at her cousins, who were introducing Libby to the others. Evidently, though, they hadn't said anything bad about her to Fern, for the girl seemed only too eager to make friends. Soon she and Alison were in the thick of a discussion on the latest fashions.

14

'Two feather-heads together,' murmured Carlotta with a grin. 'Rachel isn't going to be too pleased. Where is she, by the way?'

'She left her pencil-case in the dormitory and had to go back for it,' said Bobby. 'Here she comes now.'

Indeed, Rachel looked extremely put out when she walked in and saw her new friend engrossed in conversation with someone else. Alison spotted her and beckoned her over, wondering how Rachel would feel about making up a threesome with Fern. Alas, there was no time to find out, for Doris, standing guard at the door, hissed, 'Hush! Miss Adams is coming!'

Immediately the chattering ceased, the girls standing straight, as a short, dark young woman entered. Miss Adams, the third-form mistress, looked plain and rather dour – until she smiled, and then her whole face lit up. She smiled now, saying, 'Good morning, girls. Find yourselves desks as quickly as possible, please.'

There was the usual scramble for places in the back row, only the three new girls standing aside and waiting – as was the custom – for the others to bag their seats first.

Alison chose a middle-row desk by the window, then both Fern and Rachel made a beeline for the vacant one next to her. They reached it neck and neck, Fern placing her bag on the desk at precisely the same time as Rachel sat down on the chair.

'I was here first!' they cried in unison.

Doris nudged Libby and grinned.

'I put my bag on the desk before you sat down!' insisted Fern indignantly.

'Well, I reached the chair first, so it's mine!' said Rachel, equally determined, as she glared at her rival.

'What it is to be popular,' murmured Bobby, seated directly behind a red-faced Alison.

'Move your things!' demanded Rachel arrogantly.

'I shan't!' refused Fern, blue eyes sparkling with anger. '*You* can just move yourself!'

'Excuse me!' boomed Miss Adams, stern eyes fixed on the two quarrelling girls. 'I was under the impression that I was teaching the third form at a senior school, not a kindergarten class. And it's customary, young lady, to stand when you are being addressed by a mistress!'

Blushing furiously, Rachel shot to her feet, keeping one hand possessively on the back of the chair, as though afraid that Fern would snatch it from her.

'And you!' Miss Adams's sharp eyes switched to Fern, who had been smirking triumphantly. 'Are you wearing *nail polish*?'

Quaking, Fern stammered, 'It – it's only a clear one, Miss Adams.'

'Kindly remove it at the earliest opportunity!' the mistress ordered sternly. 'And never let me catch you wearing it in class again.'

Humiliated, and aware of the wide grins of the rest of the class – with the exception of Alison, who looked as though she wanted to sink through the floor – Fern pursed her pretty mouth. Even her own cousin thought it was hilarious, she realized, glaring at Libby, who was clinging helplessly to Doris.

'Now, the two of you have precisely ten seconds to sit down, or you will stand outside!' barked Miss Adams, looking at her watch. 'Ten . . . nine . . . eight . . .'

'Oh, move along, Rachel!' snapped Alison with unusual impatience. So much for her ideas of a threesome!

'Fern, you come and sit here by the window, and I'll go in the middle.'

'Poor Alison,' whispered Doris. 'She's like the meat in a sandwich!'

Libby giggled then, seeing the mistress's eye on her, turned it into a long cough.

'Now, if everyone's settled, perhaps we can get on?' said Miss Adams with sarcasm.

Immediately, everyone fell silent and sat up straight, wiping the grins from their faces as Miss Adams continued. 'I'm sure that all of you are keen to know who will be head of the form. Miss Theobald and I both consulted Miss Jenks, as you were in her form last year and she obviously knows you better than I do at this stage. There were a couple of you in the running and it was a very close thing but, after much consideration, our choice is . . . Carlotta Brown!' There was a moment's silence then the form erupted, cheering and yelling.

'Good for you, Carlotta!'

'Yes, well done!'

Carlotta stared blankly round. At last she said, 'Pardon?'

17

'Carlotta,' explained Hilary patiently. 'You're head of the form.'

'Who, me?' said Carlotta, eyes widening. 'No, there's some mistake.'

Miss Adams laughed at the girl's air of disbelief and said, 'There's no mistake, Carlotta.'

'Well!' exclaimed the girl, astonished. 'I really don't know what to say! It's a real honour and I'll do my best to live up to it, you can be sure.'

So Mrs O'Sullivan's prediction had come true, she realized, her head in a whirl. This was the last thing she had expected!

As Miss Adams had said, it had been a close thing. Mam'zelle had entered the staff common-room as Miss Theobald and the two mistresses were discussing the matter, giving a shriek of protest when she heard Carlotta's name mentioned.

'Ah, *non*! That Carlotta, she is too wild! She will lead the third formers into all kinds of scratches!'

'Scratches? Oh, you mean scrapes, Mam'zelle!' Miss Theobald had laughed. 'What do you think of Janet, then?'

The Frenchwoman's sloe-black eyes became sombre as she shook her head gravely, sitting down at the table with the others. 'She is too fond of the trick and the joke. It is not dignified in a head girl!'

'Both girls have their faults,' remarked Miss Jenks thoughtfully. 'Carlotta is inclined to be reckless and hot tempered, while Janet can be a little too sharp tongued and lacking in tact. Yet both are strong, determined characters and have the makings of leaders.'

'I agree,' said Miss Theobald. 'And neither of them has any mean, petty faults. I think a little responsibility might do them the world of good.'

'But how do we choose between them?' asked Miss Adams.

'I propose that we make Carlotta head girl for this term, and let Janet have her chance next term,' replied the head. 'What do you all think?'

'An excellent idea!' said Miss Jenks decidedly. Miss Adams nodded in agreement.

'*Mais oui*!' cried Mam'zelle, her earlier comments on the two girls suddenly forgotten as she was swept along on a tide of enthusiasm. 'It is as you say, Miss Theobald! It will be so, so good for the dear girls! Ah, what fine leaders they will make.'

Miss Theobald and the two mistresses found it hard to hide their smiles. How well they knew Mam'zelle's little ways! In a few moments she would have convinced herself that the whole idea had been hers, thought Miss Jenks.

'We're agreed, then,' said Miss Adams briskly. 'Carlotta Brown is to be head girl this term, and Janet Robins next.'

What a pity that the mistresses didn't let Janet in on the plan!

She, to her dismay, was feeling extremely jealous, a novel and unpleasant experience for her. Yet the girl liked Carlotta immensely and, even in the midst of her own disappointment, wanted to feel pleased for her friend and back her up. So Janet nobly swallowed her feelings, fixed

19

a smile to her face and called out, 'That's marvellous, Carlotta! You'll make a wonderful head girl!'

'Thanks! I certainly hope so,' answered Carlotta, still feeling quite overwhelmed.

'I'm sure you will,' said Miss Adams. 'Now, I've another piece of news that I'm sure will interest you all. Miss Theobald would like the third to produce an end-of-term play, to which the parents are to be invited.'

The girls sat up straight, exchanging excited glances. This was great news! Gladys put up her hand to ask, 'What kind of play, Miss Adams?'

'That's entirely up to you,' answered the mistress. 'It's quite literally your show – from the script, to the costumes and scenery. Naturally, the mistresses, including myself, will be on hand to give you any help or advice required, but the final decisions will all be yours.'

And judging from the babble of noise that broke out, there would be no lack of ideas or enthusiasm!

Miss Adams rapped on the desk with a ruler and said loudly, 'Well, I'm delighted that you are all so keen, but I suggest you wait until break-time to discuss the matter. In the meantime, I'm afraid, we have to get down to the more mundane task of making out timetables.'

The girls did their best to concentrate, but how the morning crawled by! Then, at last, it was break and the third form found a secluded corner of the playground where they could discuss this exciting news.

'There's no time to hold a proper meeting now,' said Hilary, taking charge. 'So I vote we hold one after tea . . .'

Her voice trailed off as Isabel nudged her and nodded in Carlotta's direction.

'Carlotta, I'm sorry!' she apologized, blushing. 'Old habits die hard, I'm afraid. But this is your job now.'

'No need to apologize,' laughed Carlotta. 'I haven't got used to the idea of being head girl myself yet! Well, as Hilary says, the best thing would be to hold a meeting in the common-room after tea . . .'

'Hold on!' interrupted Libby. 'Fern and I go home at tea-time, remember? We don't want to be left out.'

'Oh, yes, I forgot!' exclaimed Carlotta. 'Will your parents let you come back to school for the meeting? It will still be light when we finish and you don't have far to walk.'

'I don't see why not,' replied Libby. 'We'll ask them as soon as we get home.'

'Good! All right, girls, after tea it is,' said Carlotta, grinning round. 'Put your thinking caps on, everyone, and be sure to bring plenty of ideas with you.'

4.

A very important meeting

Carlotta perched on the edge of a table in the common-room and looked round at the third formers, all of them eagerly waiting for the meeting to begin.

'I'm really looking forward to this,' said Isabel, her eyes sparkling.

'Me too,' agreed Hilary. 'We'll all have to work hard and do our best to get things just perfect, especially as our parents are coming. We want to make them proud of us.'

'I suppose you'll be auditioning for one of the leading roles, Gladys?' said Bobby.

'I don't know about that,' said the quiet little Gladys with her usual modesty. 'It all depends on what kind of play we decide to do and whether or not I'm suitable.'

'You'd be suitable for *any* part,' Pat told her warmly. 'It's just amazing the way you can transform yourself into any character you choose.'

Gladys was a very fine little actress indeed and the girls had discovered her talent quite by chance, half-way through her first term at St Clare's. Before that she had been a miserable, timid little character with no friends. Then Mirabel had unexpectedly taken the girl under her wing after learning that Gladys's mother was seriously ill in hospital and that that was why the girl was so unhappy.

Mirabel's friendship had made a big difference to Gladys, bringing her out of her shell. It had been Mirabel who discovered that Gladys could act and had persuaded her to perform for the others; Mirabel who had been a tower of strength when the girl's mother had undergone a serious operation; Mirabel who had rejoiced with her when her mother made a full recovery. And now it was Mirabel who said loyally, 'Pat's right. You're easily the best actress St Clare's has ever had.'

Rachel had been listening to this with a rather strange, frozen expression and Alison, fearing that the girl might be offended at her own talents being over-looked, said reassuringly, 'Gladys *is* very good, but I'm sure that you will be able to give her a few pointers. With your background you're certain to get one of the leading parts.'

Bobby and Janet, standing nearby, caught the end of this and grinned at Alison's gushing tone.

Then Rachel gave a little laugh and said, 'Sorry to disappoint you, Alison, but I'm not interested in having a leading role – or *any* role for that matter.'

This was too much for Bobby, who whipped round and said scornfully, 'I suppose a mere school play is quite beneath you! Well, Rachel, this might not be the kind of grand production that you're used to, but it means a lot to us.'

'You bet it does!' called out some of the others, glaring at the new girl.

'Quite frankly,' went on Bobby, 'I think we'll manage very well without you.'

Completely taken aback by Bobby's contemptuous tone and the hostile stares around her, Rachel turned red with dismay. She *didn't* think the play was beneath her! She hadn't meant it like that at all! But what was the point of trying to defend herself? Every time she opened her mouth these days, things seemed to come out sounding all wrong. And the third formers seemed determined to think the very worst of her.

Fortunately Mirabel created a diversion then, calling out impatiently, 'Can't we get started? Gladys and I were hoping to get some tennis practice in before prep!'

'Libby and Fern haven't arrived yet,' pointed out Carlotta. 'We'll give them five more minutes, then start without them.'

Thankfully, as Mirabel was growing extremely restless, the two day girls arrived a moment later.

'Sorry we're late,' said Libby ruefully. 'What's happened? Have we missed much?'

'We haven't started yet,' said Carlotta, clapping her hands for silence. 'All right, girls, let's begin. Now, does anyone have any thoughts on what sort of a play we should do?'

Everyone did, and a dozen voices cried out at once.

'An historical drama!'

'No, comedy!'

'Better still, how about a musical comedy?' suggested Bobby. 'That would be brilliant!'

'Yes, but it might be a little ambitious,' said Isabel doubtfully. 'If it's to be all our own work, that would mean we would have to write songs and music scores, as well as a script, and none of us has any great talent in that direction.'

'I think you're right,' agreed Carlotta. 'So, that leaves us with comedy or drama.'

'I'd love to do a costume drama,' said Fern who, to Rachel's annoyance, had made straight for Alison. 'At my last school I played a princess in our play and the dress I wore was simply beautiful. White satin, with lace and . . .'

'There is a little more to acting than simply dressing up, you know,' Rachel interrupted cuttingly.

'I was speaking to Alison,' said Fern pointedly, glaring at Rachel before turning her back on the girl.

'Well, it's very rude of you to speak to *anyone* when Carlotta is trying to get on with the meeting,' said Hilary bluntly. 'For Heaven's sake, shut up and do let's get on!'

Flushing hotly, Fern subsided and Carlotta continued, 'Whatever kind of play we decide to put on, we're going to need a really good script. Does anyone think they can write one?'

'I wouldn't mind having a bash at a comedy,' replied Doris, who had a marvellous sense of humour and could send the girls into fits of laughter with her wonderful gift for mimicry.

'And I'd rather like to try my hand at drama,' volunteered Hilary, who was excellent at English.

Several more girls spoke up too and Carlotta said with

a grin, 'Well, I was afraid no one would want this particular job, but it seems that we're a form of budding playwrights! I think the fairest thing would be if everyone leaves their finished scripts on my desk – without names attached, so that I can't be accused of any favouritism. Then I'll ask Miss Adams to read through them with me and, between us, we'll pick the best one.'

'We're going to have to get a move on,' said Doris. 'Until we have a play, we can't dish out parts, paint scenery or make costumes.'

'Then we'd better set a deadline,' said Carlotta decidedly. 'All completed scripts to be on my desk – or Miss Adams's – by five o'clock, three weeks from today.'

'Three weeks!' exclaimed Hilary. 'Considering none of us has ever attempted to write a play before, that's quite a task.'

'I know, but, as Doris says, we need to get things moving,' replied Carlotta. 'If we leave it any longer, we shan't have time to rehearse properly, and that would never do! I'm sure we all want this to be a big success.'

There was a chorus of agreement at this. 'There is one thing we can do without a script,' called out Bobby. 'And that's choose a director. It'll have to be someone who can lead and keep us all in order.'

'Carlotta!' cried Doris. 'After all, she's head girl and she can probably do with a bit of practice at bossing us all around!'

'Thank you, Doris!' laughed Carlotta. 'But I don't think I ought to take control just because I'm head of the form!

Perhaps someone else would like to have a bash?'

'I think Janet would make an excellent director,' said Bobby. 'What do you say, Janet?'

Janet suddenly thought that directing would be just the kind of challenge she enjoyed – and it would make up for her disappointment at not being head girl. 'I wouldn't mind giving it a try,' she said. 'Provided the majority agree.'

'Well, there's only one way to find out,' said Pat. 'And that's to take a vote. Does anyone have any paper?'

'I've a notebook here,' said Alison, tearing off some sheets and beginning to hand them round.

'Half a minute!' called Hilary. 'The three new girls shouldn't vote, because they don't really know Janet or Carlotta yet.'

'And Janet and I can't vote either,' said Carlotta. 'So that leaves the rest of you. An odd number – that's lucky!'

Hilary collected the votes and counted them – which didn't take very long at all. Then she cleared her throat and said, 'Well, that couldn't have been much closer! The winner, by one vote, is Carlotta!'

Everyone, even those who had voted for Janet, cheered sportingly, and Janet was the first to shake Carlotta's hand, saying, 'The best girl won! Well done yet again!' Inwardly, though, she couldn't help but feel disappointed and a little resentful. This was the second time today she had lost out to Carlotta!

Quite unaware of the girl's feelings, Carlotta said sincerely, 'I don't know about being the best girl, but it certainly seems to be my lucky day.'

27

And it wasn't over yet! As the meeting broke up, Libby came across and said, 'Carlotta! I've asked Mum if you can come to tea with us on Saturday. If you come over early in the afternoon, we can get some riding in first. Do say you'll come!'

'Oh, yes!' exclaimed Carlotta, her dark eyes sparkling with anticipation. 'I'll have to get permission from Miss Adams, but I shouldn't think she'll say no. Thanks, Libby! It will be fun!'

'You can bet it will!' agreed Libby with a grin. 'I must say, I'm looking forward to having a friend who appreciates the important things in life – namely horses! I'm terribly fond of Fern, but we don't have much in common and her conversation bores me stiff most of the time.'

Carlotta felt a happy glow spreading through her. The girl was extremely popular with all of her form, but she had never had a special friend of her own. Carlotta hadn't minded, and had certainly never felt lonely at St Clare's but there was something very warming about the thought of having someone to confide in.

Alison, meanwhile, wasn't feeling quite so happy with her two new friendships. Rachel and Fern really disliked one another intensely and Alison didn't like being caught in the middle at all. She managed a few words alone with Fern, before the day girls went home, and said pleadingly, 'I do wish that you and Rachel would try to make friends. I like both of you so much and it makes things terribly difficult when you don't get on with one another.'

'Well, Alison, I can't understand what you see in Rachel, to be honest,' said Fern in her high, pretty voice. 'But as it's so important to you, I really will make an effort to be nice to her.' She smiled her sweetest smile, which a delighted Alison returned with one of her own.

Hilary, who happened to walk by just then, said to Pat later that she felt quite ill at such a display of sickly-sweetness.

But Alison was content, and made up her mind to speak to Rachel later. Perhaps they could be a threesome after all.

5.

Settling down

As the first week went by, the three new girls settled down at St Clare's in their different ways. Rachel proved to be extremely clever at her lessons, especially English, but very often she seemed to go off into some sort of day-dream – not a very happy one, to judge from her sombre expression. Her lapses in concentration sorely tried the mistresses' patience. Mam'zelle hardly knew what to make of her and was torn between delight and exaspera-tion. Delight because Rachel's grasp of French grammar and her written work were exceptionally good. Exaspera-tion because her accent was dreadful. The girls found this rather puzzling. As Doris, who could copy Mam'zelle's voice to perfection, said, 'I should have thought that an actress would be able to imitate any accent she chose.'

'Perhaps she isn't as good an actress as she makes out,' Fern had suggested with a touch of malice. She had kept her word to Alison and tried to be more pleasant to Rachel. But as Alison wasn't present when this con-versation took place, she had felt quite safe getting a small dig in at Rachel.

Fern herself, thanks to her prettiness and charming manner, had swiftly become one of Mam'zelle's favourites, although her French was not at all good. In fact, Fern wasn't very good at any of her lessons. Miss Adams's sarcastic remarks went right over her pretty head and made no impression on her at all. She was very like Alison in her dislike of any form of sport, detesting anything that made her get hot and untidy.

Her cousin Libby, however, adored swimming and had a lovely, natural style at tennis. Jennifer Mills, the new games captain, called her over after watching her practise one day and said, 'Well done, kid! Carry on like this and you could well be in a few matches this term.'

Libby couldn't help flushing with pride at the bigger girl's words, but she said frankly, 'Thanks, Jenny, but I'm afraid all my spare time is spent with the horses, so I can't put in as much practice at tennis as I would like. I mean to make a career out of show-jumping, you see, so I really must devote as much time as I can to my riding.'

Jennifer, a keen horsewoman herself, understood at once and said, 'That's a pity, because you could have done well for St Clare's. Oh, well, Libby, if you ever change your mind and decide to concentrate on tennis instead of riding, let me know!'

Libby's attitude extended to the classroom as well. She was bright and could do well at most subjects – when she bothered to make the effort! As Janet said, 'Libby will never be really whole-hearted about anything other than her horses. I'm not sure whether that's a good thing or a bad one. Still, she's ever so nice and good fun.'

The whole form agreed that Libby was a livewire,

as they put it, and the girl soon became a firm favourite with everyone.

One lunch-time the third formers had found themselves a sunny spot on one of St Clare's fine lawns and were enjoying the glorious weather.

'Mm, I could lie here all day,' sighed Hilary contentedly, stretching at full length on the grass. 'This hot weather always makes me feel so lazy.'

'Yes, it's lovely when we're outside,' agreed Bobby. 'But I just can't bear being cooped up indoors when the sun is shining. Then it has the opposite effect and makes me feel bored and restless – especially during maths and French *dictée*!'

Doris chuckled, knowing that when Bobby felt restless, it usually meant the class was in for some fun. 'Does this mean you're going to play a trick?' she asked hopefully.

'Doris! Nothing was further from my mind!' protested Bobby, making her eyes wide and innocent. 'Though, now that you mention it, there's nothing quite like a really good trick for letting off a bit of steam.'

Libby raised herself up on one elbow, an excited sparkle in her eyes. 'Who will you play it on?' she asked eagerly. 'Not Miss Adams, surely? She's far too sharp.'

'No, my dear Libby,' said Janet with a grin. 'Definitely not Miss Adams. There's really only one choice of victim when it comes to playing a trick – and that's Mam'zelle. Hey, Bobby, I wonder how many times you and I have caught her out over the years?'

'Dozens, I should think,' laughed Hilary. 'Remember

that trick you played, Bobby, when you made Mam'zelle's plate jump up and down? I thought my sides would split with laughing.'

'And that time back in the first form, Janet, when you filled her spectacle case with insects,' joined in Alison. 'Poor old Mam'zelle thought she was seeing things!'

'That one wasn't nearly so funny,' remembered Janet, pulling a wry face. 'I did it to get back at Mam'zelle for being so bad tempered that term, and it turned out that she was really ill. I felt so dreadful about it afterwards that it nearly cured me of playing tricks for good! Thank Heavens there was no harm done.'

'I just adore jokes and tricks, though I'm not very good at thinking them out,' said Libby. 'Oh, Bobby! Janet! *Do* play one on Mam'zelle! I'd just love to see her face.'

'It would be good fun,' said Bobby, her merry eyes crinkling mischievously. 'How about it, Janet?'

Janet, thinking that they would have a most appreciative audience in Libby, agreed readily. 'Though it's going to take us a little time to come up with an idea and plan it all out. I'm due a letter from my brother soon. Perhaps he'll have some ideas.'

'Janet's brother comes up with the most ingenious tricks,' explained Hilary to Libby. 'And he always passes them on to her. Which is wonderful for us, but not so good for Mam'zelle!'

'Poor Mam'zelle!' put in Fern with a pout. 'I think it's a shame to play jokes on her. She's such a decent sort!'

Libby pulled a face at her cousin. 'You only say that

because she believed that feeble excuse you made this morning about one of the horses eating your French prep! Anyway, it's only a bit of fun.'

'And dear old Mam'zelle always takes it in good part,' laughed Doris fondly.

But after Fern and Alison had moved away to join Rachel, who had just come outside, Doris said, 'Libby! That cousin of yours won't sneak to Mam'zelle, will she? That would really ruin everything.'

'Oh, Fern's all right,' Libby assured her airily. 'She can be a bit of an idiot at times, but she wouldn't tell tales.'

'Ah, Fern might not, but can we be so sure about our illustrious head girl?' said Janet slyly, nudging Bobby and nodding towards Carlotta, who was lying with her hands behind her head, half asleep.

'Hm?' The girl gave a yawn and stretched. 'What are you talking about?'

'We were just talking about playing a trick on Mam'zelle,' explained Bobby patiently. 'Fern doesn't approve – and Janet seems to think that as you're head of the form, you might not either.'

Carlotta sat bolt upright at this, saying with mock indignation, 'Does she indeed? Well, Janet, for your information, if I was head girl of the whole school I should still say go ahead and play your trick on Mam'zelle.'

Everyone laughed at this and Doris cried out, 'Good for you, Carlotta! We might have known that you wouldn't go all prim and proper on us!'

Carlotta laughed too, but she cast a sharp glance in

Janet's direction. The girl had made one or two pointed comments about her in the past couple of days and, although they had been laughed off, Carlotta couldn't rid herself of the idea that Janet was annoyed with her for some reason. Was it because she had been chosen to direct the play, perhaps? That might be part of it, but Carlotta had a strange feeling that it went deeper than that. It was all very odd, because Janet was normally every bit as frank and forthright as Carlotta herself, and would blow up if anyone upset her. Ruefully, Carlotta wished that she would blow up at her! At least it would clear the air between them, and anything would be better than this veiled hostility which wasn't Janet's style at all. Then, the next minute, Janet was her usual friendly self, punching Carlotta playfully on the arm as she reminded the girl of a trick the two of them had played on the sixth form last term. And, as Carlotta laughed with her, she began to wonder if she wasn't imagining things, and if Janet's change in attitude wasn't all in her own mind. It really was most perplexing and extremely annoying!

Equally annoying, as far as Alison was concerned, was the strained friendship between Fern and Rachel. Alison had spoken to Rachel the other night too, telling her that Fern had agreed to make an effort, and asking her to do the same.

'Well, I'll be pleasant for as long as she is,' had been Rachel's not very encouraging response. 'But *how* I dislike her! Nothing but a little feather-head, without a single sensible thought between her ears.'

Alison had bitten her lip at this and said, rather soberly, 'If only you knew how often the others have said exactly the same thing about me! And it's true. I know that I'm a bit of a dunce, and not exactly a deep thinker.' She frowned suddenly. 'But if Fern and I are so alike, how is it that you like me, but not her?'

Rachel clapped Alison on the shoulder, rather touched by her friend's little speech. 'You're only alike on the surface,' she said. 'And as for not being deep – well, at least you *have* something under *your* surface. You're warm, kind, sincere, loyal . . . everything that Fern isn't!'

'Oh!' exclaimed Alison, torn between pleasure at this glowing tribute and a wish to defend Fern. 'Well, thank you, Rachel. I'm glad that you feel like that about me. But I've always found Fern to be very warm and friendly.'

Rachel was shrewd and, unlike Alison, able to see beyond a pretty face. She had summed Fern up at a glance, had seen the spoilt, calculating girl behind the charming smile. But it was of no use to expect Alison to see Fern the same way. She would never believe ill of anyone she had taken a liking to unless she saw it with her own eyes. So Rachel summoned up a smile and said, 'Perhaps I'm being a bit hard on Fern and she'll turn out to be quite decent once I get to know her. Anyway, I'm willing to meet her half-way.'

Rachel was thinking of this conversation now as she stepped out into the bright sunshine and saw Fern and Alison laughing with a group of third formers. Alison smiled and got to her feet when she saw her, Fern following suit. But Fern's smile, Rachel noticed, didn't quite reach her eyes.

'Hi!' said Alison. 'What have you been up to? Fern and I have been out here for ages.'

'Oh, I thought I had better tidy my corner of the dormitory before Matron spotted it,' answered Rachel.

'Tidying up inside on a glorious day like this!' said Fern with a shudder. 'How dull! Still, I dare say life at St Clare's must seem pretty dull to you altogether.'

'What do you mean by that?' asked Rachel sharply.

Fern raised her finely arched brows at the girl's tone and said, 'Why, only that a school like this must seem terribly boring when you're used to mixing with theatrical types all the time.'

'Oh, I see!' Rachel seemed to relax a little. 'Well, Fern, theatrical types can be just as tiresome and boring as anyone else when you're with them every day.'

'I suppose so,' said Fern with her high little laugh. 'Which drama school did you go to, by the way?'

'The De Winter Academy,' answered Rachel. 'It's a very good one.'

'What a coincidence!' exclaimed Fern, clapping her hands together. 'A friend of mine from prep school goes there. Sara Jameson! We still keep in touch. Do you know her?'

'Yes.' Rachel had turned suddenly pale, the word forced out through stiff lips, while Fern and Alison stared at her curiously. 'Yes, I know Sara. Er . . . excuse me, would you? I've just remembered something I have to do.'

With that, Rachel sped away towards the school, leaving Alison and Fern to stare after her in surprise.

'Well, how peculiar!' exclaimed Alison, astonished. 'Did you see how white and upset she looked?'

Fern nodded while her mind worked rapidly. Rachel was obviously badly shaken by the fact that she, Fern, knew one of her fellow drama students. It was beginning to look as though the girl had something to hide. The question was, what? Fern made up her mind to find out. It was time, she thought, grinning slyly to herself, that she wrote to Sara Jameson.

6.

A wonderful day

The first week of term really flew by and at last it was Saturday, when the girls were free to do as they pleased.

Many of them went into town to spend their pocket-money, meet in the coffee shop, or see a film. Others took advantage of the fine weather to swim, play tennis or just sunbathe. Carlotta was particularly excited today, for she was to spend the afternoon at Libby's. How she looked forward to meeting her friend's family – and the horses, of course!

She arrived at the Oaks early and, instead of going straight to the house and knocking on the door, she went across to the paddock. Leaning on the gate she watched critically as a tall, thin boy, who looked very like Libby, rode a huge black horse around. The horse was obviously a wild, high-spirited creature, rearing and bucking violently in an effort to throw its rider. But the boy was a fine horseman, noted Carlotta with approval, and stayed firmly in the saddle. Suddenly he spotted Carlotta and turned the horse towards the gate.

'Hallo, there!' called out Carlotta in her friendly manner. 'You must be Will! I'm Carlotta Brown.'

To the girl's dismay, her bright smile was met with a

scowl and Will replied with a bored air, 'I know. Libby has had to pop into town with Mum and Fern, but she won't be long. She asked me to look after you until she gets back.' A task that he evidently wasn't looking forward to, realized Carlotta, feeling her temper beginning to rise.

The boy looked her up and down disdainfully, then ordered curtly, 'Wait here. I'll see if we've got a horse suitable for you.'

While Will went off towards the stables, Carlotta reached up to pat the neck of the black horse. The animal tossed its head and reared away.

'Come on, boy,' she crooned softly. 'Come to Carlotta.'

The horse became still suddenly, then moved slowly forward, until he was directly in front of her. This time when she reached up to stroke him, the animal didn't break away, laying his big head on her shoulder.

'Hey! What on earth do you think you're doing?' The angry shout, coming from behind her, made Carlotta spin round sharply. She came face to face with an absolutely furious Will. 'Don't you realize he could have bitten you?' said the boy angrily.

'Of course he won't bite me!' snapped Carlotta, getting more annoyed by the second at his manner.

'That's all you know! Rocky isn't fully broken in yet and he has a vicious temper. *You* certainly wouldn't be able to handle him. My sister is the only girl I know who can ride a horse properly, and even she can't control Rocky.'

With an effort, Carlotta swallowed a cutting retort. She wasn't going to lose her temper. Instead, she was going to teach Libby's stuck-up brother a lesson!

'I'm sorry,' she said meekly, moving away from Rocky. 'Is this the horse I'm to ride?' Carlotta nodded towards the plump, docile little mare that Will was leading and the boy said shortly, 'Yes. Have you ridden before?'

'Just a little,' she answered diffidently.

'Well, you shouldn't have any trouble handling old Maisie here,' said Will with a patronizing air that made Carlotta's hackles rise. 'Do you think you can manage to mount by yourself?'

'Oh, I'm quite sure that I can't,' said Carlotta, opening her dark eyes wide in pretend dismay. 'Don't you have something that I could stand on?'

Heaving a sigh of irritation, Will dropped Maisie's reins and turned back towards the stables to get a mounting-block. Carlotta pulled a face at his departing back, then sped across to the gate, climbing nimbly over it and into Rocky's paddock. By the time Will returned, she was on the horse's back.

'Get down from there right now, you idiot!' he cried, dropping the block and springing towards the gate. 'You'll break your neck!'

'Pah!' was Carlotta's only reply, delivered with a toss of her dark head, before she made a soft clicking sound and Rocky took off as though he had winged hooves! Indeed, the horse moved so swiftly that, for a moment, Will really feared that he had bolted with Carlotta and decided that he had better ride to her rescue. Then he noticed her relaxed, light touch on the reins and the natural grace of her posture, and realized that she didn't need rescuing at all. Rocky hadn't bolted with Carlotta. *She* had bolted with *him* and, to Will's astonishment, was very much in charge of the situation! Just then Will's mother came into the stableyard, along with Libby and Fern.

'Will!' cried out Mrs Francis in alarm. 'What are you thinking putting that poor girl up on Rocky? Ride after them this instant!'

'Don't worry about Carlotta, Mum!' laughed Libby. 'She used to ride in a circus. Wow, just look at her go!'

'A circus?' repeated Will with a groan of dismay. 'Oh, no! Libby, why on earth didn't you tell me that? Now I've just made a complete idiot of myself!'

'Well, there's nothing new in that,' giggled Libby. 'You're always making an idiot of yourself. Hey, Carlotta! Come and meet my mum.'

Carlotta reined in the horse and dismounted, coming through the gate.

'So you're Carlotta,' said Mrs Francis with a friendly smile. 'Libby's been singing your praises all week, so it's nice to meet you at last. We'll be seeing a lot of you here, I hope?'

'If you'll have me,' said Carlotta with a grin, liking her friend's mother at once.

'The children's friends are always welcome here,' Mrs Francis said. 'Now, I dare say you could all do with a cold drink, so I'll put a bottle of lemonade out on the kitchen table. Come and get it when you're ready.'

She went into the house, leaving the four young

people together. Libby said wickedly, 'I don't need to introduce you to my big ape of a brother. Obviously you've already met.'

'Big ape is right,' said Will with a rueful smile. 'Carlotta, I really am sorry for speaking to you the way I did.'

Never one to bear a grudge, Carlotta found herself smiling back, liking the boy's frankness. 'Apology accepted. And I'm afraid I ought to say sorry to poor Maisie here,' said Carlotta, going across to the placid mare and stroking her nose. 'I brushed you aside most rudely, didn't I, sweetheart?'

'Will! You surely *didn't* try to get Carlotta up on dear old Maisie?' gasped Libby, torn between amusement and dismay. 'I'm surprised that she's speaking to you at all!'

Fern, who had been hovering uncertainly on the edge of the group, looking a little bored, piped up, 'Will, we've had a brilliant time in town! Just wait until you see the new dress that Aunt Polly bought me!'

Will glanced briefly at his cousin and nodded vaguely, before saying, 'Libby, let's go and get some of that lemonade, then we can introduce Carlotta to the rest of the horses.'

'Good idea,' said Libby. 'Come on, Carlotta!'

'Oh, don't say you're going to spend *all* afternoon with the horses,' wailed Fern with her now familiar pout. 'Will, you *promised* that you'd help me with my maths prep today!'

'Later,' said Will, with an impatient wave of his hand. 'Carlotta, you must teach Libby and me some of your circus tricks! Can you ride bareback? I can't wait to tell the guys at school all about you!'

43

Carlotta grinned, but her shrewd eyes rested on Fern, who was looking extremely unhappy at the way her cousin had brushed her aside. Carlotta didn't much like the girl, but in that moment she felt a little sorry for her. She gave Fern a warm smile, and was taken aback to receive a ferocious scowl in return. Then Fern turned away and stalked off into the house.

Yet, despite Fern's sulks, it was a most enjoyable day. An afternoon spent riding and grooming the horses, then a delicious picnic tea on the lawn. Libby and Will's parents joined them and it was a very happy meal, Mr Francis keeping everyone in stitches with his jokes.

After tea Mrs Francis offered to drive Carlotta back to school, but Will said, 'I've a better idea! Let's go on horseback instead! Carlotta can ride Silver, and I'll lead him back once we've dropped her off at St Clare's.'

'That's not fair!' protested Fern. 'I won't be able to come with you.'

'Well, it's your own fault if you won't learn to ride,' said Will, with a touch of scorn. 'You're such a baby, squealing and running away every time one of the horses so much as whinnies at you!'

For a moment Carlotta thought that Fern was going to burst into tears, then Mrs Francis said sternly, 'That was very unkind, Will! Fern can't help it if she's not a "horsey" person.'

'Sorry,' mumbled Will, turning a little red.

'Why don't we walk?' suggested Carlotta. 'It won't take us very long, and then Fern can come with us.' This was really very generous of Carlotta, for she would have much preferred to go on horseback. But she realized how left out Fern must feel, living with her horse-mad cousins. The girl didn't seem very grateful, though, giving Carlotta a sour glance that made her pretty face look quite ugly for a moment. She was unusually silent on the walk to St Clare's, too, but none of the others seemed to notice, chattering happily among themselves. Carlotta felt quite flat once they reached the school gates and Libby said, 'See you on Monday, Carlotta.'

'Thanks for a lovely day,' answered Carlotta. 'Goodbye. Goodbye, Fern.'

'Come again soon, won't you?' said Will, adding with a cheeky grin, 'You're not a bad sort – for a girl!'

'And I suppose you're quite decent – for a boy!' Carlotta retorted wickedly.

What a lovely day it had been, thought the girl happily, as she went in search of the third formers. She couldn't wait to tell them all about it. And how marvellous that she had made another friend in Will. Carlotta didn't realize that she had also made an enemy in Fern, for the girl had an extremely jealous nature. A spoilt only child, Fern was used to having the undivided attention of her doting parents. When anyone she liked showed the slightest interest in anyone other than herself, she was quite unable to bear it.

Fern brooded over Carlotta on the way home. Will had treated the girl almost like a sister, she thought jealously, while he hardly paid any attention to her at all. As for

Uncle Tom, he never laughed and joked with her as he had with Carlotta. Even Aunt Polly had made a fuss of her, as if Carlotta was one of the family. It just wasn't fair! First there was that awful Rachel, trying to take Alison away from her, and now that horrible little Carlotta seemed to want to take her place with the family. Well, she would just have to do something about both of them!

7.

An announcement – and a plan

There was great excitement in the third form common-room, for Carlotta had called a meeting to announce which script had been chosen for the end-of-term play. Several of the girls had begun writing scripts, but had soon discovered that it wasn't as easy as they had thought. Pat and Isabel were among those who had fallen by the wayside, their effort – after much sighing, soul-searching and crossing out – finding its way into the wastepaper bin.

'I think we have to face the fact that we just don't have the talent to write a play,' Pat had remarked ruefully.

'After that lame effort, I'm not sure that we have the talent to write a nursery rhyme!' Isabel had said with a sigh. 'Let's just hope the others have done better, or we shan't have a play at all.'

In the end, three scripts were submitted, and Miss Adams and Carlotta read them all carefully. In spite of the fact that the writers hadn't given their names, Carlotta recognized Doris's work at once. Her wonderful sense of humour shone through every line, and Carlotta chuckled as she read it.

The second script was a very dramatic one, and certainly a praiseworthy effort. But the third, agreed

47

Carlotta and Miss Adams, was outstanding. 'Whoever wrote this has a very bright future ahead of her!' exclaimed Miss Adams. 'It really is excellent.'

'Yes, and it has a few humorous touches, as well as some dramatic moments, so it ought to please everyone,' said Carlotta, delighted.

She looked at the cover and read out the title of the play. '"Lady Dorinda's Diamonds." I wonder if this is Hilary's work? If so, she's been hiding her light under a bushel.'

But the mystery writer wasn't Hilary. In fact, it was the last person Carlotta expected!

She entered the common-room with the script under her arm and smiled round at the waiting girls. 'First of all, I'd like to thank the three of you who handed in plays,' she said, sitting down. 'They were all very good and you must have worked very hard indeed. It's a pity that we could only choose one, but here it is – "Lady Dorinda's Diamonds". I'm going to read out the first act, then we'll get the writer to come forward, and give her a round of applause!'

The girls listened attentively as Carlotta began to read, swiftly becoming enthralled as the story unfolded.

'Isn't it marvellous?' whispered Isabel to Pat.

'I'll say! Our feeble effort wouldn't have stood a chance!'

At last Carlotta came to the end of the first act and looked round expectantly, waiting for the girls' reaction. And what a reaction! There was silence for a moment, then the whole room erupted, the third formers cheering, clapping and whistling, so that Mam'zelle, marking books in the room below, thought that the ceiling was about to come down!

'Absolutely brilliant!'

'Bravo!'

'This is really going to make the parents sit up and take notice!'

'Writer! Writer!' called someone, and all the girls took up the cry, until Carlotta, raising her voice above the others, shouted, 'Yes, stand up, whoever you are!'

She glanced towards Hilary as she spoke, half expecting her to come forward. But a movement came from the other side of the room and a slim figure got to her feet. Rachel! The girls were stunned into silence for a moment. Fancy *Rachel*, who seemed to think herself a cut above the third formers, bothering to write a play for them – and such a good play, too! The girl at once went up in everyone's estimation, blushing and looking rather shy as the cheering started again, several girls reaching out to clap her on the back. Only Fern remained silent and tight lipped, resenting the attention the girl was receiving, especially when Alison called out, 'Well done, Rachel!'

'Thank you,' said Rachel hesitantly, taking her place beside Carlotta. 'I'm so glad that you like it.'

'I'll say we do!' exclaimed Carlotta, still feeling surprised that Rachel had turned out to be the anonymous writer. 'And now we can get down to the business of giving out parts and rehearsing. I'll arrange to have some copies of the script printed so that everyone can read through it properly, and we'll hold auditions in the hall next Sunday at two o'clock sharp.'

A babble of excited chatter broke out and Fern, completely forgetting that she was supposed to be making an effort to like Rachel, said spitefully to Alison, 'This is going to make Rachel even more swollen headed and unbearable. I think she's a sly creature, too. Fancy writing a play in secret and not even letting on to you, her best friend, about it.'

'Oh, she did tell me,' said Alison. 'But I promised to keep it to myself. Rachel didn't want anyone else to know in case her script was no good and she decided not to submit it.'

'Well, you *are* changing for the better, Alison,' exclaimed Janet, overhearing this. 'Not so long ago, telling you a secret was the surest way of spreading it round the whole school!'

Alison pulled a face at Janet, who laughed. Alison really was changing! A few terms ago, a teasing remark like that would have made her burst into tears. Fern, however, was not amused, hating the thought of Alison sharing a secret with Rachel and not letting her in on it. Worse still, she couldn't even punish Alison by sulking, for that would only drive her closer to Rachel. Fern really felt that life was very unfair at that moment!

As the girls began to drift away, Carlotta called out to Janet and Rachel, 'I wondered if you two would be decent enough to help me out with the auditions on Sunday? It's going to be quite a task, fitting the right part to the right person. Janet, you're always clear headed, so you ought to be a big help. And Rachel, you've had some experience at this kind of thing, so you should know how to make everything run smoothly.'

'I'd love to help,' said Janet at once, forgetting for the moment that she was still feeling a little sore with Carlotta.

'So would I,' agreed Rachel, who felt happier now than she had done in a long time. And what a difference it made, thought Carlotta, thinking how pretty and pleasant the girl looked, with her flushed cheeks and sparkling eyes.

'Great!' she said, pleased. 'It should be good fun.'

The girls were in for some fun before the auditions, too, thanks to Bobby and Janet.

The following day, Janet received a small package from her brother, and she and Bobby opened it together in the dormitory.

'Well, this doesn't look very thrilling!' said Bobby, disappointed, as she picked up what looked like a reel of thread. 'I don't see how we can trick Mam'zelle with this.'

Janet, who had been reading the letter that had come with the package, chuckled and said, 'You will! Here, read this.'

Bobby took the letter, and soon a grin spread across her mischievous face. 'Brilliant!' she cried. 'Janet, this could be our best trick yet.'

'And I think I know how to improve on it,' said Janet, opening her locker and rummaging around in it. 'Ah, here we are!' She produced a small tin with holes in the top, and Bobby said curiously, 'Whatever is that?'

'It's called a noise-box,' Janet told her. 'I've had it for ages, but haven't been able to find a use for it. I think I've found one now, though. Just listen.'

Janet turned the little tin upside down and it emitted a long, mournful wail.

'Marvellous!' breathed Bobby. 'Janet, let's play it on Friday, when Mam'zelle means to read us that French book!'

'The ghost story, you mean?' said Janet with a wicked grin. 'This just gets better and better, Bobby! Now, let's go and tell the others.'

At break that morning a group of third formers, led by Bobby and Janet, entered their classroom.

'Come on, Janet,' said Pat impatiently. 'We're just dying to see what you've got planned.'

'All right. Isabel, stand by the door will you, in case one of the mistresses comes along,' said Janet, producing the thread and the noise-box from her pocket.

'Why, it looks just like a reel of ordinary sewing cotton,' said Hilary.

'Ah, this is no ordinary cotton,' Janet said. 'Watch this!' Deftly she tied one end to the cord hanging from the blind at the window, then stepped back. 'See? The thread is almost invisible.'

'I see,' said Doris, 'Or rather, I *don't* see! Now what?'

In answer, Janet tugged on the invisible thread and the blind came whooshing down. 'We can make all sorts of things move simply by attaching a length of thread and pulling on it,' explained Bobby. 'We'll have poor old Mam'zelle believing that the room is haunted. And this will help.' She turned over the noise-box and it gave its spine-chilling wail, making Libby shiver.

'Ooh, that sounds really eerie!' she cried. 'My goodness, what a wonderful trick this is going to be!'

'We'll have to make sure that all the lengths of thread are in place before Mam'zelle comes in,' said Janet, who liked everything to be just perfect when she was planning a trick. 'A few of us will have to come in at break-time on Friday and see to that. And it won't be at all difficult to get Mam'zelle on to the subject of ghosts, seeing as we shall be reading that spooky French story.'

'I can't wait!' cried Doris excitedly. 'Roll on Friday!'

8.

A ghostly trick

The next two days seemed to crawl by, but at last it was Friday and time for the third form's French lesson.

Bobby, Janet and the twins sneaked into the classroom at break-time, cutting off long lengths of the magic thread and tying them to cupboard handles, empty chairs, the ceiling light – anything, in fact, that could be easily moved.

'Mam'zelle's always such a wonderful person to play a trick on,' chuckled Isabel in gleeful anticipation. 'She *always* falls for it, and never ever suspects that we might have anything to do with the mysterious things that are going on.'

'Well, there will be some very mysterious happenings in here today, all right,' said Pat with a grin. 'I just hope that no one gives the game away by laughing too much.'

Mam'zelle was in good humour when she entered the classroom. The morning post had brought her a long and chatty letter from one of her adored nieces, and she had just enjoyed a most peaceful and rewarding lesson with the sixth form, who were all good, hard-working girls.

Little guessing that her peace was about to be rudely shattered, she beamed round at the third formers, saying happily, 'Sit, *mes filles*. Now, today we will continue to read the ghost story which we started last week. Hilary, begin.'

'Oh, Mam'zelle, must we?' pleaded Hilary, making her eyes wide and scared. 'It really gives me the creeps.'

'Ah, it is just a story, *mon enfant*,' Mam'zelle assured her kindly. 'There are no such things as ghosts.'

'Well, I wouldn't be too sure about that, Mam'zelle,' put in Doris darkly. 'I got a book from the library the other day, which said that St Clare's itself is supposed to be haunted.'

Alison gave a realistic shudder and Doris continued, 'By a faceless monk, who roams the corridors and classrooms, wailing and . . .'

'Enough!' broke in Mam'zelle, losing some of her good humour. 'There are no monks at St Clare's, faceless or otherwise. The good Miss Theobald would never permit it!'

Mirabel gave a giggle, which she hastily turned into a cough, and Mam'zelle repeated firmly, 'There are no such things as ghosts, I tell you. Hilary, please read.'

Hilary began, and Janet waited until she was half-way down the page before operating the little noise-box which was in her pocket.

Libby squealed. 'Mam'zelle! What was that?'

The French mistress looked most astonished for a moment then, recovering herself, said briskly, 'It must have been the school cat, outside the window. Gladys, you take over the story, please.'

It was as Gladys reached a very tense, frightening part of the tale that Bobby tugged the end of the thread nearest her and the blind came down with a terrific clatter.

'*Tiens*!' exclaimed Mam'zelle, putting a hand to her heart. 'What a startle that gave me!'

'You mean a start, Mam'zelle,' giggled Isabel. 'What on earth could have caused that?'

'If you ask me, it wasn't anything on earth,' said Doris gravely. 'I think it was the ghost of . . .'

'Doris! One more word about faceless monks, and I send you outside!' threatened Mam'zelle, her glasses slipping down her nose as they were prone to do in moments of emotion. 'See, the window is open! It must have been the wind.' She conveniently overlooked the fact that it was a perfectly calm day without so much as a breeze, giving the girls a stern look that dared them to contradict her. 'Gladys,' she ordered firmly. 'Continue!'

Pat waited until Gladys made a mistake in her reading before pulling her thread. Then the door of the cupboard flew violently open, and Pat gave a well-feigned jump. 'Mam'zelle, I don't like this at all!' she cried, looking frightened. 'There seems to be something awfully strange going on in here today.'

Mam'zelle was beginning to look a little alarmed now, but said staunchly, 'Doors do not open themselves. One of you girls at the back must have pulled it open!'

'But, Mam'zelle, none of us is close enough,' pointed out Janet. 'And you can see for yourself that no one has moved from their seats.'

As she finished speaking, Janet set off the noise-box again, and poor Mam'zelle stood frozen to the spot in terror.

Doris, unable to control herself any longer, gave a snort of laughter, which set off Libby and Carlotta, both of whom hid behind their books to disguise their giggles. Then Janet caught the eyes of the girls around her and gave a little nod. Everything seemed to happen at once after that. The light above the French mistress's head began to swing back and forth. An empty chair beside Rachel suddenly toppled over backwards and the blackboard rubber flew from its ledge. And all the while a mournful wailing went on in the background. Mam'zelle gave a shriek and staggered back, almost overbalancing.

'Ah, *mon dieu*, *mon dieu*!' she cried. 'It is indeed true! The classroom is haunted.'

This was too much for the girls, who began to laugh helplessly. Isabel almost fell off her chair, while Hilary held her sides. Gladys and Mirabel clung to one another as tears of mirth poured down their cheeks.

Mam'zelle took one look at the chaos in the classroom and fled to find help. The girls gave full rein to their laughter.

'A monk with no face!' gasped Carlotta.

'Ah, *mon dieu*, *mon dieu*!' cried Doris, in a fine imitation of Mam'zelle's voice. 'Oh, I shall be sick if I laugh any more!'

Even Fern, who had been against the trick at the beginning, was doubled up with laughter, while Rachel was quite convulsed.

'Listen,' said Pat, when she could control her laughter enough to speak. 'Where do you suppose Mam'zelle went?'

'I hope she hasn't gone to Miss Theobald,' said Hilary. 'Although even if we get into a row, I shall still say it was worth it. Did you see her face when the light began to swing to and fro?'

That set them all off again and in a few minutes the whole class was helpless.

Mam'zelle, meanwhile, *had* gone to the head, quite convinced that the third-form classroom was inhabited by a ghost. The head looked up, startled, when the French mistress burst into her room without knocking, and was quite alarmed by her pallor.

'Why, Mam'zelle, you're trembling!' she cried. 'Whatever is the matter?'

'Ah, Miss Theobald, you would not believe what has happened in the third-form classroom,' groaned Mam'zelle, sinking on to a chair. 'It is haunted. There is a ghost and it is quite invisible!'

Miss Theobald, knowing Mam'zelle's excitable ways, hid a smile and said calmly, 'Perhaps you had better tell me exactly what happened.'

'It started with a truly terrible wailing noise, like a soul in torment. Then books and furniture began to fly about the room of their own accord. The poor girls are in a state of terror.'

'Really?' said the head drily. 'Bobby and Janet are in the third form, aren't they, Mam'zelle?'

Mam'zelle's glasses began to slip down her nose once more as she realized what Miss Theobald was suggesting. 'It is not a trick!' she declared firmly. 'It is quite impossible that the dear girls could have made such things happen.'

The head felt that where Bobby and Janet were concerned, nothing was impossible! Getting to her feet, she said briskly, 'Well, Mam'zelle, let's go and investigate.'

The third formers had calmed down a little by the time Mam'zelle returned, and they sobered up completely when Miss Theobald entered behind her. A deathly hush fell over the room as the girls hastily stood up.

'See, Miss Theobald!' exclaimed Mam'zelle. 'There is the chair which fell over, and see how the blackboard rubber flew through the air!'

Bobby, who had more daring than any girl in the class, still had in her hand the thread which was attached to the light, and couldn't resist a wicked impulse to give it another tug.

Mam'zelle screamed and clutched at Miss Theobald. 'Ah, the spirit is still here!' she cried.

The head looked from the swinging light to Bobby, who was wearing a most innocent expression. This alone was enough to confirm Miss Theobald's suspicions and she went across to the girl, saying coldly, 'Roberta, what is that in your hand?'

Bobby opened her hand which, at first glance, appeared empty. But Miss Theobald's eyes were sharp and, as she leant forward, she could see something against the girl's palm.

'Mam'zelle, I think Roberta can provide an explanation as to the strange goings on in here,' said the head. 'I will leave you to deal with the matter.' With that she left the room and Bobby waited for Mam'zelle's wrath to descend on her bent head.

'So!' cried the Frenchwoman. 'A trick! How was this abominable thing done?'

Bobby explained about the thread, while Janet removed the noise-box from her pocket, making it wail once more.

'I see,' said Mam'zelle, returning to her desk. The class waited with bated breath as she stared straight ahead of her, the sloe-black eyes solemn. All was silent for several moments. Then Mam'zelle began to chuckle. Softly at first, then more loudly, until she was positively roaring with laughter, her head thrown back and tears streaming down her cheeks. The girls began to grin too, liking Mam'zelle for being able to take a joke. They were relieved as well! If the French mistress could see the funny side, nothing too terrible would happen to them. But Mam'zelle wasn't letting them off scot-free.

'Ah, you bad girls!' she cried, with a twinkle in her eye. 'As a punishment, you will translate the first two chapters of the story we have been reading and have it ready for me by Monday!'

The third formers groaned inwardly, but no one dared protest out loud, for they knew that they had earned their punishment. Indeed, as Doris said later, 'If it had been any other mistress, we wouldn't have got off nearly so lightly! We can count ourselves lucky that Mam'zelle is such a sport.'

'Isn't she just,' chuckled Bobby. 'All the same, we had

better not play any more tricks on her for a bit. I don't think there's much chance of her being so lenient with us a second time.'

'No,' said Pat with a grin. 'Not even the *ghost* of a chance!'

9.

Carlotta in hot water

On the day of the auditions, Carlotta spent the morning riding with Libby. She had become a regular visitor at the Oaks and was quite one of the family, as Libby put it.

Libby and Fern were in the stableyard when Carlotta arrived and called out, 'Hi, you two!'

'Carlotta. You here again?' said Fern pointedly. 'Really, you might as well move in here and become a day girl at St Clare's, just like Libby and me.'

'Fern!' cried her cousin, quite shocked at the girl's rudeness. 'How dare you! Carlotta is a guest here – a very welcome guest – and I won't have her spoken to like that!'

'Well, she's obviously a lot more welcome here than I am!' snapped Fern. 'Perhaps you'd like me to move out of my bedroom so that she can come here permanently!'

'Well!' exclaimed Carlotta, as Fern flounced off. 'What's got into her? I know I'm not exactly Fern's favourite person, but she's never attacked me directly like that before.'

'Oh, she's just jealous because you've made such a hit with Will and my parents,' said Libby, exasperated by her cousin. 'You know how soppy she is about Will, yet he doesn't see her as anything but a perfect pest. Then you come along and he starts treating you like another sister.'

'Poor Fern,' said Carlotta. 'No wonder she's got such a down on me.'

'Poor Fern nothing!' scoffed Libby. 'She's been spoilt and pampered all her life, thanks to my aunt and uncle. It will do her good to realize that she can't wind everyone round her little finger.'

'I suppose so,' laughed Carlotta. 'By the way, where *are* Will and your parents? It seems awfully quiet here today.'

'They're out visiting friends,' Libby explained. 'Fern and I were invited too, but it would have meant missing the auditions.'

'Are you going in for one of the leading parts?' asked Carlotta.

'Heavens, no! A walk-on part will suit me,' answered Libby. 'I don't want to have to spend all my spare time rehearsing when I could be out riding. I must say, I'm rather sorry that you're director. You won't be able to come over here nearly so often.'

'You're right!' said Carlotta in dismay. 'I hadn't thought of that! I almost wish that I'd let Janet have the job now. Oh, well, I'd better make the most of the time I have got, then. How about a race?'

The two girls spent a blissful hour riding, then went into the kitchen for a simple but scrumptious lunch of crusty bread, cheese and salad, followed by cold apple pie with cream.

Fern joined them, getting up from the table as soon as

she had finished eating and saying shortly, 'I'm going across to St Clare's now.'

'Why?' asked Libby in surprise. 'The auditions don't start for ages.'

'I know, but I'm going for the part of Lady Dorinda, and Alison has promised to read through it with me so that I'm word perfect.'

'Best of luck,' said Carlotta. 'Hey, Libby, we'd better keep an eye on the time. It will never do if I'm late for the auditions.'

'The stable clock keeps good time,' replied Libby. 'Come on, let's clear up quickly, then we can get back to the horses.'

Fern was thoughtful as she stepped out into the bright sunshine. Carlotta *would* be in hot water with the rest of the form if she turned up late this afternoon. The third took their responsibilities very seriously indeed and looked to Carlotta, as head girl, for a lead. Making a sudden decision, Fern ran to the stables, getting out a small stepladder and placing it beneath the stable clock. It was set above the doors and, even on the top step, she had to stand on tiptoe, stretching her arms high above her head to reach the hands. But she managed it, setting the clock back by a full hour. Smiling triumphantly to herself, she replaced the steps, then made her way out of the yard into the lane. Even if she didn't get the part of Lady Dorinda, Fern was really going to enjoy today's auditions!

'Where on earth has Carlotta got to?' said Pat impatiently,

looking at her watch. 'It's almost quarter past two and no sign of her!'

'It really is too bad of her when the rest of us have made the effort to turn up on time,' said Janet irritably. 'Hey, Fern, do you have any idea where she and Libby could have got to?'

'Oh, you know what Carlotta's like,' answered Fern with a laugh. 'Once she gets on horseback, nothing else seems to matter. I shouldn't be surprised if she's forgotten about the auditions altogether!'

'Well, I vote we start without her,' said Hilary. 'Otherwise we're just wasting everyone's time. If Carlotta doesn't like it, that's just too bad.'

'Right,' said Janet, taking charge. 'We'll cast the part of Lady Dorinda first, as she's the main character. Fern, you can go first, then Gladys.' She took a seat beside Rachel, and the two of them watched critically as Fern took centre stage. 'She certainly looks the part,' murmured Janet. 'But she couldn't act her way out of a paper bag!'

Rachel nodded agreement as Fern flung herself about the stage, almost shouting the lines and accompanying them with dramatic gestures. Several of the watching girls had to smother giggles at the terribly refined voice Fern put on, which was quite different from her own pleasant tone. At last, unable to bear any more, Janet stood up and called out, 'Thank you, Fern! I think we've seen enough. Gladys, your turn now.'

A small, almost insignificant figure, Gladys looked pale and nervous as she took the stage, and Rachel frowned.

This mousy little creature would never be able to play the beautiful, spirited Lady Dorinda convincingly! But Rachel was wrong. Gladys didn't just *play* Lady Dorinda, she became her, her speech and movements fluid and natural. When she had finished, the watching girls applauded and cheered loudly.

'Wow, what a talent!' exclaimed Rachel, absolutely thrilled. To hear Gladys speak the words she had written, and breathe life into the character she had created, had been strangely moving. Rachel had felt a lump form in her throat. She and Janet were in complete agreement – Gladys just *had* to play Lady Dorinda!

Tall, strapping Mirabel was given the part of her absent-minded husband, while Doris was just marvellous in a comic role as a bumbling policeman. 'She'll bring the house down,' said Rachel happily. 'Doris is every bit as gifted as Gladys, though in a completely different way.'

Janet nodded, surprised and pleased at the change in Rachel, and at how well the two of them worked together. She had been afraid that the girl, with her drama school training, might have been critical and hard to please, but she was extremely sincere and generous in her praise. Slightly to her shame, Janet was also delighted by the chance to show the others how smoothly she could make things run in Carlotta's absence. And, certainly, she made the auditions run like clockwork, so that by ten minutes to three all of the leading roles had been filled and there now remained only the minor parts to cast. This was when Carlotta and Libby turned up and the sight of them, laughing and chattering away to one another as they strolled into the hall, annoyed many of the girls intensely.

'Good of you to put in an appearance!' called out Janet, with sarcasm. 'I do hope that we haven't interrupted your horse riding.'

Hearing the edge to Janet's voice, and suddenly aware of the hard stares which many of the girls were giving her, Carlotta came to an abrupt halt in the middle of the floor. 'What's up?' she asked in surprise. 'Oh, don't say you've started without us! That was a bit mean!'

'Well, it's rather mean to turn up late!' cried Bobby indignantly. 'You surely didn't expect us to sit around doing nothing for the best part of an hour while we waited for you to grace us with your presence?'

'Bobby, whatever do you mean?' said Carlotta, completely bewildered by the girl's tone. 'It's only ten to two.'

'Actually, Carlotta, it's ten to *three*,' pointed out Pat drily.

'But that's impossible!' put in Libby with a frown. 'We left home at precisely twenty to two by the stable clock.'

'Well, your clock must be wrong,' said Isabel. 'Because you're almost an hour late.'

'Oh, no!' wailed Carlotta in dismay. 'Girls, I really am sorry!'

'It's my fault,' said Libby apologetically. 'I was quite certain that the clock was right.'

'Well, it can't be helped now,' said Hilary sensibly. 'I'm afraid we just had to carry on without you, though, and most of the parts have been filled.'

'I see.' Carlotta walked across to Janet and Rachel,

looking down at the notebook that lay between them. There was a neatly written list of all the characters and, beside each one, the name of the girl who was to play the part. 'Well, the two of you seem to have done an excellent job,' said Carlotta generously, trying to keep the disappointment from her voice. 'Would you like me to take over now?'

'That's hardly fair,' protested Mirabel. 'Janet and Rachel have done all the donkey work and now you want to push them aside.'

'I don't want to do anything of the kind!' retorted Carlotta, stung. 'I was late due to a simple mistake, I've apologized, and now I want to make up for it by pulling my weight. What's wrong with that?'

Fern, in the background, almost hugged herself with glee. Her mean little trick had gone better than expected, and no one had the slightest suspicion that she had put the clock back. And there would be plenty more tricks where that one came from!

'Let's calm down a little,' suggested the steady Hilary. 'Carlotta, why don't you let Rachel and Janet finish dishing out the parts, seeing as they've done such a marvellous job? And in the meantime you can set about working out a timetable for rehearsals.'

Carlotta gave Hilary a grateful smile. 'Good idea,' she said. 'I'll just find myself a sheet of paper and a quiet corner.'

So the situation was resolved and Carlotta's lapse was forgiven. But not all of the girls forgot about it. Fern thought about it often, rejoicing at the trouble she had caused and plotting further revenge, as she thought of it, against both Carlotta and Rachel. And the incident remained in Janet's mind too. Carlotta had shown that she was unreliable and she might well do so again. The girl had better watch her step!

10.

A birthday party

Carlotta did watch her step, extremely conscious of the fact that she had blotted her copybook with the third form and anxious not to repeat the mistake. The first couple of rehearsals went smoothly, with everyone present on time and the cast enthusiastic. Everybody was looking forward to the end-of-term play enormously.

There were other things for the girls to look forward to as well. There was tennis and swimming, of course, which most of them loved. Then half-term was coming up shortly, and everyone was dying to see parents, brothers and sisters again. Best of all, there were several form birthdays coming up – and birthdays meant parties!

First was Libby's, and her parents threw a party at the Oaks one Saturday afternoon, to which the whole form was invited. She was a popular girl and everyone bought her presents, some expensive and some not so expensive. Carlotta gave her a beautiful book on horses, which she was absolutely delighted with, and the twins clubbed together to buy her an enormous bottle of bubble bath.

'So that you can soak away your aches and pains after a long day in the saddle,' laughed Isabel.

'I'm afraid I'm broke this week,' said Bobby handing

the girl a small box of chocolates. 'But happy birthday anyway, Libby.'

'Thanks awfully, Bobby,' said Libby happily, accepting the chocolates with as much pleasure as if they had been the crown jewels. 'I don't think I've ever received so many presents in my life. Thank you everyone. What a lovely birthday this is!'

And what a great party they had. First there were riotous games in the garden, then tea in the big kitchen. There were cries of 'ooh' and 'ah' as the girls gazed happily at the plates piled high with cakes, biscuits and sandwiches of every kind.

'This is what I call a party!' exclaimed Bobby in delight. 'Thanks a lot, Mrs Francis.'

The others echoed this and Libby's mother said with a smile, 'Well, just make sure you eat up every scrap of it! I don't want to see a single crumb left on these plates.'

'No problem there, Mrs Francis,' laughed Hilary. And indeed there wasn't. The girls were very hungry indeed after their energetic games and attacked the food as though they hadn't eaten in days. Libby's mother kept their glasses filled with lemonade and the party was a great success.

'Can I help you to clear away, Mrs Francis?' offered Alison politely, once tea was over.

'That's kind of you, dear, but go and enjoy yourself outside with the others,' said Libby's mother, smiling at the girl. This was the first time Mrs Francis had met Fern's friend, Alison, and she had taken a great liking to her.

Alison was like her niece in many ways, yet she had a gentle, kindly side to her nature which Fern lacked. Mrs Francis was fond of her niece, but she wasn't blind to the girl's faults, which worried her at times. It would be a good thing, she thought, if some of Alison rubbed off on Fern.

'What shall we do now?' asked Libby, once the girls were outside again.

'I don't feel like doing much of anything after that lovely tea,' said Janet, flopping down on the grass. 'I'm quite happy to just laze in the sun and chat.'

Everyone seemed to feel the same, settling down and stretching out comfortably.

'Wouldn't it be brilliant if we could do this every Saturday?' sighed Doris happily.

'Well, Isabel and I have a birthday coming up after half-term,' said Pat. 'Mum and Daddy have promised us some money, and I bet Miss Theobald would give permission for us to have a party in the common-room.'

'Who needs permission?' scoffed Bobby. 'I vote we make it a midnight feast.'

Several voices cried out excitedly.

'What a wonderful idea!'

'A feast! Oh, yes, let's!'

'It would be fun,' agreed Isabel. 'But we can't! Libby and Fern wouldn't be able to come, and I'd feel really mean about leaving them out, especially after Libby was decent enough to invite us all here today.'

Everyone agreed to this at once, but Bobby said wickedly, 'Who said anything about leaving them out? It's only a few minutes' walk from here to St Clare's, and the moon will be up. I'm sure we could work out a way for Fern and Libby to join the feast without them being caught.'

Surprisingly it was the bold Carlotta, usually ripe for any kind of prank, who sounded a note of caution. 'I'm not so sure that's a good idea. It would be bad enough the rest of us being caught. But if it was discovered that the day girls were missing from their home in the middle of the night, the cat really *would* be among the pigeons!'

'Well, it won't be discovered,' said Janet with a scornful laugh. 'We'll make sure of that. Honestly, Carlotta, you seem to have lost your sense of fun since you became head of the form.'

'I haven't!' said Carlotta hotly, rather hurt by Janet's words. 'But I could lose my position if anything went wrong.'

'Perhaps Carlotta doesn't want us at the feast,' suggested Fern slyly. She had suddenly thought of a way to cause more trouble for Carlotta and, in order to make her plan work, it was vital that she and Libby be invited to the midnight feast.

'That's not true,' protested Carlotta unhappily, hating having to be a wet blanket. 'I'd love you both to come. It's just that as head girl . . .'

'Now let's get this clear,' broke in Janet. 'Are we to understand that if Hilary was still head girl, you would have no objection to the day girls coming to our feast?'

'That's right,' said Carlotta with a frown, wondering where this was leading. She soon found out.

'I see,' said Janet smoothly. 'So you would have been

73

quite prepared to allow Hilary to jeopardize her position, but now that you are head, you aren't prepared to take any risks. Rather hypocritical, Carlotta, if you ask me.'

'Oh, Janet, that's a bit strong,' protested Pat. 'A hypocrite is one thing Carlotta has never been.'

'Why, Pat, how can you say that?' put in Fern, eager to back up Janet against a girl she saw as her enemy. 'Remember when you, Isabel and Carlotta stopped here on your way to school that first day? Carlotta actually mentioned the possibility of us attending a midnight feast then! But, of course, that was before she found out that she was to be head girl. Libby, what do you say? You'd like to go to the feast, wouldn't you?'

Poor Libby didn't know *what* to say! On the one hand she badly wanted to go to the feast. On the other, she didn't want to go against her friend.

Carlotta, who had been looking grave and thoughtful, saved her from having to answer. Her firm little chin up, she said in her frank way, 'Fern and Janet are quite right. I *have* been a hypocrite, although I didn't see it that way. I just thought that I was being a responsible head girl. Yes, Janet, I would have been prepared to let Hilary risk her position if she was in my place. And yes, Fern, you're right about what I said on that first day. So, girls, you are both very welcome at the feast and if – Heaven forbid – anything should go wrong and we're caught, I shall take full responsibility.' Carlotta grinned suddenly, looking more like herself as her dark eyes twinkled merrily. 'After all, if I *am* dropped as head girl, it won't be the end of the world!'

'Good for you, Carlotta!' called out Doris.

'Yes! And nothing will go wrong – touch wood,' said Isabel, tapping Doris on the head.

'Here, do you mind?' said Doris, with a comical expression.

Everyone laughed, then Pat spoke.

'Janet, I think you ought to take back what you said about Carlotta being a hypocrite. She's been big enough to admit that she got a bit muddle-headed about things. Now *you* should be big enough to admit that you were wrong about her.'

'Of course,' said Janet at once, turning a little red. Carlotta's forthright speech had taken the wind out of her sails a bit. It was difficult to hold a grudge in the face of such straightforward honesty. Never one to shirk an unpleasant task, Janet said bluntly, 'I take it back, Carlotta. You're no hypocrite.' Then, grinning ruefully, she held out her hand. 'No hard feelings?'

'None at all,' agreed Carlotta, returning both the grin and the handshake.

Inwardly, though, neither girl felt quite so sure. A truce had been agreed, but it was an uneasy one. Pat and Isabel discussed the matter in a quiet corner of the common-room later.

'I can see a terrific row brewing between Janet and Carlotta,' said Isabel worriedly. 'Yet they've always been such good pals up to now. I just can't understand what's gone wrong between them.'

Nor could Pat. 'I wish they would just have a blazing row and clear the air once and for all,' she sighed. 'I hate all this bad feeling in the atmosphere.'

The incident was on Carlotta's mind too when she went to bed that night, making it difficult for her to sleep. Despite her bold talk this afternoon, she was more worried than she cared to admit about the two day girls coming to the proposed feast. It wouldn't be the end of the world if she was no longer head girl, she had said defiantly. But, in reality, she would be deeply upset and feel a complete failure. She had written a long and excited letter to her father and grandmother at the beginning of term, telling them her exciting news. And they had written straight back, letting Carlotta know how proud and delighted they were. How bitterly disappointed in her they would be if this important and responsible position was taken from her!

11.

Half-term

Before plans could be made for the twins' birthday feast, there was the excitement of half-term. The third formers were up with the lark that day, fighting good-naturedly for the bathrooms before arraying themselves in their prettiest summer dresses.

'Are your parents coming to take you out, Rachel?' asked Hilary, secretly rather hoping that they were. Like most of the others, she was dying to see the famous actors in person.

'Yes, and Alison will be joining us as her parents are away.'

'Won't they be proud of you when they hear all about the play you've written!' said Bobby.

'The play?' Rachel looked blank for a moment, then said rather stiffly, 'I don't suppose I shall tell them about it.'

'Funny girl,' remarked Pat to her twin as Rachel moved away. 'I don't know quite what to make of her. At the start of term I thought she was dreadfully stuck up and conceited, then she seemed to settle down and become one of us. But she still goes all cold and distant at times.'

'Oh, never mind about Rachel,' cried Isabel, who was in high spirits. 'I'm just looking forward to seeing our own parents! Hey, Gladys, I bet you're dying to see your mum again!'

'I'll say!' answered the girl with her gentle smile. 'We're going out to lunch at a hotel with Mirabel and her parents, so it should be good fun.'

Just then Carlotta came into the common-room, looking most unlike herself – but extremely pretty – in a lovely pale blue dress, a matching ribbon confining her unruly curls.

'Hello, who's this elegant stranger?' joked Doris. 'Can we help you, young lady?'

'Idiot!' laughed Carlotta, aiming a playful punch at Doris. Then she straightened the skirt of her dress and said self-consciously, 'I don't feel like *me* at all.'

'What's this in aid of, Carlotta?' asked Hilary with a grin. 'You wouldn't be trying to impress your grand-mother, by any chance?'

'I would,' answered the girl frankly. 'You know how she always complains that I look wild and untidy. I thought that if I wore the dress she bought me for my last birthday, I might stand a chance of getting into her good books.'

'Any particular reason why you want to get into her good books?' asked Pat, amused.

'Actually, it's all for you and Isabel,' answered Carlotta with a grin. 'You see, the more grandmother approves of me, the more generous she becomes. So the size of your birthday present, twins, all depends on how ladylike I am!'

Isabel winked at her twin, saying, 'Well, if Pat and I get a stick of toffee between us, we'll know that you've misbehaved, so just mind your Ps and Qs.'

Everybody laughed, then Mirabel cried, 'Oh, look, a car has just pulled up outside! It's the first lot of parents!'

Immediately everyone rushed to the window, Doris putting her head out and calling excitedly, 'They're mine! Hi, Mum! Dad!'

'Steady on, or you'll fall out of the window and squash your poor mother flat!' laughed Janet, pulling her back.

But Doris didn't care. 'Come on!' she called out to Hilary, who was spending the day with her. 'Let's go and say hi!'

The cars arrived thick and fast after that, until the lawn was crowded with people.

'I'm rather nervous about meeting your parents,' Alison confided to Rachel.

'Why?' laughed the girl. 'They don't have two heads each, you know.'

'No, but they're famous,' said Alison rather gravely. 'They're bound to think I'm a little nobody.'

'What nonsense!' cried Rachel. 'Their faces might be famous, but my folks are just normal down-to-earth people – and here they are! Come on, Alison, and you'll see for yourself.'

Sure enough, Rachel's parents were extremely pleasant and friendly, not at all up in the air as Alison had feared, and she relaxed at once in their company. Unfortunately, Alison's decision to spend the day with Rachel had caused some coolness between herself and Fern.

Fern had asked Alison prettily if she would care to spend half-term with her. 'We'll have lunch at home,' she had said. 'Then afterwards we'll come over to St Clare's to watch the tennis and swimming and take a look at the art exhibition.'

'Oh, Fern, that's awfully kind of you, but I'm afraid I've already agreed to go out with Rachel and her parents,' Alison had replied dismayed, for she always hated to hurt anyone's feelings.

'Well, surely you can tell her that you've changed your mind,' Fern had said.

'But that would be terribly rude after she asked me first. Besides, I haven't changed my mind! I want to go out with Rachel.'

'I see,' Fern had said coldly. Then she gave the high little laugh that had begun to irritate Alison. 'I suppose the truth is that you just want to rub shoulders with her famous parents!'

'That's a terrible thing to say!' gasped Alison, feeling hurt. 'Of course I'm looking forward to meeting them, but my main reason for going is because Rachel is my friend and I like her.'

'As if anyone could like that stuck-up creature!' snapped Fern. 'Well, do as you please, Alison. I shall find someone else to spend the day with.' Then Fern had turned on her heel and stalked away.

She had made it up with Alison later, but there was still some tension between the two girls. When Alison had asked her if she had found someone to spend the day with her, Fern had given a curious little smile and said, 'Oh, yes. Someone very interesting.'

'Who?' Alison had asked curiously.

But Fern would only shake her head and give an infuriatingly smug smile. Alison knew that all of the other third formers had made arrangements of their own, and Fern didn't have any friends in another form, so she simply couldn't imagine who the girl's mystery guest could be.

She found out that afternoon. Rachel's parents were deep in conversation with Miss Adams when Alison spotted the Francis family arriving. Libby immediately took her parents and brother to meet Carlotta's father, while Fern made straight for Alison and Rachel. With her was a tall, fair girl, whom Alison had never seen before. She nudged Rachel.

'Here comes Fern. I wonder who that is with her? She looks rather nice.'

Rachel glanced across – and the colour drained from her cheeks, leaving her white as a sheet, eyes wide with horror.

'Why, Rachel, whatever is the matter?' cried Alison, alarmed. 'Do you feel all right?'

Rachel did not answer, unable to move or speak as Fern and her companion came over.

'Alison – and Rachel!' said Fern in her sweetest, most gushing tone. She was wearing her brightest smile too, realized Rachel bitterly – and unless she was mistaken, there was more than a hint of spite in it.

'Alison, I'd like you to meet an old friend of mine, Sara Jameson. Of course, there's no need to introduce her to you, Rachel, because she's an old friend of yours as well.'

'Really? Do you two know one another?' asked Alison, looking at Rachel in surprise. 'Oh, of course, I remember! Sara is the girl who was at drama school with you! Well, how nice for you both to meet again.'

Rachel didn't seem to take any pleasure in the meeting at all, though. Her tone was odd and stilted as she said, 'Hello, Sara. What brings you to these parts?'

'Oh, my grandmother lives near here and I've been staying with her for a while. When Fern found out I was in the area she asked me to spend half-term with her. Wasn't that nice of her?' If Sara found anything peculiar in Rachel's behaviour she didn't betray it, her own manner open and friendly. 'How are you settling in here?' she asked warmly. 'I must say, it looks a really nice school.'

'It is . . . I . . . I'm fine here,' answered Rachel disjointedly, looking wildly around as though trying to escape. Alison couldn't imagine what had got into her. Suddenly Rachel grabbed her arm and said hastily, 'Oh, Mum and Dad are calling us! Come on, Alison. Goodbye, Fern. Sara – nice to see you again.' Then Alison found herself being propelled across the lawn, only to find that Sir Robert and Lady Helen were still talking with Miss Adams.

'Rachel, whatever is the matter with you?' said Alison, unusually waspishly. She would have liked to spend a little longer with Fern and Sara, who she had thought a very pleasant girl. She gave Rachel a narrow, sideways glance. Surely *Sara* couldn't be behind the odd way her friend was acting?

Lady Helen happened to turn round and, putting her arm round her daughter's shoulders, said with her dazzling smile, 'Is everything all right, darling?'

'Fine, Mum,' said Rachel, her answering smile a little forced. 'Everything's just fine.'

But everything wasn't fine, thought Alison with a puzzled frown. Something had happened to upset Rachel terribly. If only she could discover what it was and help her friend.

Fern could have enlightened her! Over the half-term break, Sara, unwittingly, told her everything that she needed to know. Just having the knowledge, knowing that Rachel would see it in her eyes, gave Fern a feeling of power and that was all she wanted. It is quite likely that she would have said nothing to the rest of the third form about it if a dreadful quarrel hadn't sprung up between Rachel and herself during rehearsals after the break.

12.

A bad day for Rachel

Carlotta was finding Rachel a great help with rehearsals. She had a keen eye for detail and often spotted something that Carlotta overlooked. 'If Bobby made her entrance from the other side, she wouldn't overshadow Gladys so much,' she would suggest. Or, 'Mirabel's excellent, but it really isn't necessary for her to roar like that! If she spoke normally her performance would be far more effective.'

'I sometimes think that you should be directing instead of me,' Carlotta said one day.

Rachel had blushed and said with a laugh, 'I don't know about that, but I think it's easier for me because I visualized the play in my mind as I wrote it, so I can instantly spot anything I think isn't quite right.'

Carlotta bit her lip. Not for the first time it occurred to her that it really *would* be better for the third form if Rachel took over altogether. Yet the girls had chosen her and if she simply handed the reins to Rachel, some of them – Janet in particular – would accuse her of shirking her responsibilities.

Then, quite suddenly, the matter was taken completely out of her hands.

It was a Saturday afternoon and Carlotta was out

riding with Libby, while the other third formers were at a loose end.

'If only Carlotta was here to direct, we could fit in another rehearsal,' said Doris.

'Well, why shouldn't we rehearse just because Carlotta is too busy with her own interests?' cried Janet suddenly. 'Libby doesn't have any lines, so we shan't miss her, and Rachel can step in as director. Rachel, what do you say?'

'Well, I don't mind, so long as Carlotta doesn't think I'm treading on her toes,' answered Rachel.

'Nonsense!' said Janet. 'Anyway it's Carlotta's own fault. She spends more time at Libby's these days than she does at St Clare's.'

Fern, who had come over to the school to spend the afternoon with Alison, smiled and said sweetly, 'Yes, let Rachel take over. I'm sure that with her drama school background she'll do a marvellous job.'

Alison gave Fern an approving smile. The girl really was making an effort to get on better with Rachel. Only Rachel herself saw the sly look in Fern's big blue eyes and heard the spite behind the sweetness. Bobby sped along to Miss Theobald to get permission for the third formers to use the hall, and soon a rehearsal was in full swing.

Everything went swimmingly until it came to Fern's part. The girl was playing a maid and only had one line, but she persisted in muffing it. And Rachel was quite certain that she was only doing it to annoy her, especially when Fern kept directing smug, knowing little smiles in her direction. Rachel tried hard to keep her temper, taking the girl through the line time and time again, resisting the impulse to yell at her. But really, Fern would try the patience of a saint.

The explosion came when Janet, who along with some of the others was becoming impatient, called out, 'For Heaven's sake, let's move on to another scene or we shall have wasted a whole afternoon on Fern. Come on, Rachel, you're supposed to be in charge.'

'Oh, do let me have just one more try at it,' pleaded Fern. 'I promise to get it right this time.'

'Very well,' agreed Rachel through clenched teeth. 'But this is positively the last time.'

So yet again Fern spoke her line. And yet again she got it wrong. It was just too much for Rachel. 'For goodness' sake, how difficult can it be to learn one line?' she shouted, clenching her fists tightly at her sides. 'You're the worst actress I have ever seen! Well, Fern, I'm sacking you! You can swap parts with Libby and take her non-speaking role. At least she has the brains to string a few words together!'

'You can't do that!' protested Fern furiously, turning red. 'Only Carlotta can! You're just standing in for her, so don't get too big for your boots, Rachel.'

'Then I shall suggest it to Carlotta, and I'm pretty sure she will agree with me,' said Rachel, adding with a sneer, 'She shares my opinion that you can't act to save your life.'

There was silence for a moment, the third formers watching with bated breath as Fern glared down poisonously at Rachel from the stage. They waited for her to burst into tears, or flounce off. To their surprise Fern did neither of these things. Instead she gave a scornful laugh and said coolly, 'Well, you would know all about being a poor actress, wouldn't you? That's why you were sent away from drama school. Not because you were taking time off to be an ordinary schoolgirl, but because they didn't want you there any more – because you just can't act!'

Rachel said nothing, but turned very pale and trembled from head to foot. This was what she had dreaded. Now the others would know what a fraud she was!

Fern went on in that smooth, hateful little voice, 'Sara told me all about it at half-term. About how the principal of the drama school had to tell your parents that you would never follow in their footsteps and they would do better to take you away and send you to an ordinary school. And you thought that you could come here and lord it over all of us, didn't you? The great actress! Ha!'

Unable to bear Fern's triumphant expression any longer, and not daring to look at the faces of the others for fear of the contempt she would see there, Rachel gave a sob and fled from the hall.

'Well, now you all know what a fraud she is,' said Fern, looking round at the others. 'What do you think of your precious Rachel now, Alison?' She stopped suddenly, for there *was* contempt in the others' faces. But it wasn't for Rachel. It was for her.

'That was a rotten thing to do!' said Alison in a

trembling voice. 'Fern, how could you?'

'I'll say it was rotten,' said Hilary scornfully. 'And cunning! You deliberately provoked Rachel into losing her temper, just so that you could blurt this out in front of us all.'

'I didn't!' wailed Fern, horrified at the reaction her bombshell had produced, with even Alison turning against her. 'If she hadn't said that she was going to sack me, I would have kept quiet.'

'Perhaps, but you've just loved having a hold over Rachel, haven't you?' snapped Alison disdainfully. 'I've known something was wrong ever since you brought Sara here at half-term.'

'I don't know why you're all so angry with me!' protested Fern. 'You should be grateful to me for exposing her.'

'Yes, that's exactly what you've done,' said Pat coldly. 'Exposed her and torn away the protective shell Rachel had built up round herself. Can't you imagine how dreadful this business must have been for her? The poor girl must have been absolutely shattered when she was told that she had no future on the stage.'

'Not to mention the shame of her parents being told that the school no longer wanted her,' put in Isabel. 'She must have felt that she had let them down terribly.'

'And she was settling in here so well,' said Gladys. 'Admittedly she was a bit full of herself at first, but now we know it was just an act, her way of coping with what had happened. Since we all praised her for writing the play, she's really become one of us.'

'Yes, and you didn't like that, did you, Fern? Especially when she began getting closer to Alison,' sneered Janet. 'Now clear out! We've all had quite enough of you and your spite for one day.'

Shocked, Fern turned a pleading look on Alison who glared at her and said, 'Go away, Fern. I shall have to think carefully about whether or not I still want to be your friend after this.' She turned her back and Fern, just as Rachel had done earlier, gave a sob and ran out.

'Wasn't that just awful!' said Doris, looking unusually grave. 'I wonder where Rachel went?'

'Probably up to the dormitory,' said Hilary. 'One of us really should go and see if she's all right.'

'I'll go,' said Alison. 'After all, she is my friend.' Then, quite suddenly, she put her hands up to her face and began to cry.

'Poor Rachel!' she sobbed. 'I feel so sorry for her.'

Janet gave her a pat on the shoulder. 'Never mind, Alison. She'll be all right once she knows none of us thinks any the less of her. All the same, I don't think you're going to be a great comfort if you mean to cry all over her.'

Alison gave a watery little laugh and Isabel said, 'Carlotta really ought to be the one to deal with this, as head of the form.'

'Yes, but, as usual, Carlotta isn't around when she's needed,' said Janet drily. 'I'll go and have a word with Rachel.'

Everyone agreed to this at once. Janet might be a little sharp tongued at times, but she was good hearted and had plenty of common sense. She would need both of those qualities in dealing with poor, miserable Rachel.

13.

Another row

Janet found Rachel in the dormitory, curled up into a tight little ball and absolutely sobbing her heart out. Feeling desperately sorry for her, Janet went across and laid a hand on her shoulder.

'Leave me alone!' cried the girl, shrugging her off.

'I can't leave you like this,' said Janet calmly, sitting down beside her. 'Come on, Rachel! It's never any good bottling things up. You'll feel much better if you talk about it.'

'Oh, yes, I bet you'd just love to hear all the details of my humiliation,' stormed Rachel through her tears. 'So that you can go back and tell the others and you can all have a good laugh at me!'

'Rachel, that just isn't true!' cried Janet, shocked. 'I just want to help you. We all do.'

Rachel stopped crying for a moment and looked into the girl's warm brown eyes, feeling comforted when she saw the compassion there. Taking a deep breath she said, 'There isn't much to tell. You know it all, thanks to Fern. All my great talk of becoming an actress was empty. Last term the principal took me aside and told me – very kindly – that I just didn't have enough talent and that I would be better off setting my sights on a different career.'

'I see,' said Janet solemnly. 'That must have been shattering. But, Rachel, you should have been straight with us from the start. We would have understood.'

'I know, but I couldn't bring myself to accept it,' sighed Rachel. 'That's why I put on that stupid, conceited, stuck-up act when I first came here. Because I still desperately wanted to believe that I could be an actress. I just couldn't come to terms with the fact that I had failed and let my parents down.'

'Were they terribly disappointed?' asked Janet gently.

'They've been marvellous,' answered Rachel. 'They've told me that anything I want to do is fine by them, and they'll give me all the support they can.'

'Well, you're very lucky to have a mother and father like that,' said Janet warmly. 'And I suppose it's better for you to know the truth sooner rather than later.'

Rachel gave her an impatient look and sniffed. 'Oh, I couldn't expect you to understand! The theatre is in my blood! I've grown up with it as a big part of my life and I always expected my future to lie there.'

'Perhaps it still does,' said Janet thoughtfully. 'You just need to approach it from a different angle.'

'Whatever do you mean?' asked Rachel, curious in spite of herself.

'Rachel, you have *enormous* talent,' Janet told her earnestly. 'Not as an actress, but as a writer. This play you've written for the third is just brilliant – and you're not half bad as a director either. If you concentrate on those things, I really think you could have a big future in the theatre.'

Rachel stared at the girl for a moment, then gasped, 'Janet, do you really think so?'

'I *know* so!' laughed Janet. 'But don't take my word for it – ask Miss Adams. I overheard her talking to the head after she had looked in on our rehearsal the other day.'

'Yes?' prompted Rachel, eagerly. 'What did she say?'

But Janet shook her head and grinned. 'I'm not going to tell you, my girl, because I don't want you getting swollen headed! All I will say is that she shares my opinion.'

Rachel gave a shaky laugh. 'I can't quite believe this! Do you know, for the first time since leaving the academy I feel that my future isn't looking quite so bleak. Thanks, Janet.'

Janet grinned. 'Glad to have been of help. Now, how about coming back to rehearsal. Hey, won't your parents be thrilled when they come to see our play and find out that it's been written by you?'

'Yes, but . . .' Rachel bit her lip. 'Janet, I can't face everyone just yet. Fern . . .'

'Fern has gone,' said Janet, her face hardening. 'Everyone is absolutely disgusted with her and told her so in no uncertain terms.'

'Honestly? Even Alison?'

'*Especially* Alison!' Janet assured her. 'You have a very loyal friend there. Now listen, Rachel, I've been thinking. You have much more flair for directing than Carlotta so, if it's all right with you, I'm going to suggest that she lets you take over completely.'

'Oh, but I couldn't push Carlotta out like that!' exclaimed Rachel. 'It just wouldn't be fair.'

'To be honest, I don't think Carlotta will mind,' said Janet. 'It will give her more time to spend riding, which is all she really seems interested in.'

'But what about you?' asked Rachel, looking at Janet curiously. 'You only lost out to Carlotta as director by one vote, remember. If anyone takes over it should be you.'

'I wouldn't do nearly as good a job as you, and I see that now,' said Janet with her usual frankness. 'Well, Rachel? What do you say?'

Rachel gave a laugh, a genuinely delighted one this time. 'I really would love to do it,' she said. 'But only if Carlotta agrees.'

'Good,' said Janet. 'I'll speak to her about it as soon as she gets back.'

What a pity that Janet didn't use the same tact in dealing with Carlotta as she had with Rachel! When Carlotta returned, she said to her, 'Could I have a quick word with you in the common-room?'

'So long as it *is* quick,' answered Carlotta. 'I'm starving!'

The common-room was empty when the two girls entered, most of the third form having gone in to tea.

'Well, you certainly missed some excitement this afternoon,' began Janet, and quickly explained about the quarrel between Fern and Rachel.

Carlotta listened, astonished, and exclaimed at the end, 'Well! What a spiteful creature Fern is! And poor Rachel! Is she all right?'

'She is now,' said Janet, and repeated the conversation she had had with Rachel.

'Well, Janet, I think you gave her some very sound advice,' said Carlotta sincerely. 'Good for you!'

'Thanks,' said Janet. 'Look, you don't mind us holding a spur-of-the-moment rehearsal without you?'

'Of course not,' laughed Carlotta. 'I'm sure that Rachel stood in for me admirably.'

'She did,' said Janet, giving Carlotta a narrow look. 'More than admirably. The thing is, Carlotta, we've decided – Rachel and I – that it might be better if she took over from you as director.'

Carlotta felt dismayed and a little angry when she heard this. It was true that she had been thinking about giving Rachel the job. But it was one thing for her to make the decision – quite another to have it taken out of her hands like this. 'Well!' she exclaimed. 'You *have* been busy while my back has been turned. Have you been plotting anything else against me that I ought to know about?'

'Oh, Carlotta, don't be so melodramatic,' laughed Janet. 'No one's plotting against you! We just want what's best for the play. Surely you want the same?'

'Of course,' agreed Carlotta stiffly. 'But I'd like to have been consulted, rather than told what has already been decided. Really, Janet, anyone would think that *you* were head of the form!'

Janet flushed a little and said coldly, 'Well, you can't blame me if I sometimes forget that *you* are. You don't seem to care about anything except enjoying yourself over at Libby's house. You should have been the one to comfort Rachel this afternoon but, as you weren't here, I had to step in.'

'It's not true that I don't care about anything!' cried Carlotta, taken aback and feeling very angry. 'How was I to know that a quarrel would spring up this afternoon? I think you're being most unreasonable, Janet.'

Then it suddenly occurred to Carlotta that she would not be involved in the third's play at all. She hadn't bothered auditioning for any of the parts as she had assumed that she would have her hands full with directing. Now that was being taken away from her and she – head of the form – was to be completely left out of the play. 'I shouldn't be surprised if you planned this just to push me out,' she said wildly. 'You haven't backed me up in anything this term, and you've lost no opportunity to undermine me.'

'What nonsense!' cried Janet, though she couldn't help feeling a bit ashamed. She *hadn't* backed up Carlotta as she should have but somehow she hadn't been able to help herself, letting these horrible, jealous feelings take hold. 'You can take Fern's part,' she offered, in a conciliatory tone but Carlotta, in a fine temper now, brushed this aside, snapping, 'I thought *Rachel* was going to direct, not you! Surely that should be her decision – or do you intend to issue your orders through her?'

Janet's eyes glittered angrily, all thoughts of reconciliation forgotten, as she glared at Carlotta. And into this tense situation walked Rachel herself. She realized at once that she had interrupted a row and said awkwardly, 'Sorry. I was just looking for Alison.'

'I expect she's gone in to tea,' said Janet. 'Which is what I intend to do, instead of wasting my time here.' And, throwing one last glare at Carlotta, she left the room.

Carlotta reminded herself that she had no quarrel with Rachel, putting on a wide smile and saying brightly, 'So, you are to be our new director! Congratulations!'

'Well, it was really Janet's idea,' faltered Rachel, seeing straight through Carlotta's forced, jolly manner to the hurt beneath. 'I told her that I would only consider it if you didn't mind. But you mind terribly, don't you, Carlotta? That's why you and Janet were rowing. This is just what I was afraid would happen! I'll go to Janet at once and tell her that I intend to stand down.'

'You'll do nothing of the sort!' cried Carlotta, giving Rachel a clap on the shoulder, all the fight going out of her. 'Janet and I don't see eye to eye about very much these days, but we agree that you're the right girl for the job.'

'Well, if you're absolutely sure?' said Rachel, still a little uncertain.

'I am,' Carlotta assured her. 'By the way, I'm sorry about what happened with Fern today, and sorrier still that I wasn't here to deal with her! Don't worry, though, I shall see to it personally that she apologizes to you.'

Rachel gave a laugh. 'Actually, Fern has done me a favour although she didn't mean to. I feel much more comfortable now that my dark secret is out!'

'I'm glad,' said Carlotta sincerely. But she was determined that Fern would apologize. She might not be director of the play any more, but Carlotta was still head girl and meant to have her way over this!

An apology – and a birthday

Fern did apologize to Rachel. Not because of anything Carlotta said to her or because she felt that she had done anything wrong. Simply, she felt she had to make things right with Alison, who had treated her very coldly since the fateful rehearsal. As Pat said to her twin, 'At least something good has come out of this awful business and Alison sees Fern for what she really is.'

Isabel had nodded. 'Poor Alison. I think she was quite shocked to discover what a spiteful little cat Fern can be.'

Alison *had* been shocked. Silly and feather-headed she might be, but there was no spite in her nature, and she had been truly dismayed by Fern's behaviour.

On Monday morning Fern arrived at school early, waylaying Rachel as she came out of the dining-room after breakfast, and offering her a prettily worded apology.

Rachel accepted it graciously and several of the third formers, who were present, thawed towards Fern a little, feeling that at least she had been decent enough to try to put things right. Alison made things up with her because she really did enjoy having someone to chatter with about fashions and hair-dos, things that Rachel wasn't at all interested in. Yet, somehow, the two girls couldn't quite get back on their old footing. Something had gone out of their friendship, realized Alison sadly, and she didn't know whether it would ever come back again. Still, Alison had to give Fern full marks for trying. The girl really seemed determined to make everyone forget her cattiness, behaving most pleasantly to all the third formers – even Carlotta – over the next few days, and being particularly sweet to Rachel.

When Doris, who was quite broke, needed some money to have her tennis-racket mended, it was Fern who lent it to her. Then when Gladys went down with flu and had to be dropped from an important school tennis match, Fern was the first to visit her in the sickbay. Even when Rachel, who felt that she had to back up Janet, informed Fern rather awkwardly that Carlotta would now be taking over her role in the play, Fern took it well. The others expected sulks and tantrums, perhaps even tears, but Fern said warmly, and with a charming smile, 'I'm sure that Carlotta will be excellent in the part. Perhaps I could help out backstage on the night, with make-up and hairdressing? I'm quite good at that kind of thing, if I do say so myself.'

'Thanks, Fern,' said Rachel, surprised and pleased by how well the girl had taken the news. 'That will be a big help.'

'I must say, Fern really is behaving very well over all this,' said Bobby to Janet. 'Perhaps we've misjudged her a bit.'

Janet, who could be very shrewd and far-seeing,

wasn't so sure. 'There's just something about her I don't trust,' she said. 'Still, perhaps I'm wrong. Only time will tell!'

Soon it was the twins' birthday and the third got down to the thrilling business of planning the birthday feast.

'Let's get out the hamper that Mum gave us at half-term,' said Isabel. 'Then we can see exactly what we've got and what else we need to buy.'

The rest of the form gathered round in anticipation as the twins opened the large box.

'Wow! Look at all these goodies,' exclaimed Doris. 'I should think there's enough here for two midnight feasts!'

'Tinned prawns!' cried Janet ecstatically. 'My favourite.'

'And tuna, pineapple, fruit cake,' said Hilary. 'And don't these chocolates look delicious!'

'Our gran's sent us some money so that we can buy a lovely big birthday cake, too,' said Pat happily.

'Well, we others ought to contribute something,' said Bobby. 'It's only fair. Janet and I will buy the lemonade.'

'And I'll get some candles for the cake,' offered Mirabel.

One by one all the girls agreed to bring something for the feast and Rachel said, 'Now the only thing to decide is where and when.'

'When is easy,' said Isabel. 'Friday, because that's when our birthday is. Should we hold it in one of the dormitories?'

'The common-room would be better,' said Carlotta. 'Because it's further away from the mistresses' rooms and we shall be able to talk quite normally instead of whispering.'

'I can't tell you how much I'm looking forward to it,' said Libby, hugging herself. 'My party was fun, but a secret midnight affair with no grown-ups around will be too marvellous for words.'

'Have you and Fern worked out how you're going to get away?' asked Janet.

'It'll be as easy as pie,' said Fern confidently. 'Our room is at the other end of the landing from Aunt Polly and Uncle Tom's, and they both sleep like logs. We'll sneak down the stairs and out of the back door.'

'Yes, Mum and Dad sleep at the front of the house, so there's no fear of us waking them,' added Libby. 'We'll leave the door on the latch so that we can get back in again. My brother is awfully jealous about the feast, because nothing like this ever happens at his day school.'

'You surely haven't told your brother about it?' said Janet. 'I hope he can keep a secret. Mine is the most awful blabbermouth.'

'Will won't say a word,' Libby assured her. 'He's a good sport. Mind you, I may have to bribe him with a piece of birthday cake!'

'I dare say we can spare one,' laughed Pat. 'Only a few days to go! I can hardly wait!'

All of the girls found time to go into town over the next couple of days to buy everything that was needed for the feast. The twins hid all the goodies in a little cupboard near the common-room.

'It makes my mouth water just to look at all this marvellous food,' said Isabel. 'Oh, look, sausage rolls! How wonderful! I always say that a feast isn't a proper feast without sausage rolls.'

The day before the party, Fern came up to Pat carrying a large tin. 'Aunt Polly has been baking,' she explained. 'And she said that I could have some cakes for your party. Oh, I didn't tell her it was going to be a midnight one, of course. She thinks it will be a tea-time affair.'

'Great!' said Pat, removing the lid from the tin and looking at the little cakes with their pink and white icing. 'These look scrumptious. Thanks, Fern – and do say thank you to your aunt as well.'

'Of course,' said Fern pleasantly. 'I'm really looking forward to this feast, Pat.'

This was quite true. But she wasn't looking forward to it in quite the same way as the other third formers were. For Fern meant to spoil the feast! She had worked out a cunning plan and was confident that no one would ever suspect she had anything to do with it, especially as she had behaved so well lately. And if everything went just as she hoped, Carlotta would not be head girl for much longer. At the very least she was sure to lose her privileges and be confined to school for some time. That in itself would be something, thought Fern, for at least she wouldn't keep popping over to the Oaks and sucking up to her aunt and uncle, not to mention Will. Whatever happened, Fern was determined to emerge the victor from this little episode.

Two girls were absent from school on the morning of the feast. One was Carlotta, who awoke with a dreadful sore throat and felt weak and shaky. She managed to make her way down to breakfast, but Miss Adams took one look at her and packed her straight off to Matron.

'You've got this horrid summer flu that's been going around,' said Matron after she had examined Carlotta and taken her temperature. 'A dose of medicine and a few days in bed for you, my girl.'

'Oh, Matron, no!' wailed Carlotta in dismay.

But Matron was already opening a large bottle of medicine and pouring out a spoonful, insisting that the girl swallow it.

'Ugh!' Carlotta grimaced. 'Horrible!'

'It will do you the world of good,' said Matron briskly. 'Now, get into your night things and straight into bed with you. This flu bug is very nasty, but it normally only lasts for a couple of days or so. With luck you could be back at school by Monday.' Carlotta did not move, staring at Matron in horror.

'Matron, I can't possibly spend the weekend in bed!' she cried. 'I'm going riding with Libby tomorrow, and I so much wanted to . . .' The girl broke off, biting her lip. She had almost let slip about the twins' feast.

'So much wanted to what?' prompted Matron.

'Oh . . . have a swim this afternoon.'

'A swim!' cried Matron, throwing up her hands in horror. 'With the dreadful cold you've got? Absolutely out of the question. Now, do as you're told, Carlotta.'

The girl sighed and gave in, knowing that it was useless to argue with Matron once she had made her mind up.

But why did she have to fall ill today of all days? It really was the most rotten luck!

The other invalid was Fern – though, in her case, the illness was feigned, a part of her carefully thought-out plan to spoil the third's feast.

'Goodness, you do look rather hot and flushed!' exclaimed Mrs Francis. Little did she know that the colour in her niece's cheeks had been brought on by excitement rather than illness.

'I really do feel terribly poorly,' moaned Fern. Indeed the third form, who had been so scathing about her acting talent, would have been quite astonished by her performance now. Her aunt was completely taken in, saying worriedly, 'Perhaps I should telephone the doctor.'

'Oh, no, Aunt Polly!' said Fern hastily. 'I'm sure that if I just spend the day quietly in bed I shall be all right.'

'Very well, dear,' said Mrs Francis. 'Libby, you can explain to Miss Adams that your cousin is unwell.'

Libby nodded and, once her mother had left the room, whispered, 'Fern, you'll miss the feast tonight. What a shame!'

'I know,' groaned Fern, as though she was genuinely disappointed. 'But I really do feel dreadful.'

After Libby had gone to school, Fern settled back against the pillows and picked up a book. What a long, dull day it was going to be with no one to talk to. But it would all be worth it in the end!

The third formers felt very sorry for the two absentees

but, on this, the twins' birthday, nothing could dampen their spirits for long. The twins were delighted with the presents they received from their friends and found it very hard to concentrate on their lessons. Of course, all of the mistresses knew that it was their birthday and tried to make allowances, but even the kind-hearted Mam'zelle flew into a rage when she spoke to Isabel three times without getting any response. The girl was gazing dreamily out of the window thinking pleasant thoughts about the night's feast, and didn't even hear the French mistress. At last Mirabel nudged her and Isabel looked round, startled, to find Mam'zelle glaring down at her.

'Oh, I beg your pardon. Were you speaking to me, Mam'zelle?' she asked.

'Three times have I spoken to you! And three times have you ignored me. I will not have it, Isabel. It is not like you to be so fluffy headed!'

'You mean *woolly* headed, Mam'zelle,' Hilary corrected her with a grin.

'Fluffy, woolly, what difference does it make?' said Mam'zelle impatiently. 'I know what you are thinking about, Isabel, you bad girl!'

Isabel stared at the Frenchwoman in alarm. How could she possibly know anything about the midnight feast?

'Ah, yes,' went on Mam'zelle. 'You think of birthday presents and cards. Yes, and a fine big cake with candles on it. Well, *ma petite*, there is a time for such thoughts and that time is not during my lesson, you understand?'

Relieved that Mam'zelle hadn't guessed about the feast after all, Isabel said meekly, 'Yes, Mam'zelle.' The girl did not dare let her attention wander after that, though it was most difficult. *How* she wished that midnight would come!

15.

Midnight feast

At last midnight *did* come and Janet's little alarm clock, which she had placed beneath her pillow to muffle the noise, went off. She slipped out of bed and went round from one girl to another, whispering and shaking them gently.

'Midnight feast!'

'Come on, sleepyhead, it's time.'

'Bobby! Come on, Bobby, wake up!'

Then Pat crept into the dormitory next door and roused all the girls there. Soon they were making their way silently to the common-room. The twins, along with Bobby and Janet, fetched all the food from the cupboard, while Hilary slipped along to the side door where she was to wait for Libby and let her in. Fortunately she didn't have to wait very long and the two girls joined the others in the common-room.

'Ah, good, you made it!' said Pat to Libby.

'Yes, everyone was fast asleep when I left the house,' said Libby with a grin. 'And I'm starving, I can tell you. Mum thought I was sickening for something, too, when I refused seconds at tea today.'

'Well, let's tuck in,' said Isabel. 'Mirabel, start dishing

up, would you – and try not to make too many crumbs! Gladys, you can open that tin of tuna.'

Soon all the food was ready and the girls had the most marvellous feast!

'Mm, these prawns are delicious,' said Doris happily.

'So is this pineapple,' said Pat. 'Especially when you dip it in lemonade. Try it, Isabel.'

'What a pity that Carlotta and Fern are missing all the fun,' sighed Libby.

'Yes, it's tough luck on them,' said Isabel. 'Pat and I went to see Carlotta for a few minutes this afternoon and she was really down in the dumps. We promised to save her a slice of birthday cake, though, and that cheered her up a bit. We'll give you some to take back to Fern as well.'

'It's a good job that you bought such an enormous one,' said Alison, looking at the huge confection, covered in yellow icing and sugar roses. 'Don't forget that you've promised Will a slice too. Rachel, pour out some more lemonade and we'll drink a toast while the twins cut the cake.'

So the candles were lit and the twins blew them out and cut big slices of cake, while the form drank their health in lemonade.

'Happy birthday, twins!'

'And many more of them!'

While the third formers enjoyed their feast, Fern was out of bed too. Tiptoeing softly along the landing, she listened outside the door of her aunt and uncle's room for a moment. To her satisfaction, the only sound that came to her was a gentle snore from Uncle Tom. All was quiet in Will's room too, and Fern padded softly down the stairs. A pang of conscience smote her when she reached the sitting-room. It really was a shame that Libby and Alison had to be involved in this and would get into trouble as well. But her dislike and jealousy of Carlotta had reached the stage where she just had to do something about it and, if other people got hurt along the way, it was just too bad. Anyway, she would find a way of making it up to Libby and Alison somehow.

Fern didn't know, of course, that Carlotta was in the sickbay and wasn't even at the feast. If only she had known, what a lot of trouble she would have saved the third formers – and herself! Going to the telephone, she picked up the receiver and dialled a number.

Miss Theobald was away that evening and it was Mam'zelle, who often sat up late, who heard the telephone ringing in the head's study. '*Tiens*!' she exclaimed, startled. 'Who can be telephoning at this late hour?' She went into the study and lifted the receiver, saying sharply, ''Allo?'

'Miss Theobald?' came a deep, muffled voice from the other end of the line.

'Miss Theobald is not here,' said Mam'zelle. 'Can I give her a message?'

Fern recognized the French mistress's voice and grinned to herself. This was even better! Mam'zelle had a hot temper and was very strict indeed about the girls getting a good night's sleep and remaining in bed after lights out. This really spelt trouble for Carlotta!

'I thought you should know that the third form are having a feast in their common-room at this very minute,' said Fern in her disguised voice.

Mam'zelle gave a shocked gasp and demanded, 'Who are you? How do you know this?' But there was no reply, for Fern had gone, satisfied with what she had done.

Mam'zelle, meanwhile, screwed up her face in distaste, wondering who the cowardly, anonymous caller could have been. How she disliked such low, underhand people! But she also disliked this very English custom of midnight feasts. How could the girls be expected to do their best work if they were awake half the night? Ah, such a thing would never happen in her beloved France! Suddenly Mam'zelle remembered that it was the twins' birthday. She recalled, too, Isabel's inattention in class and the excitement that had seemed to be in the air that morning. Undoubtedly the caller had been telling the truth.

'*Méchantes filles*!' she said angrily under her breath before going out into the corridor. Ah, what a shock those wicked girls would get!

The feasters weren't the only ones in for a shock. For as Fern put the receiver down, a triumphant smile on her face, she heard a sound behind her and, turning sharply, came face to face with Will. It was obvious from the expression of disgust on his face that he had heard every word!

'You horrid little sneak!' he said scornfully. 'How could you do such a thing? To tell on your own cousin is just about the lowest thing I ever heard of.'

Fern turned paper white at the contempt in his tone and stammered, 'I never meant Libby any harm! I . . .'

'No, I know who you meant to harm, because I can see right through you,' hissed Will furiously. 'Carlotta! Because you're jealous of her. Well, you've gone too far this time, Fern!' He turned abruptly and walked to the door.

'Where are you going?' whispered Fern hoarsely.

'I'm going to ride to St Clare's and see if I can't get Libby out of this mess somehow,' he answered shortly. 'And you're going to have some explaining to do tomorrow morning. Just hope that Mum and Dad don't get to hear about this. Because, if they do, I'll see to it that they find out about your part in it too, you little sneak!'

Turning his back on his cousin, Will slipped silently out of the house and sped towards the stables. Thank goodness Carlotta had shown him how to ride bareback so that he didn't need to waste time saddling a horse! Within seconds he was on his way to St Clare's. He had no idea what he was going to do once he got there, but he just couldn't sit back and do nothing when his sister and Carlotta were in trouble.

It was fortunate for Will that Mam'zelle was delayed on her way to the common-room, which was at the other end of the building. She had walked half-way there when she suddenly remembered that she had left the light on in the head's study and, with an exclamation of annoyance, she retraced her steps. Then she encountered one of the school cats, who did not like being cooped up indoors on a warm night like this. His demands to be let out were loud enough to wake the entire school, so the irate French mistress had to go and open a window for him. All of this gained Will precious minutes.

Leaving his horse at the school gates, Will ran across the lawn. Libby had shown him her common-room at half-term, so he was able to go directly to the right window. The third formers were sitting around sucking chocolates and telling silly jokes that had them all in stitches, when a soft tapping noise came at the window. This stopped their laughter most effectively, Alison clutching at Rachel in terror, while Gladys jumped so violently that she spilt lemonade on her nightie.

'What was that?' asked Isabel, looking scared.

The tapping came again and the girls stared at one another, frightened.

'Perhaps it's a burglar,' suggested Doris in a shaking voice.

'Nonsense!' said the down-to-earth Bobby. 'Burglars don't knock!' And, getting to her feet, she pulled aside the curtain and exclaimed, 'Why, it's your brother, Libby!'

Astonished, Libby went across and pulled open the window. 'Will, what's wrong? Oh, don't say that Mum and Dad have discovered I'm missing!'

Will shook his head and said hastily, 'You have to come with me now, Libby. One of your mistresses knows that there's a feast and she's on her way here.'

There was a collective gasp of horror, voices demanding, 'How could anyone have found out?' And, 'How do you know all this, Will?'

'No time to explain,' he said hastily. 'Libby can tell you everything tomorrow. Come on, sis, out through the window!'

'No,' said Libby stubbornly. 'I've joined in the feast, so if we are to be caught I shall share in the punishment.'

Just then the girls heard the unmistakable sound of footsteps along the corridor – the kind of footsteps made by large, flat shoes. Mam'zelle!

'Libby, this is no time for heroism,' hissed Janet, almost pushing the girl out of the window. 'Any punishment we get will be ten times worse if you're found here as well! For Heaven's sake, go!'

Seeing the sense of this, Libby scrambled hastily on to the window-ledge, jumping down on to the grass just as the door burst open and Mam'zelle stormed in. The brother and sister could hear her scolding angrily as they ran across the grounds.

'Phew, I wouldn't like to be in their shoes!' murmured Will. Then, suddenly, he stopped abruptly, pulling Libby to a halt. 'Carlotta!' he exclaimed. 'I forgot all about her. I didn't see her in the common-room. Where is she?'

'Oh, Carlotta's in the sickbay,' explained Libby. 'She was taken ill this morning, poor thing, and couldn't come to the feast.'

'Well, thank goodness for that!' said Will, beginning to walk on. 'So Fern's nasty little scheme backfired after all.'

'What!' cried Libby, clutching at her brother's arm. 'Do you mean to tell me that Fern was behind this?'

Her voice sounded very loud in the still night and Will

hissed, 'Sh, idiot! You'll bring that fierce French mistress of yours out here and I don't want that.'

'Then tell me,' demanded Libby, lowering her voice. 'Was it Fern?'

'Yes,' said Will, sounding unusually grave. 'She telephoned the school – anonymously, of course – and gave the game away. I heard her moving about, came downstairs to investigate and overhead the whole thing. And didn't I tell her what I thought of her!'

'The mean, deceitful little sneak!' hissed Libby, trembling with anger. 'Your ticking off will be nothing compared to what I intend to say to her when we get home!'

They had reached the gates by this time, and Will patted the horse's neck, saying, 'I wouldn't say anything to her tonight if I were you, otherwise it'll end in a full-scale row and we're likely to wake the parents. Save it for tomorrow. Now come on, climb up behind me and let's go home. I don't know about you, but all this excitement has tired me out.'

Libby felt too blazingly angry at that moment to be tired, her mind working furiously as she mounted the horse. How she was going to control herself and keep from flying at Fern tomorrow, she just didn't know!'

16.

A very angry third form

Mam'zelle was absolutely furious with the third formers, of course, giving them a really dreadful ticking off before escorting them back to their dormitories.

'You are all wicked girls!' she cried. 'Tomorrow you will clear up the common-room after breakfast, then you will go to Miss Theobald.'

'Yes, Mam'zelle,' answered the girls meekly as they got into bed feeling subdued. What a horrid ending to such a wonderful day.

'Now I go,' said Mam'zelle. 'And if I hear one sound from either of these dormitories tonight, you will all do one hour's extra French prep every evening next week.'

The girls would have loved to discuss the extraordinary events of the evening, but they knew Mam'zelle well enough to be certain that she would carry out her threat. Not one of them, even the daring Bobby, had the courage to utter a single word after she had gone.

Next morning, though, they had plenty to say as they tidied up the common-room, removing all traces of the feast. They felt extremely tired, and groaned as they went about their work.

'Thank goodness Libby managed to get away,' said

Hilary. 'If her parents had found out that she had sneaked out there would have been fireworks!'

'And Carlotta is in the clear, too,' remarked Pat. 'At least that's something to be thankful for.'

'Yes, but there are a couple of things that are very puzzling,' said Isabel. 'How did Mam'zelle find out about our feast? And how did Will know that *she* knew, and manage to get here in the nick of time? It's all most mysterious!'

'I daresay that Libby has found out what happened by now,' said Bobby. 'We'll just have to be patient until she comes over.'

At the Oaks, meanwhile, Fern had managed to avoid Libby so far. Last night she had pretended to be asleep when her cousin had returned from the feast, and this morning she had stayed close to her aunt. Now, though, Mr and Mrs Francis had gone out, and Fern could no longer put off the inevitable confrontation.

Libby wasted no time, waiting only until her parents' car had pulled away before going up to her cousin and pushing her roughly. 'What have you got to say for yourself, you horrid little sneak?'

'I'm sorry, Libby,' muttered Fern, hanging her head. 'I didn't mean *you* any harm.'

'No, you meant to harm Carlotta!' said Libby, her lip curling. 'Well, your miserable little plan failed, because Carlotta wasn't at the feast! She was in the sickbay!'

Fern felt sick too when she heard this. She was in disgrace with both of her cousins and it had all been for nothing!

'I can't understand you, Fern!' cried Libby. 'I was at the feast, your own cousin – not to mention Alison, who is supposed to be your friend! Yet you were willing to sacrifice both of us just so that you could get at Carlotta.'

Fern made no attempt to defend herself. There was really nothing she could say. She decided that her best chance of getting round Libby was by being meek and apologetic. Her eyes downcast, she said in a subdued tone, 'You've every right to be angry with me. What will you do now?'

'I shan't do anything,' answered Libby, and a gleam of satisfaction shone in her cousin's eyes. Libby wasn't going to betray her to the others! But Fern had rejoiced too soon, for Libby went on coolly, 'Your punishment must be left to the other third formers – the ones who were caught out and punished themselves, thanks to your mean trick.'

'Libby, you surely don't mean to tell them that it was me who spoilt the feast!' cried Fern, her meek pose forgotten now. 'You can't! I'm your cousin and you ought to be loyal to me, not them!'

'Don't you dare talk to me about loyalty!' growled Libby, sounding so fierce that her cousin shrank back. 'You don't know the meaning of the word! I've thought long and hard about this and I don't see why I should cover up for you. The others have a right to know who was the cause of the trouble they are in, and sending you to Coventry for a time might make you stop and think.'

Looking at the determination in her cousin's face, Fern knew that it was no use trying to make Libby change her mind. But how would she face the others and stand their contempt?

Reading the girl's thoughts, Libby said harshly, 'You can think yourself lucky that it's the weekend and you don't have to face the girls for a couple of days. And don't think of trying to get out of going to school on Monday by pretending to be ill again, or I shall tell Mum everything, even if it means getting into trouble myself. Now I'm going across to St Clare's to find out what happened after Mam'zelle stopped the feast.'

The third formers, a subdued lot that afternoon after a stern talk from Miss Theobald, were pleased to see Libby, for they were longing to know what Will had had to say. They were gathered by the swimming-pool when the girl arrived, calling out, 'Hi, everyone! What happened? Is everyone OK?'

'Miss Theobald says we aren't allowed to leave the grounds for a fortnight,' said Doris mournfully. 'By which time she hopes we will have learnt to behave in a more "mature and responsible manner".'

'Oh, no, that's too bad!' exclaimed Libby. 'It was only thanks to Will that I wasn't caught too.'

'Yes, what happened about that, Libby?' asked Bobby curiously. 'How did Will know that Mam'zelle was going to stop the feast?'

Libby told her, and the third formers listened in gathering wrath.

'The nasty little sneak!'

'How low can you get? She deserves to be sent to Coventry for the rest of the term.'

'She deserves worse than that!' cried Janet. 'If I had her here now, I'd throw her in the swimming-pool!'

Janet felt particularly guilty about the feast going wrong because it was she who had goaded Carlotta into saying that the day girls could come. Libby had escaped being caught by a whisker and if Carlotta hadn't been taken ill, she would certainly have been held responsible. Janet still felt a little resentment towards Carlotta, but coming so close to disaster had made her realize that she didn't want the girl to lose her position because of anything she had done.

'Well, I'll leave the rest of you to discuss what's to be done with Fern,' said Libby. 'I'm going to pop along to the sickbay and see if Matron will let me spend some time with Carlotta.'

'I expect she needs a bit of cheering up,' said Isabel. 'Pat and I went along earlier to give her some birthday cake but she was asleep so we had to leave it with Matron. Do give her our love.'

Carlotta was, in fact, feeling very much better when Libby – after a stern warning from Matron not to stay too long or over-excite the patient – entered the sickbay. 'Oh, how marvellous to see someone other than Matron,' she sighed happily. 'I've been bored to tears all day and just dying to hear about the feast. Do sit down and tell me all about it, Libby. I'll bet it was fantastic. How I wish I had been there!'

'Well, as it turns out, it's a very good thing that you weren't,' said Libby drily and at once launched into the tale of the spoilt feast and Fern's part in it, Carlotta interrupting with many astonished questions and exclamations. By the end of the story, her dark eyes sparkled angrily and she said in a low, trembling voice, 'So! Fern wanted to hurt me so badly that she was prepared to get the entire form into a row. How she must hate me!'

Carlotta felt hurt as well as angry. This wasn't the first time that she had come up against spite and jealousy, but she had never met anyone who loathed her as intensely and bitterly as Fern did.

Seeing her flushed cheeks, Libby became alarmed and cried, 'I shouldn't have told you yet! What an idiot I am! Matron warned me not to excite you, so I promptly go and do just that. Oh, I could kick myself!'

Seeing that Libby was really worried, Carlotta forced herself to calm down and even managed a smile. 'Don't worry, Libby,' she said. 'I'm not about to have a relapse. In fact, I fully intend to be fit for school on Monday – fighting fit!'

Before she could say any more, Matron came in and shooed Libby away. She was thoughtful as she made her way back to the others. Libby had got to know Carlotta very well and, although she had heard tales of the girl's fiery temper, she had never before seen such a blaze of anger in her eyes. Fern was really going to get it hot on Monday!

But there was no time to brood on that now, for when she returned to the swimming-pool, Rachel called out,

'Right, everyone! Now that Libby's back, how about fitting in another rehearsal?'

The form was divided on this, some girls thinking it an excellent idea, while others called out, 'Oh, no! It's too hot!'

'Well, we could do with something to take our minds off all the nasty things that have been happening lately,' said Rachel with sound good sense. 'And we're going to have some spare time on our hands for the next fortnight as we can't go into town, so I vote we put it to good use. Come on!'

'You know, you're becoming quite a slave driver!' said Janet, half amused and half admiring Rachel's determination as the girls filed indoors.

'I'm a real dragon once I get going,' laughed Rachel. 'Before long you'll be begging Carlotta to come back.'

Of course, Rachel wasn't a slave driver or a dragon. The girls were only too keen to do their best for her, spurred on by her drive and enthusiasm. For a while, the girls were able to forget their woes – and their anger – as they threw themselves whole-heartedly into the rehearsal.

But several of the third formers discussed Fern's behaviour after prep in the common-room.

'She's going to have to be hauled over the coals about this,' said Pat. 'I only hope that Carlotta is back in class on Monday, then she can call a form meeting to decide how to deal with her.'

'I know how I would like to deal with her,' said Bobby menacingly. 'Horrid creature!'

'Yes, but we mustn't put ourselves in the wrong,' pointed out Isabel sensibly. 'Hey, Alison, I hope you're going to back us up on this, and not let Fern charm her way back into your good books!'

'No fear of that, Isabel,' said Alison with unusual firmness. 'She's no friend of mine! And I'm looking forward to seeing that she gets her come-uppance on Monday.'

17.

A hard time for Fern

Fern was afraid. She had delayed coming to school that morning until the last possible moment, sidling into the classroom seconds before Miss Adams. It was impossible for the third formers to say anything to her then, but they still made their feelings plain, with hard stares and scornful glances. Fern remembered the day of the auditions, when she had put the stable clock back to make Carlotta late. How she wished that she could *really* turn back time now, and never make that ill-fated telephone call.

At break-time Miss Adams was surprised when Fern, whom she considered spoilt and lazy, offered to stay in and help her tidy out the cupboard in the classroom. But when lunch-time came it was impossible for the girl to avoid the others any longer.

Carlotta, whom Matron had declared well enough to return to class, approached her in the courtyard and said coldly, 'The girls would like you to come to the common-room. There is something we would like to say to you.'

'I . . . I can't come,' stammered Fern. 'I'm busy.'

'No you're not!' cried Libby, coming up at that moment. 'You're just trying to wriggle out of facing us!

You just come along now and don't make us even more ashamed of you than we already are.'

Fern's heart sank. There was nothing for it but to go with the two girls. She felt even more miserable when they entered the common-room and she saw cold unfriendly faces all around her. She glanced at Alison, hoping for a flicker of sympathy, but Alison stared right through her.

Carlotta took the floor. A very angry Carlotta. But she had made up her mind to hold on to her temper and not stamp her foot or fly into a rage, as she would have done a few terms ago. She was head of the form and, as such, would handle this affair with the dignity her position demanded. Indeed, her demeanour surprised and very much impressed the others. 'You know why you are here, Fern,' she began, looking contemptuously at the girl. 'You played a very mean, spiteful trick on the girls the other night and must be punished for it.'

Although she felt frightened, Carlotta's scornful tone stung Fern and she retorted, 'I won't be punished by *you*! You weren't even at the feast, so this has nothing to do with you!'

'Oh, yes it does!' said Pat angrily. 'We all know that you planned the whole thing to get at Carlotta because you're jealous of her!'

'Jealous of *her*?' sneered Fern, with an incredulous laugh. 'What nonsense! Carlotta is nothing but a common, low-down . . .' But she was not allowed to continue, a chorus of angry voices shouting her down.

'You're the one who's low down! Rotten sneak!'

'Carlotta is worth a dozen of you!'

Carlotta herself gave a scornful laugh. Fern's insults meant nothing to her at all. 'You are being punished by the whole of the form, not just me,' she told the girl harshly. 'We've all talked about this and agreed what we have to do. As from now, you are in Coventry, Fern. None of us wishes to speak to you or have anything to do with you. We don't want you coming here at weekends or joining in any of our after-school activities. Whether we change our minds nearer the end of term depends upon how well you learn your lesson and whether or not you are truly sorry.'

That was the beginning of a horrid time for Fern. Never in her pampered life had she been treated like this. It was very hard to be met with silence and blank stares everywhere she went, just dreadful to have no one to chatter and laugh with. Things were just as bad at home, too, with both Libby and Will against her. In fact the only people who ever gave her a kind word were Aunt Polly and Uncle Tom. Once she bumped into Alison in the corridor. She was alone and Fern, desperate for a smile or a friendly word, approached her.

'Alison, I'm sorry!' she said, making her eyes wide and trying her best to sound sincere. 'I know it was a dreadful thing to do, and I just wish I could put things right between us.'

Carlotta and Rachel came round the corner, just in time to hear the end of this plea, and Alison turned to them, saying with a puzzled look, 'Did either of you two hear a noise just then?'

Rachel shook her head. 'Not a thing.'

'Me neither,' said Carlotta. 'Must have been the wind!'

And with that the three girls walked away, leaving Fern to stare after them, torn between despair and anger. Alison *would* have made it up with her, Fern was quite convinced, if only that horrible Carlotta and that awful Rachel hadn't turned up. It was *their* fault! In fact, they were to blame for everything bad that had happened to her since coming to this dreadful school! Foolish, jealous Fern couldn't see that she was her own worst enemy.

There was now just over a week left until the end of term and preparations for the play were in full swing. The girls knew their parts off by heart, the costumes were almost finished and handwritten invitations had been sent out to all the parents of the third formers. Then a series of mishaps occurred which put the future of the play in jeopardy.

First, Doris caught the same flu bug which had laid Carlotta low. Unfortunately, in her case, it led to a very bad throat infection which left her barely able to croak. Matron insisted that she rest her voice completely and did not attempt to speak for several days, which meant, of course, that she was unable to rehearse.

'This is a disaster!' wailed Rachel in despair. 'Doris is one of our stars and quite irreplaceable.'

'Well, if she takes Matron's advice and rests her voice, she may not need to be replaced,' pointed out Hilary with her customary common sense. 'Do try not to get too down in the dumps, Rachel, when there may not be any need.'

Isabel stood in for Doris during rehearsals, but she lacked Doris's comic touch and felt very second-best, as she said to her twin. Isabel, almost more than Rachel, hoped devoutly that Doris would be all right on the night.

Then another blow fell. The girls had gratefully accepted a generous offer from the second formers to paint some scenery for the play. The second did a marvellous job and when they had finished, Rachel said, 'Thank you all so much! You really have been a big help.'

'Just make sure that we get good seats on the night, Rachel,' laughed Grace, head of the second form. 'Now we really ought to put this somewhere safe to dry.'

'Stand it outside against the garden wall,' suggested Bobby. 'It will dry beautifully over night.'

Alas, in the early hours of the following morning there was an unexpected downpour, so that the scenery was quite ruined. The third formers were distraught.

'We'll never have time to paint it again,' groaned Pat.

'We have to find time!' said Rachel with determination, though inwardly she felt dismayed. She might have known that everything had been going too smoothly! And now it all seemed to be falling apart.

'I wonder what next?' said Mirabel. 'Things like this always seem to happen in threes.'

'Thanks for that optimistic thought, Mirabel,' said Janet drily.

'Oh, that's nonsense anyway,' said the down-to-earth

Pat. 'Surely nothing else terrible can happen?'

But, sadly, Mirabel was proved right. Something terrible did happen – and to her!

Mirabel, a very fine tennis player, was in a school match that weekend. The entire third form turned out to watch her, their cheers and applause filling the air every time she scored a point. Her opponent was an excellent player too, and the match a close one. In the final set, Mirabel's opponent made a magnificent serve, sending the ball soaring over her head. Mirabel, though, believed in fighting for every point, however hopeless it seemed, and leapt backwards, her racket stretched upwards. Suddenly she stumbled and fell awkwardly, letting out a cry of pain.

'Oh, no, I don't like the sound of that!' said Janet.

'She'll be all right,' said Rachel, with more confidence than she felt. 'Just a nasty twist, I expect.'

'Mirabel wouldn't squeal if she had just twisted her ankle,' said a grave Gladys, who knew her friend well. 'Something is badly wrong.'

Indeed it was. Mirabel had a very nasty sprain and would have to rest her foot completely for a couple of days. Even then it would be a while before she could put her weight on it completely. Naturally, everyone's first concern was for Mirabel, who really was in quite a lot of pain. But once the third formers were satisfied that no lasting damage had been done, their thoughts turned to the play.

'I've just had the most awful thought!' exclaimed Janet in the common-room that evening. 'Mirabel can't possibly play the part of Lord Derwent if she can't walk properly! It's such an active role.'

As Lady Dorinda's clumsy husband, Mirabel had to stumble around the stage, tripping over, bumping into furniture and knocking things down. Her ankle would never stand the strain. Seeing the look of despair on Rachel's face as the realization of this sank in, Alison said hastily, 'Perhaps you can rewrite Mirabel's scenes so that she can do them sitting down.'

'Impossible!' sighed Rachel, her expression bleak. 'She can't create all the chaos that Lord Derwent is supposed to by sitting in a chair throughout. It's almost as though there's a jinx on the play.'

Fern, although the others would not speak to her, kept her ears open and heard all about the so-called jinx. She also overheard Miss Adams say to Miss Walker, the art mistress, 'I feel so sorry for them! They have all worked terribly hard. But if one more thing goes wrong, I really think that will mean the end of the third's play.'

Fern thought about this long and hard. Empty headed she might be in many ways, but the girl could be cunning when she wanted something badly. And Fern wanted nothing more than to hurt Carlotta and Rachel. If she could spoil Rachel's play and make it look as though Carlotta was responsible, she would have a fine revenge on both of them. Suddenly everything became clear to Fern. She knew exactly what she had to do!

18.

Fern is foolish

Sunday was yet another gloriously sunny day, and the afternoon saw all the girls playing tennis or splashing about in the swimming-pool. It was an easy matter for Fern to slip unseen into the school. She went first to Carlotta's dormitory and, going to the girl's locker, removed a pair of pearl-handled embroidery scissors. Carlotta did not use these very often, for needlework was not one of her talents, but Fern – along with the rest of the form – knew that she treasured them because they had belonged to her mother.

The dainty scissors in her pocket, Fern slipped stealthily downstairs and made her way to the storeroom behind the hall where the costumes for the play were neatly hung up. There was the elegant dress Gladys was to wear as Lady Dorinda, a man's suit for Mirabel and Doris's policeman's uniform. A real feeling of spite welling up in her, Fern removed the scissors from her pocket and got to work, slitting seams, removing buttons and making long slashes in the material. Within a short time, the costumes were ruined. Surveying her handiwork gleefully, Fern dropped Carlotta's scissors on the floor and slipped away.

How she rejoiced as she made her way home, thinking

of what would happen when the third formers discovered their spoilt costumes and saw Carlotta's scissors nearby. With one blow she had hit back at both her enemies. Rachel would be devastated. And Carlotta would know what it was like to be shunned, for the others would certainly want no more to do with her. But Fern's euphoric mood was short lived. The first thing she saw on returning home were Libby, Will and Carlotta, chatting together companionably as they led their horses into the paddock. None of them appeared to have noticed her slip away, and not one of them glanced round now as she returned. Carlotta said something in her funny little up-and-down voice, which made the others shout with laughter, and Fern felt certain that the remark had been about her. Bitterness welled up in her as she watched the three mount. Carlotta cantered off at once, Will close behind as he called out, 'Show us that trick you did the other day, Carlotta! It was just great.' Even Fern had to admit, grudgingly, that Carlotta made a charming picture on horseback, her lightly tanned cheeks glowing and her eyes sparkling with pleasure. Fern remembered all the times over the years that Will had offered to teach her to ride but she had always refused. If only she had accepted his offer, she might be riding round the paddock now, and her cousin's words of praise would be for her, instead of that hateful Carlotta. The three riders turned their horses and trotted past the gate where Fern was standing. They did not look at her, or acknowledge her presence in any way.

Suddenly Fern felt quite unable to bear being ignored any longer. Anger boiled inside her, so fierce that it made her tremble, taking hold of her. She would *make* her cousins notice her – and Fern knew exactly the way to do it! Anger lending her courage, she marched to the stables and unbolted one of the doors. There stood the big black horse that Carlotta sometimes rode. And anything Carlotta could do, Fern could do. After all, the girl was no bigger or stronger than she. Hesitantly she reached out and stroked the horse's velvety nose, feeling reassured when he whinnied softly and gently nudged her shoulder.

Rocky had calmed down a great deal over the last few weeks and now loved to be petted by almost anyone. However there were still only two people he would allow on his back – Will or Carlotta. Fern, who had never taken any interest in the 'horse talk' her cousins were so fond of, didn't know this. Doubtfully she looked at the bewildering array of tack that hung from the stable wall and abandoned the idea of trying to saddle the horse. She simply didn't have the first idea how to go about it and would only waste time. She had seen Carlotta ride bareback dozens of times, so it couldn't be that difficult. Standing on an upturned bucket and clutching the horse's mane, Fern managed to hoist herself up on to the horse's back. Once there, she didn't feel quite so confident. The ground seemed an awfully long way down, and when Rocky made even the tiniest movement she felt that she would fall off. Rocky was really behaving in an unusually docile manner, and when Fern made the same clicking noise with her tongue that she had heard the others do, he walked forward obediently. That was when the girl realized that she had bitten off more than she could chew. She began to slide sideways and grabbed hard at the horse's mane, giving a frightened little squeal which Rocky didn't like at all! Suddenly he seemed to realize that the person on his back wasn't his beloved Carlotta or his adored Will, but a stranger, and his aim was to unseat her at all costs. He bucked sharply and Fern squealed again but hung on for dear life, her fingers firmly entwined in the horse's mane. That was when Rocky decided to show her who was boss and, tossing his black head with an air of contempt, cantered through the stable yard, past the paddock where the others were riding, and into an open field, Fern shrieking wildly all the time. She achieved her object, however – the others took notice, all right! Libby pulled her horse up sharply, her cheeks turning white.

'Oh, my goodness!' she gasped. 'Rocky's bolted with Fern. What on earth is she doing on his back anyway?'

'Never mind that now,' said Will grimly. 'The important thing is to get her off, the little idiot! Carlotta, come with me and we'll try to pull him up. Libby, you stay here. We may need you to call for an ambulance!'

Libby turned paler still at this, her eyes wide and staring, as Rocky became a black dot in the distance.

Carlotta looked worried too as she urged her mount forward and sent him leaping over the fence that divided the paddock from the field. 'Whatever possessed her to mount Rocky?' she cried over her shoulder to Will as he caught up.

'Oh, Fern wouldn't have known that he was dangerous,' answered Will. 'She knows nothing about the horses, and one is just like another to her.'

Neither of them questioned why Fern had found it necessary to take a horse at all, for they knew – she was absolutely desperate for attention.

'We're gaining on them!' called Carlotta. 'Come on, Silver! Oh, my word, that was close!'

This last remark came as Rocky stumbled and Fern was jolted so badly that she almost lost her grip. The shock of losing his footing seemed to confuse Rocky and he circled round, heading back towards the paddock. Carlotta seized the opportunity, turning Silver deftly and edging closer and closer until the two horses were almost neck and neck.

'Hello, Rocky,' she crooned softly.

The horse recognized her voice at once and slowed, turning his head and whinnying in pleasure. Fern, by this time, was a crumpled, sobbing heap, her knuckles white from the effort of holding on, and it was evident that she could not do so for much longer. Carlotta edged forward, so that she was almost standing in the stirrups, and leant across to pat Rocky's neck. Then she tugged gently on his mane, he stopped abruptly and Fern half fell and half slid to the ground.

It was unfortunate that, as this drama was taking place, Mr and Mrs Francis, who had been out, drove into the stable yard. Libby ran to them as soon as they got out of the car and told them quickly what had happened. Both of them were horrified, running to the gate and watching in terror as Fern landed on the ground. Mrs Francis did not realize that Carlotta had the situation under control and ran towards her niece.

'It's all right!' called Carlotta, who had dismounted and was bending to help Fern up. But Mrs Francis was so frantic with worry that she did not hear, moving forward and crying sharply, 'Fern! Oh, my goodness! Are you all right?'

Rocky, disliking the sudden noise and flurry of movement, reared up and flailed his hooves. One of them struck Carlotta on the back of the head and she keeled over, unconscious.

'Oh, no!' cried Libby, tears springing to her eyes. 'Carlotta!'

While these dramatic events were unfolding, the third formers were preparing to go in to tea at St Clare's.

'Half a minute!' said Rachel. 'I've just remembered that I promised to take Gladys's dress to Miss Stratton this afternoon for a small alteration. I'll just fetch it.'

Miss Stratton was the needlework mistress, whose help with the costumes had been quite invaluable.

'All right, but hurry up,' said Janet.

The others waited outside while Rachel went into the little storeroom. She was gone a long time and when she emerged she looked rather pale and upset.

'You've been ages!' complained Bobby. 'And you still haven't got Gladys's dress, goof! Hey, whatever's up? You look awfully strange.'

'Come with me,' said Rachel in a rather strangled voice. 'There's something I think all of you ought to see.'

Puzzled, the girls followed her, gasping in horror when they saw the ruined costumes.

'They're all spoilt!' cried Pat, shocked. 'Whatever can have happened to them?'

'Not what. Who?' said Hilary coming forward to examine them. 'They have been cut deliberately.'

'But who could have done such a dreadful thing?' gasped Isabel in dismay.

Janet's sharp eyes had spotted the scissors on the floor and she picked them up, holding them out in answer. Every girl recognized them at once.

'Carlotta's!' exclaimed Alison. 'No, I don't believe it! She would never do such a thing.'

'I agree,' said Pat stoutly. 'Why, what possible reason could she have?'

'Perhaps she felt more angry than she let on about being replaced as director,' suggested Janet coolly.

'No!' protested Isabel. 'When Carlotta feels angry she lets people know about it! This certainly isn't her work.'

'Well, they're certainly her scissors,' said Hilary uncomfortably. 'But everyone knows where she keeps them and any one of us could have slipped into the dormitory and taken them. I certainly wouldn't be prepared to accuse her without much stronger proof than this.'

Suddenly the door opened and Miss Theobald entered looking unusually grave. The girls at once fell silent and realized that they were late for tea. In fact, they had forgotten all about it thanks to this act of sabotage. But it seemed that Miss Theobald had not come to give them a telling off. She was here on a much more serious matter indeed.

19.

Bad news – and good news

'I am sorry to have to tell you all that there has been an accident at the Oaks, involving Carlotta and Fern,' said the head seriously.

The girls stared at her in silent horror for a moment, then everyone spoke at once.

'Are they all right?'

'What kind of accident?'

'Miss Theobald, Carlotta isn't badly hurt, is she? What happened?'

'I am afraid that I don't have any details at the moment,' said Miss Theobald. 'I am going to the hospital now, to meet Mr and Mrs Francis and find out what the situation is.'

The girls felt badly shaken when they heard this. Fern and Carlotta must be in a bad way if they were in hospital.

'Libby is in the common-room,' the head went on. 'Apparently she witnessed the accident and is, naturally, extremely shocked and upset. Her parents thought it best to leave her among friends and I have assured them that you will take good care of her.'

'You can rely on us, Miss Theobald,' said Hilary seriously. 'Come on, girls, let's go and cheer Libby up a bit.'

None of the girls felt at all like tea now, their appetites completely destroyed by this piece of shocking news. Libby was huddled on a sofa in the common-room, looking very pale and trembling from head to foot. At once, Pat went across and took her hand, saying kindly, 'Poor Libby! You really have had a shock.'

'Do you want to tell us what happened?' asked Isabel gently.

Her voice quivering, and close to tears at times, Libby told the whole story.

'Poor Carlotta!' exclaimed Gladys. 'She rescued Fern so bravely, only to be injured herself! How is Fern, by the way?'

Libby gave a bitter laugh. 'Absolutely fine, apart from a few bruises. She's gone to hospital in the car with my parents. Mum insisted that the doctor check her over, just to be on the safe side, but I think she's perfectly all right. It's Carlotta I'm worried about. She had to be taken by ambulance, and my brother Will went along with her. He said that it was so that she would see a familiar face if she came round on the journey, but I think he just wanted a ride in an ambulance!' Again Libby laughed, but it broke in the middle and she began to sob. 'Carlotta looked so white and still! Oh, I do hope that she'll be all right.'

'Of course she will,' said Pat, sounding more confident than she felt.

'This is just terrible!' said Rachel, looking very upset. 'And now I find it harder than ever to believe that Carlotta was to blame for destroying our costumes. A girl with enough courage and nerve to stop a runaway horse couldn't possibly be guilty of that kind of mean-spirited behaviour. Not that I've ever considered Carlotta mean spirited. Quite the reverse, in fact!'

'Whatever are you talking about?' asked Libby, distracted from her worries for a moment.

The third formers told her about the costumes, and the girl exclaimed hotly, 'Of course Carlotta wouldn't do such a thing! But I think I know who would!'

'Who?' asked Alison, her blue eyes wide.

'Isn't it obvious?' said Libby scornfully. 'The same person who has been behind all the upsets in the third form this term!'

'Fern!' cried everyone.

'Yes, Fern,' said Libby grimly. 'And now that I come to think of it, she disappeared for a while this afternoon. Quite long enough for her to come over here and carry out her spiteful little plan.'

'I expect it seemed a marvellous opportunity to get back at Carlotta and me,' said Rachel thoughtfully.

'What a despicable trick!' said Bobby. 'To make it look as though Carlotta was to blame! And how ironic that Carlotta should save Fern after she had done such a mean thing to her.'

'That girl needs a thorough shaking up!' said Mirabel.

'I think she's had one,' said Libby. 'She really was terribly shocked and upset when Carlotta was hurt. I just hope that she's learnt something from all this.'

'And I just hope that Miss Theobald has good news for us when she comes back,' said Pat.

The others echoed this heartily as they settled down for a long wait. Never had time passed so slowly as all the girls prayed silently for their friend. Suddenly the ruined costumes, even the play itself, didn't seem important. All that mattered was that Carlotta should get better.

It was after seven o'clock when Miss Theobald, accompanied by Libby's mother, returned to St Clare's, and it was obvious from their anxious expressions that the news was not good. The girls felt their hearts sinking.

'Carlotta has still not regained consciousness,' said Miss Theobald heavily. 'I have telephoned her father and he is on his way to the hospital now. I'm afraid all that we can do is wait.'

One or two of the girls looked close to tears and Mrs Francis said gently, 'She is in the best possible hands. We must all try to be strong. Come on now, Libby. You must be exhausted. Let's get you home.'

'Oh, Mum, no!' protested Libby. 'I can't! I just can't face Fern after what she's done!'

'Why, Libby!' cried her mother in astonishment. 'I know it was very naughty and thoughtless of Fern to ride Rocky, but she meant no harm.'

'It isn't only that, Mum,' said Libby. 'Fern isn't just thoughtless – she's spiteful and cunning. It was she who sneaked to Mam'zelle about the third's feast, and now she has deliberately ruined our costumes for the play and tried to blame it on Carlotta. I tell you, she's bad!'

The two grown-ups looked at one another in amazement. There was an awful lot here that needed looking into, but now was not the time.

'We would be happy to offer Libby a bed here for the night,' said the head to Mrs Francis. Lowering her voice, she added, 'Perhaps you could have a talk with Fern in the morning, when she has calmed down a little, and let me know the outcome?'

'Yes, of course,' said Libby's mother, looking and sounding extremely worried. She had always been aware of Fern's jealous streak, but the things that Libby had accused her of were really dreadful.

'You don't mind me staying, do you?' said Libby to the others, once the grown-ups had left. 'But the thought of sharing a room with Fern is just too much to bear.'

'Of course we don't mind!' said Hilary warmly. 'Oh, you don't have any night things! Never mind, I'll lend you a nightie.'

'And I've a spare toothbrush you can have,' put in Isabel.

'How about getting some fresh air before bedtime?' suggested Bobby. 'It might tire us out a bit – I think we're all going to find it hard to sleep with this on our minds.'

'Good idea,' said Mirabel, standing up carefully and trying to keep the weight off her injured ankle. 'But I'm afraid I'll have to lean on you, Gladys.'

One girl had taken the news of Carlotta's accident particularly badly. Janet. Unusually for her, she had remained silent while the others talked. She did not follow them outside now, but remained behind in the silent and deserted common-room, feeling as though the weight of the world was on her shoulders. Only now, with Carlotta desperately ill, did Janet realize just how fond of the girl she was, her resentment and bitterness of the last few weeks disappearing and leaving behind only remorse. Every bit as brave in her own way as Carlotta, Janet faced up honestly to the petty way she had been behaving. Even when the damaged costumes had been discovered, Janet had been unable to stop herself making a snide remark about Carlotta, although she had known, in her heart, that the girl was not capable of such spitefulness. No, Carlotta was not a spiteful person. Nor was she, Janet, as a rule. But envy had made her behave like one. It was a sobering and unpleasant thought.

A movement by the door caught her eye and she looked up to see Mam'zelle standing there.

'I was looking for Miss Adams and thought that she might be here,' said the French mistress. 'But I see it is not so.'

She looked closely at Janet and, seeing her bleak expression, came into the room, saying anxiously, 'What is the matter, *ma chère*? You look very – how is it? – down in the face.'

'You mean down in the mouth, Mam'zelle,' said Janet, with the ghost of her usual smile. 'Yes, I was just thinking about Carlotta.'

'Ah, yes!' The corners of Mam'zelle's mouth turned down, her sloe-black eyes became sombre. 'The poor Carlotta! But she will be all right. I feel it here!' She put a hand to her heart. 'What a dreadful end to her term as head girl. I hope that you will have a better time when it is your turn next term, *ma petite*!'

Janet stared at Mam'zelle and said, 'Why, whatever do you mean?'

Mam'zelle looked sheepish suddenly and cried, '*Oh, là là*! Now I have let the cat out of his sack and put him among the sparrows!'

'You mean, let the cat out of the bag and . . . oh, never mind, Mam'zelle. But what *do* you mean?'

Mam'zelle sighed and shrugged expressively. 'I may as well tell you now. But, please, Janet, it must be a secret between the two of us for now, *oui*?'

'*Oui*,' agreed Janet at once, bursting with curiosity.

Mam'zelle told her of the head's decision that the two girls take turns at being head girl. 'So you see,' she finished. 'You are to be head of the form next term.'

Janet listened with mixed feelings. At any other time she would have been thrilled by this news. But now, knowing that her resentment of Carlotta had been for nothing, she could not find it in herself to feel happy.

'We must keep up our chins,' declared Mam'zelle stoutly, patting Janet's cheek. 'And pray for the dear Carlotta. Ah, Miss Theobald told me all about Fern and her wickedness. To think that she is responsible for all this. Truly, jealousy is a terrible thing!'

Yes, jealousy *is* terrible, agreed Janet silently. And, in her own way, she was every bit as bad as Fern, for she had allowed it to eat away at her. But Janet was a strong character and had learnt a valuable lesson. Never again, she vowed, would she allow jealousy to take control of her. She would conquer it, and become a better person as a result. And once Carlotta was well, she would make things up to her in every way she could.

As Janet was thinking these thoughts, Bobby suddenly burst into the room, crying, 'Janet, there you are! Why didn't you come outside? Oh, excuse me, Mam'zelle! The thing is, we've just seen Miss Theobald and she's had the most marvellous news! The hospital telephoned her to say that Carlotta has come round and she's going to be all right. Isn't that wonderful?'

A lump suddenly formed in Janet's throat and she said huskily, 'I'll say! The best news in the world!'

20.

Things are sorted out

The third formers were all thrilled at the news of Carlotta's recovery, and found it hard to contain their high spirits the next day. Jennifer Mills, the games captain, was almost knocked off her feet by the twins as they ran helter-skelter along the corridor, and she called out sternly, 'Hey, you kids! Watch where you're going, can't you?'

'Sorry, Jenny,' apologized Pat meekly. 'We're just so delighted about Carlotta that we can't seem to keep still.'

'Yes, I heard about that,' said Jenny, her face softening. 'I'm pleased that everything's turned out all right. She's a good kid. Now buzz off, you two and, for Heaven's sake, *walk*!'

The mistresses were very pleased too, for Carlotta was popular with all of them.

'It's extremely good news,' agreed Miss Adams, after the class had spent the first five minutes of their geography lesson that afternoon discussing their friend's recovery. 'But now we really must get on with some work! The head is coming in later to speak to you all, so we will lose quite enough of our lesson as it is.'

'I wonder what Miss Theobald wants to speak to us about?' said Hilary curiously.

'No doubt we will find out in good time,' answered the mistress firmly. 'Now, open your books at page twenty-seven, please.'

The head came into the classroom half-way through the lesson and went across to say something in a low voice to Miss Adams, while the girls got politely to their feet.

'You may sit down,' Miss Theobald said. 'Well, girls, I have some news for you. Mrs Francis came to see me this morning and informed me that Fern has owned up to damaging your costumes, among other things.'

There were several angry murmurs at this and Miss Theobald held up her hand for silence.

'Mrs Francis also told me that she had received a letter from Fern's parents this morning, and that they are returning to England at the weekend. This means that she will be going to live with them, and both her aunt and I agreed that it would be in everyone's best interests if she did not return to St Clare's in the meantime. You have seen the last of her.'

The third formers were glad to hear it. Bobby muttered to Janet, 'Good riddance!'

'I am assured that she feels extremely remorseful about Carlotta's accident,' went on the head. 'We must hope that she will learn from this experience and never be quite so foolish again.'

The third weren't really interested in what happened to Fern, so long as they didn't have to put up with her any longer. They were pleased when Miss Theobald moved on to the subject of Carlotta.

'I visited her in hospital earlier,' she said. 'And I am pleased to report that she is very much better and some of you will be able to visit her tomorrow. Carlotta will be in hospital for several more days, as she needs to rest, but she asked me to tell you all that she is quite determined to be back at school in time for the play.' Miss Theobald's serene face looked grave all of a sudden. 'Naturally I did not tell her about this latest set-back and that the future of the play was looking doubtful, as I felt it would upset her too much.'

'Of course,' said Hilary. 'Thank you for telling us all this, Miss Theobald.'

'Well, I will leave you to get on with your lesson now,' said the head. 'Thank you, Miss Adams.'

'Girls!' cried Janet as the door closed behind Miss Theobald. 'We just *have* to make sure that the play goes ahead somehow! We owe it to Carlotta.'

'I don't see how,' said Isabel gloomily. 'We've no scenery, no costumes, Mirabel can barely walk and Doris can't speak!'

'Oh, yes I can!' piped up Doris, sounding a little husky. 'Matron gave me the all-clear earlier today.'

'Oh, that's wonderful!' exclaimed Pat. 'At least that's one thing we don't have to worry about.'

'Yes,' said Janet thoughtfully. 'Now, if only we can do something about the scenery and . . .'

'Ahem!' broke in Miss Adams, turning a stern look on the class. 'I am delighted that Doris has regained her voice. I am thrilled that you are all so committed to the play. And

I will be positively ecstatic if you can just show a *little* interest in your geography!' After that no one dared mention the play again, but Janet – although she bent her head studiously over her books – did not put it out of her mind. She had a most determined streak in her nature once she set her mind to something, and she intended to see that, one way or another, the third would perform their play.

When afternoon school was over, Rachel said dismally, 'We're meant to be having a rehearsal now, but I don't suppose there's much point.'

'The show must go on!' declared Janet. 'Isn't that what you theatrical folk say?'

'Yes,' laughed Rachel. 'But we're going to have our work cut out, with only a few days left to the end of term. We need a miracle!'

'Well, perhaps we'll have one,' said Janet cryptically. 'Go on with the rehearsal, Rachel, and I'll be back shortly.'

With that she sped away, leaving Rachel to stare after her in surprise. The rehearsal was not a great success at first, for most of the girls felt that they were wasting their time and went through their performances rather woodenly. Then Janet returned, grinning from ear to ear, and Isabel called out from the stage, 'Wow, what's happened to you? You look like a Cheshire cat!'

'Girls,' announced Janet triumphantly. 'The play is saved.'

'So you did work a miracle after all,' said Rachel. 'But how?'

The others demanded to know as well, climbing down

from the stage and crowding round Janet excitedly.

'Well,' she explained. 'I simply asked Miss Walker if it would be possible for all her classes to work on our scenery over the next few days. She's very fond of Carlotta, you know, and agreed at once. Then I took our costumes to Miss Stratton and she thinks that they can be patched up. She pointed out that the audience won't be able to see them close up, so it won't matter too much if the repairs are a bit rough and ready.'

'Fantastic!' cried Pat. 'Well done, Janet. You've really saved the day!'

'But there's one more thing,' said Rachel, frowning. 'And that's Mirabel's part. It's far too late to expect someone else to learn it, yet she can't possibly stand for all that time. I really don't see a way out.'

The solution came from an unexpected source. Alison, who had been listening thoughtfully, piped up, 'I've an idea. You know Matron keeps a couple of wheelchairs in the sickbay? Well, I'm sure she would let us borrow one, then Mirabel would be able to sit down during the play yet still move about the stage, bump into everything, knock tables over and . . .' she broke off suddenly, aware that everyone was staring at her, and turned red. 'Oh, well,' she mumbled. 'Perhaps it wasn't such a good idea, after all.'

'No, it's not a good idea,' said Rachel. 'It's a *brilliant* one! Alison, I could hug you! And next time anyone calls you a feather-head, they'll have me to answer to!'

'And the rest of us!' called out the others. 'Well done, Alison.'

'Come on, then!' Rachel clapped her hands together. 'Why are you all standing around here when you should be on stage? Pat, you're not in this scene, so would you be an angel and pop along to Matron for the wheelchair? The rest of you, places, please!'

The third formers all made time to visit Carlotta over the next three days, and Janet was one of the first. She took with her a huge bar of chocolate and a book she knew Carlotta wanted to read. 'How are you?' she asked gently.

'Oh, miles better,' said Carlotta, who certainly didn't look any the worse for her adventure. 'I seem to have spent most of this term in bed, what with the flu, and now this. I just can't wait to get back to school. Oh, are those for me? How lovely! Sit down and tell me all the news.'

Janet pulled up a chair and began to talk. As the play had been saved, she felt that it was all right to tell Carlotta about Fern and the costumes.

'So,' said Carlotta at last. 'Fern won't be returning to St Clare's. Well, I can't say that I'm sorry. Having so much jealousy directed at you is pretty horrible, you know.'

'I can imagine,' said Janet gravely. 'And you've had a double dose of it – from Fern and from me.'

'*You*, jealous of me?' said Carlotta incredulously. 'Is that the reason you've been so off-ish with me all term? But Janet, *why*?'

'Because you were made head girl,' answered Janet in a small voice. 'I had got it into my mind that I ought to be head of the form, and I felt absolutely *green* when you were chosen!'

'Oh, Janet, if only you had told me!' groaned Carlotta. 'I just couldn't imagine what I had done to offend you.'

'You hadn't done anything,' said Janet. 'It was my own stupid pig-headedness that was to blame. I feel pretty mean about it now, though, especially since Mam'zelle let it slip that I'm to be head girl next term.'

'Really?' exclaimed Carlotta. 'Oh, Janet, I am pleased for you. I'll back you up all the way, you can be sure.'

'I know that you will,' said Janet with unusual humility. 'And it's more than I deserve after the way I've behaved this term.'

'Oh, nonsense!' said Carlotta. 'Now what say we put all this behind us and start afresh next term. And my behaviour hasn't been all that it could be, you know. I've had a lot of time to think while I've been lying here, and I realize that I didn't face up to my responsibilities very well.' Carlotta gave a grimace. 'I got too wrapped up in my friendship with Libby and my horse riding and didn't take as much interest in the affairs of the third as I should have. Well, Libby is leaving at the end of term, so I shall be able to settle down and become a proper member of the form again.'

'Oh, yes, I'd forgotten that Libby was off to America!' exclaimed Janet. 'You'll miss her, won't you? Not to mention the horses!'

'Yes, though I shall still go to the stables and ride with Will from time to time,' answered Carlotta. 'But I shan't

153

be spending so much time over there next term. Instead I shall be with my *old* friends. I've learnt a lesson this term as well, Janet.'

21.

A marvellous play

Alison was feeling a little unhappy. Rachel was so busy with last-minute preparations for the play that she seemed to have very little time for her friend. There also seemed to be something guarded and off-hand in her manner these days, and Alison was puzzled and rather hurt by it.

The twins noticed that their cousin looked down in the dumps and wondered why, Pat asking, 'Anything wrong, Alison? You're going round looking like a wet weekend just lately.'

'Yes, do cheer up!' said Isabel. 'We've got such an exciting time ahead of us. The play tomorrow night, then school holidays! Lovely!'

Alison sighed. 'I just can't seem to work up much enthusiasm for anything at the moment. Rachel's being so cold and stand-offish and I can't think why.'

'Rachel's just very tied up with the play right now,' said Pat. 'She'll be her normal self once it's over.'

'That's right,' agreed Isabel. 'We're all feeling pretty nervous about it, wanting to get everything just right, and it must be a hundred times worse for Rachel because it's all in her hands, so to speak.'

Alison so much wanted to believe the twins, who both

had a great deal of common sense. Their cousin didn't have quite so much, but she did feel things deeply – and her feelings still kept on telling her that something wasn't right. But she had to put it to the back of her mind for now as there was so much going on.

The first thing was that Carlotta arrived back at school while the third formers were sitting down to lunch. She slipped in quietly and the first the girls knew of her presence was when they heard her laughing voice saying, 'I hope you've left some for me.'

Then what a hubbub there was, girls scrambling out of their seats to greet Carlotta noisily, even Miss Adams patted the girl on the shoulder and exclaimed that she was happy to see her back. Mam'zelle went a step further, bustling over from her table to envelop Carlotta in a great hug.

'Ah, *ma chère* Carlotta!' she cried, her dark eyes suspiciously moist. 'How good it is that you are well again!'

'Thanks, Mam'zelle,' said Carlotta with a grin. 'It's great to be back.'

'Just in time for dress rehearsal, too,' said Libby, moving up to make room for her friend. 'I hope you've been practising your lines while you've been in hospital, Carlotta.'

'The nurses were sick and tired of hearing me repeat it,' laughed Carlotta. 'And I can't wait for dress rehearsal.'

Dress rehearsal was, in fact, a disaster. Gladys, most unusually for her, was a bundle of nerves and couldn't stop shaking during the entire thing. Bobby tripped as she made her entrance, almost knocking over Pat and sending the others into fits of giggles so that the rehearsal was held up for five minutes while the third formers laughed themselves silly. Then Hilary seemed to forget her lines completely. Rachel, rather to the surprise of the others, wasn't at all put out by this and seemed quite cheerful.

'It's an old theatre superstition,' she explained. 'A good dress rehearsal means that the actual performance will be a disaster – and vice versa.'

'Well, if that's true, we ought to be a roaring success tomorrow night,' laughed Doris.

'We will be!' said Rachel confidently. 'I just know it.'

And Rachel was right! All seemed chaos backstage, with everyone milling about, getting changed and putting their make-up on. The noise was terrific!

'Gladys, do you *really* want to put blue greasepaint on your lips?' called Janet. 'I'm sure you'll find this red one much more suitable.'

'Oh, I'm so nervous I hardly know what I'm doing!' exclaimed Gladys, taking the stick from Janet.

'You'll be all right once the lights go down and you're centre stage,' said Mirabel. 'Then you'll just get right into character and forget everything else.'

'Miss Stratton has done a terrific job with these costumes,' said Doris, donning her policeman's tunic.

'Yes, and Miss Walker's classes have done wonders with the scenery,' said Hilary. 'Whatever would we have done without their help?'

'Looks as if we've got a full house,' said Bobby, peering through the curtains. 'I can see my parents – and yours, Alison. They're right at the front.'

'Oh!' wailed Alison nervously, dropping the pins with which she had been putting up her hair, and scattering them all over the floor. 'I wish you hadn't told me that, Bobby! Now I just *know* I shall fluff my lines. Oh, where did those hairpins go?'

'Here, let me help,' said Rachel, scooping up the pins and deftly coiling Alison's curly hair. The girl looked very pretty indeed in the part of a beautiful society lady.

'You'll do just fine,' said Rachel, giving her a clap on the shoulder. 'And your folks will be proud of you.'

Rachel sounded so much like her old, friendly self that Alison steeled herself to ask hesitantly, 'Rachel, I haven't done anything to upset you, have I? Only you've seemed so distant the last couple of days.'

'Oh, Alison, of course not!' cried Rachel. 'I know that I've been acting a bit strange, but it's nothing that you've done, honestly. Look, we'll have a chat after the play and I'll explain everything to you. Now, come on – it's time!'

Then the lights went down, the audience fell silent and the curtains swished back. They were on! Rachel stood in the wings, fingers crossed as she watched apprehensively. For the past hour she had bustled around backstage giving a reassuring word here and a piece of advice there to the nervous actors. And how confident she had sounded! None of the third form had realized that Rachel was far more nervous than any of them, for the play meant a great deal to her. She watched the audience as much as the cast, looking for signs of boredom or restlessness. She found none. Everyone was absolutely enthralled. The lower school held its breath at the dramatic moments, while parents, mistresses and girls absolutely roared at Doris's hilarious performance. Mam'zelle was in the front row and her shrieks of laughter tickled everyone almost as much as the antics on stage. Mirabel was very good too, crashing around in her wheelchair, which she had learnt to manoeuvre most skilfully, while Gladys was just wonderful. Rachel spotted her own parents, saw her mother's eyes widen at Gladys's polished performance, then watched her whisper something to her father. Sir Robert, his eyes fixed on the small figure on stage, nodded agreement. Rachel guessed that they were praising Gladys and, where a short while ago she would have felt intensely bitter and jealous, now she felt absolutely delighted for the girl. Well, that just showed how a fine school like St Clare's could change attitudes!

At last it was over and the audience clapped and cheered its thunderous approval. Mirabel got an extra-loud cheer when she took her bow, still in her wheelchair, while Doris and Gladys both had standing ovations. But the loudest applause of the evening was reserved for Rachel who, at the insistence of the third formers, walked hesitantly on to the stage, looking rather shy. She felt that she ought to make some kind of speech, but found suddenly that there was a big lump in her throat which made it quite impossible for her to say a word, especially when she looked towards her parents once more and saw their faces glowing with love and pride.

'Three cheers for Rachel!' called out Carlotta, and the

whole audience joined in, almost raising the roof. Then the cast tripped off stage to change and remove their make-up.

'What a great night this is!' said Bobby happily.

'And the best part is still to come,' said Hilary. 'The after-show party! I don't know why, but acting always gives me a tremendous appetite!'

The others heartily endorsed this, making haste to get back into their own clothes.

'Wait a bit, Alison,' said Rachel in a low voice as the others made their way to the dining-room, where supper for the third formers and their parents had been laid out. 'Let's have that talk before we join the party.'

'All right, Rachel,' agreed Alison, looking at the girl curiously. 'Something has happened, hasn't it?'

Rachel nodded. 'I've wanted to tell you for days, but I was afraid you would be upset. You see, I shan't be returning to St Clare's next term. I'm going back to my old drama school.'

'But, Rachel, I thought you had given up all idea of becoming an actress,' said Alison, torn between surprise and dismay.

'I have,' replied Rachel. 'But Mum found out that the school is starting a new course next term, specializing in writing, directing and the technical side of things. Oh, Alison, I'll miss you terribly, but I've thought things out and decided that this is what I really want to do.'

Alison said nothing for a few moments, looking down at the floor. She was very upset, for she had grown extremely fond of Rachel. But she was not quite so silly and selfish as she had once been, and she knew that her friend had to take this opportunity. Alison certainly wasn't going to spoil their last day together with tears, so she lifted her chin, smiled bravely and said honestly, 'I'll miss you, too, Rachel. But I'm really thrilled for you – and we can write, and perhaps meet up occasionally.'

'That would be great!' said Rachel, pleased at the way Alison had taken the news. 'In fact, Mum said I could ask you to come and stay with us for a week during the holidays. Would you like to?'

'Oh, of course!' exclaimed Alison, delighted. 'That will be just marvellous! Now let's go and find your parents so that I can thank them for the invitation myself. And they must be just dying to congratulate you on your play.'

My play! How good that sounded, thought Rachel. And if it wasn't for St Clare's, she might never have discovered this hidden talent in herself.

22.

Home for the holidays

'Rise and shine, sleepyheads!' called out Pat, as she awoke next morning. 'The holidays start here!'

One by one the girls sat up, excitement making them throw off their usual early-morning sluggishness as they realized that it was the end of term.

'And what a term it's been,' said Hilary.

'Yes, it's certainly had its ups and downs,' remarked Isabel. 'The ups, like our trick on Mam'zelle, and the play last night, were just brilliant.'

'But the downs have been dreadful,' said Pat with a grimace. 'There was all that horrid business with Fern, then the rift between Carlotta and Janet. Thank Heavens it's all sorted out now.'

'We shall miss Libby,' said Bobby. 'And Rachel. Funny how none of us was keen on her at first, except for Alison, of course, but she turned out to be a really good sort. It was quite a shock when she announced at the party last night that she wouldn't be back next term.'

'Well, I'm really pleased for her,' said Janet. 'And I hope that she makes a success of this new course. She certainly deserves to.'

The others agreed whole-heartedly with this.

'I must say, I thought Alison took the news very well,' said Isabel. 'This hasn't been an easy term for her. First she had to face up to the fact that Fern wasn't all that she seemed, and now she's to lose Rachel.'

'Poor Alison,' said Pat. 'Still, I think that Rachel inviting her home in the holidays softened the blow a little.'

'I wonder who your cousin will find to worship next term?' said Hilary drily.

'Don't even joke about it!' said Pat with a shudder. 'Oh, look at the time! We'd better get a move on. Our parents were going to a hotel in town after the play last night and they promised to get here early.'

'Mine too,' said Bobby, beginning to throw things frantically into a suitcase.

'Well, I don't think they'll be too pleased if you take this guy home with you,' chuckled Isabel, removing one of the school cats, which had sneaked unseen into the dormitory and lain down in Bobby's case for a snooze.

Extremely cross at being disturbed, he mewed grumpily at Isabel and went off in search of peace.

In the dormitory next door, Carlotta had finished packing when she heard her name being called from outside. Going to the open window she looked out. There on the lawn stood Libby and Will – with Rocky!

'Come down for a minute, Carlotta!' called Libby. 'We've come to say goodbye.'

Carlotta sped down the stairs and out through the front door, where she went straight up to Rocky, flinging her arms about his neck.

'Rocky wants to apologize for hurting you,' said Libby. 'I wasn't sure that you would want to see him, but Will said that you would.'

'Of course I do,' said Carlotta. 'What happened certainly wasn't his fault. Hey, Libby, you must be so excited about going to America after the holidays.'

'You bet! I shall be staying at a big ranch, you know, and helping out with the horses,' answered Libby.

'How marvellous!' exclaimed Carlotta. 'It's all going to be very different from St Clare's.'

'I'll miss being here, though,' said Libby seriously. 'I never expected to settle in so well – or to make such a good friend.'

'Here! You two aren't going to start howling, are you?' put in Will, looking alarmed. 'Because if you are, I'm off!'

'Of course we're not!' said Libby indignantly. 'Oh, I almost forgot! I have something here for you, Carlotta. It's from Fern. Her parents are coming to fetch her later, and Mum intends to have a serious talk with them.'

Carlotta took the piece of paper that Libby held out to her and unfolded it. This is what it said:

Dear Carlotta,
I am so pleased that you recovered from your dreadful accident, and am terribly sorry for the way I behaved towards you. I would not have been able to forgive myself if you hadn't got well again, and I just hope that you can forgive me. Libby told me that the play was a great success and I am glad of that as well. Please give Rachel my congratulations and tell her that I'm sorry for being so

horrible to her too. I see now that it was my stupid jealousy to blame, and I mean to work really hard at conquering it, because I really have learnt my lesson.

Best wishes,

Fern

'Well, perhaps there is hope for her, after all,' said Carlotta seriously.

'She's certainly behaved a lot more sensibly just lately,' said Libby. 'If only she can keep it up.'

'We'd better be off, sis,' said Will. 'We promised Mum that we wouldn't be long. Carlotta, you will still come over for a ride now and then next term, won't you?'

'Try and stop me!' answered Carlotta with a grin. 'And, Libby, I shall expect lots of postcards from America. Have a wonderful time! Goodbye! Goodbye, Will – and Rocky!'

The usual end-of-term bustle was much in evidence when Carlotta went back into the big entrance hall. Laughing, chattering girls were everywhere and mistresses did their best to keep some kind of order.

'Jane, *must* you yell like that?' called Miss Jenks, the second-form mistress, in exasperation. 'And, Harriet, if I trip over your night-case once more, I shall . . . oh, I don't know what I shall do!'

'Ah, the dear girls! They are so, so excited,' said Mam'zelle. 'Soon they will be with their beloved parents again.'

'And we shall have a little well-earned peace,' said Miss Jenks dryly.

A group of third formers descended the stairs at that moment and Rachel called out, 'Mam'zelle, let me give you my address. You will write, won't you?'

'*Certainement*! I go to visit my family in France tomorrow and will send many letters and postcards. To you, Rachel, and Doris, and Hilary – ah, yes, even one to you, Janet, though you do not deserve one! All the tricks and jokes you play on me, you bad girl!'

'Well, Janet shan't be playing tricks next term, Mam'zelle,' laughed Pat. 'She won't be able to fool around once she's head girl.'

'Very true,' said Mam'zelle, nodding. 'She must – how you say it? – mind her ABCs.'

'You mean her Ps and Qs, Mam'zelle,' said Bobby with her cheeky grin. 'Goodness, I shall have my work cut out next term.'

'How so?' asked the French mistress, puzzled.

'I shall have to play *twice* as many tricks to make up for Janet,' Bobby replied wickedly. 'I must put my thinking cap on during the holidays and come up with some really brilliant ones.'

'*Non*!' cried Mam'zelle. 'There will be positively no tricks next term, Bobby, or I give you double French prep every evening!' But there was a twinkle in her eye and the third formers laughed. Then there came the sound of a car pulling up outside and someone opened the big front door.

'Parents!' called Doris. 'Hey, twins, they're yours.'

Quickly Pat and Isabel picked up their cases, saying their last goodbyes.

'*Au revoir*, Mam'zelle!'

'Goodbye, Rachel! Remember us when you're famous, won't you?'

'Goodbye, everyone! See you next term. Goodbye!'

Then the twins walked out into the sunshine and Pat said happily, 'Holidays! At last!'

'Yes,' agreed Isabel. 'But do you know what will be just as good? Coming back to St Clare's next term.'

Contents

1.

Where's Pat?

Isabel O'Sullivan and her cousin Alison sat in the small station café drinking cups of tea and eating jammy buns. Both girls were waiting for the train that would take them back to St Clare's after the holidays.

'Mummy dropped us off here far too early,' complained Isabel, who was bored with the wait and Alison's company, and longing to see some of the other third formers.

'That was my fault,' said Alison sheepishly. 'I thought that the clock in your kitchen was slow. Sorry.'

Isabel swallowed the last of her tea then, glancing out of the window, brightened as she saw a group of girls in the familiar St Clare's uniform walk by. But they turned out to be top formers and sailed past without so much as a glance at the two younger girls, which made them feel very small indeed. Isabel sighed. 'I shall miss Pat terribly,' she said for about the fiftieth time.

'Well, you have plenty of other friends in the third form, and Pat will be back in a couple of weeks,' pointed out Alison with commendable and – for her – unusual common sense.

1

Isabel nodded, though she still felt miserable. She did have lots of friends at St Clare's – good friends. But it just wasn't the same as having her twin with her. Alison just didn't understand what it was like to share everything, even thoughts and feelings – to be so close to someone that they were almost a part of you. How she had hated leaving Pat this morning. And how Pat had hated being left behind!

'You will write, won't you?' her twin had said anxiously that morning. 'Every week. And tell me all the news.'

'Of course. But what a pity you won't be able to write back.' Isabel had tapped the plaster cast on Pat's right arm.

'Don't worry about that, Isabel,' Mr O'Sullivan had said. 'Pat can dictate her letters to me and I'll write them out for her. I shall be her secretary!'

That had made both girls laugh, but when the time came for them to part they had felt more like crying.

'Now we must be sensible about this,' Pat had said briskly, seeing Isabel's chin begin to tremble. 'We shall be together again very soon, after all. Besides, if we start crying that will set Alison off. You know how she loves a good blub!'

Alison had taken the teasing in good part, laughing and punching her cousin playfully on her good arm, so the twins had parted on this lighter note. But, for Isabel, some of the pleasure she always felt in going back to St Clare's was gone.

'I say, Isabel!' cried Alison suddenly. 'Isn't that Bobby and Janet over there?'

'Yes – and Hilary too!' said Isabel, forgetting her woes for a moment and jumping to her feet so hastily that she almost upset the table. 'Come on, Alison, let's go.'

The two girls dashed out on to the platform, calling out, 'Hi, Bobby, Janet! Hilary, wait for us!'

The little group of third formers turned round, their faces breaking into delighted smiles as they saw their friends.

'Hallo, Isabel. Hallo, Alison. Nice to see you again!'

'Had good hols?'

'Isn't it grand to be going back to school! I say, where's Pat?'

'She's broken her arm,' explained Isabel dismally. 'It's her right one, so Mummy decided there wasn't much point in her coming back to school until it's healed.'

'Golly, what rotten luck!' exclaimed Hilary. 'How on earth did she manage that?'

Isabel grinned. 'She took it into her head to pay a visit to the old tree-house that Daddy made for us when we were little. I warned her that the branch wouldn't bear her weight and I was right.'

'Ouch!' said Bobby. 'Poor Pat.'

'Most undignified behaviour for a third former,' said Janet, pretending to be shocked. 'Seriously, though, I'm terribly sorry. How long until she comes back?'

'Two or three weeks, the doctor thinks,' answered Isabel. 'So you others will have to put up with me hanging around you until then.'

'Well, I daresay we can put up with you if it's only for a short while,' said Bobby with her wicked grin. 'Oh look, here comes Jenny.'

The third formers turned to see Jennifer Mills of the sixth coming towards them, a pleasant smile on her kindly face.

'Hallo, you lot,' she greeted them cheerily. 'I expect you've all heard that I'm to be head girl this term as well as games captain. So if you have any worries or problems I'm always on hand to help.'

'Thanks, Jenny,' said the third formers rather shyly. They all looked up to her enormously. Yet, as Hilary said, when the older girl had moved away, 'There's something so lovely and warm about Jenny, even though she's so sensible and dignified. You really feel as if you could tell her your problems and she would listen and take an interest.'

The others agreed, then Janet said, 'Now there's someone I wouldn't like to share my troubles with – Margaret Winters.'

The others looked round as another sixth former approached. Margaret was a remarkably good-looking girl, with straight dark hair cut in a dramatic bob, unusual violet-coloured eyes and high cheekbones that gave her a rather exotic appearance. She also looked extremely haughty and it seemed as though she would pass by the third formers without a word. Then her glance fell on Alison and she saw the way the girl was staring up at her, eyes wide with admiration. Margaret liked admiration. She bestowed a dazzling smile on the girl, said 'Hallo, Alison' and favoured the others with a brief nod before passing on.

'My word, Alison, you're honoured!' exclaimed Hilary. 'Fancy Margaret, of all people, speaking to a mere third former.'

Alison said nothing, staring raptly at Margaret's retreating figure.

Bobby nudged Isabel and said slyly, 'Looks as if your cousin has found someone else to worship. Alison, don't say you're going to lose your silly heart to Margaret Winters.'

Alison's habit of idolising the most unsuitable people was a standing joke among the third formers and the girl turned red, saying defensively, 'Nothing of the sort. Though I admire her tremendously, of course. She's so attractive and has such poise and self confidence!'

'Yes, it's just a pity her character doesn't match up to her looks,' said Janet dryly.

'That's a terrible thing to say!' cried Alison. 'I'm sure I don't know what you've all got against her.'

'She's sly,' said Hilary. 'And spiteful. Last term she made one of the first formers learn a great long speech of Shakespeare's and recite it to her, simply for cheeking her a little bit.'

'Quite right too!' said Alison indignantly. 'Some of those kids are far too full of themselves and they need to learn a little respect for the top formers.'

'Don't waste your time,' murmured Isabel, as Hilary opened her mouth to say something else. 'You know what Alison's like once she's decided that someone's worthy of her adoration. The more you try to put her off Margaret, the more she will stick up for her!'

'I suppose you're right,' said Hilary with a rueful grin. 'I say, isn't that our train along there? May as well find ourselves good seats before the crush starts. Come along everyone!'

The girls hurried along the platform, then Janet suddenly tapped Bobby's shoulder and said, 'I wonder what's going on over there? Looks like some kind of row.'

The third formers turned their heads and saw two new girls standing facing one another. Both had their hands on their hips and, judging from the angry scowls on their faces, were exchanging heated words, while their embarrassed parents tried to calm them down.

'Friendly looking pair,' said Bobby wryly. 'I suppose they must be sisters, although they don't look much alike.'

Indeed they didn't. One girl was fair and slightly plump, while the other was dark and slim.

Suddenly Miss Jenks, the second-form mistress, bustled across and said something to the girls' parents. The sisters themselves immediately fell silent, quite awed by her authoritative tone and air of dignity.

'Helen, you come with me and I'll introduce you to some of the second form,' said Miss Jenks to the fair girl. Then she glanced across and spotted Janet, beckoning her over. 'Janet, this is Amanda Wilkes, who is to be in your form this term,' she said, placing a hand on the dark girl's shoulder. 'Take her under your wing for a bit, would you?'

'Of course, Miss Jenks,' answered Janet proudly. She was to be head of the form this term, and making the new girls feel welcome was one of her duties. She waited patiently while the two girls said goodbye to their parents, then Miss Jenks led Helen away and Janet took Amanda's arm in a friendly way, saying, 'It looks as if the others have boarded the train. Let's join them and I'll introduce you to everyone.'

The third formers looked up with interest when Janet came into their carriage with the new girl. She looked a little nervous, and no wonder, thought Isabel, giving her a friendly smile. It must be quite an ordeal starting at a new school where the others had all known one another for ages.

'Everyone, this is Amanda Wilkes,' said Janet. 'Amanda, meet Isabel, Alison, Hilary and Bobby.'

'Nice to meet you, Amanda,' said Hilary. 'Is this your first time at boarding school?'

'Yes, and I've been looking forward to coming to St Clare's so much,' replied the girl. 'I just wish Helen didn't have to tag along and spoil everything for me.'

The girls were rather shocked at this. What a terrible thing to say about one's own sister. Isabel couldn't imagine ever feeling like that about Pat and said, 'I should have thought it would help you settle in, having your sister with you.'

'Helen isn't my sister!' said Amanda, obviously horrified at the very thought. 'We aren't related at all really.'

'Oh,' said Bobby. 'When we saw you both together with the two grown-ups, we just assumed that you must be sisters.'

'She's my *step*sister,' explained Amanda. 'You see, my father died when I was a baby, and Helen was only little when her mother died –'

'Then your mother met Helen's father and the two of them hit it off,' said Janet.

'That's right,' said Amanda gloomily. 'They married a few months ago.'

'Well, you don't sound awfully thrilled about it!' said Alison. 'Don't you get on with your stepfather?'

'Oh yes, he's a dear,' said Amanda. 'And Helen absolutely adores Mummy. It's just one another that we can't bear!' Suddenly the girl became silent and looked around, giving a self-conscious little laugh and turning red. 'Heavens, just listen to me! I've only known you for five minutes and here I am telling you my life story. You must think I'm simply dreadful!'

'Ah well, we're such kindly souls that few people can resist confiding in us,' said Bobby, making everyone laugh.

'And it's certainly broken the ice,' said Janet. 'You're one of us now, so you can tell us anything you please and know that we won't pass it on.'

'Gosh, thanks awfully!' exclaimed Amanda, turning pink with pleasure at being so readily accepted by these jolly, friendly girls. 'I must say, it is good to get it all off my chest. You see, my stepfather is very wealthy and he's spoilt Helen all her life, letting her have everything she wants. She's the most frightful little snob as well.'

'I shouldn't worry about that,' chuckled Isabel. 'She'll soon have her corners knocked off at St Clare's.'

'Yes, the second formers will sit on her all right,' said Hilary. 'You just wait, Amanda! In a few weeks' time she'll be a much nicer person.'

2.

An unusual schoolmate

The train girls switched to a coach once they arrived at the little station near St Clare's, and after a short journey their beloved school was in sight.

'Look, Amanda,' said Janet. 'If you look to the left you can just see St Clare's in the distance – that big white building.'

'Yes, I see!' cried Amanda excitedly. 'My word, it looks simply enormous.'

'That's what Pat and I thought when we first arrived,' said Isabel. 'But once you know your way around it doesn't seem quite so huge.'

Amanda's stepsister was sitting a couple of rows in front and, overhearing this, said to the second former beside her, 'Poor Amanda! She simply can't get used to living anywhere too big. Of course, she and her mother lived in the *tiniest* little cottage before they moved in with Daddy and me. I remember it took her simply ages to find her way around our house.'

Amanda turned red with fury, her brown eyes glittering as she opened her mouth to make an angry retort.

'Steady,' said Janet, laying a hand on her arm. 'If Helen knows that she's annoying you it will only make her worse. Leave it to her own form to put her in her place.'

Janet was right, for the next moment Grace, the second form's sensible head girl, said coolly, 'Come off your high horse, Helen. None of us are impressed by your big house or your father's wealth.'

Helen looked put out, but one look at Grace's stern little face was enough to warn her against saying any more.

'I told you,' said Janet. 'Just ignore her and she'll soon get bored with baiting you like this.'

Amanda nodded. How much easier it was to deal with Helen when she had people like Janet and Isabel to back her up and offer sound advice.

At last the coach turned into the long drive that led up to St Clare's, the girls' noses pressed up against the windows as they looked out. Isabel frowned. Normally on the first day of term there were girls wandering around simply everywhere. But today there was something different. A huge crowd was gathered on the lawn and there seemed to be some sort of commotion.

'I say, whatever is going on over there?' said Hilary.

'Let's find out,' replied Bobby, standing up and grabbing her night-case from the luggage rack.

The others followed suit and, as soon as the coach stopped, everyone scrambled out and ran to join the crowd gathered on the big lawn. In the middle of it stood Mam'zelle, the French mistress, wagging her hands towards the sky as she always did when agitated. And opposite her stood a small girl with a cap of shiny

11

red curls, a smattering of freckles and the merriest, naughtiest blue eyes the girls had ever seen. But it wasn't she who was the cause of the commotion. In her hand she held a lead and, at first, the third formers thought she had brought a dog to school with her. Then they edged to the front of the crowd and saw that the animal on the end of the lead wasn't a dog, but a small black-and-white goat.

Suddenly Janet spotted their fellow third formers, Carlotta Brown and Doris Elward, who had arrived by car some time earlier, and moved towards them. 'Carlotta! Doris!' she cried. 'What's going on and who on earth is that?'

'Begorrah, 'tis our new girl, Kitty Flaherty,' said Doris, in a fine imitation of an Irish accent, her humorous eyes twinkling. 'She's an absolute scream!'

Then Mam'zelle spoke, her voice shrill as she said, 'This is a school for young ladies, not a farm! And a farm is where this horrid, fierce animal belongs!'

'Bless you, Mam, McGinty is the gentlest creature you could wish to meet,' said Kitty Flaherty, in an accent exactly like the one Doris had adopted. 'Sure and he'll be no trouble. No trouble at all, Mam.'

Mam'zelle stared perplexedly at the girl before her. Why did she speak in this strange manner? And why did she keep calling her Mam?

Just then Jennifer Mills and her friend Barbara Thompson came over, along with Margaret Winters. Jenny and Barbara seemed much amused by the

12

situation, but Margaret was most disapproving. She walked right up to Kitty and, pointing at the goat with an expression of disgust, said, 'What is that?' Margaret was as cool and authoritative as any mistress, even Mam'zelle falling into subdued silence at her presence.

Kitty, however, did not seem at all worried. 'Why, 'tis a goat,' she replied, looking at Margaret in surprise. 'Did you not know? It's a few nature study lessons you need, I'm thinking.'

The listening girls roared with laughter, Janet clutching at Doris and gasping, 'Oh, she's simply priceless!'

Everyone waited for Margaret, not noted for her sweet temper, to explode, but she contented herself with a sharp, 'Don't be cheeky! I can see that it's a goat. What I want to know is, what is it doing on school premises?'

'Ah, yes!' put in Mam'zelle, recovering herself. 'That is what I, too, wish to know. A school is no place for goats! The good Miss Theobald will be most upset and angry when she hears of this.'

'But Miss Theobald knows all about McGinty,' said Kitty. 'Sure and I have her written permission to keep him at St Clare's, Mam.'

'And do not call me Mam!' cried Mamzelle, feeling that she was losing control of the situation. 'I am Mam'zelle, do you hear?'

At this point Miss Theobald herself, having been alerted by someone, arrived on the scene. The first day of term was always an extremely busy one for her, and she looked annoyed at being interrupted. 'What on earth is going on here?' she demanded. 'Goodness gracious, a goat! Would someone care to give me an explanation?'

Mam'zelle and Kitty both obliged at once, the Frenchwoman's exclamations of 'Tiens' and 'Mon dieu' mingling with the Irish girl's 'Begorrahs'. Miss Theobald clapped her hands over her ears and said sternly, 'Enough! I presume that you are Kitty Flaherty and that the goat belongs to you?'

'Indeed he does, Mam. But 'twas yourself wrote to Mother and gave permission for me to bring him to school,' said Kitty, her merry eyes earnest for a moment.

'But I did nothing of the sort,' said the head, looking puzzled. 'I am afraid, my dear, that there has been some kind of mix-up.'

'Did Mother not write and ask you if I might bring my pet goat to school with me?' asked Kitty, looking crestfallen.

'I don't recall any such letter,' replied Miss Theobald. 'One moment, please.'

Miss Theobald went off to her study, returning moments later with a sheet of paper in her hand. Looking rather dismayed, she said, 'This is the only letter I have received from your mother, Kitty. She asks if you might bring a black and white *coat* to school with you – or so I thought! I believed that she was making enquiries about the clothes you were allowed to bring to school, and replied that this would be all right for your leisure time.'

'Ah, that would be Mother's handwriting,' said Kitty

blithely. 'Sure and it's dreadful! You see, Mam, if you look closely you can just see a little tail on the g there.'

Then McGinty snatched the letter from the astonished Miss Theobald's fingers and, with a very droll expression on his face, began to eat it! The watching girls were in absolute fits of laughter. Tears streamed down Doris' cheeks, while Carlotta held her sides. Even Jenny and Barbara, the two dignified sixth formers, held their hands tightly across their mouths to stop themselves laughing out loud.

'You bad fellow, McGinty!' cried Kitty, though her eyes twinkled. 'What's to be done with you? I'm very sorry, Miss Theobald, but you can see that he won't cost much to feed, for he'll eat anything.'

Miss Theobald could also see that little Kitty Flaherty was going to be quite a handful! But there was something about the naughty, merry little girl that one just couldn't help liking. Hiding a smile, the head said, 'It appears that we have no choice but to accept McGinty as a member of St Clare's. You are responsible for him, Kitty, and if he causes any trouble I shall have to contact your parents and ask them to take him away. You are only to see him during break times and after school, and he is not to disrupt your lessons in any way. Now I suggest you go along to the gardener and he will find McGinty a home in the old stables.'

'Ah, bless you, Mam!' said Kitty, beaming at the head mistress. 'You'll not regret this, I promise you.'

'I hope not,' answered Miss Theobald, smiling back.

'And, Kitty, it is customary to address the mistresses by their names rather than as Mam.'

'Sure and I'll remember that, Mam,' Kitty said happily. 'Come on, McGinty, me boy, let's find you a home.'

Miss Theobald and Mam'zelle, who was still muttering disapprovingly, walked back to the school together and the crowd that had gathered around Kitty began to disperse, until only the third formers were left.

'Hallo there!' said Bobby with a grin. 'Well, you've certainly made a spectacular entrance.'

Kitty grinned back and Janet said, 'Let's help you get McGinty settled in. I'm Janet Robins, by the way, head of the third form. This is Amanda Wilkes, another new girl. Then we have Bobby Ellis, Hilary Wentworth, Isabel O'Sullivan and her cousin Alison. Doris and Carlotta you've already met, of course.'

'O'Sullivan,' repeated Kitty, looking at Isabel with interest. 'Would you be after having a bit of the Irish in you?'

'Yes, Alison's father and mine were both born in Ireland,' said Isabel with a smile. 'What part are you from, Kitty?'

'Ah, the most beautiful little village called Kilblarney,' sighed Kitty wistfully. ''Tis a little bit of heaven on earth. My parents have had to move to London for a little while, because Father – he's a writer, you see – needs to do some research for his latest book. And the big city wouldn't have suited young McGinty here at all, for he's a country boy. It wouldn't have suited me either, for that matter, so I'm afraid you're stuck with the pair of us for the next term.'

The girl's Irish lilt was most musical and quite fascinating to listen to, and Janet said, 'Well, we won't mind that at all. In fact, it's a pity you can't stay longer. I've a feeling we're going to have some fun with you, Kitty Flaherty!'

3.

The deputy head girl

The third formers all had to report to Matron and be allocated dormitories. They were rather surprised – and not too pleased – to find that, instead of having two dormitories between them, extra beds had been squeezed into one dormitory and they were all in together.

'I say, this is going to be a bit of a crush!' complained Hilary. 'And it means that none of us will be able to get away from Mirabel's snoring.'

Mirabel Unwin, who had just arrived with her quiet little friend, Gladys Hillman, pushed Hilary playfully. 'I wonder who's having the dorm next door?' she said. 'It certainly seems odd, cramming us all in here like sardines.'

It was Janet who found out the reason for this. While the others showed Kitty and Amanda round the school before tea, she, as head of the form, had to go and see Miss Theobald. She felt extremely nervous as she knocked on the door, a most unusual thing for the bold Janet. Normally she was daring enough for anything, but she was well aware of the honour of being head of the form, as well as the responsibilities it would bring.

Miss Theobald, however, put her completely at ease, smiling her most charming smile and inviting the girl to sit down.

'Well, Janet, this is a very important term for you,' she began. 'I feel confident that you will do your best to be a good head girl.'

'I certainly will, Miss Theobald,' said Janet, feeling very proud indeed.

'I am afraid that you will be coping in somewhat difficult circumstances this term,' the head went on. 'You will have already noticed that all the third formers are to be together in one dormitory instead of two?'

'Yes, and I'm afraid some of the girls aren't too pleased about it,' said Janet, with her usual honesty.

'I can understand that,' said Miss Theobald. 'But it is purely a temporary measure. You see, there is some building work taking place at the moment in the second form's quarters. Their dormitories and common-room are really far too small and are being extended. Obviously it is quite impossible for the girls to use those rooms while work is going on, so the only solution is for them to use one of the third-form dormitories. They will also be sharing your common-room for a while.'

Janet felt most dismayed at this. The second formers weren't a bad crowd on the whole, but the third certainly wouldn't want them sharing in any of their secrets.

'I realise that it's going to be rather cramped and uncomfortable for a while,' said Miss Theobald. 'But the builders have assured me that they will complete the work as soon as possible. In the meantime I can only ask you all to be patient and do your best to get along together.'

Janet responded with a polite 'Yes, Miss Theobald', but she wasn't looking forward to breaking the news to the others that they would have to share their common-room with a lot of noisy, unruly second formers!

The rest of the third form, meanwhile, had finished giving the new girls the 'Grand Tour', as Doris called it, and were pleased when the bell rang for tea.

'Good, I'm starving,' said Hilary. 'Hope it's something nice!'

'I've forgotten the way to the dining-room already,' said Amanda, looking rather forlorn. 'There's so much to remember, I don't think I'll ever find my way around.'

'I'll see to it that you don't get lost,' laughed Isabel, taking her arm. 'Actually I'm feeling at a bit of a loose end myself, without Pat here to turn to.'

'Oh yes, you mentioned someone called Pat earlier,' said Amanda. 'Who is she – your friend?'

'She's my twin,' answered Isabel. 'But she broke her arm and won't be back for a while. You simply can't imagine how queer it is being back at St Clare's without her, because Pat and I do absolutely everything together.'

Amanda was rather sorry to hear this, for she had taken a great liking to Isabel and had hoped that she might become her best friend.

Just then Bobby called out, 'I say, Kitty, where do you think you're going?'

Kitty, who had wandered off towards the big front door, turned and said, 'Why, to check on McGinty. The poor fellow's probably feeling a wee bit lonely on his own in the stables.'

'Well, do be quick or you'll get into a row for being late,' said Hilary. 'Here, Bobby, perhaps you had better go with her to make sure that she doesn't spend all night in the stables with McGinty.'

'Kitty's quite potty about that goat,' chuckled Doris as Bobby and the little Irish girl went outside. 'If the dorm wasn't so overcrowded I bet she'd ask Miss Theobald if he could sleep in there with her!'

McGinty seemed perfectly content where he was, however. Really, he was almost like a dog, thought Bobby, watching in amusement as he wagged his stumpy tail when his mistress approached. He allowed Bobby to pet him too, gently butting her hand and nibbling at the sleeve of her blazer.

'He's awfully sweet,' said Bobby, as she and Kitty walked back to the school. 'You're jolly lucky that Miss Theobald allowed him to stay.'

'Sure, Bobby, I'm always lucky!' said Kitty with an impish smile, her bright eyes twinkling merrily.

A moment later, though, it seemed as though Kitty's luck might have run out, for Margaret Winters was standing at the door of the dining-room. In her hand was a notebook, in which she was busily jotting down the names of all latecomers.

'You two are almost ten minutes late,' she said coldly

to Kitty and Bobby. 'I shall be giving out lines to anyone who is late more than once a week.'

'Sure and I thought that nice, fair girl I met earlier was head girl, not you,' said Kitty, meeting the bigger girl's cold, violet eyes with an innocent stare.

'I've already had to tick you off once today for being insolent,' snapped Margaret. 'Not a very good start for a new girl. And, for your information, Miss Theobald has just made me deputy head girl. Jennifer is very busy with her duties as Games Captain, so she needs someone to assist her.'

And didn't that gladden her spiteful, self-important nature, thought Bobby in dismay. The girl simply couldn't imagine what had made Miss Theobald pick Margaret, for she was everything a head girl shouldn't be, and would be sure to use her power wrongly. And Bobby was quite right, for at that moment Alison – who, as usual, had spent far too long doing her hair – came along and said breathlessly, 'I'm terribly sorry that I'm late, Margaret. I say, I've just heard about you being deputy head girl and I think it's simply marvellous.'

'Why, thank you, Alison,' said the top former, with her attractive smile. 'Go on in now, while there's still some food left.'

'She didn't write Alison's name in the book!' fumed Bobby, as she and Kitty made their way to their table. 'Talk about favouritism!'

'Sure and that one wants taking down a peg or two,' said Kitty, with a thoughtful gleam in her eye.

Strangely enough, Margaret was thinking exactly the same thing about the little Irish girl. She was still smarting over the way Kitty had cheeked her earlier, in front of the whole school, and was determined to get her own back. Little Miss Flaherty had better watch her step!

As Miss Adams, the third-form mistress, was not due back until late that evening, Mam'zelle was at the head of the table and she beamed round, saying happily, 'Ah, how good it is to see everyone back again, all of you refreshed after your break and ready to work hard – especially at your French.'

'If we manage to get any studying done,' said Janet ruefully, deciding that this was as good a time as any to break the bad news to the others. Quickly she explained to them about having to share their common-room with the second form, unsurprised at the outcry that followed. Amanda felt particularly upset, saying dismally, 'Blow! That means I shall have to spend my free time with Helen after all.'

'I daresay we shall get along with most of them all right though,' said Isabel. 'They're a pretty decent lot.'

'Yes, but some of them can be a bit rowdy,' pointed out Hilary.

'Well, we shall just have to sit on them good and hard,' said Janet firmly. 'After all, we are senior to them and it is our common-room.'

'This isn't much of a start to the term,' Doris said glumly. 'Crammed into one dormitory, having to share our common-room and, to top it all, Margaret Winters as deputy head girl.'

'Miss Theobald is usually such a good judge of character,' said Carlotta with a puzzled frown. 'I can't think what possessed her to choose Margaret.'

'Well, you can't deny that she has an air of authority,' sighed Bobby. 'Kitty and I have already fallen foul of her! And she puts on a very different manner for the mistresses from the one she uses with us small fry. They can't seem to see through her at all and think she's just too wonderful for words.'

'What is this you are talking about?' demanded Mam'zelle, who had only caught a few words and hated to be left out.

'Oh, we were just discussing Margaret Winters, Mam'zelle,' said Isabel.

'Ah yes, the dear Margaret,' said the Frenchwoman. 'What a fine deputy she will make. So just and fair!'

'See what I mean?' muttered Bobby under her breath. 'She's pulled the wool right over Mam'zelle's eyes.'

'I agree, Mamzelle,' said Alison raptly, glancing over at the sixth-form table, where Margaret was now seated. 'I think that Margaret will do a super job.'

'Trust Alison,' said Bobby scornfully. 'I did think she had learned some sense after all that business with Fern last term, but she still has to find someone to trot round after like a little dog.'

Fern had been a new girl the previous term, whom Alison had made friends with. But she had caused a lot of trouble for the third and left St Clare's under a cloud at the end of term.

Some of the girls had begun to yawn during tea and they were all glad when bedtime came, tired out after their long journeys and the excitement of the first day back at school. But, thanks to the cramped conditions, getting ready for bed proved to be quite a task!

'Hi, Mirabel, get your elbow out of my face!' protested Doris.

'Alison, those are *my* pyjamas you're putting on,' said Gladys, snatching them back. 'Yours are under the bed, for some reason!'

'Ow, that's my foot you're treading on, Doris!' cried Kitty. 'Sure and McGinty would feel quite at home in here, for it's like a farmyard!'

Isabel caught Amanda's eye and the two of them laughed.

'Settling in OK?' asked Isabel in her friendly way.

'Yes, everyone's been so kind to me,' said Amanda. 'I really think I'm going to like it here.'

'Good,' said Isabel, pleased at this praise of her beloved St Clare's. But she wasn't quite so pleased a few moments later, when Amanda took the bed next to hers, which she had been planning to save for Pat. It seemed mean and unfriendly, though, to ask the new girl to move, especially as she and Isabel had been getting on so well together. Oh well, Amanda seemed a reasonable girl, and no doubt she would agree to move when Pat came back.

'Goodnight, Isabel,' whispered Amanda.

'Goodnight,' Isabel whispered back.

'No more talking now,' came Janet's voice through the darkness. No one really felt like talking anyway, most of the girls falling asleep immediately.

Isabel, drifting pleasantly off, realised that, although her twin was still very much in her thoughts, she didn't feel at all gloomy now. How could she, when there was a whole new term to look forward to, and people like Kitty and Amanda to get to know? It was just impossible to be down in the dumps for long at St Clare's.

4.

Isabel makes a friend

There was so much to do that the first few days of term simply flew by. There were timetables to make, new books to give out and a hundred and one things. Amanda settled in well, though she seemed to find some of the lessons difficult and, while she worked hard, never got very good marks. She seemed to attach herself particularly to Isabel, and Isabel had mixed feelings about this. She liked Amanda enormously and it was very nice to have someone to talk to and share a joke with whilst her twin was away. Yet she couldn't help feeling that she was being disloyal to Pat.

'What nonsense!' scoffed Janet, when Isabel mentioned this to her. 'As if anyone could ever come between you and Pat. I'm sure she's delighted to think that you're not moping about without her. Besides, we've only been back a few days and you've already written to her twice, so she's hardly likely to take it into her head that you've forgotten her!'

So Isabel, reassured by Janet's common-sense words, was able to relax and enjoy her new friendship with Amanda.

Kitty, too, settled down in her own way.

'Although perhaps settled isn't the right word,' remarked Bobby, when she and some of the others were discussing the new girls one day. 'Kitty's so restless and mischievous that she seems positively *uns*ettled!'

The third had quickly taken the little Irish girl to their hearts, for she was a real character – warm-hearted, fun-loving and very funny in a completely natural way. Kitty didn't have a particular friend of her own, but she didn't seem to want or need one, mixing quite happily with all of the girls. She had absolutely no shyness in her nature and could chatter nineteen-to-the-dozen with almost anyone.

'No wonder Kitty doesn't have a special friend,' remarked Carlotta shrewdly. 'She would be just too much for one person! Her personality is so big that she needs to spread it around everyone.'

Most of the mistresses couldn't help liking Kitty either, though she drove them to distraction at times. As Miss Adams said, she could work well enough when she chose to – it was just a pity that she didn't choose to more often! The girl had a habit of staring out of the window, a dreamy and angelic expression on her face. But as Miss Adams had swiftly learned, the more angelic Kitty looked, the more mischief she was likely to get up to!

'Kitty!' the mistress would say sharply on these occasions. 'Have you listened to a single word that I have been saying?'

'I have and all, Mam,' Kitty would reply solemnly.

'Sure, me eyes might be out there in the garden, but me ears are in here all right.'

Then Miss Adams would shake her head in despair, while the rest of the form struggled to contain their giggles.

Mam'zelle – who as well as being the kindest-hearted mistress in the school was also the most hot-tempered – frequently became exasperated with Kitty too. The Irish girl would make no attempt at a French accent, and the language, spoken in her soft Irish brogue, sounded very funny indeed to the other third formers. Unfortunately, Mam'zelle did not agree with them.

'Ah, Keety! Never have I taught a girl as stubborn as you!' she would cry. 'The poor Doris, now she is slow, but at least she makes an effort. You, though, will not even try! You are as stubborn as that goat of yours!'

'Why, 'tis donkeys that are stubborn, Mam'zelle, not goats,' Kitty would reply, her eyes twinkling, and the Frenchwoman's wrath would descend on her auburn head.

'You'll drive Mam'zelle too far one day,' warned Doris, after a lesson which had almost reduced Mam'zelle to tears. 'Honestly, Kitty, I thought my French accent was bad, but you take the biscuit.'

Then the Irish girl astounded everyone by reciting a few lines of the French poem they had been learning, in rapid, perfectly accented French.

'Kitty, you fraud!' exclaimed Amanda. 'Your accent is the best in the class!'

'But why have you been pretending that you're no good at French all this time?' asked Carlotta, perplexed.

'Sure and I like to see old Mam'zelle fly into a paddy,' answered Kitty with a broad grin. 'It brightens up the lessons no end.'

'Well, you certainly brighten up life at St Clare's,' chuckled Bobby. 'I thought I was cheeky and don't care-ish but, my goodness, you can teach me a thing or two, Kitty!'

The person who came down hardest on Kitty was Margaret Winters. She would pull the girl up over the slightest misdemeanour, even something as trivial as running in the corridor, or having a crooked tie, and would dole out a punishment. The other third formers grew most indignant on Kitty's behalf.

'It's most unfair!' cried Hilary. 'She's doing exactly what a deputy head girl shouldn't – using her position to vent her own personal feelings of spite.'

'Never mind, Kitty old girl,' said Doris. 'I'll do half of those lines for you. My handwriting is a bit like yours – untidy!'

'Ah, you're a good friend, Doris,' said Kitty, handing the girl a sheet of paper.

'Margaret really ought to be reported to Jenny for this,' said Isabel. 'I'm sure she would put a stop to her persecuting poor Kitty.'

'Now, Isabel, don't you go worrying your head about me,' said Kitty, in her usual relaxed manner. She never seemed to get upset about anything, and the girls had yet to see her lose her temper. 'Telling tales isn't my way.'

There was a certain roguish look in Kitty's eye that made Gladys ask curiously, 'And just what is your way, Kitty?'

'Why, I'm thinking that if Margaret is going to punish me over these silly little things, then I may as well do something to really earn the punishment,' answered Kitty.

'Just what do you have in mind?' asked Mirabel, much amused.

'Nothing – yet,' replied the girl. 'But I'll come up with something, to be sure.'

With Kitty in the class the third was a very lively and exciting place to be that term. There was only one fly in the ointment – and that was the second formers. The girls really did find sharing a common-room with them very trying. They talked long into the night after lights-out too, and the sound came through the wall of the third form's dormitory, keeping them awake.

At last Janet lost her temper and got out of bed one night, going to the second-form dormitory and flinging open the door. The second formers fell silent at once, afraid that it was a mistress who stood there, and Janet snapped, 'Well, that's the quietest you've been all night! For goodness' sake, shut up and let us get some sleep! We third formers are tired, even if you lot aren't!'

Without giving the errant second formers a chance to speak up for themselves, Janet shut the door with a slam and went back to her own bed, hoping that her outburst would do the trick.

Sure enough, there wasn't another peep out of the second formers that night and the following morning, when Janet came out of the dormitory, she found Grace, their head girl, waiting for her.

'Sorry about last night, Janet,' said the girl, rather sheepishly. 'It won't happen again, I promise you.'

'Well, I'm glad to hear it,' said Janet frankly. 'I'm sorry that I had to blow up at you like that, but while we're all living together so closely it's important that we consider one another's wishes and feelings. Anyway, so long as it doesn't happen again we'll say no more about it.'

Isabel had a letter from Pat that morning, and she read parts of it out to the third formers at the breakfast table.

'She sends you all her love and says she can't wait to come back,' said Isabel. 'Kitty, she's absolutely longing to meet you – and McGinty, of course.'

'Tell her that we all miss her when you write back, won't you?' said Hilary.

'I will,' replied Isabel. 'I'll try and write the letter at lunchtime, then I can post it this afternoon.'

'I should,' said Carlotta gravely. 'It must be at least two days since you last wrote. Poor Pat must be feeling quite neglected!'

The others laughed – all except Amanda, who was strangely quiet. She was feeling rather put out, because Isabel's twin seemed so keen to meet Kitty, yet she hadn't mentioned her, Amanda, at all. In fact this was

Isabel's fault, for she had carefully avoided saying too much about the girl in her letters to Pat, still feeling a little guilty over her new friendship.

Isabel wrote her letter during the lunch break but, just as she was about to go and post it, she was called to Matron's room over the matter of some missing stockings.

'Blow! Matron will keep me for simply ages, and the post is collected in fifteen minutes,' said Isabel in dismay. 'I did so want to get my letter off today.'

'I'll take it for you,' offered Amanda, holding out her hand. 'I've a letter of my own to post anyway.'

'Would you? Oh thanks, Amanda, you're an angel.' So Isabel handed over the letter and went off to see Matron, while Amanda dashed off to the postbox, which was just outside the school gates. She posted her own letter to her mother, then, just as she was about to put Isabel's into the slot, she stopped, looking thoughtfully at the letter in her hand. Things would be different between Isabel and herself once Pat returned to school, she thought. Twins were so close that she was bound to be pushed out, and Amanda wasn't looking forward to that at all. She liked Isabel so much – how she wished that she didn't have a twin! Then an idea came into her mind. Suppose Pat didn't receive Isabel's letter? She would be sure to think that her twin was settling down at school without her. And if Amanda could intercept any further letters from Pat to Isabel, then Isabel would begin to think that her twin was behaving coldly towards her, and perhaps a rift between them would open up. Amanda shook herself. She couldn't do such a thing – it was wicked! But was it really so wicked to want to keep a friend, whispered a little voice in her head. She knew, from listening to the others, that Pat was extremely popular, and she would soon find someone else to chum up with. She had to make a decision quickly, for here was the postman cycling along the road on his way to empty the box. Hastily, her fingers trembling, she stuffed Isabel's letter into the pocket of her blazer and slipped back in through the school gates.

How guilty she felt later, when Isabel asked, 'Did you remember to post my letter, Amanda old girl?'

'Of course, Isabel,' she answered, quite unable to look her friend in the eye for fear that Isabel would see the guilt on her face.

Two days later another letter arrived for Isabel, and Amanda, who came down to breakfast before the rest of her form, saw it lying next to the girl's plate. She looked round swiftly to make sure that no one was watching, then slipped it quickly into her pocket, turning red as she did so. How she hated doing this! Yet somehow she couldn't seem to stop herself.

5.

Alison makes an enemy

On the following afternoon, which was a Saturday, the third form had the luxury of having their common-room all to themselves while the second form were out on a nature walk.

'Isn't it nice to be able to spread ourselves out a bit, instead of feeling so overcrowded,' said Carlotta, stretching out on a sofa.

'I'm just glad to get away from that beastly stepsister of mine,' said Amanda with feeling. 'Stuck-up little madam!'

Janet looked at the girl sharply. Amanda and Helen were the cause of a lot of ill feeling and tension when the two forms were together in the common-room. Most of it was Helen's fault, for she would usually start things by making some sly, sarcastic remark at her stepsister's expense. Then Amanda would retaliate, and it would end with the two of them having a full-scale row, until the head girls intervened to calm things down. It really was most unfair on everyone else, and extremely trying.

There were other things which caused problems too, such as one form wanting to listen to the radiogram, whilst the other wanted to play a gramophone record, or the second formers getting to the common-room first and bagging all the most comfortable seats. It really was a very unsatisfactory situation. Which made it all the more enjoyable now for the third form to have the room to themselves, and they were determined to make the most of it.

'Let's have a dance,' cried Doris, jumping up from her seat and going to the gramophone. Moments later a lively dance tune filled the air, and the girls leapt to their feet. Everyone was in stitches watching Kitty capering about doing a comical Irish jig, when the door opened and Margaret Winters entered. Immediately Kitty stopped dancing, and Gladys hurriedly turned the gramophone down.

'Oh!' said Margaret blankly. 'I was looking for Helen Wilkes of the second form. It's her turn to do my jobs this week.'

It was the custom at St Clare's for the first and second formers to wait on the top-form girls and do their little jobs, such as lighting fires in their studies or making their tea. The third formers all felt thankful that their turn at doing this was behind them and they could now look forward to the time when they were top formers and it would be their turn to be waited on.

'The second formers are all out on a nature walk, Margaret,' Janet said in a coolly polite tone. 'I'm afraid you'll have to get someone from the first form to help you out.'

Margaret didn't look too pleased at this, and Alison

piped up, 'I'd be more than happy to do your jobs for you, Margaret.'

'Why, Alison, that is kind of you!' said Margaret, with her most charming smile. 'Are you quite sure that you don't mind?'

'Oh no!' said Alison, looking worshipfully up at the older girl. 'It will be my pleasure.'

'Sure and that cousin of yours is completely mad,' Kitty remarked to Isabel, when the door had closed behind Margaret and Alison.

'I'll say she is!' agreed Bobby. 'Golly, when I think of the fuss Alison used to kick up about doing the older girls' jobs when she was in the first form – and now that she doesn't have to do it she goes and volunteers!'

'She wouldn't have volunteered if it had been anyone but Margaret,' said Isabel with a grin. 'I don't know why Alison persists in thinking that she's absolutely wonderful, but it's clear that she does!'

'Well, Alison's welcome to Margaret as far as I'm concerned,' said Doris with a grimace. 'Horrid creature! Anyway, why are we wasting a free afternoon talking about her? Turn that gramophone up, Mirabel, and let's have some fun!'

Alison was gone for simply ages, and it was obvious from the blissful expression on her face when she returned that she had had a wonderful time. 'I've been having a chat with Margaret in her study,' she said, rather smugly. 'She really is nice once you get to know her. Look, she gave me this hairslide too, and we've agreed that I'm going to do her jobs all the time from now on.'

'Alison, you are silly,' said Hilary, exasperated. 'Can't you see that Margaret is just making use of you?'

'She is not!' retorted Alison indignantly, turning red. 'In fact she refused my offer at first and I had to talk her into agreeing to it.'

'More fool you,' said Janet scornfully. 'I don't think Miss Adams will be too pleased about it either.'

'What I do in my free time has nothing to do with Miss Adams,' said Alison stiffly. 'I just feel thrilled and terribly honoured that Margaret enjoys my company so much.'

The others gave up. As Bobby said later, there was no doing anything with Alison once she had decided to make a slave of herself for someone. Little did the third form realise that Alison's adoration of Margaret was to lead to a bust-up between them and the second form.

Helen, whose turn it had been to do Margaret's jobs, went straight to the sixth former's study when she returned from her nature walk. She, like Alison, greatly admired the girl and enjoyed working for her. 'Sorry I couldn't come earlier, but we had to go on a nature walk,' she explained rather breathlessly. 'I can stay now, though, and do whatever you want me to. Would you like me to put the kettle on?'

'That's all right,' said Margaret off-handedly. 'Alison O'Sullivan has already done everything. She'll be coming permanently from now on, so I shan't be needing you again, Helen.'

Margaret far preferred Alison's kind of admiration to Helen's. Alison was quite happy to sit in open-mouthed, adoring silence while Margaret talked about herself, speaking only to put in a remark like 'Oh, Margaret, how wonderful!' or 'Oh, Margaret, how clever of you!'. Helen, on the other hand, was far too conceited and full of herself to really worship anyone else whole-heartedly, and was far too fond of talking about her own talents and achievements for Margaret's liking.

The second former felt both angry and humiliated now, as she recalled how she had boasted to the others about how friendly she was becoming with Margaret. How they would laugh when they learned that she had been cast aside in favour of that silly Alison O'Sullivan. Well, Helen was certainly going to tell Alison what she thought of her!

The common-room was extremely crowded that evening, the girls engaged in various activities. Isabel and Amanda were doing a jigsaw together, while Hilary and Janet pored over a crossword. Grace settled down with some embroidery, and others read, listened to the radiogram, or just chattered. Suddenly the door burst open and Helen stalked in, a scowl on her face.

'I say, what's up with you?' asked Harriet of the second form, looking at her in surprise.

Helen ignored her, walking straight over to Alison. 'Well!' she exclaimed, her hands on her hips. 'I just hope that you're pleased with yourself, Alison O'Sullivan!'

'Whatever do you mean?' asked Alison, completely taken aback and quite unable to imagine why Helen was so angry with her.

'Don't put on that innocent expression with me!' snapped Helen. 'It doesn't fool me one little bit. You know what you've done, you mean beast! *I* was supposed to be doing Margaret's jobs for her, but you had to go behind my back and start sucking up to her.'

Now Alison was an extremely gentle-natured girl, who hated rows of any kind. But she certainly wasn't going to let this second former – and a new girl at that – get away with speaking to her so rudely.

'How dare you!' she said, getting to her feet. 'Just who do you think you are talking to?'

Helen, who had thought that Alison would be quite unable to stand up for herself, was most astonished at this, and shrank back, looking alarmed.

'If Margaret doesn't want you around any longer, I'm sure it's no wonder,' went on Alison. 'Your conceited, stuck-up ways are quite unbearable.'

The whole of the second and third form were gathered round now, watching with bated breath, and Amanda, thrilled at seeing that beastly stepsister of hers in a row, called out, 'That's it, Alison! You tell her!'

'Mind your own business!' shouted Helen, turning on Amanda. 'This is between Alison and me. If it isn't just like you to come sticking your nose in!'

Janet, who had been listening to all this in growing

anger, now pushed her way to the front of the group of girls that were gathered round Alison and Helen, her face quite white with fury. 'I've heard enough of this!' she cried, glaring at Helen. 'How dare you speak to third formers in this way? I insist that you apologise at once!'

Helen, who was secretly a little afraid of the sharp-tongued Janet, turned pale and was almost prepared to back down.

Then Grace came forward and said sharply, 'Now look here, Janet, you might be head of the third form, but *I* am head of the second and it's up to me to tick Helen off, not you!'

'Then do it!' snapped Janet, rounding on Grace at once. 'What's the use of being head girl if you can't keep your form in order.'

This really wasn't very fair, for Grace was a very good head girl, but Janet was in such a rage now that she didn't care what she said. Poor Grace looked most upset and there were angry mutterings among the second formers.

'Honestly, you kids!' said Janet scornfully. 'You really ought to be in kindergarten, the way you behave sometimes.'

'Well, Janet, to hear you talk anyone would think that you were in the sixth form, not just the third,' Grace retorted. 'You're only a year older than us, after all, and you really have no right to order us around.'

'Yes, and you third formers are fine ones to accuse *us* of behaving like kids,' put in Harriet, eager to stick

41

up for her form. 'Just look at some of the pranks Kitty plays! And as for Carlotta, why, Jenny Mills had to tick her off for turning cartwheels on the playing field the other day. If that isn't childish I'd like to know what is!'

This was a mistake, for Carlotta, who was half Spanish, had a very fiery temper indeed. She walked over to the unfortunate Harriet, shaking her fist in the girl's face and raging, 'Who are you to criticise my behaviour? Do it again and I will slap you!'

Hilary, seeing that things were rapidly getting out of hand, took Carlotta's arm and pulled her away, while a shaken Harriet retired into the background. It was at this point that the door opened and Miss Jenks, the second-form mistress, appeared. The girls, intent on their quarrel, didn't even notice her at first, as insults and accusations continued to fly back and forth. At last Miss Jenks raised her voice and shouted, 'What on earth is going on in here?'

Everyone fell silent at once, looking most dismayed to see the mistress standing there.

Janet cleared her throat. 'We – er – we were just having a slight disagreement, Miss Jenks.'

'A *slight* disagreement? It sounded as if war had broken out!' said Miss Jenks, obviously displeased. 'Do you realise that you can be heard right at the other end of the corridor?'

'Sorry, Miss Jenks,' everyone muttered sheepishly.

'I should think so! Now kindly find a more civilised

way of settling your differences in future,' said the mistress coldly.

Silence reigned once she had left. The quarrel had ended, but the hostility that had sprung up between the two forms was only just beginning. For the rest of the evening it was as though an invisible line had been drawn down the middle of the common-room, with third formers on one side of it and second formers on the other. Janet wondered where it would all end. What bad luck that this beastliness had all boiled up during her term as head girl.

6.

The feud

The row was at the forefront of everyone's minds the following day, and the third formers could talk of little else.

'Cheeky little monkeys!' said Bobby indignantly. 'They can't be allowed to get away with this kind of behaviour.'

'Sure and they need to be taught a lesson,' agreed Kitty. 'Fancy them accusing me of playing pranks! Did you ever hear the like? Now, I think we should let McGinty loose in their dormitory.'

'Yes, fancy them accusing you of playing pranks, Kitty,' said Hilary dryly.

'I'm not going to resort to tricks of that kind,' declared Janet suddenly. 'They're silly, childish and . . .'

'Great fun,' put in Bobby.

'Well, they are, of course,' agreed Janet with a grin. 'But the thing is, I don't want them to be able to accuse us of starting anything. I intend to treat the whole situation in an adult and dignified manner. Unless, of course, they try any tricks on us! Then they had better watch out!'

Alison had been particularly upset by the row, and

still felt very sore with Helen. She poured the whole story out to Margaret in the girl's study that afternoon. For once the sixth former didn't mind not being able to talk about herself, for this was just the kind of thing that she loved listening to. If there was trouble between the second and third forms, Margaret might be able to turn it to her advantage in some way. The girl had an extremely spiteful streak in her nature, and she was both shrewd and clever. There might be a way here to get back at that dreadful Kitty Flaherty, and one or two others in the lower forms who had treated her with a lack of respect. So Margaret was extremely interested in what Alison had to say, taking her side against Helen and sympathising with her warmly. Alison, who was a terrible chatterbox anyway, blossomed under this treatment and promised to let Margaret know if the feud went any further.

It was as Alison was leaving the sixth former's study that Jennifer Mills came in, to borrow a book from Margaret. The head girl looked rather surprised to see Alison there and, as the door closed behind her, she said to Margaret, 'What was Alison doing here? Surely she's not in any kind of trouble?'

'No, she's doing my jobs for me this term,' answered Margaret airily.

'But the first and second formers are supposed to do that,' pointed out Jenny, with a frown. 'Alison's a third former.'

Margaret laughed and said, 'My dear Jenny, I can

45

assure you that I haven't forced Alison into doing anything that she doesn't want to do. She seems to have taken a liking to me and I thought it would be cruel to turn her away.'

Jenny's frown deepened at this. She knew Margaret well, and it was most unlike her to consider the feelings of a mere third former. 'Is it true that there was some sort of bust-up between the second and third forms last night?' she asked. 'Did Alison mention anything about it?'

'Not a word,' lied Margaret, looking surprised. She certainly wasn't going to let the head girl in on any of the lower school secrets Alison shared with her. Jenny was such a goody-two-shoes that she was quite likely to call Janet and Grace to her study and insist that they shake hands and make up. But that wouldn't suit Margaret at all. The girl was already turning over several cunning schemes in her head.

'You know what these kids are like,' she said to Jenny now. 'Probably just a storm in a teacup.'

'I daresay you're right,' agreed Jenny. 'Whatever it was about, I expect that it's all blown over by now.'

But the row hadn't blown over at all. The second and third formers continued to studiously ignore each other in the common-room that evening, but there was an air of excitement among the younger girls, and a good deal of whispering and giggling.

'They're up to something,' murmured Janet to Bobby. 'The question is, what?'

The third formers found out at bedtime. Swiftly they changed, brushed their teeth and got into bed. But they didn't get very far, for the girls found that, no matter how they tried, they simply couldn't push their legs down into their beds.

'I say!' roared Bobby. 'The mean beasts have made us all apple-pie beds!'

Then came the sound of laughter from the other side of the wall that separated the two dormitories, infuriating the third formers even more. Bobby, Carlotta and one or two others were all for marching into the second form's dormitory there and then, to give the pranksters a good ragging. But Janet, every bit as furious as they were, said firmly, 'No. Things are bound to get out of hand and we shall end up with some perfectly horrid punishment.'

'You surely aren't suggesting that we ignore it!' cried Mirabel indignantly.

'Shh! Keep your voice down, idiot!' hissed Janet. 'I'm certainly not suggesting anything of the kind. I know I said that we weren't going to resort to childish tricks, but this changes everything. The second form have struck the first blow, and I intend to retaliate! Gather round, everyone, and let's make some plans. And for heaven's sake, let's do it quietly. We don't want them getting wind of what's in store for them. Now, does anyone have any ideas?'

'We could get hold of Helen's books and hide them somewhere,' suggested Amanda rather spitefully. 'Then we could fill her pencil-box with insects, because she's simply terrified of them, and –'

But Janet broke in, to say sharply, 'This isn't just an excuse for you to get back at your stepsister, you know. It's a form feud now, and we're all involved.'

Amanda looked put out, as did Alison, who had rather liked the idea of getting back at Helen for all the mean things she had said to her.

'We could play some sort of trick on Miss Jenks and make it look as if the second form are responsible,' said Bobby thoughtfully. 'She would be simply furious! You know how Miss Jenks prides herself on never letting anyone get the better of her.'

'That's more like it,' said Janet. 'But it would take us a while to plan, and we really need something that we can put into action quickly, so that the second formers know they haven't got away with this.'

The third formers racked their brains, and at last Bobby said, 'Got it! Janet, do you still have that trick ball that your brother sent you last term?'

'Yes, it should be in my locker. Hold on a minute.' Janet sprang down from the bed and rummaged around in her locker for a few moments. 'Here it is.'

The ball that she held up looked much like any other, but as Bobby explained, 'It has a weight inside, which makes it roll round all over the place when it's hit, instead of going in a straight line.'

'And you've thought of a way to trick the second formers with it?' said Gladys.

Bobby nodded, a mischievous grin on her freckled face and, in a low voice, explained her plan to the others. There were many stifled chuckles as she spoke and, when she had finished, Isabel said, 'Bobby, it's a simply marvellous idea! My goodness, I can't wait to see the second formers' faces when we spring this on them!'

'Nor can I,' said Hilary. 'But right now, we'd better make our beds properly and get some sleep, otherwise we shall be too tired to play this wonderful trick tomorrow.'

So the girls sorted out their beds and settled down to sleep, their thoughts pleasant ones. Just wait until tomorrow, you second formers!

The second form had hockey practice the following afternoon and were keen to make a good showing, as Jennifer Mills was coming to watch, and there was a good chance that some of them would be picked for the junior team. The third form, however, had chosen that moment to take their revenge and were quite determined that no one from the second form would be given a place on the team.

Just before practice began, Isabel, Amanda, Gladys and Mirabel slipped into the changing room and removed all the laces from the second formers' hockey boots. 'We'll put them back later,' said Isabel, slipping the bundle of laces into her bag. 'This is just to stir Miss Wilton up – she hates being kept waiting!'

Next Janet and Bobby carried out their part of the

plan. Whilst Miss Wilton, the games mistress, and Jenny were waiting for the second form to emerge from the changing room, Bobby ran on to the field on the pretext of speaking to them about practice times for the third formers. Janet, meanwhile, sneaked up behind them and slipped the hockey ball into her pocket, replacing it with her own very special one!

'What *is* taking those girls so long?' said Miss Wilton, impatiently, to Jenny, glancing at her watch. 'It seems to be taking them ages to get changed.'

The third formers, all of whom had turned out to watch what promised to be a most entertaining practice, grinned and winked at one another. They knew what was taking the second formers so long, but they weren't telling!

At last the second form came running out on to the field, and Miss Wilton heaved an exasperated sigh. 'Grace! Why are you all wearing plimsolls? What has happened to your hockey boots?'

'Our laces have all gone missing,' answered Grace, glaring in the direction of the third form.

'What, *all* of them?' exclaimed the games mistress, in disbelief. 'How can that have happened?'

Grace knew exactly how it had happened, but she said nothing. The St Clare's girls had very strict ideas of honour and, even in the middle of a feud like this, simply refused to sneak.

'Come along, then – we've wasted quite enough time already,' said Miss Wilton, briskly. 'Take your places, girls, and practise shooting at goal.'

Harriet gave the ball a terrific whack that should have sent it straight into the goal. But instead it simply veered round in a big circle and ended up back at Harriet's feet.

Doris gave one of her explosive snorts of laughter, which was fortunately drowned as Miss Wilton called sharply, 'Do stop fooling around! Helen, stop hanging back and trying to make yourself invisible! Come forward and try to hit the ball *somewhere* near the goal.'

Helen detested all games and, as she was not very good at them, always hated coming to the attention of Miss Wilton. She stepped forward reluctantly and gave the ball a feeble tap. It moved forward a few inches, then rolled back to its starting place. Jenny shook her head in despair, while the third formers clutched at one another gleefully as they tried to stifle their giggles.

'What a super trick!' exclaimed Gladys. 'Oh, I say, do look at Grace!'

Grace was only feet away from the goal, and getting the ball in should have been a simple matter. But as soon as her hockey stick touched it, the ball veered sharply to the left and went wide of the posts.

'Well!' said Jenny. 'What a sorry looking bunch! You lot are going to have to pull your socks up if you hope to stand any chance of getting into the team. Extra coaching for all of you!'

Helen, in particular, looked absolutely aghast at this, for the girls had to give up their free time to attend

Jenny's coaching sessions. She scowled fiercely at the third formers, and Amanda chuckled. 'It looks as if my dear stepsister is going to be taking some more exercise, whether she likes it or not.'

'I vote we make ourselves scarce,' said Hilary. 'Miss Wilton keeps looking at us most suspiciously every time we laugh. If we aren't careful we shall give the game away.'

So, reluctantly, the third formers left, congratulating themselves on an extremely successful trick. But, as Bobby said, 'They are sure to try and get back at us in some way, so we shall have to be ready for them. We can't possibly let the second formers get the better of us. The honour of the third is at stake!'

7.

An unexpected arrival

'I say, Isabel, have you had any word from Pat lately?' asked Doris one day. 'When is she coming back?'

Isabel shrugged and said rather stiffly, 'Your guess is as good as mine. She hasn't written to me for days.'

Amanda, sitting nearby, overheard this and turned pink. In fact, Pat had written to her twin several times lately, but she had managed to intercept the letters. The girl had also conveniently forgotten to post several of Isabel's letters to Pat as well. But how wretched Amanda felt at seeing poor Isabel looking so down in the dumps.

'Cheer up,' said Bobby. 'I'm sure there's a simple explanation. Perhaps your father has grown tired of writing everything out for her. I wouldn't blame him! He's probably got writers' cramp with the amount of post you and Pat send back and forth.'

Isabel shook her head. 'No, Daddy always sticks by his word and he knows how much those letters mean to me. I think it's Pat who's grown tired of dictating them.'

'Heavens, I hope you and Pat aren't going to fall out,' said Hilary. 'We've quite enough trouble on our hands at the moment with the second formers.'

'Yes, why don't you write to Pat and tell her all about

that?' suggested Alison. 'If that doesn't get a response, nothing will.'

'I don't think I shall bother,' said Isabel, rather huffily. 'If she can't make the effort to write I don't see why I should!'

As it happened, Pat returned to St Clare's the very next day, feeling every bit as put out as Isabel at her twin's long silence. She had written to tell Isabel what time she would be arriving and quite expected a reception committee from the third form. But when she arrived there was no one to greet her at all. It really was most odd, thought Pat, feeling very hurt.

After reporting to Matron, Pat went to the dormitory to unpack. She knew which was Isabel's bed at once, for there was a photograph of their parents on the locker beside it. But the bed next to Isabel's appeared to have been taken, a neatly folded dressing-gown on top of it and some personal belongings on the locker. Pat began to feel very upset indeed. She and Isabel had *always* slept next to one another. What was her twin thinking of to let someone else take her place?

It was as Pat was brushing her hair in front of the mirror that Amanda came in and exclaimed, 'There you are, Isabel! I've been looking everywhere for you. Listen, I had a postal order from Mummy this morning, so I thought I might treat us both to tea in town. It's my turn, as you paid last time.'

Pat stiffened. So, this was the reason Isabel hadn't written for so long! Well, she certainly hadn't wasted much time in making a new friend. Rather coldly, Pat said, 'I'm not Isabel. I'm her twin.'

Amanda turned a little pale. Soon she would discover whether or not her scheme had worked. Taking a deep breath, she said, 'How do you do? I'm Amanda Wilkes, Isabel's friend. I expect she's mentioned me?'

Pat stared at the girl. She seemed pleasant enough, yet Pat disliked her intensely because she had come between her twin and herself. 'No,' she said shortly. 'Isabel hasn't mentioned you at all.'

And with that she swept past Amanda and out of the room. She found most of the third formers in the common-room, though Isabel was not among them, and got an extremely warm welcome.

'Pat! Marvellous to see you again. How are you?'

'You should have let us know you were coming!'

'I say, won't Isabel be pleased! Have you seen her yet?'

'Hallo, everyone,' said Pat, smiling round. 'It's nice to be back. No, I haven't seen Isabel yet, but I did write and tell her that I was coming.'

'Well, how odd that she didn't let on to us,' said Carlotta.

'Isabel's behaviour has been rather odd altogether these past few weeks,' said Pat, with a harsh laugh. 'She hasn't written in simply ages, and now I find out that she's chummed up with this Amanda.'

'This is all jolly queer,' said Janet, looking mystified. 'Isabel says that *you* haven't written to *her*! Obviously there's been a mix-up somewhere. Anyway, the two of you can thrash it out when you get together. Now, do sit down and we'll tell you all the news.'

Pat sat in between Janet and Bobby on the sofa and said, 'Where are the second form? Isabel mentioned in her first letter to me that you were sharing the common-room with them.'

'The poor little dears are having extra hockey coaching,' said Bobby with a grin, and at once launched into the story of the feud. There was other news to catch up on too, then Kitty had to be introduced and the girls insisted on taking Pat outside to meet McGinty. So it was not until teatime that Pat finally caught up with her twin. Isabel was already seated at the table with Amanda when the rest of the third form entered, and she looked up at Pat rather apprehensively.

'So there you are,' said Pat. 'I thought you were having tea in town with your new friend.'

Isabel flushed, stung by her twin's tone. Pat had no right to object to her being friendly with Amanda when she hadn't even bothered to write for ages.

'Amanda found me in the library and told me that you were back,' she answered. 'Naturally I wouldn't go out to tea on your first day back.'

'Well, I suppose that's something,' sniffed Pat. 'You might have come along to the common-room to say hallo.'

'I did, but by the time I got there you had gone,' said Isabel indignantly.

'That must have been when we popped outside to see McGinty,' put in Hilary quickly, anxious to avert a quarrel. 'Pat, do have something to eat. You must be starving after your journey.'

Pat was, so she sat down as far away from Isabel as possible.

Janet pursed her lips. She liked the twins enormously and knew how close they were. What a shame it would be if they fell out over this. It was a very strange business, each of them claiming not to have received the other's letters. Janet began to feel that there was something fishy going on. And as head girl it was her duty to sort it out.

But she had no time to bend her mind to the problem that evening, for the second formers were up to their tricks again. They made sure that they were first in the common-room, and the door was slightly ajar when the third form arrived. Amanda pushed it open – then what a squeal she let out! For the wicked second formers had carefully balanced a bucket of water on top of the door, and Amanda received the contents all over her. The second formers laughed uncontrollably and Helen drawled, 'I always said you were a drip, Amanda.'

'You horrid little beast!' spluttered Amanda, wiping the water from her eyes. 'I bet you were behind this.'

'How could I possibly have known that you would be first through the door?' laughed Helen. 'That was just bad timing on your part.'

Pat had to turn away to hide a smile at this. Naturally she was on her form's side in this feud, but she couldn't help feeling pleased that the person who

57

had received an unexpected shower was Amanda.

'I should go and get changed if I were you,' advised Doris. 'Before Matron or one of the mistresses comes along and catches you in those wet clothes.'

With one last glower in her stepsister's direction, Amanda stormed off and Janet said scornfully, 'Rather a juvenile trick. Still, what can one expect from a bunch of kids?'

Grace flushed angrily, well aware that the tricks she and her form had come up with weren't nearly so ingenious as the one the third had played on them the other day. She wondered what they would come up with next.

Janet was intent on revenge, she and the rest of the form going into a huddle once Amanda returned in dry clothes.

'That idea you came up with, Bobby, for playing a trick on Miss Jenks would be absolutely super,' Janet said.

'Yes, but it's going to be terribly difficult to play a trick under the eyes of Miss Jenks and the whole of the second form,' said Bobby thoughtfully.

'Come on, thinking caps on, everyone, and let's see if we can't come up with something between us.'

'If we could only get the second form out of their classroom for a while we'd have a clear field, so we would,' said Kitty thoughtfully.

'Golly, that would be a fine trick in itself – to make an entire form disappear,' said Hilary. 'I'm afraid it's a bit of a tall order, though.'

'It is that,' agreed Kitty, an impish twinkle in her eyes. 'But not impossible, I'm thinking.'

'Kitty, you've got a plan, haven't you?' said Alison excitedly. 'What is it?'

'Yes, do tell!' begged Amanda.

'Shush now.' Kitty glanced warningly towards the second formers, who were looking across at them most suspiciously. 'I need to think this out a bit. Come to the stables tomorrow morning while I'm giving McGinty his breakfast and I'll tell you what I have in mind.'

'Why the stables, Kitty?' asked Janet, amused and very curious. Knowing Kitty's mischievous, don't-care-ish nature, any trick she came up with was sure to be simply splendid.

'Because there's something in there that I think might be of use to us,' Kitty answered with a grin. 'I'm saying no more now. Just wait until tomorrow morning.'

The third formers were bursting with curiosity when they got to the stables after breakfast the following morning.

'I say, where's Kitty?' asked Doris. 'I do hope she won't be long or we shall be late for English.'

'She'll be here soon,' said Hilary. 'She's just gone to get some scraps from Cook for McGinty.'

Both Kitty and her pet had quickly become firm favourites with the kitchen staff, and the girls often complained jokingly that McGinty was better fed than they were. The third formers had all grown very fond of the little goat, and there was never any shortage of volunteers to feed him, or walk him on his lead, if Kitty was busy. Even Alison, who had been a little afraid of him at first, now loved to pet him, and she stroked his wiry head as everyone waited for Kitty. At last she appeared, carrying a bucket of scraps, which she placed on the ground before McGinty.

'There you are, me boy,' she said gaily, and at once the goat lost interest in the girls, intent on his breakfast.

'Well?' said Isabel impatiently. 'What's this plan of yours, Kitty?'

In answer the Irish girl went into the empty stall next to McGinty's. In it had been dumped old bits of furniture and boxes of all kinds of odds and ends that were no longer wanted. Kitty went to one of the boxes and pulled something out, holding it aloft for the others' inspection.

'What on earth are we going to do with *that*?' asked Bobby, puzzled.

'Sure, Bobby, and we're going to teach the second form a lesson they'll never forget,' replied Kitty cheerfully. 'Gather round and I'll tell you how.'

8.

The third form hatch a plot

The object that Kitty held was an old fire bell, very rusty now for it had been in the stables for some time, and Pat asked, 'How are we going to get the second form to disappear from their classroom with that?'

'Ah, we're not, Pat. We're going to get them to disappear from their dorm,' replied Kitty. 'Tricks aren't just for the classroom, you know. You have midnight feasts here, don't you? Well, tonight we're going to play a midnight trick.'

There were gasps of surprise and delight at this. How simply thrilling!

'Go on, Kitty,' said Mirabel eagerly. 'Tell us the plan.'

'Well, at midnight – or thereabouts – one of us will sneak out on to the landing and ring the fire bell,' Kitty explained. 'It still works, but not loudly enough to wake anyone further away, so the only people it will disturb will be the second formers.'

'Then what?' asked Doris, who was jumping up and down in excitement.

'Then the fun really starts,' chuckled Kitty. 'The second formers will follow the fire drill, of course, and go downstairs and out of the side door.'

'But won't they wonder why *we* haven't heard it and aren't taking action ourselves?' said Gladys, with a frown.

'But we will be taking action, Gladys,' answered Kitty. 'We'll put on our dressing-gowns and follow the second form downstairs, all the while acting very surprised and scared. Then, once they've slipped outside, we bolt the door behind them, run back to our dorm, and wait for the person on duty to discover that they're missing.'

'Kitty!' exclaimed Carlotta, delighted. 'It's marvellous!'

'I'm not so sure,' put in Hilary, looking doubtful. 'If Miss Jenks catches the second formers out of bed they'll be in real trouble. And they were decent enough not to sneak on us yesterday morning after hockey practice.'

There were a few murmurs of agreement, and Kitty exclaimed, 'I knew there was something I'd forgotten to mention! You see, I happened to overhear Miss Jenks telling Miss Adams that she would be away tonight, so that nice Jenny Mills is on duty instead.'

'That settles it, then,' said Doris happily. 'Jenny's a decent sort. She'll give the second form a jolly good ticking off, but she won't report them to Miss Theobald.'

'Golly, it will be sport!' said Janet. 'Well done, Kitty. Now come along, everyone, or we shall be late.'

Laughing and chattering, the girls moved away and, as always, Pat turned automatically towards Isabel, so that they could discuss the trick together, forgetting for a moment that there was any coolness between them. Isabel grinned at her twin and opened her mouth to speak. Then, suddenly, Amanda was at her side, taking her arm and saying excitedly, 'My word, what a trick this is going to be! I do like Kitty so much, don't you?' The smile was wiped from Pat's face, replaced by a cold look as she turned her back on her twin and went off to catch up with Hilary. Isabel felt deeply hurt. Why was Pat behaving like this? She was the one who was in the wrong, for not having replied to any of Isabel's letters, and she was being perfectly beastly to poor old Amanda.

Janet noticed this little incident too, and frowned heavily. She had hoped that the coolness between the twins would blow over and they would make up, but instead a real rift seemed to be opening. Janet made up her mind that tomorrow, once this trick was out of the way, she would tackle Pat and Isabel. If she could get to the bottom of this business of the letters perhaps she could bring them together. Being head of the form certainly had its fair share of problems!

Bedtime couldn't come quickly enough for the third formers that evening, though all of them were quite certain they wouldn't get a wink of sleep, spirits high at the prospect of the trick that was to be played. It had been extremely difficult to keep their minds on their work during lessons, and Miss Adams had found it necessary to call several of them to order.

'Doris!' she had barked. 'Why do you keep grinning to yourself in that idiotic way? Do you find my method of teaching maths so amusing?'

Doris, who didn't find maths at all amusing, at once

63

made her face perfectly serious and said meekly, 'No, Miss Adams.'

'I'm glad to hear it! Now, if Bobby would kindly refrain from whispering to Carlotta and give me her attention also, we might get some work done,' said the mistress dryly.

Bobby had fallen silent immediately, sitting up straight in her seat, and Miss Adams had no further trouble with her class.

Kitty, though, grew extremely restless during French, bringing Mam'zelle's anger upon her.

'Kee-ty!' cried the French mistress, as the little Irish girl gazed out of the window. 'Twice have I asked you to stand up and recite a verse of this so-moving French poem, and twice have you ignored me! What is outside that fascinates you so?'

'Ah, 'tis nothing, Mam,' answered Kitty, her lips twitching humorously. 'I thought I saw McGinty out there, but I must have been mistaken.'

'McGinty?' repeated Mam'zelle, her glasses slipping down her nose.

'My little goat,' explained the girl. 'I could have sworn I saw him in the flowerbed outside the window of the mistresses' common-room.'

'How can this be?' demanded Mam'zelle. 'That goat is in the stables.'

'Sure, but he's a clever one, Mam. If he wanted to slip out and have a taste of those delicious-looking flowers he would find a way.'

Mam'zelle gave a shriek of dismay. The tiny flowerbed was her pride and joy, and she had planted many of the seeds herself, tending them lovingly whenever she had a spare moment.

'This is abominable!' she wailed. 'And you, Kee-ty, *you* are abominable! If that creature has eaten my beautiful flowers I will have him expelled!' With that she rushed from the classroom to go in search of McGinty and, as soon as the door closed behind her, the class exploded into laughter.

'Poor old Mam'zelle,' gasped Amanda, holding her sides. 'Kitty, you're wicked.'

'Yes, and the funny thing is, I was looking out of the window too,' said Carlotta with a grin. 'Yet I didn't see hide nor hair of McGinty.'

'Ah well, I did say I could have been mistaken,' said Kitty, her blue eyes gazing innocently around the class. 'But once old Mam'zelle gets an idea into her head there's no stopping her.'

The others roared. They had needed an excuse to release some of the laughter that was bubbling up inside them, and Kitty had provided it. The third formers chatted happily amongst themselves until Gladys, standing guard by the door, hissed, 'Shh! Mam'zelle's coming back.'

Instantly there was silence, and Gladys scuttled back to her seat as the French mistress entered, her sloe-black eyes fixed angrily on Kitty. 'There was no goat in the flowerbed,' she declared. 'He is safely locked away in the old stables.'

'Ah, that's a relief, Mam,' said Kitty solemnly. 'It's terrible worried I've been.'

'Your worries are just beginning, Kee-ty! Tonight you will learn the French poem, and tomorrow you will recite it to me perfectly, with not one mistake.'

Kitty, who was blessed with an amazing memory and already knew the poem off by heart, bowed her head to hide a smile and answered meekly, 'Yes, Mam.'

'And do not call me Mam!'

Alison was still smiling to herself over this incident when she went to Margaret Winters' study after tea that afternoon. Because they were so angry with Helen, she and Amanda were looking forward to tonight's trick more eagerly than any of the third form.

'You look happy, Alison,' remarked the sixth former pleasantly. 'Is it your birthday or something?'

Alison hesitated. She liked Margaret so much and would have loved to tell her what was going to take place that evening. But as silly as she was, Alison knew that the others would not take kindly to her sharing third-form secrets with a sixth former – especially Margaret. So she muttered something about having got good marks for her English prep and set about boiling the kettle for Margaret's tea. The sixth former, however, wasn't fooled. Margaret was shrewd, and she could sense Alison's excitement. The third formers were up to something, and Margaret badly wanted to know what.

'Sit down and have a cup of tea with me, Alison,' she invited sweetly. 'I've got some chocolate biscuits, too.'

Alison turned quite pink with pleasure, hardly able to stammer out her thanks. What an honour, for a mere third former to be invited to have tea with the deputy head girl! Just wait until she got back to the common-room and told the others – silly little Helen would be green with envy! Alison didn't realise that she was smiling to herself at these pleasant thoughts, but Margaret's sharp eyes noted it and, her voice full of concern, she said, 'I do hope that things are all right between you and Helen now, Alison. I feel simply terrible that I'm the cause of ill feeling between you. But I do enjoy your company so much, and when you offered to carry on doing my jobs I'm afraid I simply couldn't resist saying yes.'

And Alison simply couldn't resist flattery! She beamed with delight as Margaret went on, 'And Helen is so full of herself that I couldn't bear having her around. It's a pity you third formers haven't come up with a plan for taking her down a peg or two.'

Alison bit her lip, longing to tell the older girl about the trick her form was planning for tonight. Margaret was such a wonderful person, so understanding and easy to talk to. It was such a shame that the others couldn't see it. Of course, she could be a little sharp-tongued with people like Kitty and Bobby at times, but they were so disrespectful to her that it was quite their own fault.

Margaret could certainly turn on the charm when she wanted something, and now she gave Alison her most dazzling smile, saying, 'I remember when I was in the third form. My word, what tricks we used to get up to! Of course, I have to behave myself now that I'm a prim and proper sixth former, but I do so enjoy hearing about all your pranks.' Margaret's smile became slightly wistful, and suddenly the strain of keeping her secret became too much for Alison. Before she could stop herself, the girl was pouring out the whole story of the fire bell trick. Margaret listened avidly, her violet eyes sparkling with excitement, and Alison thought how pretty she looked.

'What a simply marvellous trick!' exclaimed the sixth former, when Alison came to the end of her tale. 'You must come along tomorrow and tell me how it went. But now, I'm afraid, I must get on with my prep. Be a dear and clear the table before you go, Alison.'

'Of course, Margaret.' Eagerly the girl jumped to her feet and did as she was told. 'Shall I wash the cups out?'

'Oh no, don't bother about that. I'll do it later.'

Now that Margaret had learned the third form's secret, she wanted Alison out of the way as quickly as possible, for she had a plan of her own. A plan that would get her just what she wanted, as long as she thought it out carefully. As soon as the door closed behind Alison, Margaret went across to a cupboard in the corner of the room and took something out. Then she smiled to herself. The third formers weren't the only ones who were going to enjoy themselves tonight!

9.

A very successful trick

The third formers had planned their trick well. Earlier that day, Mirabel had overheard Jennifer Mills talking to her friend Barbara.

'I don't want to be too late getting to bed, or I shall never get up in the morning! On the other hand, I suppose I'd better make sure that the little beasts aren't planning a midnight feast or something.'

'Yes, some of those second formers are quite a handful.' Barbara had laughed. 'Though I suppose we were just the same at their age! I should check on them soon after midnight, then you can be tucked up in bed by half past twelve.'

Jennifer had agreed that this was a good idea, and Mirabel had raced off to report to the others.

'Well done, Mirabel,' Janet had said. 'We'd better sound the fire bell at ten minutes to twelve. That leaves plenty of time for the second form to get outside.'

'And for us to get back to bed, so that it looks as if we're fast asleep when Jenny comes round,' Isabel had finished with a grin.

At a quarter to twelve the little alarm clock that Carlotta had placed under her pillow went off. The girl sprang from her bed and went round quickly and quietly waking the others. A few girls had been too excited to sleep, but most had dozed off and yawned and stretched sleepily as they sat up.

'Doris!' hissed Carlotta. 'Doris, wake up! We need to get a move on or our trick will be ruined.'

Grumbling to herself, Doris emerged from beneath her lovely warm quilt and groaned.

At last everyone was awake and, shining her torch round, Janet whispered, 'Kitty, have you got the fire bell?'

Kitty nodded and Janet said, 'Good, then let's . . . Amanda, where are you going?'

Amanda, already in dressing-gown and slippers, was heading for the door. She stopped and said, 'I thought we were going to gather on the landing.'

'Not until Kitty has sounded the fire bell! If the second form come out and find us all ready and waiting they'll be very suspicious. We have to act as surprised and scared as they will be.'

'Idiot!' muttered Pat, glaring at Amanda, who flushed.

'Right,' Janet went on briskly. 'Kitty, you know what to do. Everyone else, get into your dressing-gowns and slippers.'

Quietly opening the door, Kitty darted out on to the landing and placed the fire bell in a dark corner. Then she set it ringing and, hands over her ears, rushed back into the dormitory, closing the door behind her.

'My goodness, that sounds dreadfully loud,' said Hilary. 'It'll be a wonder if it doesn't wake the whole building.'

70

'It won't,' Bobby assured her. 'We're miles away from the rest of the school, and once the second formers are safely out of the way we can stop it.'

Through the wall the girls could hear cries of alarm and bustling noises, then came the sound of a door opening. Winking at the others, Janet went out on to the landing, making her voice very scared as she asked, 'Grace, is that you? You'd better get your form out quickly.'

'They're all ready,' replied the second former, her voice shaking a little. 'Where do you suppose the fire is, Janet? I can't smell any smoke.'

'We don't have time to worry about that now. Let's just concentrate on getting everyone out safely.'

All the St Clare's girls knew the fire drill well, and Grace felt proud of her form as they filed quickly down the stairs, all of them appearing much more calm than they felt. The third formers followed close behind, Janet calling out, 'Unlock the door, Grace, and let everyone out into the garden.'

Grace obeyed, her fingers trembling a little as they slid back the heavy iron bolt. She pulled open the door and the second form made their escape, all of them relieved to be outside. But their relief soon turned to bewilderment, for Carlotta, the first member of the third form to reach the bottom of the stairs, swiftly pushed the door closed behind them, slipping the bolt back into place. Grinning up at her friends, she said, 'Now let's get back to bed. And Kitty, for heaven's sake

71

turn that fire bell off before Jenny gets here.'

Chuckling to themselves, the third formers sprinted back up the stairs, the muffled tones of the second formers following them.

'I say, what's going on?'

'We've been tricked, that's what!'

'The mean beasts! We'll get them for this!'

'Oh no you won't,' thought Janet, a determined smile on her face. No one was going to get the better of the third form while she was head girl! Certainly not a bunch of half-baked kids like the second form.

On the landing Kitty stopped the fire bell and stowed it safely in her bedside locker, and everyone sighed thankfully as the persistent clanging abruptly stopped.

'Are you all right, Alison?' whispered Pat to her cousin, as they slipped back into their beds. 'You've been awfully quiet tonight.'

'I'm fine,' replied Alison, sounding a little subdued. 'Just tired, that's all.' In fact, Alison's conscience was troubling her, and she now wished wholeheartedly that she had never told Margaret Winters about the trick. It had all seemed so *right* earlier, so natural to confide in her. But the others would never forgive her if they knew that she had given away the third form's secret. And to the deputy head girl, of all people! What if Margaret decided to report them to Miss Theobald after all? Alison shifted uncomfortably in her bed, reminding herself firmly that the sixth former had given her word not to sneak. And Margaret would not go back on her word, for she was a decent and loyal person, no matter what the others said! All the same, Alison would be glad when the trick was over. She hadn't long to wait.

Moments later, footsteps could be heard on the landing, and Jennifer's tall, slender figure was silhouetted in the doorway. All was silent until Doris gave a very loud, very realistic snore, grunting to herself as she turned over in bed. Isabel stuffed a corner of the pillow into her mouth to stifle her giggles, but Jennifer seemed perfectly satisfied that all was well and shut the door softly behind her. The third formers lay there with bated breath as she moved on to the second form's dormitory. They heard Jennifer enter, a moment's silence, then an angry exclamation, and the girls sat up in their beds as the head girl's brisk footsteps faded into the distance.

'I bet she's heading for the common-room, to see if they're having a midnight feast,' said Hilary.

'I say, are you absolutely sure Jenny won't wake one of the mistresses?' said Gladys anxiously. 'I know the second form are little beasts, but I wouldn't want to get them into real trouble.'

'Of course she won't,' Bobby assured her. 'Jenny's a good sport. Now, if it had been Margaret Winters who was on duty . . .'

Everyone groaned – except for Alison, whose guilty feelings made her speak out in defence of her idol. 'Why are you all so horrible about Margaret?' she cried, the easy tears starting in her large blue eyes. 'You don't know her like I do, but –'

'We don't *want* to know her!' interrupted Bobby rudely. 'Honestly, Alison, when are you going to take off those rose-tinted glasses of yours and see our dear deputy head girl as she really is?'

Alison opened her mouth to retaliate, but before she could speak Bobby went on, 'She found out that the first form were holding a feast last term and made sure they were caught. The poor things weren't allowed out of the grounds for a fortnight.'

'That was all a misunderstanding!' said Alison hotly. 'Margaret explained it all to me, and what happened was –'

'We know what happened,' said Janet scornfully. 'Your precious Margaret couldn't resist stirring up trouble. And I, for one, don't want to waste any more time talking about her.'

'Hear hear!' put in Isabel. 'Come on, everybody! Jenny's safely out of the way, so let's take a peek out of the window and see what's going on.'

This sounded like an excellent idea, and the third formers scrambled out of bed, padding over to the big window at the end of the room.

'There are the second formers!' said Mirabel, pointing. 'Over by the gardener's shed. My word, don't they look cold!'

The watching girls laughed at the sight of the shivering second formers, all huddled together by the big shed. It was a cold, clear night, the moon lighting the scene beautifully, and Kitty said, 'Sure, it's as good as a play. Let's see if we can hear what they're saying.'

With that she slid the window up a few inches, and the still night air carried the second formers' voices up to the watching girls.

'I'm frozen! What if they leave us out here all night?' Amanda recognised Helen's tearful, high-pitched voice and grinned.

'They wouldn't dare!' said Grace. 'That would be going too far, even for the third form.'

'Suppose Miss Jenks comes along and finds our beds empty?' said Katie fearfully, unaware that the mistress was away for the evening. 'Shall we go and bang on the door?'

'We'll wake the whole school!' said Harriet. 'No, we'll just have to wait until the third formers decide to unlock the door and let us back in. They won't leave us out here too long, I'm sure.' Harriet was trying her best to sound confident, but the listening girls heard the note of uncertainty in her voice.

Then another voice joined the throng outside – a stern, angry voice. 'What on earth are you kids doing out of your beds?' it said, and the second formers almost jumped out of their skins. Jennifer Mills had sneaked around the other side of the shed and crept up on them from behind. 'Well?' she demanded now, folding her arms and glaring at the frightened girls. 'I'm waiting for an explanation.'

'Oh, Jenny, we've been tricked!' began Helen. 'It was those awful –' But she got no further, for Grace elbowed her sharply before she could sneak on the third form.

Bravely, Grace faced up to the head girl and said frankly, 'We're sorry, Jenny. It was . . . it was just a prank that went wrong, and somehow we ended up getting locked out.'

'Are you going to report us to Miss Theobald?' asked Katie, her eyes big and scared looking.

'I ought to,' said Jenny crossly. 'You youngsters deserve –'

But the second formers never found out what they deserved, for two things happened at once. Katie began to cry, and a window overlooking the garden was thrown open. A large, angry head appeared and everyone recognised Mam'zelle's distinctive voice as she cried, 'Who is there? If you are burglars, be warned! I go to call the police!'

The second formers looked at one another in horror and, thinking quickly, Jennifer ushered them into the shadows, putting an arm around the weeping Katie.

'Good old Mam'zelle,' chuckled Doris, enjoying the scene hugely. 'Every time she hears the slightest noise in the night she thinks it's burglars.'

'She won't call the police,' said Janet. 'As long as Jenny can keep those kids quiet and out of sight for a few minutes, Mam'zelle will think she's imagining things and go back to bed.'

At that moment a small movement in the bushes down below caught Alison's eye, but she could see no one. It was probably the school cat on one of his night time prowls. Or perhaps a rat or a mouse! Even from a distance, the thought of rats and mice made Alison shudder, and she stepped back from the window.

Mam'zelle, meanwhile, as Janet had predicted, had grown tired of uttering threats to the empty air and closed the window.

'Right, kids,' said Jenny briskly. 'Make a run for it while the coast is clear and head for the side door. I came out that way, so it should still be unlocked. Go straight up to your dorm and don't stop for anything.'

The second formers didn't need telling twice, sprinting across the lawn until they disappeared from the view of the watching third form, while Jennifer followed at a more dignified pace.

'Show's over,' said Carlotta, closing the window. 'We'd better get some sleep.'

And what a show it had been, agreed everyone. One of the best tricks they had ever played! Simply super!

And Alison felt happier than any of them, breathing a sigh of relief as she listened to the second formers returning to their dormitory. It was over, and Margaret hadn't let her down. The older girl could so easily have interfered and got the whole of the third form into hot water, but she hadn't. For once Alison had been proved right about someone, and it was a very pleasant feeling.

10.

A shock for the second form

Following the success of the trick, Janet felt that she could afford to be generous and decided to offer a truce to the second formers. But Grace, angry at being duped, irritable from lack of sleep and still smarting from a painful interview with Jennifer Mills, was in no mood to forgive and forget. 'We're not interested, Janet,' she said coldly. 'Your form made complete idiots out of us last night, and we shan't rest until we've got our own back.'

Janet laughed. 'Just as you like, Grace. But you kids will never get one over on us third formers. We're far too clever for you.'

And it seemed that Janet was right. Helen, finding herself alone in the common-room one morning, decided to steal Amanda's maths book and hide it. But Carlotta came in and caught her in the act, ticking the girl off so fiercely that Helen fled in terror. An attempt to get Kitty into trouble by setting McGinty free also backfired, when the little goat spotted Harriet's French prep sticking out of her satchel and promptly ate it. Finally they made the mistake of trying to play the same trick twice, by balancing a bucket of water on top of the common-room door. The alert third formers spotted it from the corridor and, after a whispered conference, decided to spend the evening at a slide show in the hall. So the second form were left alone to gaze hopefully at the door all evening, a pastime of which they soon grew heartily bored.

'Poor,' said Bobby later, shaking her head gravely. 'Very poor. These youngsters just don't have our ingenuity.'

Grace, who overheard this, simmered with rage and became more determined than ever to get revenge on the third form. She would be seeing her older brother at half-term – perhaps he could come up with an idea.

The third formers were looking forward to half-term. It would be such fun to see parents, brothers and sisters again, and find out what was going on at home. There was great excitement at St Clare's in the few days leading up to the holiday, and the girls found it very hard to sleep the night before.

But, at last, the big day arrived, the entrance hall and the lawn outside thronged with happy, chattering girls as they waited excitedly for their parents to arrive. Pat and Isabel were among them, but they were not so happy as the others. Of course, it would be simply wonderful to see their mother and father again, but things still weren't right between the two of them. So instead of gaily discussing their plans for the day, Pat and Isabel made polite, rather stiff small talk, punctuated by long, awkward silences. It was a situation the twins had never found themselves in before, and it felt most uncomfortable. Fortunately for them, their parents were among the first to arrive. Naturally it didn't take Mrs O'Sullivan long to realise that something was wrong, for she knew her daughters very well indeed. She was extremely dismayed because, although the twins had their squabbles, like all sisters, she had never known them to be so cold and distant towards one another before.

For most of the girls, though, half-term was a very happy time. Carlotta's father and grandmother were unable to come, so she was delighted to be asked out by Kitty, whose parents turned out to be every bit as mad as their daughter. They went for a picnic because, naturally, McGinty had to come as well. The little goat thoroughly enjoyed his day out, being spoiled and petted by the two girls and eating all the leftovers from the picnic.

As Hilary's parents were abroad, Doris invited her to spend the day with her people. They had a simply marvellous time, Mr and Mrs Elward treating the two girls to a slap-up lunch at a restaurant before taking them to see a show.

Amanda's pretty mother and Helen's father, a tall, good-looking man with a humorous face, also turned up, each parent warmly hugging both girls. But Amanda glared furiously at Helen when Mrs Wilkes put an arm round her, while Helen eyed Amanda jealously as she joked with Mr Wilkes. How silly they both were, thought Gladys, walking by arm-in-arm with her own mother. Didn't they realise how lucky they were to have two kind, loving parents?

Alison was happy to see her people again, spending a very pleasant day with them. And, just when she thought things couldn't get any better, she bumped into Margaret Winters, who was showing her parents round the grounds.

'Alison, do come and meet my people,' said the older girl, putting a hand on her shoulder. 'Mummy, Daddy – this is Alison, the girl I was telling you about. She does all my little jobs for me and is an absolute angel!'

Alison turned red, partly from pride and partly because she felt quite over-awed in the presence of this grand-looking couple. Mrs Winters, although perhaps a little over-dressed for the occasion, was the most elegant person she had ever seen, and it was easy to see from whom Margaret had inherited her good looks. She greeted Alison with a polite smile and a regal nod of the head. Mr Winters, who looked most distinguished, was more friendly, shaking Alison's hand and recommending her not to allow Margaret to work her too hard. But his eyes twinkled as he spoke, and it was plain that he adored his daughter. Alison walked away with her head in the clouds, thrilled to think that she was the only member of the lower school who had had the honour of being introduced to the deputy head girl's parents.

But, all too soon, half-term was over and, as the third formers prepared for bed that evening, Doris said glumly, 'Back to the old routine. Why does half-term always seem to fly by so quickly?'

'Cheer up, Doris,' said Bobby. 'We've all had a simply marvellous day. I can't remember when I last enjoyed myself so much.'

'That goes for me, too,' added Hilary, climbing into bed. 'It was jolly kind of you and your people to invite me along, Doris.'

'I wonder if the second half of the term will be as eventful as the first?' mused Janet, sitting up in bed and hugging her knees. 'It's been a strange sort of term so far, what with one thing and another.'

'Yes, it has,' agreed Hilary. 'For my part, I hope things settle down a bit now. I've had quite enough excitement for one term.'

But things weren't about to settle down at all. The third formers, worn out and happy, drifted off to sleep one by one, all of them blissfully unaware of the shock they had in store for them the following day.

It all started with a rumour. 'I say!' exclaimed Amanda, sitting down next to Isabel at breakfast. 'Have you heard about Jenny Mills?'

'What about her?' asked Carlotta, buttering a slice of toast.

'Apparently . . .' Amanda leaned forward over the table and lowered her voice. 'Apparently Miss Theobald has asked her to resign as head girl.' She sat back and folded her arms, waiting expectantly for the reaction to her bombshell. But Amanda was disappointed, as the girls were distinctly unimpressed.

'Nonsense!' said Pat scornfully. 'Miss Theobald thinks the world of Jenny. You've got hold of the wrong end of the stick, Amanda.'

'I'm quite sure I haven't!' retorted Amanda, stung. 'I heard a group of first formers chattering about it in the corridor, and they said –'

'First formers! They're just babies,' said Janet loftily. 'What do they know?'

'I expect someone was pulling their leg, Amanda,' Isabel said. 'And they fell for it.'

'Yes, there are always rumours of some sort or another flying around in a school of this size,' said Hilary. 'And nine times out of ten they turn out to be untrue.'

'Oh,' said Amanda, looking rather crestfallen. Not that she wanted Jennifer to lose her position as head girl, of course, for she liked the top former enormously. But it would have been rather a thrill to be first with the gossip.

The third formers thought no more about Amanda's story until morning break, when Carlotta and Kitty, on their way back from a visit to McGinty, spotted Jennifer and Barbara Thompson walking towards them. Normally the two top formers would have called out a friendly greeting, but today they didn't even notice the younger girls, walking past them as if they simply didn't exist. Both of them wore unusually grave expressions, and Jennifer in particular looked pale and strained, her eyes suspiciously red. Carlotta and Kitty exchanged worried glances.

'It *can't* be true!' Carlotta said, with a frown. 'Why, Jenny is one of the most popular head girls St Clare's has ever had.'

'Of course she is,' said Kitty. 'Don't go worrying yourself now, Carlotta. Perhaps Jenny's had a falling out with one of her friends, or something.'

But by lunchtime the rumour had spread like wildfire. Everyone in the school had heard the story and, reluctantly, a lot of the girls began to believe that it must be true. To make matters worse, there was also a tale going round that Margaret Winters, as deputy head girl, had now been asked to step into Jenny's shoes.

'Can things get any worse?' groaned Doris, her head in her hands.

As it happened, they could – and did. Shortly after tea, Grace was summoned to the head's office. The second formers weren't particularly alarmed by this, as Miss Theobald often sent for the form heads to discuss various matters with them. Besides, like the rest of the school, they were far more worried about the prospect of having Margaret Winters as their head girl.

The atmosphere in the common-room was very subdued that evening, the second and third formers too preoccupied to even bother goading each other. Then Grace came back from her talk with Miss Theobald.

'What did the head want?' asked Harriet, glancing up from her book.

'You've been absolutely ages, and . . . I say! Whatever's the matter, Grace?'

Everyone looked round. Grace was trembling, and as white as a sheet. Through clenched teeth, the girl said, 'She knows. Miss Theobald knows.'

'Knows what?' asked Helen, looking bewildered. 'Grace, what on earth are you talking about?'

'Miss Theobald knows about us being out of our beds last week, and thinks we were up to no good. That's why she's suspended Jenny as head girl, because she knew and didn't report it.' Grace paused and looked round the room, her eyes hard. 'Someone's sneaked!'

11.

A truce – and more trouble

The third formers looked at one another in horror. Never had they guessed for one moment that a simple trick would lead to so much trouble! Tricks were supposed to be fun, but no one felt like laughing now. A perfect hubbub broke out among the second formers.

'Who split on us, Grace? Did the head tell you?'

'Whoever it was is a mean beast! How I wish I could get my hands on her!'

'What's going to happen to us, Grace? Will we be punished?'

'Miss Theobald didn't tell me who the sneak was,' answered Grace angrily. 'And yes, Katie, we're being punished all right. No trips to town for a fortnight. And when Miss Jenks finds out about it, no doubt she'll have a punishment of her own to add too.'

'No!' Janet stepped forward suddenly. 'You won't be punished. I'm going to see the head now, and I'll tell her it was all our fault.'

'That's decent of you, Janet, but you don't have to do that,' said Grace.

'Oh yes I do,' Janet said firmly. 'The third form can't stand by and watch you kids suffer for something we did.' She looked round at her form, and everyone nodded in agreement.

'I'll come with you,' said Hilary.

'And me,' added Isabel.

In the end, the whole form volunteered to go with Janet. Even Amanda, not because she had any real wish to get the second form out of trouble, but because she always followed Isabel's lead.

'We can't all go,' said Janet. 'Miss Theobald will think that she's been invaded! Hilary, you come with me, and the twins.' She grimaced. 'It's not going to be pleasant, so we may as well get it over with.'

Their heads held high, but all of them feeling very nervous indeed, the four girls trooped off to Miss Theobald's office.

The head was looking unusually grave when they entered, saying in her clear voice, 'Well, girls? What can I do for you?'

'It's about the trouble that the second form are in,' began Janet, bravely looking Miss Theobald in the eye, though inwardly she was quaking.

'What has that to do with you, Janet?' asked the head, frowning.

'Well, you see, Miss Theobald, it was all our fault. We found an old fire bell in the stables and set it off as a joke.' Once Janet had begun, the words came tumbling out, and soon Miss Theobald knew the whole story.

'I see,' she said at last, looking very serious. 'Rather a childish and irresponsible trick, Janet.'

The third formers blushed to the roots of their hair and looked at the floor.

'We're truly sorry, Miss Theobald,' said Hilary. 'It was only meant to be a bit of fun.'

'I daresay,' said the head dryly. 'But your bit of fun has led to serious consequences, Hilary. However, I am extremely glad that you have had the courage to own up. I see now that the second formers were not to blame and were, in fact, acting very sensibly in following the fire drill. When you return to the common-room you may tell them that their punishment has been lifted.'

'Yes, Miss Theobald,' said Janet, feeling half relieved and half apprehensive. Relieved because the second formers would not, after all, be punished. And apprehensive because she knew that her own form would not get off so lightly. And she was right.

'As for you third formers, you will receive two punishments,' said Miss Theobald, making the waiting girls' hearts sink even further. 'You will not be allowed to leave the school grounds for a fortnight, and you will also be given an extra thirty minutes prep every evening for the next week.'

The girls had to stop themselves from groaning aloud at this. But each of them knew that they were being given the extra punishment for the trouble their trick had caused, and they realised that Miss Theobald was being perfectly just.

'That is all,' finished the head, turning her attention to the pile of papers on her desk. 'You may go now.'

Pat, Isabel and Hilary turned towards the door, but Janet remained where she was, looking down at Miss Theobald's bent head. She cleared her throat and said hesitantly, 'Miss Theobald?'

The head looked up sharply. 'What is it, Janet?'

'It . . . it's about Jenny Mills. We're all so sorry that she's been suspended as head girl. What happened that night was nothing to do with her, and –'

'I'm afraid that my decision regarding Jenny must stand,' said the head briskly, though there was a note of regret in her voice. 'The rule about girls remaining in their dormitories at night is a strict one, and there are very good reasons why it must be kept. As head girl, Jenny should have reported the incident and she knows this.'

'But she only acted as she did to keep the second formers from getting into trouble,' protested Pat, turning to face Miss Theobald once more. 'Please, Miss Theobald, couldn't you give her another chance?'

'Not at the moment, I am afraid. I understand Jenny's reasons for not reporting the second formers,' said the head, her tone softening slightly. 'But, as head girl of the whole school it is her duty to stick to the rules. Believe me, Pat, I regret having to suspend her as much as anyone.'

Isabel, who had been frowning thoughtfully, asked suddenly, 'Miss Theobald, how did you know about the second formers being out of their beds that night?'

'Someone took it upon herself to inform me of the

fact,' replied the head, sounding rather scornful. 'And please don't ask me who it was, for even if I knew I would not be able to tell you.'

'Even if you knew?' repeated Hilary, looking puzzled.

'Yes. I am afraid that the person responsible did not have the courage and sense of honour that you girls have shown tonight, but left the information anonymously.'

'You mean that she sent you a letter, Miss Theobald?' said Janet. 'But if that's so, how could you have known that she was telling the truth and not simply making up a story to get Jenny and the second formers into trouble?'

'Because she left me proof,' replied Miss Theobald solemnly. 'Now really, girls, I can't discuss this with you any further. Please return to your common-room now.'

The four girls left, each of them silent until they were out of earshot of the head's room. Then they had plenty to say!

'Miss Theobald said that she couldn't change her mind about Jenny at the moment,' said Isabel, trying hard to look on the bright side. 'Which means that she might at some time in the future. A suspension is only a temporary thing, isn't it?'

'Let's hope so,' said Janet. 'What's puzzling me is what kind of proof the sneak could possibly have given Miss Theobald.'

But none of the others could imagine.

'There's something that doesn't add up about all this,' said Isabel thoughtfully. The others looked at her and she went on, 'We played that trick over a week ago. Why did the sneak wait all this time to go to Miss Theobald?'

'I was wondering that,' said Hilary with a frown. 'It doesn't make any sense at all.'

'I thought of something else, too,' said Janet, looking troubled. 'The sneak has to be a second or third former. No one else knew about the trick.'

'I don't believe for a minute that it's anyone from our form!' cried Isabel, shocked. 'None of them would dream of doing such a sly, underhand thing.'

'What about the new girl, Amanda?' suggested Pat, unable to resist the opportunity to plant doubts in Isabel's mind about her new friend. 'None of us really knows her that well.'

'I do!' protested Isabel, glaring at her twin. 'And I know that she wouldn't dream of doing such a thing! And I notice that you don't mention Kitty. She's new as well, so it could just as easily have been her.'

But no one could really believe that the open, likeable Kitty would be capable of such meanness.

'I suppose it could have been that stepsister of Amanda's – Helen,' said Janet, wrinkling her brow. 'I don't much like her – conceited little beast!'

'I agree, but just because she's conceited that doesn't make her a sneak,' said Hilary. 'Besides, why would she sneak on her own form and get herself into trouble? She couldn't possibly have known that we third formers would own up to Miss Theobald and save their skins.'

'Oh, I don't know! The whole thing's a complete

mystery,' said Janet. 'Anyway, we'd better hurry along to the common-room and tell the others what's happened. I expect they're on tenterhooks.'

Indeed they were! The second and third formers pounced on the four girls as they entered, all of them talking at once.

'What happened, Janet? What did the head say?'

'Yes, tell us what our punishment is.'

'Did Miss Theobald tell you who the sneak is?'

Quickly Janet told them what had happened. There were groans from the third formers when they learned of their punishments, but Grace stood up and said in her clear voice, 'Thank you, Janet – and the rest of you third formers. It was jolly decent of you to take the blame and get us out of trouble.'

'Hear hear!' shouted her form-mates.

'Perhaps now we can put this silly feud behind us,' said Janet, looking at Grace. 'After all, we have more important matters to deal with now.'

Grace nodded and said solemnly, 'I agree. If it wasn't for our quarrel, poor Jenny would still be head girl. I think we should do all we can to get her reinstated.' Her face broke into a grin suddenly. 'I must admit though, Janet, that was a simply splendid trick you played on us – even if it did end up causing so much trouble.'

'Well, at least something good has come out of it,' said Doris happily. 'It will be nice to go to bed tonight without having to check first to see if one of you second formers has put a frog or something in it!'

This was said with such a comical expression that everyone burst out laughing, and suddenly all the ill feeling that had boiled up between the two forms vanished completely.

But there were still very serious matters to discuss, and the laughter soon died when talk returned to the sneak.

'It's horrible to think it might have been one of us,' said Katie, looking round. 'Someone who might be here right now. Ugh!'

'None of us want to think that, Katie,' said Hilary. 'But who else could it have been?'

'Well, who had the most to gain from this?' asked Carlotta, who perched on the edge of a table, swinging her legs.

'What do you mean, Carlotta?' asked Pat, with a frown.

'I mean that maybe we're looking at this from the wrong angle. Perhaps the sneak wasn't out to get us into trouble, but Jenny Mills.'

'Oh, that's impossible!' cried Mirabel. 'Who could have a grudge against old Jenny?'

'No one,' answered Bobby promptly. 'Everyone simply adores her.'

'But there is one person who has got something out of this whole business,' said Carlotta. 'Think about it.'

'Margaret Winters!' cried several girls in unison.

'Of course!' said Pat. 'But how could Margaret do something like that to a member of her own form?'

'I think that Margaret would stop at nothing to get her

own way,' put in the quiet little Gladys. 'And everyone knows that she's always wanted to be head girl.'

'Yes, but how could she possibly have known about the trick we played on the second form?' Isabel asked.

Alison, who had taken no part in this discussion, could have told her cousin exactly how Margaret knew. It was fortunate for her that no one chose to glance in her direction, for Alison's guilty face would certainly have given her away!

'She could have overheard us discussing it,' Kitty was saying now. 'Listening outside doors would be just her style.'

'I suppose so,' said Janet. 'Well, we can't talk about it any more tonight – it's almost bedtime. But I think we should have a meeting in here tomorrow night to plan what we do next.'

Everyone agreed at once, and the girls made their way to bed, all of them in thoughtful mood. But for two girls their thoughts were particularly unhappy, and kept them awake long after the others had gone to sleep.

One was Amanda, whose conscience was troubling her increasingly over what she had done to Pat and Isabel. 'Sly and underhand' – that was what her form had said about the sneak. What would they say about her, Amanda, if they knew how she had intercepted the twins' letters, and that they were hidden away in the locker beside her bed? And how would the twins themselves feel? 'How could she do that to a member of her own form?' That was the question Pat had

94

asked about Margaret Winters, the look of disgust on her face plain to see. Yet what Amanda had done was just as bad – perhaps worse, for she had made her friend unhappy too. Because Isabel was clearly *very* unhappy about the rift that had grown between herself and her twin, no matter how hard she tried to hide it.

And as if that wasn't bad enough, Amanda was also terribly worried about her schoolwork. At her old school she had always been near the top of the class, but the work here was so much more difficult, and no matter how hard she tried she always seemed to be near the bottom. Every week she seemed to fall further behind the others. What if she never caught up, and was kept down next term instead of going up into the fourth with them? It was just too horrible to think about!

The other third former who couldn't sleep was, of course, Alison. No matter how often she told herself that Margaret wasn't the sneak, a niggling little doubt persisted. And if she owned up to the others that she was responsible for letting Margaret in on their secret they would be simply furious with her! Alison didn't think she could bear that. She wouldn't say anything, she decided, until she had seen Margaret tomorrow. Alison was certain that she would be able to tell from the older girl's manner whether she was guilty or not, for surely Margaret wouldn't be able to look her in the face if she had sneaked. Feeling slightly better now that

she had made this decision, Alison closed her eyes and
tried to get to sleep. Oh dear, what a troublesome term
this was turning out to be!

Alison makes a discovery

Alison didn't have long to wait before she encountered Margaret. She was going downstairs to breakfast the very next morning when she heard her name called and, turning, saw the new head girl behind her.

'Alison, I just wanted to say how sorry I was to hear that the third form had got into trouble,' said Margaret, a sympathetic expression on her face. 'Miss Theobald has just told me what happened. What a perfectly horrid ending to such a marvellous trick.' She laid a hand on Alison's shoulder as she spoke, and the girl felt a warm glow spread through her. Margaret sounded so sincere, she couldn't possibly be putting on an act.

'It was rather horrid,' said Alison. 'I just wish we could find out who sneaked.'

'I don't suppose you will, though. I just hope that whoever it was feels thoroughly ashamed of herself,' Margaret said, her eyes sparkling with indignation. 'Oh well, I suppose we'd better go in to breakfast. As head girl I shall be accused of setting a bad example if I'm late. Come and see me after tea, would you, Alison? I've a couple of little jobs for you.'

The girl nodded eagerly before rushing into the big

dining-room to join the rest of her form, feeling more light-hearted than she would have thought possible a short while ago.

The other third formers, however, felt far from light-hearted. Tomorrow was Saturday, and normally they would have been looking forward to going into town to spend their pocket money, or have tea and cakes at the little tea shop. Instead they were to be confined to the school grounds.

Carlotta, who had just opened a letter lying beside her plate, exclaimed, 'Oh, my goodness!'

'What's up, Carlotta?' asked Isabel. 'Not bad news?'

'Far from it, Isabel. My father's just sent me a simply enormous postal order to make up for not being able to visit at half-term. Look!'

'Ooh, you lucky thing!' said Isabel enviously. 'What will you do with all that money?'

'I know what I'd like to do,' replied Carlotta at once, her vivid little face glowing. 'Throw a party!'

'What a marvellous idea,' said Bobby, looking over her shoulder at the postal order. 'My word, Carlotta, I should think you'd be able to feed the whole school with that amount of money!'

Carlotta laughed. 'Well, I wasn't planning on inviting the whole school, Bobby, but it would be nice to ask the second formers, to celebrate the end of our feud.'

There were oohs and aahs at this. 'What a super idea,' said Janet. 'But a party's out of the question until this beastly punishment is over. For one thing we can't go into town to buy the goodies. And for another, Miss Theobald wouldn't allow it while we're in disgrace.'

'No, but there's nothing to stop us planning something for a couple of weeks' time, is there?' said Pat. 'Goodness knows we could do with something to look forward to.'

Everyone agreed to this eagerly and Carlotta said wistfully, 'What a pity we can't hold a midnight feast.'

'Why can't we?' asked Kitty, with a frown. 'Sure, that sounds like a grand idea to me.'

'Kitty, we daren't,' said Hilary. 'It's just too risky. We're already in trouble, and if we're caught I don't like to think what would happen to us.'

'And don't forget that Margaret Winters will be watching us like a hawk,' put in Mirabel, pulling a face. 'She'll just be waiting for a chance to make trouble for us.'

'*More* trouble, you mean,' said Bobby. 'I bet she was absolutely delighted when she found out that Miss Theobald had confined us all to school.'

There were murmurs of agreement at this, but Alison piped up, 'Oh no, you're all wrong! I've just spoken to Margaret, and she told me how sorry she was that we'd all got into trouble.'

'Hmm,' said Janet doubtfully. 'I just bet she was!'

'Honestly, Janet, she was so sincere, and –'

'Oh, Alison!' Isabel interrupted, shaking her head in exasperation. 'You're such a goof that you believe every word Margaret says. And as for her feeling sorry for us – huh!'

Alison's eyes glinted with angry tears, but before a quarrel could erupt Hilary said hastily, 'Kitty, you'd better dash if you're going to give McGinty his breakfast before Geography.'

'So I had,' said the little Irish girl, getting to her feet. 'It's awful grumpy he gets if he's kept waiting for his food.'

'Hold on a minute, Kitty,' said Amanda, rummaging in her satchel. 'I've a couple of apples in here for McGinty. I know how he loves them.'

'Sure, that's awfully kind of you, Amanda. But why don't you come and give them to him yourself?'

Amanda, who was a great animal lover and very fond of McGinty, agreed at once, and the two girls set off together.

The little goat was very pleased to see them, and even more pleased with the bucket of scraps they had brought him.

'You'd think he was starving!' declared Kitty as he polished off the lot.

Amanda laughed and pulled out the brown paper bag containing the apples. But before she had the chance to feed him one, McGinty made a sudden lunge and wolfed down the lot, bag and all.

'Why, I believe he's enjoying the paper more than the apples!' said Amanda, chuckling at the comical appearance McGinty presented, as he stood there with shreds of paper hanging from the corner of his mouth.

'He probably is,' said Kitty, with a grin. 'There's no greater treat than a nice, tasty bit of paper as far as

McGinty's concerned. Come on, boy, just time to take you for a little walk.' She slipped McGinty's lead on and led him to the door. 'Amanda, are you coming?'

Amanda had been staring at the little goat thoughtfully. So, McGinty liked paper, did he? Well, she knew where there was plenty of the stuff, and how to dispose of it was a problem that had been preying on her mind for some time. Maybe McGinty was the answer to her problem. She followed Kitty outside, watching as the goat ate a chocolate wrapper someone had dropped, before nibbling at a patch of grass.

'You know, Miss Theobald really ought to pay me to keep McGinty here,' said Kitty thoughtfully. 'Sure and he earns his keep, getting rid of litter and keeping the grass tidy.'

Amanda opened her mouth to reply, but shut it again quickly, for Margaret Winters was striding towards them, a haughty expression on her face.

'You girls, hurry up!' she commanded briskly. 'Get that animal back where it belongs, or you'll be late for class.'

Looking at Margaret with dislike, Kitty said firmly, 'McGinty is a he, not an it. And if I took him back where he belonged, I would have to travel all the way back to Kilblarney. Then I really would be late!'

Margaret bristled. 'Don't be cheeky, unless you want an order mark. Ugh!' She shuddered and backed away as McGinty raised his head and gently butted his head against her arm. 'I don't know what Miss

Theobald was thinking, to allow such a badly behaved creature at St Clare's!'

Kitty looked up at the head girl, a hurt expression in her blue eyes. 'Ah now, Margaret, that's unkind. Sure and I'm trying so hard to be good!'

Amanda turned her head away, lips clamped tightly together to prevent herself exploding with laughter. Margaret, however, did explode – with anger! At the end of her lecture Kitty was left in no doubt that she was the most insolent, unruly, disrespectful girl ever to darken the doors of St Clare's.

'You'd better be careful, that's all,' Margaret finished, glaring at the younger girl. 'I've got my eye on you – and that goat of yours. If either of you puts a foot wrong –'

'Or a hoof,' broke in the irrepressible Irish girl.

'Kitty,' Amanda said quickly, before a red-faced Margaret could give vent to her fury. 'We really ought to be going, or we shall be awfully late.'

Margaret glanced at her watch and realised that she, too, would be late for class if she didn't hurry. So, contenting herself with a last, angry scowl in Kitty's direction, she stalked off towards the school.

'Kitty, you're dreadful!' said Amanda, as they escorted McGinty safely back to the old stables. 'I wouldn't dare speak to the head girl the way that you do.'

'Ah, as far as I'm concerned, Jenny's still head girl,' answered Kitty, bolting the door firmly behind McGinty. 'And I'm thinking maybe it won't be long before we have her back again!'

Both girls were unusually quiet as they made their way to the Geography lesson, each of them occupied with her own thoughts and schemes. Life at St Clare's was about to get very interesting indeed!

Margaret appeared to be in good humour again when Alison went to her study that evening, behaving so sweetly that the girl was more convinced than ever that she couldn't possibly be the sneak.

'I'm afraid I have to dash off to a meeting now,' said the top former, after she and Alison had drunk their tea. 'Be a dear and clear that pile of books away before you go, would you?'

Alison set to work eagerly once Margaret had gone, picking up the books that had been left on the table and stacking them neatly on a shelf in the cupboard. There was also a cardboard box on the shelf and, as she moved it aside to make room, the lid fell off. Alison saw that the box contained photographs, and couldn't resist taking a peek. There was one of Margaret and her parents, smiling happily at a family party. And another of her with a tall, good-looking young man, who looked so like her that he must be her older brother. Alison sifted happily through the photographs, and was about to put them away when she realised that there were two more in the box, hidden under some negatives. Alison moved the negatives and saw that the last two photographs were different from the others. Margaret and her family weren't on them at all and Alison blinked as she picked them up, hardly able to believe her eyes, then gave a gasp. Hearing a noise in the corridor, she hastily thrust the two photographs and the negatives into her pocket, putting the others back into the cupboard. There was a grim look on her pretty face as she left Margaret's study. She had to speak to the others at once – and it wasn't going to be pleasant!

The common-room was crowded when Alison entered. Girls sat around chattering, one or two reading, some knitting or sewing, while in the corner of the room the radiogram played a lively dance tune.

Alison stood in the doorway for a moment, looking round, before she raised her voice. 'Doris, could you turn the radiogram off, please? There is something I have to tell you all.'

Doris did as she was asked, with a curious glance at Alison. She looked awfully white! Whatever could be wrong?

'What's up, old girl?' asked Isabel, concerned. 'You look terribly pale. Don't say you've fallen out with Margaret!'

Alison's legs suddenly felt dreadfully weak and shaky. She sat down in the nearest armchair and reached into her pocket. 'Take a look at these,' she said, handing the photographs to Janet. 'I found them in Margaret's study.'

The second and third formers crowded curiously round Janet as she looked at the photographs. There was silence for a moment, as they took in what they were seeing.

The first photograph was of the second formers, all in their dressing-gowns, as they huddled together in the grounds, looking furtive. In the middle of them stood Jenny Mills, looking just as guilty as the rest, with her arm round a distressed Katie. The second was even more incriminating, for here Jenny was peering around the corner of the shed, holding a warning hand up to the others. They had obviously been taken on the night of the fateful trick.

'So, this is what Miss Theobald meant by proof,' said Hilary. 'Margaret must have been lying in wait with her camera.'

'I knew that she was the sneak!' said Bobby angrily. 'I just knew it!'

'Good work, Alison!' cried Mirabel.

'Thank goodness we know for certain that no one from the second or third forms was the sneak,' said Grace.

'Yes, but there's just one thing that's puzzling me,' said Janet, who had been looking thoughtful. 'If Margaret was lying in wait, she must have known what we had planned. The question is – who told her?'

Alison swallowed and took a deep breath. Then, in a small voice, she said, 'It was me.'

13.

Amanda is caught out

With many tears from Alison, and much angry prompting from the others, the whole sorry story unfolded.

'Alison, you're an idiot!' Carlotta told her roundly, when she had finished. 'Fancy telling Margaret, of all people, what we were planning. Why, you might just as well have gone to Miss Theobald herself!'

Alison said nothing, merely sniffed and dabbed at her eyes. The twins were quite as angry with Alison as everyone else, but she *was* their cousin, and they tried to stick up for her.

'Alison didn't *mean* to cause trouble,' said Isabel.

'And Margaret can turn on the charm when she wants to,' put in Pat. 'I've seen her!'

'Yes, let's not be too hard on Alison,' Kitty added. 'She's owned up, which can't have been easy. And she's made up for her mistake by bringing us these photographs.'

'I'll bet Miss Theobald won't be too impressed if we tell her that the cowardly, anonymous sneak turns out to be the head girl of St Clare's,' said Isabel. 'It might end in Margaret being suspended too. You know how Miss Theobald hates anything underhand.'

'We can't go to the head,' sighed Janet. 'We've no

proof that Margaret took these photographs. It's just our word against hers, and you can bet Margaret will lie her way out of this as she always does.'

'You don't mean that we're just going to let her get away with it?' cried Bobby indignantly.

'It's the last thing in the world I want to do,' Janet said. 'But at the moment, I just can't think of a way to catch her out.'

'This explains why there was such a delay before she snitched on us to the head,' said Grace, who had been looking at the photographs thoughtfully. 'Margaret must have taken the film to the chemist's shop in town to have it developed, and she would have had to wait for the photographs.'

'Alison, you'll have to put them back where you got them from at the earliest opportunity,' said Hilary. 'If Margaret notices that they're missing she'll realise that we're on to her.'

'It's a pity we don't have the negatives,' said Grace, frowning. 'Then I could make a copy of them – just in case dear Margaret takes it into her head to destroy the evidence.'

'But I do have them!' cried Alison, reaching into her pocket once more. 'Is it possible to make a copy from them though?'

'It is if you're a member of the school photography club,' said Grace. 'Which I am. I can slip into the darkroom at break tomorrow morning. There shouldn't be anyone around then.'

'Sure and I'll come with you, Grace,' said Kitty. 'I'm thinking of taking up photography myself.'

The roguish gleam in her eyes made Janet look at her sharply. 'Kitty! You've got something up your sleeve, haven't you?' she said. 'A way of catching Margaret out.'

'Ah now, maybe I have, and maybe I haven't,' Kitty answered, with a teasing smile. 'I don't want to say too much, for I need to think about it and it may not come to anything yet. If my plan is to work, though, I'll be needing accomplices. Alison, you play a very important part.'

Alison, still red-eyed, looked rather alarmed, and the Irish girl went on, 'It's important that Margaret doesn't suspect anything, so you must carry on doing her jobs, and being just as friendly towards her as you've always been. Can you do that?'

'Oh, Kitty, I don't think I can!' said Alison dolefully. 'I feel so betrayed and let down that I really don't think I can even look at her again.'

'Don't be such a goof, Alison!' said Janet sharply. 'You got us all into this mess – the least you can do is help us to get out of it.'

'Janet's right,' said Pat. 'You owe it to all of us to try and put things right.'

'Yes, come on, Alison!' Doris cried bracingly. 'This is your chance to be a heroine.'

This instantly appealed to Alison's sense of the dramatic, and the thought of getting back into the others' good books cheered her enormously. 'Very well,' she said, squaring her slim shoulders. 'It won't be easy being pleasant to Margaret but, for the sake of our two forms, I shall sacrifice my pride.'

One or two of the girls had to turn away to hide their smiles at this, but Kitty said, 'That's the spirit, Alison! And there's something else that I want the rest of you to do.'

'Anything, Kitty,' said Bobby promptly. 'If it's going to help us show Margaret Winters up for the sly, deceitful creature she is, I'm all for it!'

'Good. Because I want you all to go ahead and organise that midnight feast we were talking about earlier. Goodness knows we need something to cheer us up a bit!'

There was silence as the second and third formers looked at one another in amazement. This was the last thing they had expected Kitty to ask of them.

At last Hilary spoke. 'Kitty, are you quite mad? As I explained this morning, it's just too dangerous. If Margaret starts snooping round . . .'

'Ah now, don't you go worrying your head about Margaret,' said Kitty soothingly. 'She'll not be doing any snooping, I promise you. Not if my little scheme comes off.'

The girls were in two minds. On the one hand, they certainly didn't want to get into any more trouble. But on the other hand, a midnight feast would be too wizard for words! As always, they looked to their head girls for a lead.

'I vote we do as Kitty says,' said Grace firmly. 'Janet?'

Janet looked at the Irish girl thoughtfully for a moment, her head on one side. 'I trust you, Kitty,' she said at last. 'Though I don't know why, for you do the craziest things! A feast it is, then – but just make sure you don't let us down.'

'That was a very brave thing you did earlier,' said Amanda, coming up to Alison in the dormitory that evening. 'It must have been difficult, owning up to what you had done in front of everyone like that.'

'I don't feel as if I'm a very brave person,' said Alison honestly. 'But once I'd discovered those photographs I really didn't have much choice in the matter. I do feel better for it, though – as if a great weight has been lifted from my shoulders.'

Amanda could understand that, for she, too, had been carrying a great weight around with her for quite a while, and it seemed to get a little heavier each day. She looked at Alison's pretty, kindly face and, for a moment, thought about confiding in the girl. Alison might be silly at times, but she was kind-hearted and sensitive to the feelings of others. But she was also the twins' cousin, a little voice in Amanda's head reminded her. It was highly probable that Alison's loyalty to Pat and Isabel would make her run straight to them and blurt out her, Amanda's, secret. No, she could not risk letting Alison know what troubled her.

But Amanda would have to find some way of easing her conscience, which was beginning to cause her sleepless nights. And then she was tired and stupid in class, and got even further behind with her work, which made her worry about that as well! Perhaps getting rid of those wretched letters would ease the burden a little. It wouldn't change what she had done, but at least they wouldn't be there in her locker, right beside her as she tried to sleep, a constant reminder of her deceit and wickedness. Yes, tomorrow – with McGinty's help – she would dispose of them.

'Well, this is no way to spend a Saturday afternoon,' grumbled Bobby the next day, as the third form sat rather listlessly in the common-room. Even the luxury of having it all to themselves didn't cheer them, when they thought of the second formers happily shopping and having their tea in town. And the fact that they only had themselves to blame for their confinement didn't make the punishment any easier to bear.

'It's the first fine day we've had all week, too,' sighed Carlotta, looking wistfully out of the window.

'Well, why don't we go outside?' suggested Hilary, brightening suddenly. 'Miss Theobald said we weren't allowed outside the grounds, but there's no reason why we have to stay cooped up indoors.'

'Good idea,' said Janet. 'Let's get our coats and go for a walk round the gardens.'

The others leaped to their feet eagerly, only Amanda remaining in her seat.

'Come on, Amanda!' cried Isabel. 'Let's get some fresh air.'

'Actually, Isabel, I think I'll just stay here and finish my book,' said the girl. 'I've got a bit of a cold coming on.'

'I thought you'd been looking a bit peaky lately,' Isabel said. 'Would you like me to stay and keep you company?'

'Thanks, Isabel, but I'll be fine,' said Amanda, smiling wanly. 'You go off with the others and enjoy yourself.'

So Isabel left and, after a few moments, Amanda went to the window. She could see the third formers heading towards the playing fields and breathed a sigh of relief. The coast was clear.

Running up to the dormitory, Amanda pulled on her hat and coat, before taking the twins' letters from her locker. The girl shuddered as she stuffed them into her satchel. Just a few sheets of paper – but what a lot of trouble they had stirred up!

In a few minutes Amanda had reached the old stables. Looking around furtively to make sure no one was about, she slipped inside and received a warm welcome from McGinty.

'Are you hungry, boy?' she whispered. 'Well, not for much longer. I have a special treat for you.'

With that, Amanda pulled a couple of the letters from her satchel, McGinty snatching them from her and making short work of them. Amanda fed him another, then another, so intent on what she was doing that she didn't even notice one of the envelopes fall from her bag and on to the floor. Nor did she hear the door open softly behind her.

'Nearly finished now, McGinty,' murmured Amanda. 'Have you room for one more?'

Again she reached into her satchel, giving a gasp when she found it empty. Amanda was certain that there had been one more letter! Suppose she had dropped it in the grounds on the way here? Worse still, what if it was lying on the floor in the dormitory, where anyone could find it? A shiver went down her spine. She had to retrace her steps at once and find that letter. Quickly Amanda turned – and came face to face with Janet!

'Looking for this, Amanda?' said Janet coolly, holding out her hand. In it was the missing letter.

Amanda turned white, but tried to bluff it out. 'Wh – what's that?' she asked, her voice sounding unnaturally high with nerves.

'You know what it is!' Janet said scornfully. 'So don't try to act all innocent with me. I know what you've been up to, Amanda, and I saw you feeding the twins' letters to McGinty, so you may as well do the decent thing and own up.'

At once Amanda saw that there was no point in lying. She had been caught red-handed!

14.

A very unhappy girl

As Janet stood watching her, arms folded and a stern expression on her face, the only thing Amanda could think of to say was, 'I thought you had gone for a walk with the others.'

'That was what you were supposed to think,' Janet said. 'Actually I told them that I'd changed my mind and decided to stay behind with you. Then I hid round the corner by the common-room and waited to see if my suspicions were correct. I had a feeling you'd want to get rid of those letters pretty soon.'

All at once Amanda's legs seemed to turn to jelly, and she sat down on a rickety old chair that had been dumped in the stables. 'But how did you know?' she whispered, staring at Janet in bewilderment. 'What made you suspect me?'

'Actually, it was something Carlotta said,' Janet told her. 'The day Jenny Mills was suspended. "Who had the most to gain?" she asked. Do you remember?'

Horrified, Amanda nodded.

'That got me thinking,' Janet went on. 'And I asked myself who had the most to gain from ensuring that the twins didn't receive their letters to one another. The answer was you, Amanda. I began to watch you, and noticed how nervous and unhappy you seemed – and how uncomfortable you looked whenever anyone brought the subject of those letters up. That's when I knew that I was right.'

'Janet, please don't tell Pat and Isabel,' begged Amanda. 'I would lose Isabel's friendship and I couldn't bear that.'

'That's why you did it, isn't it?' said Janet. 'You were afraid that, once Pat came back, Isabel wouldn't want you around any more.'

Miserably Amanda nodded. 'It was terribly wrong of me, I know, but, you see, I've never really had a friend of my own before.'

'Haven't you?' said Janet, surprised and a little disbelieving. Surely everyone had friends! 'Why ever not?'

'Well, when it was just Mummy and I, we lived in a little cottage in a remote village. I went to day school in the nearest town, which was where most of the other girls lived. But because our cottage was such a long way out, I could never invite anyone home to tea, or go to their birthday parties. Soon people became fed up with me refusing their invitations all the time and just left me alone. I think they thought I was a bit stuck-up and didn't want to make friends when, actually, I was desperately lonely. I would have given anything for someone to laugh and joke with, and share secrets with.'

'Golly, how awful!' said Janet, beginning to feel a

little sorry for Amanda. 'But why didn't you try to make friends with Helen when your parents got married? Surely that would have been a perfect solution.'

Amanda laughed bitterly. 'I was so thrilled when Mummy announced that she and Helen's father were getting married and that I was to have a stepsister. I tried so hard to be her friend, and to make her like me. But Helen never gave me a chance. She looked down her nose at me from the start, and made it very plain that we were never going to be friends.'

It just went to show, thought Janet, that things were never quite as they seemed. She had come in here prepared to tear Amanda off a strip, before hauling her in front of the third form so that they could decide on a punishment. Now, though, although what Amanda had done was very wrong, Janet felt that the girl needed helping rather than punishing. At last she said, 'It seems to me, Amanda, that you have done a bad thing for a good reason. But Pat and Isabel have to be told. It's only fair.'

Amanda nodded unhappily and said, 'Will you have to tell all the others as well?'

'That will be for the twins to decide,' answered Janet, moving towards the door. 'Wait here and I'll go and find them.'

'You're going to bring them here now?' squeaked Amanda, in alarm.

Janet nodded. 'I think you should own up to them yourself, Amanda – and the sooner the better. Just be honest, and tell them exactly what you have told me. They're both fair and decent, and although they will probably be angry at first, I don't think that they will be too hard on you.'

Then she was gone, leaving poor Amanda alone with her own thoughts. They were not pleasant ones, and the next few minutes seemed to pass very slowly indeed. At last Janet returned with the twins, Isabel looking puzzled, and Pat looking displeased at having her walk interrupted.

'Janet said that you wanted to speak to us,' said Isabel. 'What's up, old girl?'

The concern in her voice made Amanda feel guiltier than ever. She glanced at Janet, who nodded encouragingly. So, taking a deep breath, she began. The twins were silent for a few moments when they learned that it was Amanda who had caused the rift between them. Isabel found her voice first. She was so shocked to learn of her friend's deceit that she had scarcely taken in the other things Amanda had admitted to – her feelings of loneliness, and her fear of losing her first true friend.

'How could you, Amanda?' she cried, two angry spots of colour on her cheeks. 'I trusted you and thought we were friends. But you're no friend of mine.'

This was exactly what Amanda had feared, and she began to sob, burying her face in her hands. Someone moved across to her, placing a comforting arm about her shoulders, and Amanda lifted her head, giving a shocked gasp when she saw who it was. Pat! But why? Amanda knew how bitterly Isabel's twin resented her, for she had not attempted to hide her hostility. Yet here she was offering her comfort! Amanda could not understand it. Nor could Isabel, who cried, 'Pat, how can you feel sorry for her after what she's done to us?'

'Because, believe it or not, I can understand *why* she did it,' said Pat, keeping her arm around the weeping Amanda. 'You and I have been lucky, Isabel. We've always had one another, as well as our friends here at St Clare's. But Amanda didn't have a friend in the world until she met you.'

Isabel's brow puckered thoughtfully and Pat went on, 'I can sympathise with her, because, for the past few weeks, I've felt that I was in danger of losing you too.'

'Oh, Pat,' said Isabel, tears starting to her eyes. 'You'll never lose me! No matter what happens, you and I will *always* have one another.'

Janet, who had remained in the background petting McGinty, joined the other three now, and said in her forthright way, 'Well, you don't know how glad I am to hear that!'

The twins laughed, rather shakily, and Pat said, 'But what are we going to do about Amanda?'

'I was rather wondering that myself,' came Amanda's plaintive voice, as she pulled a handkerchief from her pocket and dabbed at her eyes.

'I don't think we should tell the others,' said Pat firmly. 'That would only turn them against Amanda, which would make matters worse.'

'I agree,' said Isabel. 'We'll just tell them that we've sorted out the mix-up over the letters and that everything is all right between us now.'

'Do you mean that?' gasped Amanda, beginning to look more hopeful. 'It's more than I deserve after I played such a mean trick on you both.'

'It *was* a mean trick,' said Isabel gravely. 'But everyone deserves a second chance.'

'Come on, Amanda,' said Janet, taking the girl's arm and pulling her to her feet. 'You'd better wash your face, or the others will start asking questions if they see you with red eyes at the tea-table. And I rather think that the twins have things to talk about.'

'We do,' said Isabel, as Janet led Amanda away.

But, as she reached the door, Amanda turned and said, 'Isabel! Are we still . . .'

'Yes, we're still friends,' said Isabel. 'Pat?'

'I'd like to be friends with you too, Amanda,' Pat said with a smile. 'You see, that's the thing with twins – if you're friends with one, you have to be friends with the other too. I hope you don't mind.'

'Mind?' repeated Amanda incredulously. 'Why, I'm thrilled. Having both of you as my friends will be too marvellous for words!'

'Thank heavens for that!' laughed Janet. 'Now Amanda and I are going indoors, and you two had better not be far behind unless you want to be late for tea.'

As the door closed behind the two girls there was silence for a moment then, at the same time, both Pat and Isabel cried, 'Let's never quarrel again!'

They laughed and Pat said, 'I'm sorry I doubted you, old thing.'

'And I'm sorry too,' said Isabel. 'I should have known that you wouldn't have suddenly stopped writing to me for no reason.'

'I'm so glad we're friends again,' said Pat happily, slipping her arm through Isabel's. 'I just wish there was something we could do to help Amanda.'

'So do I,' sighed Isabel. 'If only she and Helen could settle their differences I really think that the pair of them would be much happier.'

'Yes, we must put our thinking caps on and see if there's something we can do to bring the two of them together.'

But, as things turned out, Pat and Isabel didn't need to put their thinking caps on at all!

In the common-room that evening Helen was in an extremely bad temper, having been given several stockings to darn by Matron. 'I hate darning,' she complained, for about the twentieth time, and Grace rolled her eyes.

'If you concentrate on what you're doing, instead of moaning about it, you'll get it done much more quickly,' she said sensibly.

'Katie, can't you help me?' pleaded Helen. 'You're good at needlework.'

'No,' Katie said bluntly. 'I've finished my own

mending and I've no intention of doing yours as well.'

Helen's expression was so sulky that Amanda, sitting nearby, laughed. The second former glared at her, then said, 'Of course, if I was at home I would simply throw these old stockings away and get Daddy to buy me new ones. Amanda, perhaps you could give me a hand. After all, you're used to having to mend things and go on wearing them when they're worn out and shabby.'

'That's enough!' said Grace sharply. But it was too late.

Amanda laughed and said, 'Do you know, Helen, I often wonder how someone as kind and sweet-natured as your father came to have a daughter like you. I really feel sorry for him at times.'

'Well, I feel sorry for your mother,' retorted Helen angrily. 'Being poor *and* having to live in a tiny cottage with only *you* for company must have been simply dreadful. Thank heavens Daddy came along and rescued her.'

'Here we go again,' muttered Janet under her breath, as the quarrel grew more heated. She and Grace exchanged glances, and were just about to step in and break things up when Gladys suddenly got to her feet and shouted, 'Will you two SHUT UP!'

The stepsisters were so astonished at being yelled at by the timid little third former that they did just that!

'The two of you ought to be ashamed of yourselves,' Gladys went on, looking angrier than the girls had ever seen her. 'You are both so lucky to have two parents to love you and take care of you, but you're so intent on rowing with one another that you don't appreciate it at all! Why, if my mother met a nice man who could be like a father to me, and if I had a sister or brother to share my happiness with, I would think myself the luckiest girl in the world!'

Everyone knew that Gladys's father had died when she was small, and that her mother had struggled to bring her up alone. Remembering this, Amanda turned red, and even Helen looked shame-faced.

'Gladys is perfectly right,' said Carlotta, going across and giving the girl a pat on the shoulder. 'I only have a father, because my mother died when I was a baby, and I feel just as Gladys does. You two should learn to count your blessings. And if you can't manage to do that, save your quarrels for when you're alone and stop making everyone else feel uncomfortable!' She glared fiercely at the two girls, who didn't dare resume their quarrel after that.

Helen finished her darning in silence, while Amanda buried her head in a book. But everyone noticed that, when bedtime came, they managed to say goodnight to one another in quite a civil manner.

'Good old Gladys,' murmured Pat to Isabel. 'Let's hope that this is a new beginning for Amanda and Helen.'

It was. At breakfast the next morning, Amanda opened a letter from her mother, and gave a gasp as she read it. 'Oh my goodness! I don't believe it!'

'Don't believe what?' asked Doris, looking quite alarmed.

'It's my mother,' said Amanda. 'And Helen's father. They're going to have a baby. I'm going to be a sister!'

Pat looked up sharply, curious to know how Amanda felt about the news. One look at the girl's face left her in no doubt – Amanda was beaming from ear to ear! As the third formers called out their congratulations, Helen, at the second-form table, let out a cry and it was obvious that she, too, had received the news.

'Amanda!' she called, standing up and waving the letter in the air. 'Have you heard?'

'Yes, isn't it simply marvellous?' Amanda called back.

'I'll say,' laughed Helen, whose genuinely happy smile made her look really pretty. 'The most thrilling news ever.'

Mam'zelle, who was at the mistresses' table, stood up and called both girls to order.

'Sorry, Mam'zelle,' said Amanda, unable to stop grinning. 'But, you see, we've just learned that our parents – Helen's and mine – are expecting a baby!'

'Ah, that is indeed good news!' cried Mam'zelle, clapping her hands together and smiling. 'A dear little *bébé*. Amanda, you may take your meal over to the second-form table. You and Helen will wish to talk about your new brother or sister.'

Amanda picked up her plate at once, while Helen moved up to make room for her. The others looked on in amusement.

'I do hope it's a boy,' said Helen, as Amanda sat down. 'It would be such fun to have a little brother.'

123

'Yes, though a girl would be nice too,' Amanda said. 'Or twins – one of each!'

'Well!' said Isabel, with a laugh. 'It looks as though this new baby has done the trick.'

'You don't mind, do you?' said Pat. 'Amanda going off with Helen, I mean.'

'Not a bit,' said Isabel happily. 'I'm just glad that the two of them finally seem to be getting on. And, to be honest, it will be nice to have you to myself for a bit.'

Pat grinned and said, 'When breakfast's over let's find a quiet corner and go and have a good old chat before lessons start. Just the two of us.'

'Yes,' said Isabel. 'Won't that be nice? Just the two of us.'

15.

Kitty's secret plan

The third form's two weeks of punishment were up, and plans for the midnight feast were in full swing.

'We'd better hold it in here,' said Janet, looking round the common-room one evening. 'Neither of the dorms is big enough.'

'And we can use the big cupboard over there to store all the goodies,' said Bobby, rubbing her hands together. 'Whoopee, I can't wait! When's it to be?'

'How about next Saturday?' suggested Hilary.

Kitty, who had been looking at the calendar on the wall, turned and said, 'Sure, Friday would be better.'

'Oh? Why's that, Kitty?' asked Mirabel.

'There will be a full moon, for one thing,' answered Kitty.

'What difference does that make?' Doris asked, puzzled. 'We shall all be indoors anyway.'

'*You* will be,' said Kitty. 'But I'll be spending part of the evening outside and it'll be good to have some light. Alison, do you think I could have a word with you?'

'Of course,' said Alison, getting up and following the Irish girl into the corridor.

Kitty looked up and down then, satisfied they could

not be overheard, said, 'Did you know, Alison, that some people believe the full moon causes madness in animals?'

'Er, no, Kitty, I didn't know that,' said Alison, frowning. 'It's very interesting, but surely you didn't bring me out here to tell me that?'

'I did. For I want you to make sure Margaret knows that McGinty is prone to moon madness,' said Kitty with a grin. 'Tell her that it's awful worried I am that he might escape from his stable and go on the rampage on the night of the full moon.'

Alison nodded, her eyes wide, and Kitty went on, 'Then I want you to tell her that he's been misbehaving dreadfully, and that Miss Theobald has told me he's on his last chance at St Clare's. If he gets into one more scrape he's to be sent away. Now, have you got all that, Alison?'

'Yes, but *why* do you want me to tell Margaret all this?' asked Alison.

'Ah, never you mind,' said Kitty. 'You and all the others will find out soon enough. Now, I must go and speak to Grace.'

Kitty had been spending quite a lot of time with Grace lately, learning all she could from her about photography. The others knew that this had something to do with Kitty's great plan, and were simply bursting with curiosity. But Kitty, enjoying herself enormously, would tell them nothing, merely saying infuriatingly, 'All in good time!'

Gradually the big cupboard in the common-room began to fill up, as preparations for the feast went ahead. The twins opened the door one day to put away a tin of biscuits they had bought, and Isabel's eyes lit up as she saw all the good things piled up there.

'Tins of pineapple, prawns and sardines – yummy! And just look at this simply enormous box of chocolates! My word, what a feast this is going to be.'

'I'll say,' said Pat. 'And that big iced cake looks simply gorgeous. I wonder who bought that?'

'Amanda and Helen bought it between them,' said Isabel. 'Who would have thought that they would become so close all of a sudden – and all thanks to a baby!'

'Well, this baby will be brother or sister to both of them,' said Pat. 'So at last they will have something they can share.'

'And a jolly good thing too,' said Isabel. Then she gave a laugh. 'I wonder how long it will be before the two of them are arguing over whose turn it is to babysit!'

But, for the moment, the stepsisters were the best of friends, and seemed to have put their differences behind them. Helen's happiness seemed to have made her forget her snobbish ways and, as a result, she was much more popular with her form too. In fact, the whole of the second form and the whole of the third form were getting on together very well indeed. So much so that, when Miss Theobald came into the common-room that evening, to make what she thought would be a happy announcement, there was consternation.

Everyone rose to their feet when the head entered, and Helen immediately turned off the gramophone.

'Sit down, girls,' said Miss Theobald, smiling round. 'I shan't take up much of your evening. I have just come to tell you that work on the second form's quarters is finished. I know it has taken a little longer than we expected but, for the last week of term, you third formers will have your common-room to yourselves again. The new dormitory has yet to be painted, so I'm afraid your sleeping arrangements will remain as they are for the rest of the term.'

'Thank you, Miss Theobald,' said the two head girls, in rather a subdued manner. It was funny, but after all the complaints about being cramped, and having no privacy and, of course, the big feud, each form now realised that it was going to miss the other.

Miss Theobald, who had expected cheers, was most surprised at the way the girls received the news. But, after being head of St Clare's for many years, she had learned that girls often behaved unexpectedly!

'Amanda, my dear,' she said. 'I wonder if you could come to my room for a few moments. There is something I need to discuss with you.'

'Yes, Miss Theobald,' said the girl politely, feeling surprised and rather nervous. Whatever could the head want to speak to her about?

'Well,' said Janet, flopping down into an armchair, after Miss Theobald and Amanda had left. 'It's going to be jolly quiet in here without you second formers.'

'I thought you couldn't wait to get rid of us,' said Grace, with a grin.

'So did I,' said Janet, with her usual honesty. 'But now that it's almost time for you to leave, I'm not so sure I like the idea.'

'I daresay you'll soon get used to being without us,' said Grace. 'It is going to be strange for a while though. You third formers aren't really such a bad lot, you know.'

'Thanks,' said Janet, with a smile. 'I say, I wonder what Miss Theobald wants with Amanda?'

'I was wondering that too,' said Helen, frowning. 'I do hope she's not in any trouble.'

But Amanda wasn't in trouble, although what Miss Theobald had to say was very important. She wasted no time in getting straight to the point. 'Miss Adams has been speaking to me about you, Amanda, and she is a little concerned that you are finding the work of the third form too difficult. This is no reflection on you, as she tells me that you are an extremely hard worker and always try your best. However, as you are a little younger than most of the third, it is perhaps not surprising that you have found it hard to keep up with them. You really should have been in the second form from the start, but your mother felt that you might settle in better away from your stepsister. I understand that the two of you don't get on?'

'We *didn't* get on,' admitted Amanda. 'But that's all been sorted out now. Helen and I realised how silly we had been and have made friends now.'

'That is very good news,' said Miss Theobald with her charming smile. 'And it makes it very much easier to tell you why I have asked you here. You see, my dear, Miss Adams feels that you aren't ready to join the fourth form with the others next term – and I agree with her. So, we have decided that it is for the best if you remain in the third form, along with the second formers, who will be going up after the holidays. How do you feel about that?'

'It's funny,' said Amanda, wrinkling her brow. 'I always dreaded that this would happen, and now that it has – I don't actually mind. I shall miss being with Pat and Isabel and the rest, but I'm quite looking forward to spending more time with Helen. Though I expect we will still argue from time to time.'

'I expect that you will,' laughed Miss Theobald. 'I believe that all sisters do. I am very pleased with your sensible attitude to this, Amanda. Now you may go and join the others.'

'There you are!' said Isabel, when Amanda returned to the common-room. 'What did Miss Theobald want?'

Amanda told her, the others gathering round to listen.

'What a shame!' cried Hilary. 'It would have been sport if you could have come up into the fourth with us.'

'Well, your loss is our gain,' said Grace, clapping Amanda on the shoulder. 'I know it's a bit early, as you won't actually be joining us until after the hols, but welcome to our form.'

'Golly, what a good thing we aren't feuding any

more,' said Harriet. 'You wouldn't know whose side to be on, Amanda.'

Everyone laughed, and the twins came up on either side of Amanda, each of them taking one of her arms.

'She's still a member of our form, for now,' said Pat grinning. 'Come and help Isabel and me with this jigsaw, and never mind these kids.'

Amanda smiled too, feeling a warm glow inside. How lovely it felt to be wanted! And she had so much to look forward to, as well – a new brother or sister, the holidays – and, of course, the midnight feast!

Part of Kitty's plan seemed to be to annoy Margaret, which she did most effectively and at every opportunity. Whenever the head girl appeared, Kitty would start running in the corridor, or yelling loudly, earning herself a stern ticking off. The final straw, for Margaret, came two days before the feast was to take place, when Kitty arrived in the dining-room ten minutes after the bell had gone for tea.

'Kitty Flaherty!' thundered Margaret, as the Irish girl sauntered in. 'This is the third time this week you've been late for tea. Report to my study at six o'clock.'

'Yes, Margaret,' said Kitty meekly, her laughing eyes downcast.

'I bet she'll give you lines,' said Carlotta, as Kitty took her place at the table.

'Sure and I'm not bothered about that,' Kitty said, helping herself to a sandwich. 'It's all going to be worth it in the end, Carlotta. You'll see.'

Margaret was poring over her maths prep when Kitty reported to her, and she stared at the girl coldly. 'Well?' she snapped. 'What have you got to say for yourself?'

'I'm sorry I was late, Margaret,' said Kitty politely. 'But it took me longer than usual to settle McGinty. He's become awful restless lately, because –'

'I'm not the slightest bit interested in that animal,' Margaret interrupted. 'I want you to write me a five-hundred-word essay on punctuality, and hand it in to me on Sunday.'

'Very well, Margaret,' said Kitty, sighing heavily. Then she frowned. 'Ah, there's a fly just landed on your maths book there! Let me swat it for you.' And, flapping her hands wildly, Kitty leaned over the desk – knocking Margaret's ink bottle all over her neatly written prep!

'You idiot!' shrieked Margaret, jumping to her feet before the ink could drip on to her skirt.

'Oh, Margaret, I'm so sorry!' exclaimed Kitty, putting her hand up to her mouth in horror. 'Ah, it's awful clumsy I am!'

'Clumsy? I believe you did it on purpose!' cried the head girl, quite beside herself with rage. 'I spent hours on that prep, and now I shall have to do it all again.'

'Let me clean it up,' said Kitty contritely. 'Ah, this old cloth will do the job!'

Before Margaret could stop her, the Irish girl snatched up a piece of cloth that was hanging over the back of a chair and began mopping up the spilled ink with it.

132

'Stop!' yelled Margaret. 'That old cloth happens to be my best scarf!'

'Oh no!' wailed Kitty, dropping the scarf instantly and clutching at Margaret's arm. 'Now what's to be done?'

'Get off me, you stupid girl,' Margaret hissed, brushing Kitty's inky hand away. 'You're getting ink stains all over my sleeve now. Oh, just get out before you do any more damage!'

Lowering her head to hide a grin, Kitty said in a very subdued tone, 'I really am sorry, Margaret.'

'Oh, don't put on that meek and mild act with me!' snapped Margaret. 'I know that what you did was deliberate, and I'll get back at you somehow, Kitty Flaherty!'

This was just what Kitty wanted to hear, and she hummed to herself as she washed the ink from her hands before joining her friends. Margaret would well and truly have it in for her now – and that was going to be her downfall!

Alison played her part the following evening. Margaret couldn't wait to pour out the story of Kitty's dreadful behaviour, and Alison listened open-mouthed. 'Well!' she said at last, when Margaret had finished. 'I thought Kitty looked pleased with herself last night, and now I know why.'

Margaret gasped. 'That just proves that the little beast did it on purpose. I honestly don't think she cares tuppence for anyone's opinion!'

'She doesn't,' said Alison, with a sniff. 'I think all she

cares about is that horrible goat of hers. Of course, she's awfully worried about him at the moment. He's been in a few scrapes lately, and Miss Theobald has warned Kitty that if he causes any more trouble, she will have to send him away from St Clare's.'

'Really?' said Margaret, her eyes narrowing keenly.

'And, of course, Kitty's got this silly idea that he's going to go mad tomorrow night, because of the full moon,' Alison went on.

'Full moon?' repeated Margaret, baffled.

Alison nodded. 'Apparently some animals go completely potty when there's a full moon – and McGinty is one of them. Kitty says he becomes completely uncontrollable, and she's terrified that he'll escape from the stables and run wild.'

'And if he does, he's for the high jump,' murmured Margaret.

'That's right,' said Alison. 'And so is Kitty.'

Margaret seemed distracted after that, and soon found an excuse to get rid of Alison. She needed to be alone, to think and to scheme. That Irish girl had gone too far this time, and now she was going to pay for it.

Alison, for her part, was extremely pleased with the way she had duped Margaret. Really, she ought to be an actress, for the head girl had believed every word she said. Alison felt quite smug when she went to find Kitty, saying triumphantly, 'She fell for it, hook, line and sinker. And I'm betting she means to make things pretty hot for you and McGinty.'

'Let her try,' said Kitty with a grin. 'I'm afraid our dear head girl is about to find out that she's bitten off more than she can chew!'

Alison laughed. 'I don't know what I'm more excited about, Kitty – our feast, or your revenge on Margaret. Oh, I can't wait for tomorrow night!'

16.

Midnight fun

The second and third formers were in a state of great excitement the following day, and not in the mood to concentrate on their lessons at all. Miss Jenks grew so exasperated with her form that she threatened to set them an extra hour's prep that evening. This made them sit up and pay attention at once, as their plans for that evening most definitely did not include extra prep!

Pat, Isabel and Amanda whispered together almost continuously through their English lesson, and Miss Adams became extremely annoyed. 'If I hear one more whisper, or one more giggle, from you three girls, I shall send you all out of the room,' she snapped.

'Sorry, Miss Adams,' chorused the three, trying their best to look serious.

'So you should be,' said the mistress crisply. 'Now, instead of talking among yourselves, please listen to what I have to say and you might actually learn something!'

But not even Miss Adams' short temper could dampen the girls' high spirits as they waited eagerly for bedtime.

At last it arrived, and the girls trooped upstairs.

Janet said, 'Grace, don't forget to set your alarm

clock. It would be simply awful if you all slept through the feast.'

'No chance of that, Janet,' laughed Grace. 'We'll be there all right. Now, come along, everyone. Let's try and get some sleep.'

Janet and Grace were to be responsible for waking everyone – all except Kitty, who slipped out of bed an hour before everyone else and put on her coat and outdoor shoes. She had no idea what time Margaret would show up, and didn't want to risk missing her. That would ruin everything!

'Kitty?' whispered Bobby, who was still awake. 'Is that you?'

'Yes, I've something important to do,' Kitty whispered back. 'Now don't worry if I'm not back in time for the start of the feast, Bobby. But save me some food, for I'll be hungry.'

'All right. Take care, Kitty.'

And, with a wave, the girl slipped from the room, ran down the stairs and out into the night.

At midnight the others awoke, making their way quickly and quietly to the common-room. Carlotta and Doris lit candles and placed them around the room. Hilary, Mirabel and Gladys pushed the furniture back against the walls to make more space. And the others got the food from the store cupboard and began setting it out.

'This looks delicious!' said Katie, when everything was ready.

'I should say,' agreed Harriet. 'Jolly decent of you third formers to invite us to share.'

'Hear, hear!' chorused the rest of the second form, all of them raising tooth mugs of ginger beer to the third form.

'Tuck in, everyone,' said Janet, sitting on the floor and opening an enormous tin of pineapple. 'Don't forget to save a little bit of everything for Kitty, though.'

'We won't,' said Bobby. 'I wonder what she's doing now?'

Kitty was, in fact, hidden in an empty stall in the old stables. It was a chilly night and, despite a thick coat, scarf and gloves, she felt extremely cold. She felt stiff, too, from sitting in the same position for so long, and thought enviously of the others enjoying their feast. But despite the cold and discomfort, Kitty was determined to stay where she was, absolutely certain that Margaret would take the bait and walk right into her trap. Kitty just hoped she wouldn't have to wait too much longer.

Five minutes later her patience was rewarded. A beam of torchlight played on the floor as a shadowy figure appeared. Kitty held her breath, sure that the intruder must be able to hear her heart pounding. The figure advanced into the stables and Kitty was able to see quite clearly who it was. Margaret!

McGinty made a bleating sound as the head girl approached and she hushed him, getting his lead down from the wall and slipping it round his neck.

'You're coming with me,' she said, producing a carrot

from the bag she carried and dangling it in front of him. 'Hurry up!'

The carrot did the trick and McGinty trotted along beside Margaret, trying to snatch the treat from her hand. Eventually he succeeded and, once he had eaten it, refused to budge another inch until she had produced more food. It soon became apparent that she was heading for the little kitchen garden, and Kitty followed, moving stealthily under cover of the trees and bushes. The short walk took some time, as McGinty's demands for food were frequent, but at last Margaret reached her destination. She removed McGinty's lead and opened the little gate, saying under her breath, 'Go on then, you greedy creature – help yourself.'

The garden was full of herbs and vegetables and, normally, McGinty would have been in seventh heaven. Now, however, he moved slowly through the gate and sat down.

'What's the matter with you?' Margaret hissed, prodding him with the toe of her shoe. 'Get up!'

But, alas for Margaret, she had fed the goat so well that he simply wasn't interested in the contents of the kitchen garden. All he wanted to do was sit quietly for a while and let his unexpected supper go down. Kitty grinned to herself in the darkness. Oh dear! What was Margaret going to do now?

For a moment the head girl seemed at a loss, then her lips tightened determinedly and she stepped through the gate, muttering, 'Well, I'll just have to do the job myself. You and your mistress will still get the blame, which is all that matters!'

And, under Kitty's astonished, horrified gaze, Margaret began to destroy the little garden. Plants were trampled, broken, uprooted and scattered everywhere, the head girl so intent on making trouble for Kitty that she cared nothing for the destruction she caused. The expression of spite on her face made Kitty shiver.

At last, panting from her exertion, Margaret stood back and leaned on the fence, a triumphant smile on her face as she shone her torch beam over the ruined garden. Now all that remained was for her to shut the gate so that McGinty couldn't get out. Tomorrow he would be discovered – and banished from St Clare's. And no one would ever dream of suspecting that the head girl had had anything to do with it. Even Kitty would assume that the goat's 'moon madness' had got the better of him. Margaret yawned, feeling quite worn out. Longing for her bed, she turned to go through the gate. But the torch slipped from her fingers and, with an exclamation of annoyance, she bent to pick it up. McGinty, who was beginning to feel a little more lively, got up and watched her. Despite the fact that she had fed him well, McGinty didn't care for Margaret. He didn't like the way she spoke to him, and he certainly didn't like the way she had prodded him with her toe earlier. Suddenly, the sight of her bending over to retrieve her torch was just too tempting. McGinty lowered his head, pawed the ground – and charged!

Kitty thought that she would burst with the effort of keeping her laughter in, as Margaret squealed, pitched forward and landed face down in the compost heap! It had been a soft landing, but the smell was revolting! Margaret, certain that she had swallowed some of the horrible stuff, felt sick. Giving a groan, she slowly picked herself up, prodding herself gingerly and wrinkling her nose in disgust at the smell. Fighting back angry tears, she hissed, 'You evil little brute!' She began to walk towards McGinty, but he stood his ground and gave Margaret a menacing glare, before lowering his head threateningly again. Margaret stopped in her tracks. Perhaps there was something in this moon madness nonsense after all, and the goat was about to go wild. She certainly didn't want to risk being butted again. Besides, she was cold, tired – and now she needed a bath too! This time she didn't make the mistake of turning her back on McGinty, walking backwards out of the gate and shutting it carefully. Then, limping slightly, she walked away, back towards the school.

Kitty waited for a few minutes before coming out of her hiding place to release McGinty. 'Well done, boy,' she said, bending to hug him. 'You certainly showed *her*! Now, let's get you away from here and back to bed.'

The others, meanwhile, were having a simply marvellous time at their feast, and Amanda was now cutting the big cake that she and Helen had bought.

'Just a small slice for me, please, Amanda,' said Alison, holding her stomach. 'I'm absolutely full!'

'Me too,' said Doris. 'It's been simply super though, hasn't it?'

'I'll say it has,' agreed Janet. 'Though I wish that Kitty would hurry up and come back.'

'Yes, I hope everything has gone according to plan,' Hilary said, looking rather anxious. 'If anything has gone wrong . . .'

'Shh!' Isabel said suddenly, holding up a warning finger. 'I thought I heard a noise in the corridor.'

At once everyone became silent, faces tense and watchful as they listened. There it was – the unmistakable sound of footsteps. But was it Kitty returning? Or was it one of the mistresses? The girls held their breath as the footsteps got closer, stopping right outside the door. Slowly the handle moved, the door creaked open and . . .

'Kitty!' gasped Doris, heaving a sigh of relief. 'Thank heavens!'

Kitty beamed round, her eyes sparkling and cheeks rosy from the cold night air. Then her eyes fell on the plate of food the others had put aside for her and she said, 'Ah, good, I'm starving.'

Flinging her coat aside, she sat down and began to eat hungrily. The others nibbled on their cake and sipped their ginger beer, all of them dying to know what she had been up to.

'Well?' said Janet impatiently, as soon as the girl had cleared her plate. 'How did it go?'

'Very well indeed,' answered Kitty brightly. 'Better

than I could have hoped, in fact. Harriet, do you think that I might have a piece of that chocolate, please?'

Harriet handed the chocolate over and Kitty broke a large chunk off, seeming lost in her own thoughts as she ate it.

'Kitty, we'd quite like to know what happened,' Carlotta prompted her.

'And so you shall, Carlotta, so you shall,' Kitty assured her, before taking a sip of ginger beer.

'Yes, but *when*?' asked Bobby. 'We're simply dying of curiosity.'

'Ah, be patient now, Bobby,' said Kitty. 'Just you wait until tomorrow night.'

'Tomorrow night!' repeated Helen in dismay. 'Kitty, we can't wait that long.'

'Of course we can't,' said Alison. 'Kitty, you must tell us now.'

But Kitty could be as stubborn as McGinty at times. 'Tomorrow,' she said firmly. 'Trust me, it will be well worth the wait.'

'It had better be, you wretch,' said Grace. 'I shan't be able to sleep tonight.'

'Oh yes you will, my girl,' Kitty told her. 'You and I need to go to the darkroom, bright and early!'

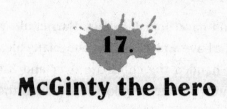

17.

McGinty the hero

'I don't think I can face breakfast this morning,' said Alison, with a shudder, as she brushed her hair. 'I ate far too much last night and I feel quite sick now.'

'Serves you right for eating half a packet of chocolate biscuits,' said Bobby, with a grin. 'Gosh, I'm tired. I wish I could go back to bed for an hour instead of going down to breakfast.'

Most of the second and third formers felt either sick or tired, or – in a few cases – both. Only Kitty was her usual bright and breezy self, brushing her hair and getting dressed in record time, and singing all the while.

'Kitty, do you *have* to be so lively – and so noisy – this early in the morning?' groaned Amanda, who was having great difficulty in keeping her eyes open. 'It quite wears me out just to look at you.'

'Ah, but it's a wonderful day,' said the Irish girl, skipping over to look out of the window. 'And I've a feeling it's going to get better. I'm just going to pop next door and see if Grace is up yet.'

'Yes, you go and annoy the second formers,' murmured Doris, who had yet to get out of bed. 'Take your time and don't hurry back.'

'We'll have to try and eat something,' said Hilary, without enthusiasm. 'The mistresses will be most suspicious if we're all off our food.'

'Yes – at the very least we'll be sent to Matron,' said Janet, with a shudder. 'And we all know what that means!'

The others did know. It meant a large dose of extremely nasty-tasting medicine! So the girls made a heroic effort to get through breakfast without arousing suspicion.

'I must say, Kitty,' said Isabel, as she pushed her plate away. 'Whatever happened last night doesn't seem to have had much effect on Margaret. Just look at her.'

At once all eyes turned to the sixth-form table, where Margaret was drinking coffee and chattering to her neighbour as though she hadn't a care in the world.

'Don't all stare at her like that!' hissed Kitty. 'She'll guess that something is up. You see, girls, Margaret doesn't realise yet that she's been caught out. But she'll know all about it before today is over – and you are all going to be there when it dawns on her!'

This sounded good, the third formers exchanging excited glances.

'You know that Mam'zelle's giving a slide show in the hall tonight,' went on Kitty, and a groan went up. Mam'zelle had recently taken a holiday in France, and had been threatening ever since the beginning of term to show everyone her slides. And tonight the whole school had been invited to see them.

'I'd forgotten all about that,' sighed Janet. 'I suppose we'll have to go, though, or old Mam'zelle will be terribly hurt.'

'I'm quite looking forward to it,' said Hilary. 'Mamzelle gets so carried away when she's talking about her beloved France – it might be quite fun.'

'It *will* be fun,' promised Kitty, with a secretive smile. 'Just make sure you're all there.'

And before they could question her further, she slipped from her seat and darted across to the second-form table, to pass the message on to the girls there.

The French mistress walked by just then, and Grace called out to her, 'Mam'zelle! We're so looking forward to your slide show tonight. If you like I could help to lay out the slides for you in the hall beforehand.'

Grace was one of Mam'zelle's favourites, and the mistress beamed down at her, saying, 'Ah, that is indeed kind of you, *ma petite*. Come to the mistresses' common-room after tea and I will give them to you.'

And, patting the second former's head, she went happily on her way, failing to notice the sly wink that Grace directed at Kitty.

It was as the girls were about to leave the dining-room that Miss Theobald entered, looking very stern indeed. 'Girls, please stay where you are,' she called out. 'I am afraid I have some very serious news.'

'Gracious, whatever can have happened?' whispered Isabel.

'I don't know,' answered Pat, with a frown.

'Something bad, by the look of things.'

Miss Theobald began to speak. 'I am sorry to have to tell you all that someone has – apparently deliberately – damaged the school's kitchen garden.'

A gasp went round the room, and someone called out, 'Who did it?'

'I would very much like to know the answer to that,' answered Miss Theobald grimly. 'But unfortunately there are no clues.'

Kitty stole a glance at Margaret, smiling to herself at the look of utter bewilderment on the girl's face. She had, of course, expected Miss Theobald to name McGinty as the culprit and couldn't, for the life of her, understand why she hadn't done so. Instead she was saying, 'If anyone knows anything about this dreadful act, I would like them to come and tell me about it, for I am quite determined to track down the person – or people – responsible.'

But how dreadful to think that any of the St Clare's girls would do such a thing! Janet put up her hand and said, 'Miss Theobald, could someone from outside have got in and damaged the garden?'

'It's possible, I suppose, though I can't imagine what motive they would have had,' replied the head. 'Hopefully we will soon find out. That is all I have to say at the moment.'

A babble of voices broke out as the head departed, and it was left to the mistresses to restore order.

Margaret Winters followed Miss Theobald out,

catching up with her outside her study. 'Miss Theobald!' she said. 'Something has just occurred to me.'

'Yes, Margaret?' said the head.

'Well, I don't want to accuse anyone – or anything – unjustly,' said Margaret, at her most earnest. 'But – well, I don't suppose that goat of Kitty Flaherty's could have had anything to do with this, could he? You see, I was reading something the other day, and apparently some animals are affected by the full moon and go quite mad. There was a full moon last night, and perhaps it caused Kitty's goat to run riot in the garden.'

Miss Theobald smiled faintly. 'That was the first thing that occurred to me, too, Margaret. This full-moon madness sounds like a lot of superstitious nonsense to me, but McGinty's healthy appetite and mischievous nature made me suspect him instantly. As soon as the damage was discovered I sent the gardener to check on him. But McGinty was safely in his stall, with the door securely bolted, so it cannot possibly have been him.'

Margaret almost reeled with shock, but managed to hide this from the head, saying lightly, 'Oh well, it was just a thought.'

'And a very good one,' said Miss Theobald. 'I appreciate your concern, Margaret, and if you have any more ideas as to who the culprit could be, please share them with me.'

The head went into her study and Margaret, her mind in a whirl, walked away. She desperately needed to think. It was just possible that McGinty might have managed to jump the fence and make his way back to the stables. But there was no way on earth that he could have locked himself back in! Margaret fretted and puzzled over the mystery, but could not work out how the goat had managed to put himself in the clear like that. The only thing that she was certain of was that her cunning scheme to get both him and his mistress into trouble had failed!

The entire school, girls and mistresses alike, turned up to Mam'zelle's slide show. Hot-tempered the French mistress might be, but she was also big-hearted and everyone was extremely fond of her.

A big screen had been rigged up on the stage and in front of it stood a projector on a table. Grace was there, carefully arranging piles of slides, and she looked up and grinned as the second and third formers filed in. They all knew that she and Kitty had spent a long time in the darkroom that morning, and realised that whatever they had been doing had something to do with the surprise Kitty had planned for Margaret tonight. They took their seats near the front, just behind the chattering first formers. Soon the big hall was filled to bursting and a huge cheer went up when Mam'zelle walked on to the stage and, thoroughly enjoying being the centre of attention, she beamed round for a moment, before holding up her hands for silence.

'Thank you all for coming!' she cried. 'Tonight I take you on a tour of *la belle* France. Miss Adams, if you would be good enough to turn off the lights, we shall begin!'

Miss Adams obliged, and Mam'zelle showed the first slide, which was of the main street of a pretty little French town.

'This is where I grew up,' explained Mam'zelle, a note of pride in her voice. 'And where many of my family still live.'

She went back to the projector and the picture changed. 'Here is the house where I was born. My brother Pierre lives there now, with his wife and their many children.'

And so it went on. The views of France were most interesting, but soon Mam'zelle began to introduce more and more slides of her family, accompanying them with long anecdotes, and some of the girls began to grow a little restless.

'Now I shall show you a picture of my youngest brother,' said Mamzelle proudly. '*Regardez* Alphonse!'

She clicked the slide into place and a shout of laughter went up. '*Tiens*!' cried Mam'zelle, most offended. 'Why do you laugh at the so-handsome Alphonse?'

'It isn't the so-handsome Alphonse, Mam'zelle,' called out a cheeky first former. 'It's the not-so-handsome McGinty!'

Mamzelle spun round so quickly that she almost overbalanced, and saw at once what had made the audience laugh so uproariously. For there on the screen, instead of her brother, was indeed a picture of McGinty. He was in his stall and, bending over him, was a dark figure, its back to the camera.

'*Mon dieu!*' Mamzelle exclaimed. 'How can this be? Never have I taken a photograph of this bad goat!'

Bustling over to the projector she changed the slide – and McGinty appeared again! This time the figure with him was turned towards the camera, and a murmur broke out as everyone recognised the head girl.

'Grrrace!' shouted Mam'zelle angrily. 'You have done this on purpose. It is abominable! The show must be abandoned!'

But Miss Theobald chanced to look round at Margaret. The girl was huddled in her seat, red-faced, looking as if she wanted the ground to open up and swallow her. 'No, Mam'zelle,' said the head, standing up. 'I would like you to carry on. Please show the next slide.'

The second and third formers caught one another's eyes, alight with excitement. Clever little Kitty! Margaret had stirred up trouble for their forms by using her camera – and now Kitty had turned the tables on her! Several slides followed, each more shocking than the last. There was Margaret, entering the kitchen garden, pulling McGinty behind her. Then shocked gasps and angry murmurs ran round the hall as the head girl was caught in the act of ripping a plant from the ground, an expression of real spite on her face as she did so.

At the back of the hall, Jenny Mills and Barbara Thompson exchanged shocked glances. Neither of them particularly liked Margaret, but they would never have believed that she was capable of such meanness. But the mood in the hall changed completely when the final picture appeared on the screen. Kitty had caught the moment perfectly, and the school was treated to the sight of Margaret sprawling in a most undignified manner on the compost heap, while McGinty stood triumphantly nearby. A great cheer arose, and a group of excitable first formers cried, 'Hurrah for McGinty!' Then the screen went blank, and Miss Adams turned the lights back on.

The French mistress, still a little dazed and bewildered by the turn of events, blinked, while Miss Theobald said, 'A most interesting and informative evening, Mam'zelle. Margaret, I will deal with you tomorrow.'

With that the head left, in her usual calm, dignified manner. Margaret, meanwhile, felt far from calm and dignified as she got to her feet and faced the hard, scornful eyes of her fellow pupils. Even the mistresses looked at her with utter contempt. It was more than she could bear and, with a sob, she fled from the hall.

'Something got your goat, Margaret?' Doris called after her, and everyone roared with laughter.

'Phew!' said Pat. 'That was quite a show!'

'Wasn't it just!' exclaimed Janet. 'And to think I was worried that it was going to be boring.'

Isabel looked across at Kitty, who was being clapped on the back by a group of fourth formers, and laughed. 'Nothing is ever boring when Kitty Flaherty is around!'

18.

Margaret in disgrace

Kitty was the heroine of the hour. Word had soon spread that she was responsible for Margaret's disgrace and, as the girls gathered in the dining-room for cocoa and biscuits before bedtime, many of them came up to congratulate her.

'It's about time that someone showed Margaret up for the sly creature that she is. Well done, Kitty!'

'How I wish I could have been there when McGinty butted her into the compost heap. Priceless, Kitty!'

'Thanks to you we won't have to put up with her as head girl any longer, Kitty. Good work!'

'My goodness,' murmured Hilary to the twins. 'Much more of this and Kitty's head will be so big that she won't be able to get through the door.'

But Kitty, as usual, seemed quite unaffected by the praise heaped upon her, saying modestly, 'Ah, it was nothing, to be sure. I couldn't have done it without Grace, for she lent me her camera and taught me how to use it, as well as doing all the hard work in the darkroom.'

So Grace received three cheers as well, then the mistresses decided that there had been quite enough excitement for one evening and ushered the lower forms off to bed.

'Do you suppose Margaret will be expelled?' asked Alison, as she changed into her pyjamas.

'It will serve her right if she is,' said Mirabel. 'I've seen some rotten tricks but, my word, that one takes the biscuit!'

'Yes, to destroy the garden was downright wicked – and then to try and blame it on poor McGinty. Horrible!' said Gladys, wrinkling her nose in distaste.

'Well "poor" McGinty certainly stuck up for himself all right,' said Bobby, with a grin.

'He did that,' agreed Kitty. 'Sure and I was proud of him!'

'Come on, everybody – into bed!' called Janet. 'Lights out in a minute.'

There was some grumbling, but everyone obeyed, secretly quite glad to settle down after all the fun and games. What an evening it had been!

Margaret did not appear at breakfast the next morning and no one was very surprised.

'I wouldn't want to face the whole school if I had behaved as she has,' said Hilary. 'Just imagine how humiliated she must feel.'

Margaret did indeed feel most humiliated – and frightened as well. She had barely slept at all that night, trying to think of some way to explain her extraordinary behaviour to Miss Theobald. At last she had realised that it was pointless to try and talk her way out of it. She would just have to accept whatever punishment the head decided to give her. And it was certain to be a big punishment! And all because of that wretched Kitty Flaherty. Margaret could not see that she had brought everything on herself, thanks to her own spite. For that would have meant admitting to a fault – something Margaret would never do. This was the end of her brief career as head girl, she knew. Never again would Miss Theobald trust her. She might even be expelled. That thought caused a chill to run down Margaret's spine. The disgrace would be simply unbearable, and her parents would be so angry, and so bitterly disappointed in her. She was not looking forward to her interview with Miss Theobald at all.

But before the head dealt with Margaret, she sent for Kitty.

'Good morning, Mam,' the Irish girl greeted Miss Theobald politely as she entered the study.

'Good morning, Kitty,' replied the Head. 'Please sit down.'

Kitty did so, and Miss Theobald looked at her thoughtfully for a moment, before saying, 'I am going to ask you something, Kitty, and I would like a truthful answer. Were those slides last night your work?'

'Indeed they were, Mam,' answered Kitty at once, looking the headmistress straight in the eye. 'And, as you'll have guessed, I wasn't in my bed when I should have been. I know I'll probably be punished for that but, you see, I knew Margaret was going to try and have

McGinty sent away and I had to save him. What's more, Mam, I wanted you and everyone else to know what kind of person Margaret is. Sure and I'm awful sorry about the garden, and if I'd known she meant to damage it like that then perhaps I would have come up with another plan, but there, she started pulling the plants up, and throwing them around, and there was no stopping her!'

And there was no stopping Kitty when she had a tale to tell, thought Miss Theobald, amused despite the seriousness of the situation. Now that the girl had paused to take a breath, the head opened her mouth. But before she could utter a word, Kitty was off again. 'And there's something else you should know, Mam. Margaret was the one who caused all that trouble for Jenny Mills and the second form. Though, of course, the second formers didn't get punished in the end, for we third formers owned up and –'

'Kitty!'

'Yes, Mam?' said Kitty, looking a little surprised at the interruption.

'Do stop for a moment, my dear, for my head is quite in a whirl!' said Miss Theobald. 'Now, please explain everything to me calmly and clearly.'

Kitty did her best, though Miss Theobald had to interrupt once or twice when she got carried away! But, at last, the head knew the whole story. 'Well!' she said at last, sitting back in her chair and looking quite astonished. 'It seems that Margaret has been behind quite a lot of the unpleasantness that has occurred at St Clare's this term.'

Kitty nodded, then said impulsively, 'Mam, will you make Jenny head girl again now?'

'I would like to very much, Kitty,' answered the head, looking thoughtful. 'But I must bear in mind that she, too, did wrong.'

'Yes,' said Kitty. 'But what Jenny did was a – a good wrong!'

'A good wrong?' repeated Miss Theobald, puzzled.

'Well, you see, although Jenny broke the rules, she did it with good intentions,' explained Kitty. 'She only wanted to protect the second formers and keep them out of trouble. Whereas everything Margaret did . . .'

'Was intended to deliberately cause trouble for others,' the head finished for her.

'Exactly!' Kitty leaned forward and said confidingly, 'You know, Mam, I think that here at St Clare's we need a head girl that everyone likes, and trusts, and can look up to. And, in Jenny, that's exactly what we had.'

'I can see that you have given the matter a lot of thought, Kitty,' said Miss Theobald, smiling, but thinking privately that there was a great deal of wisdom and truth in the girl's words. 'And I shall give it some thought too. I shall let the heads of form know what I decide.'

Kitty stood up, but before she left the room, she said, 'Am I to be punished, for being out in the grounds the other night, Mam?'

Miss Theobald looked hard at the girl for a moment. At last she said, 'No, Kitty. For what you did was also a "good wrong", as you like to call it. Without your intervention I would probably never have seen Margaret's true character.'

Exactly what passed between the head and Margaret, no one ever found out. But one of the fourth formers reported seeing the girl come out of Miss Theobald's room in tears later that morning. That afternoon her parents were sent for, prompting rumours that Margaret had been expelled. But, after a long talk with Miss Theobald, Mr and Mrs Winters left alone, both of them pale and grim-faced.

'As Margaret only has one more term left at St Clare's, she is being allowed to stay,' announced Janet in the common-room that evening. She and Grace, along with the other form heads, had been summoned to Miss Theobald's study earlier, and had just returned with the news. 'I rather think she has her parents to thank for that. They are going to pay for the damage to the garden, and Mr Winters has promised to try and talk some sense into her during the holidays.'

'Well, let's hope he succeeds,' said Hilary. 'Perhaps Margaret can learn something from this and become a nicer person as a result.'

'I saw her outside earlier,' said Alison. 'She looked awfully pale, and so red-eyed that I almost felt sorry for her.'

'Alison!' shouted everyone, exasperated.

'I said *almost*,' huffed Alison. 'Then I remembered how she betrayed my trust, and caused trouble over our trick, and how she tried to get McGinty sent away. So I don't feel sorry for her at all any more.'

'Thank heavens for that!' said Pat. 'Janet, did Miss Theobald say anything about who is to be head girl now?'

'Yes, I was just coming to that,' said Janet, smiling broadly. 'Jenny Mills is to be head girl for the rest of this term *and* next term. And Barbara Thompson is going to be her deputy.'

'That's marvellous!' cried Doris. 'It will be wonderful to have Jenny back again, and Barbara's a good sort too.'

Everyone agreed heartily with this, and both forms felt highly honoured when, just before bedtime, the head girl herself dropped into the common-room.

'I just wanted to thank you all,' said Jenny, smiling round. 'I know it's because of you kids that I'm head girl again, and I can't tell you how thrilled I am. Kitty, you deserve a medal!'

Kitty laughed and said, 'Sure, Jenny, and it's McGinty you ought to be thanking. He's the real hero.'

'Yes, I've already been to see McGinty, and taken him some biscuits as a treat,' said Jenny. 'Judging by the way he snatched them from my hand I think he enjoyed them!'

'Well, wasn't that nice of her?' said Amanda, once Jenny had left. 'You know, now that everything has turned out right, I think I'm going to enjoy the rest of the term.'

'What's left of it,' said Carlotta. 'Only one week to go d then it's home for the hols.'

Kitty sighed. 'It's home for good as far as McGinty and I are concerned.'

'Golly, so it is!' cried Isabel. 'I'd forgotten you were only with us for one term, Kitty. You've fitted in so well it feels as if you've been here forever.'

'We shall miss you both,' said Bobby, looking glum. 'I don't suppose your people will decide to stay in London a bit longer, so that you can spend next term with us too?'

Kitty shook her head. 'I'm afraid not. Father's finished his research, so they're coming to collect me on the last day of term, then it's back to Kilblarney for all of us. I'm looking forward to going home and seeing my old friends, of course, but McGinty and I will really hate saying goodbye to St Clare's.'

'Everything's changing,' sighed Grace. 'Tomorrow night we second formers are moving into our new common-room.'

'Ooh yes!' said Doris brightly. 'Well, that's good news, anyway. It'll be nice to come in here and be able to bag a seat without you great, lazy lumps hogging all the comfy chairs. Ow! No, Grace, don't! I was only joking!'

Everyone laughed as Grace began pummelling Doris with a cushion, and the atmosphere in the room brightened again.

19.

Home for the holidays

'Peace, perfect peace!' sighed Hilary happily, putting her feet up on a sofa and stretching out.

'Yes, isn't it grand,' said Pat, gazing round the common-room, which seemed very much bigger now that it was only occupied by one form. 'Although I must admit, I got to like most of the second formers very much in the end.'

'Me too,' agreed Janet. 'Who would have thought that we'd actually grow quite fond of the little beasts?'

'I say, has anyone seen Amanda?' asked Isabel. 'She promised to lend me a book to read, but I haven't seen her in simply ages.'

'She's probably in the second form's common-room,' said Carlotta. 'I saw her arm-in-arm with Helen a little while ago. Those two are almost inseparable these days.'

'Oh well, I'll just have to come and chat to you, Pat,' said Isabel cheerfully, going to sit by her twin.

'You know, Isabel, it's only natural that Amanda should want to spend more time with the second form, and get to know them better, as she's going to be joining them next term,' said Pat, watching her twin closely. 'And it's a very good thing that she and

Helen have become such good friends.'

'Absolutely,' agreed Isabel at once. 'The news about the baby has worked wonders on both of them.'

'Well, I must say, you're taking it awfully well,' said Pat.

Isabel looked puzzled for a moment, then her brow cleared and she laughed. 'Pat, I like Amanda enormously, and I'm pleased to have her as a friend. But I don't mind at all that she's spending more time with the second form.'

'Really?' said Pat.

'Really,' said Isabel. 'I think you and I have both learned a valuable lesson this term. That no matter how many friends we make, no one will ever come between us.'

Pat nodded solemnly. 'You're quite right, old thing. I say, won't it be fun next term to come back to school together, and to have our beds next to one another again.'

'I'll say,' agreed Isabel. 'But let's not talk about next term just yet. We have the holidays to enjoy first, and I'm looking forward to them so much.'

All of the girls were looking forward to the holidays, and the last few days of term simply flew by. Then – all of a sudden, it seemed – it was the last day of term and everyone was packing to go home.

In the third form's dormitory there was complete chaos, and girls hunted high and low for missing stockings, lost toothbrushes, and a dozen other things that seemed, unaccountably, to have disappeared.

Hilary, who was always very well organised, and had packed most of her things the night before, was looking out of the window. Suddenly she cried, 'Good gracious, someone's parents have arrived early. Why, Kitty, I do believe they're yours!'

'No, mine wouldn't turn up at this hour, Hilary. They know that it always takes me ages to pack.'

Carlotta, who had joined Hilary by the window, looked out and said, 'They *are* yours, Kitty. I recognise your father's red hair.'

'Now, what do you suppose they're playing at?' said Kitty, sounding mildly annoyed. 'Ah well, I suppose I'd better go down and greet them.'

The rest of the third form, glad of an excuse to abandon the task of packing for a while, followed the Irish girl downstairs, where they found Mr and Mrs Flaherty in the big entrance hall. They looked rather lost, but their faces lit up when Kitty appeared, and she ran towards them, hugging first one, then the other.

'But, Mother, what are you doing here so early?' asked the Irish girl at last.

'Why, you asked us to collect you soon after breakfast, dear,' said Mrs Flaherty.

'No, I didn't,' said Kitty, puzzled.

'Ah now, you did,' said her mother, reaching into her handbag. 'Sure and here's a letter from you that came a few days ago. See, it says "Looking forward to seeing you soon after breakfast".'

Kitty took the sheet of paper, frowning over it for a

moment. Then she gave a laugh and said, 'It says "Looking forward to seeing you soon". Then there's a full stop and a new sentence, which begins "After breakfast" – and then I went on to tell you about something I was doing that day. Honestly, Mother!'

The watching third formers laughed as Mr Flaherty peered over Kitty's shoulder and said, 'Sure and it is a full stop. I can see it now. Ah well, we're here now, so what's to be done?'

At that moment Matron came bustling into the hall, crying, 'You third formers should be upstairs packing!' Then she spotted Kitty's parents.

'Hallo there. Have you come to collect one of the girls?'

'We have indeed, Mam,' said Mr Flaherty. 'But it seems we're a little early.'

'My goodness, there's no need to ask whose parents you are,' said Matron, her plump face creasing into a smile. 'Now you come along with me, Mr and Mrs Flaherty, and we'll see if we can find you a cup of tea. And you girls, go and finish your packing – unless you want to spend the holidays at school!'

Much as they loved St Clare's, no one did wish to spend the holidays there, and the girls sped away.

Seeing her parents seemed to have spurred Kitty on, for she finished her packing in record time, then dashed out of the room.

'I say, where's Kitty gone in such a hurry?' asked Bobby. 'I hope she hasn't left without saying goodbye.'

'No, for she's left her case here,' said Gladys. 'I

daresay she'll be back shortly.'

Kitty was back shortly, but she wasn't alone – for she was accompanied by McGinty, looking very jaunty at the prospect of new surroundings. The girls greeted him warmly and Janet laughed, 'If Matron comes in and sees him she'll blow her top!'

'No, boy, you can't come home with me,' said Mirabel, as the little goat tried to scramble into her case. 'And I hope your hooves aren't muddy, for you've just trodden all over my pyjamas!'

'Now behave yourself, McGinty,' said Kitty sternly, pulling him away. 'Oh dear, perhaps bringing him in here wasn't such a good idea.'

'Well, we'll have to leave in a minute, so he won't have time to get into much mischief,' said Pat, shutting her case. 'Are you ready, Isabel? The coach will be here soon.'

Downstairs was a hive of activity as girls ran around saying goodbye to mistresses, exchanging addresses and making arrangements to meet in the holidays, all at the tops of their voices.

Matron appeared and clapped her hands over her ears, crying, 'My goodness, I've never heard such a dreadful racket! I thought there was a riot going on in here.' Then she caught sight of McGinty and shouted, 'Kitty Flaherty! What is that goat doing here?'

Mr Flaherty, who – along with his wife – had followed Matron into the hall, said, 'Don't you worry, Mam. We'll take Kitty and McGinty off your hands now.

And I daresay you'll be glad to see the back of them, for they're troublesome creatures, the both of them!'

'Well, I don't know about that,' said Matron, her face softening. 'They've certainly brightened things up around here.'

'Have I given everyone my address?' asked Kitty, picking up her case. 'Now, don't forget, everyone, if you're ever in Kilblarney be sure to drop in.'

'Kee-ty!' came a voice from behind her, and the girl turned to see Mam'zelle coming towards her, arms outstretched. 'So, the time has come for you to leave us,' she said, giving the astonished Kitty a big hug and planting a smacking kiss on each of her cheeks. 'Ah, what trouble you have caused us this term, you and that bad goat. But we shall miss you.'

Then, to Kitty's further amazement, the French mistress bent down and tickled the little goat under his whiskery chin. This was exactly where he liked to be tickled most, and McGinty decided that Mam'zelle, who had never been a great favourite of his, wasn't such a bad sort after all. A bowl of freshly cut flowers stood on a low table nearby and, turning his head, the goat plucked one out. Holding it between his teeth, he gently nudged Mam'zelle, the watching girls helpless with laughter as she took it from him and tucked it behind her ear. The spectacle was so comical that even Miss Jenks and Miss Adams couldn't hide their smiles, as a delighted Mam'zelle cried, 'See! He is not a bad goat after all, but a good one!'

'Sure and he is that, Mam,' said Doris, imitating Kitty's accent to perfection and making everyone laugh even louder.

'Goodbye, Kitty – don't forget to write! Goodbye, McGinty!'

And, amid a chorus of farewells and a sea of waving handkerchiefs, Kitty, her parents and McGinty left.

Hilary sighed. 'Blow! I do wish Kitty could have stayed on. She was such fun.'

'Cheer up, Hilary,' said Isabel, patting her on the shoulder. 'I know it's not going to be quite the same without her, but I daresay there will be more new girls to meet next term.'

'Pat! Isabel!' said Amanda. 'You will write to me in the hols, won't you?'

'Of course we will,' Isabel assured her. 'Well, I certainly will – and Pat will, as long as she doesn't go falling out of any more trees and breaking her arm again!'

'No fear of that,' said Pat. 'I'm going to sit quietly and not move from the sofa at all during the holidays, so I shall be perfectly safe.'

'Come on, Amanda!' called Helen, rushing up to the third formers. 'Mummy and Daddy are here.'

'Marvellous!' said Amanda, smiling widely. 'I can't wait to see them both. Wonder if they've thought of any names for the baby yet.'

And, arm-in-arm, chattering happily, the two stepsisters walked off.

'Well, if you'd told me at the beginning of term that

those two would end up being the best of friends, I would never have believed it,' said Bobby.

'It's been a strange term altogether,' said Pat. 'Who could have guessed that Jenny would resign as head girl? Or that Margaret would get up to such mean, underhand tricks?'

'Or that you and Isabel would fall out,' put in Carlotta.

'Thank goodness everything turned out all right in the end,' said Isabel. 'And Pat and I are never going to quarrel again!'

'Come along, train girls!' came Matron's booming voice. 'The coach has arrived to take you to the station.'

And, with a flurry of last-minute goodbyes, the girls left St Clare's to go home for the holidays.

'Let's hope that we don't have as much trouble as we have had this term when we come back,' said Isabel, as the coach moved away. 'I could do with a nice, peaceful term.'

'I don't expect you'll get one,' laughed Pat. 'I don't know why, but there *always* seems to be something happening at St Clare's!'